Praise for of Award-winning Author
LINDA LAEL MILLER

Caroline and the Raider

"Funny, exciting and heartwarming, *Caroline and the Raider* is a delight—another romance that's as wonderful and hot as you'd expect from Linda Lael Miller!"

—*Romantic Times*

Emma and the Outlaw

"Ms. Miller's unique way of tempering sensuality with tenderness in her characters makes them come alive and walk right off the pages and into your heart. . . . Emma and her outlaw will captivate and enchant you."

—*Rendezvous*

Lily and the Major

"Earthy and sensuous, these two lovers are another wonderful hero and heroine presented to us from Ms. Miller's fertile and very creative imagination. If all the girls' stories are this delicious, have we got a treat in store? Darn tooting!"

—*Rendezvous*

"An absolutely joyous book; it will warm every reader's heart."

—*Romantic Times*

Moonfire

"Linda Lael Miller continues to prove that she is one of the hottest romance authors writing today. This is a novel filled with passion, mystery, drama, humor and powerful emotions. Her love scenes sizzle and smolder with sensuality."

—*Romantic Times*

"Sizzling love scenes and excellent characterization make *Moonfire* a delectable morsel of romantic fiction."

—*Affaire de Coeur*

"Dynamic, sensual, very emotional . . . Ms. Miller's explicit account of events is stimulating."

—*Rendezvous*

Angelfire

"FIVE STARS—HIGHEST RATING! . . . Linda Lael Miller is a most talented craftsman with the written word. Her characters step out of the pages majestically and the reader is soon on very intimate terms with them."

—*Affaire de Coeur*

"One of Linda Lael Miller's hottest, most sizzling romances . . . Readers will be captivated by these headstrong, vulnerable lovers, their heartwarming love story and the scorching sensuality that pervades every page."

—*Romantic Times*

My Darling Melissa

"[An] adorable, sprightly romance. Melissa is a delight—probably the most stubborn heroine of the season. Her determination to succeed, her unbridled sensuality and special brand of humor will capture your imagination."

—Romantic Times

"A fast, entertaining read. Ms. Miller's incorporation of the suffrage movement and the returning Corbin characters gave an added dimension to the story."

—Rendezvous

"Unsinkable fun. The author dishes up her favorite fare: plucky women with the strength to reason and the passion to follow their hearts; powerful men who find an independent woman infuriating yet irresistible; countless love sequences that leave plenty to the imagination; and a flavorful, 1890s setting."

—Publishers Weekly

Books by Linda Lael Miller

Yankee Wife
Daniel's Bride
Caroline and the Raider
Emma and the Outlaw
Lily and the Major
My Darling Melissa
Angelfire
Moonfire
Wanton Angel
Lauralee
Memory's Embrace
Corbin's Fancy
Willow
Banner O'Brien
Desire and Destiny
Fletcher's Woman

Published by POCKET BOOKS

LINDA LAEL MILLER

YANKEE WIFE

POCKET **STAR** BOOKS

New York London Toronto Sydney Tokyo Singapore

An *Original* Publication of POCKET BOOKS

A Pocket Star Book published by
POCKET BOOKS, a division of Simon & Schuster Inc.
1230 Avenue of the Americas, New York, NY 10020

Copyright © 1993 by Linda Lael Miller

ISBN: 0-671-73755-4

First Pocket Books printing June 1993

10 9 8 7 6 5 4 3 2 1

POCKET STAR BOOKS and colophon are registered trademarks of Simon & Schuster Inc.

Cover art: wreath by Jean Restivo Monti, couple by Alessandro Biffignandi

Printed in the U.S.A.

For Jayne Ann Krentz,
blazer of trails,
with affection and gratitude

1

*L*YDIA MCQUIRE WAS DESPERATELY HUNGRY, AND A night's piano playing had earned her enough for a bed at Miss Killgoran's boardinghouse *or* a meal, but not both. She squinted to read the bill affixed to the wall outside the supper club, her blue eyes still stinging from the dense cigar smoke within.

WANTED: ONE WIFE FOR A GOOD,
SOBER, AND PROSPEROUS MAN.
CONTACT DEVON QUADE,
ROOM 4, THE FEDERAL HOTEL

Lydia sighed. The Federal Hotel was just a few blocks from where she stood, yet it might as well have been in another world. There, people slept on crisp linen sheets, drank hot, strong tea with all the milk and sugar they could want, ate full meals without first examining the fare for mold and weevils. Perhaps if she went to see this Devon Quade, he would offer her some small refreshment during the interview—coffee and rolls, perhaps. Even that sounded like a feast to Lydia, who hadn't eaten since the day before, when a kindly bartender had given her two hard-boiled eggs that had somehow been over-looked in the mad scramble of hungry, thirsty patrons.

She started automatically toward the hotel, picking up speed as she walked. It was dawn, and there were only a few carriages and wagons in the brick-laid streets; a Chinaman wearing a round, pointed hat, his trousers and shirt made of black silk, hurried along on the opposite sidewalk. A policeman strolled his beat, looking bored and weary, his nightstick making a clunk sound against each lamp post he passed.

It occurred to Lydia that she would probably rouse Mr. Quade from a sound sleep, arriving at his door so early, but she proceeded anyway. Perhaps he would be impressed by her industry and initiative and overlook her tattered dress, her mussed blond hair, the smell of smoke that had permeated her skin and grown stale there.

Her resolve was beginning to fade, so she walked faster. It was only when she reached the front door of the Federal Hotel that Lydia realized she was holding the advertisement for a wife in one hand. She didn't recollect pulling it from the wooden wall where she'd found it.

Standing on the sidewalk, drawing in deep breaths, Lydia folded the bill into neat quarters and then tucked it into her pocket with the two pitiful coins she'd received for entertaining that lot of sodden, pinching drunks. Briefly, she considered the idea of actually applying for the post of wife to this forthright stranger, but she soon discarded it again. In time she would find an honest position as a governess, or she would scrape together enough money to take a room in a boarding-house where there was a piano. That way, she could give lessons and earn a dignified if modest living.

The hotel doorman, looking like an officer in an army of rich soldiers in his maroon suit, gold epaulets, and gleaming brass buttons, peered at her from under the brim of his cap. The expression in his eyes revealed both admiration and contempt as he took in Lydia's compact figure, her moderately pretty face and her one glory, her rich, honey-gold hair.

"There something you want, ma'am?" he inquired,

with an acid politeness that stung Lydia. It was obvious, even to a woman who'd never had an intimate experience with a man, that he thought she was a lady of the shadows, seeking lowly commerce.

Lydia wanted to run, but her hunger left her too weak, and discouragement had robbed her of all aplomb. She took the handbill from her pocket and held it out. "I'm here to see Mr. Devon Quade," she said, with her last shred of pride.

The doorman looked her over again, then smiled. It was not a friendly expression, but he granted her entry with a gesture of one arm.

Lydia walked into the lobby, with its potted palms and brass fixtures and lovely Oriental carpet, and for a few moments she was filled with such aching weariness that her throat closed tight and her eyes filled with tears.

She blinked, and sniffled, looked at the handbill again, made a mental note that Mr. Quade was housed in Room 4, and proceeded toward the stairs. The door she sought, prominently marked with a brass numeral, was all too easy to find.

She had only to knock.

Lydia bit her lower lip. She was tired, hungry, and dirty, and the last thing on the face of God's earth she would ever want was a husband, so what was she doing here? She didn't know; there was nothing in her knowledge or experience to explain the strange instinct that had propelled her through grimy streets to this place. It was far more than the hope of coffee and rolls, she concluded.

She raised her hand to knock, heart thundering against her rib cage, stomach grinding out a reminder that it was empty, held her breath and pounded at the door.

The instant she'd done that, Lydia was overcome by terror. She glanced in one direction, then the other, ready to flee down the hallway and escape, but her legs wouldn't take orders. She was frozen there on the threshold of a strange man's quarters, with little or nothing to say for herself.

There was grumbling inside the room. Lydia contin-

3

ued to struggle against her own inertia, but to no avail. She was rooted to the spot like a willow tree planted in good ground.

Then the door opened and he was standing there, tall and classically handsome, his tawny-gold hair sleep-rumpled. His indigo-blue eyes went narrow and he scowled. "Yes?"

Lydia offered the advertisement with a shaking hand. The man was clearly prosperous, as the poster claimed, and no doubt sober, given the hour, but whether or not he was good remained to be seen. Such fine-looking men were often rogues.

She realized she was staring and forced herself to speak. "Mr. Quade? My name is Lydia McQuire and I—I've come about your . . . proposal." It was plain he wasn't going to offer refreshment, clad in his dressing gown and barely awake as he was, but Lydia felt she had to make some explanation for interrupting his sleep, so she pretended she wanted to be a stranger's bride.

Ink-colored eyes looked her over speculatively, but not with the same insulting presumption the doorman had employed. "Come in, Miss McQuire," he said, stepping back.

Lydia swallowed. Somehow, perhaps because of her desperation, she hadn't anticipated this awkward development. She intertwined her fingers and twisted them until they ached. "I don't think—"

Suddenly, a blinding smile burst over his face, like early morning sunshine on the surface of a clear lake. "Of course," he said. "I've been living among lumberjacks so long, I've forgotten my manners. Give me fifteen minutes, and I'll meet you downstairs in the dining room. We'll talk while we're having breakfast."

Lydia's stomach rumbled loudly at the prospect; she could only hope Mr. Quade hadn't heard. She nodded and stood there in the hall, still as a marble monument, long after he'd closed the door. Then, driven by the thought of food, she broke free of her frenzied thoughts and dashed for the stairs.

The dining hall was just opening up for a day's business, and when Lydia told the waiter she was joining Mr. Devon Quade of Room 4, she was immediately escorted to a table. Coffee appeared, sending fragrant steam from the spout of a silver pot, and a crystal plate towering with fresh pastries was set before her.

Lydia's eyes went wide as she watched the rich brown liquid being poured into a delicate china cup.

"There you are, madame," the waiter said kindly. Then he went away.

Lydia's hand trembled as she reached for the pots of sugar and cream. She treated the coffee with generous portions of both and took a noisy slurp, too eager to honor convention by sipping. A gray-haired matron, the only other customer in attendance, gave her a look of censure.

Lydia took two more gulps of the coffee—oh, Lord, it was delicious—then reached for a pastry. Her mouth was stuffed full when Devon Quade materialized in the doorway of the restaurant, looking so startlingly handsome that she nearly choked. With frantic haste, Lydia began to chew and swallow; her face bright red when Mr. Quade reached the table, because she knew she hadn't deceived him for a moment. He'd clearly guessed that she'd put three-quarters of a sweet bun into her mouth in a single bite, and he was amused.

The same waiter reappeared, as if by magic, to draw back Mr. Quade's chair before he had even reached the table. Menus were presented, more coffee poured.

Although Lydia still had plenty of room for breakfast, she was no longer quite so ravenous. For the moment, her stomach was occupied with the roll she'd just consumed, and she could study Mr. Quade as he scanned the menu.

He startled her by looking up suddenly and catching her staring. "You are a very lovely woman," he said. "I confess to wondering why you haven't found a husband in a more traditional way."

Lydia blushed and was momentarily overwhelmed by an acute yearning for long-gone, innocent days. "The war

5

didn't leave many eligible men," she said. "Those who did survive are wounded, either inside or out, or already married."

Mr. Quade seemed sincerely chagrined. "Of course. I'm sorry." He gestured for the waiter, who came instantly, and Lydia felt a sting of envy, wondering what it would be like to be so effortlessly important as her breakfast partner. He ordered a large meal for the both of them, and when they were alone again, studied Lydia with a pensive frown. "Tell me about yourself," he said.

Her natural tendency toward rebellion made her want to counter with a demand that Mr. Quade tell her about himself first, but she wanted to eat her breakfast before she took any such risk. That way, she could use her pitiful night's pay to hire a bed and bath.

"I'm twenty-five," she said, squaring her shoulders. "I was born in Fall River, Massachusetts. My father was a doctor, and my mother died when I was very young. I am educated, and I can cook and clean as well as the next woman, though I admit I'd rather read or go out walking. When the war began, my father felt compelled to join up—on the Union side, naturally."

"Naturally," Mr. Quade said benignly, one side of his mouth tilted upward in a semblance of a grin.

Lydia resettled herself in her chair and smoothed her disgracefully rumpled skirts. "Papa hadn't been gone a week when he wired me from Washington City that he was in urgent need of my assistance. I immediately answered his summons. I worked side by side with my father and the other surgeons, as a nurse." She paused a moment, remembering the horrors that had eventually become commonplace. "We followed the battles, and it was in Virginia that Papa suffered a fatal heart seizure and collapsed. He died within a few hours and I—I—" She stopped again, took a few deep breaths, marveling that she'd reached such depths that she would willingly endure such wretched recollections for a few scraps of food. "I stayed on with the hospital corps, having no reason to return home."

Mr. Quade was silent for a long time. He looked deep

into her eyes. The meal was delivered, and Lydia used the last of her self-control to keep from scooping eggs and sausage and toasted bread up into her hands and devouring them like an animal.

"Your father must have owned a house in Fall River," Mr. Quade finally said.

Lydia shook her head, her mouth full of fried potatoes, which she gulped down before she answered, "Papa was never a practical man. We had rooms above a butcher shop, and we were two months behind in the rent when he enlisted."

Mr. Quade began spreading jelly on his toast, averting his eyes. "How did you end up in San Francisco?"

It was agony to hold her fork suspended, with all that delicious food sitting before her, fragrant and hot, but Lydia succeeded long enough to say, "I came around the Horn with an elderly lady, acting as her companion. I'd planned to start a music conservatory once I'd settled in California and saved the necessary funds, but Mrs. Hallingsworth died and her son and daughter-in-law had no need for my services. I was, in a word, stranded."

"When did this happen?"

"Last month." Lydia got in a few hasty bites, then went on. "I've been surviving by playing piano in supper bars."

Mr. Quade sipped his coffee. "I see," he said finally. "Is there anything you'd like to ask me?"

Lydia swallowed more eggs. "You must not live in San Francisco, or you wouldn't be staying in this hotel," she observed. "Where are you from?"

He sat back in his chair, hooking his thumbs in the pockets of a brocade vest. "My brother and I operate a timber concern up near Seattle, in the Washington Territory."

She gave a small, involuntary shudder. The territories were filled with bloodthirsty Indians and highwaymen, she'd heard, and in the mountainous places there were said to be wildcats in every tree, waiting to pounce on the unwary sojourner.

"You couldn't have grown up in Washington Territory," she said. "It hasn't been settled even twenty years, and you are an educated man."

He smiled. "Brigham—that's my brother—and I were raised in Maine. We came out here by wagon train as soon as we were old enough to claim our small inheritances."

"Aren't there any women in Seattle?" Lydia asked. She immediately regretted the indelicacy and bluntness of the question, but it was too late to call back her words.

"None to speak of," Mr. Quade replied. He really was handsome, with his leonine head of golden hair and strong jawline, which might have been carved, like his nose, by a master sculptor. He was cultivated, too. He would probably be very kind to the candidate he selected for his wife. "Women are at a premium in the Northwest. Why, I'll bet you couldn't walk from the harbor to Yesler's Mill without getting at least six marriage proposals."

Lydia swallowed. She had only bargained for coffee and rolls, not a barrage of amorous lumberjacks and mill workers. "Did you have a large response to your . . . advertisement?" she asked, unable to look at him. She was staring down at the few remaining crumbs of her breakfast.

"The majority of them were unsuitable," he admitted. "The Puget Sound area is still largely untamed and very primitive. It's no place for timidity or a hysterical temperament. On the other hand, it's beautiful country, and a woman bearing the Quade name would lack for nothing of any true significance."

The whole insane idea was beginning to sound good to Lydia. Appealing as this man was, she felt no particular attraction to him, but she imagined she could adjust to being his wife. That would certainly be preferable to some of her other options, like starving to death or taking up the lewd profession.

Mr. Quade reached for the silver pot, refilled Lydia's coffee cup with as much elegant deference as if she were a duchess instead of a homeless wretch with two tarnished coins in her pocket. "Would you like to come to Quade's

Harbor with me, Lydia?" he asked. "We'd be sailing in three days, and I would, of course, put you up here at the hotel in the interim. I would give you an advance on your allowance, as well, since you'll probably need a few things."

Lydia just sat there, gaping. This proposal had been unlike any she'd read about or heard of, but it wasn't without appeal. She could eat, sleep in a safe, warm, clean place, even buy herself "a few things." She didn't think beyond that; she was too dazed by the sudden turn her fortunes had taken.

"Yes," she said, bold in her desperation. "Yes, Mr. Quade, I would like that very much."

"Very well," he replied, with another of his boyish, endearing smiles, taking a wallet from the inside pocket of his coat. He removed a few bills and passed them to Lydia. "You'll need clothes for a rainy climate," he said. "I'll make arrangements at the desk for a room to be prepared, and you can spend the day as you like. Just have your meals and anything else you want billed to me." With that, Mr. Quade pushed back his chair, stood, and after a polite nod, walked away.

Lydia briefly considered ordering another breakfast, remembered the money lying on the table, and gathered it up.

Surely it was improper to accept funds from a man, not to mention a hotel room and food, but Mr. Quade had not made any unseemly demands. He clearly did not expect her to take up residence in his chambers, and he had been the soul of good manners from the very inception of their acquaintance.

Lydia folded the bills carefully and tucked them into her skirt pocket. Then, barely able to contain the sudden surge of energy that possessed her, she finished her coffee, rose, and left the dining room with sweeping dignity.

At the desk the clerk was deferential. Yes, quarters had been reserved for a Miss Lydia McQuire. He handed her a key and told her that Room 10 would be ready in half an hour.

"Thank you," Lydia said. It wasn't until she reached the sidewalk out front that she gave a cry of glee and did a little jig. The doorman looked at her suspiciously but offered no comment.

For a long moment she couldn't decide which way to go. She could simply disappear, after all—Mr. Quade had given her enough money to last for weeks, if she lived frugally—or she could have an adventure. It was an enormous risk, of course, traveling to Washington Territory with a stranger, becoming his bride, no less, but Lydia believed in bold undertakings. That was why she'd assisted her father in those dreadful field hospitals during the war, and it was the reason she had come to San Francisco with Mrs. Hallingsworth, seeking a new start in life.

Lydia headed toward the two-story mercantile on the next corner, and there was a little spring in her step now because she'd eaten and she had money and she had a future, uncertain and dangerous though it might be. Furthermore, for the first time in a month, she didn't have to worry about finding a place to sleep or having enough food to sustain her.

There would undoubtedly be challenges, but she would handle those one at a time, as they presented themselves. There was no sense, as her father had often told her, in letting one's mind get ahead into next week, next month, or next year. Better to plant oneself firmly in the moment and make the best of whatever might be offered.

Lydia bought several sensible dresses at the mercantile, along with a hooded cloak for the rainy climate Mr. Quade had mentioned and several sturdy pairs of shoes. She yearned for the pretty satin dancing slippers on display, but practicality wouldn't allow the purchase, even though she could have afforded it. She bought warm underwear, and stockings, and two modest flannel nightgowns. Her own things, stashed in a trunk in the storeroom of the supper club where she played piano, were hardly worth going back for. Because of the stringencies of the war, she had not had a new garment in five years, and everything she possessed was worn thin and painfully out of fashion.

That last thought made Lydia chuckle. When had she, daughter of the well-intentioned but chronically impoverished Dr. Wilkes McQuire, ever concerned herself with fashion? Her one luxurious purchase was a book—she'd read the volumes tucked away in her trunk until the pages of most of them were coming loose from their bindings. Still flush with money, Lydia returned to the hotel and marched herself bravely up to Room 10.

The chamber proved to be very spacious, with a large mahogany-framed bed, a settee and chairs upholstered in spotless blue taffeta, and a white marble fireplace. On the mantel stood a crystal vase filled with spring flowers.

Charmed, Lydia closed the door with her foot, set her packages carefully on the settee, and stood in front of the fireplace, touching a blossom thoughtfully. There were red and yellow zinnias, pert daisies, irises and tulips and crocuses, creating an explosion of color made double by the reflection in the mirror above the mantel.

Lydia was not accustomed to such luxuries, and their sudden appearance in her life was overwhelming. It seemed incredible that, only a few hours before, she had been faced with a choice between two such basic needs as food and shelter.

Now she was ensconced in a fancy hotel room, with money to spend, new clothes to wear, a book to read, and a kitchen staff virtually at her beck and call.

She made her way to a chair and sat down, frowning. If there was one thing life had taught her, it was that everything had a price. Sooner or later an accounting would have to be made.

Lydia closed her eyes and held fast to the arms of the chair. It was even possible that Mr. Quade wasn't the gentleman he seemed; he could be a procurer. Perhaps she was bound for some backwoods harem, or even an opium den in the Orient!

She sighed, opened her eyes.

It was also possible, she concluded, with some relief,

that she would simply end up in a sturdy log cabin somewhere in the timberlands to the north, keeping house for Devon Quade. She would live out her life in peace, raising three or four children along the way, and then it would be over and the world would go right on as if she'd never existed at all.

Hardly comforted, and no less confused for all her deliberations, Lydia rose with resolution and explored her surroundings. There was a small room reserved for bathing and other hygienic necessities, and after careful thought, she turned up the gas jet beneath the huge tank over the bathtub. While the water heated, Lydia unwrapped her parcels and laid out all her new things on the bed, as much to admire as to choose what to wear. She had bought nothing frivolous, just plain, practical, woolly things, but she felt rich and dissolute all the same. This must be what it was like to be a kept woman, she decided.

Finally, after an hour, Lydia turned a spigot on the tank in the bathroom and warm water began to flow into the tub. She hastily undressed, enjoyed a luxurious soak, something she had not had since before the war, then scrubbed her body and shampooed her hair.

When she climbed out of her bath, she felt like a woman resurrected and restored to glory. She dried her hair, combed out the tangles, and put on fresh new underthings and a prim gray-and-white-striped dress with a high collar. With this, she wore new stockings, ribbed and scratchy, and a pair of plain black shoes. She stuffed her old things into the trash basket in the bathing room.

By that time, Lydia was getting hungry again. She dined in the same restaurant where she and Mr. Quade had taken breakfast—there wasn't a sign of him anywhere about—then set out for the supper club where her trunk was stored.

Jim, the bartender, was in the rear storeroom, unpacking a crate of Irish whiskey, when Lydia came in through the door leading into the alley. He grinned and gave a low whistle of appreciation when he saw her new clothes.

"Well, then, Miss McQuire," he said. "What's happened to you? Have the Little People taken a liking to you?"

Lydia smiled. "It would seem that they have. I'm going north, to Seattle, where I'm to be the bride of a lumberman."

Jim's wise eyes seemed troubled. He was a solidly built man, middle-aged, with brown hair parted in the center and a thick mustache. "I see. Well, you want to be careful about these bride-buyers, miss. We've had some scandals where such matters are concerned."

Lydia had no doubt that Jim's words were true as the peal of a silver bell, but she couldn't stay in San Francisco, living from hand to mouth, never knowing where she would sleep when night descended or when she would have her next meal. Fate had offered her an opportunity, and she had to take it, even if there was some risk.

"I'll be careful," she promised softly, making the vow to herself as well as to Jim. It hurt to realize that even if she should travel to Seattle and then disappear into the dregs of immorality, no one would miss her. Probably there wouldn't even be anyone to ask, "Whatever happened to Doc McQuire's girl?"

"You've come for your trunk, then," Jim said, with resignation.

"There are only a few books and personal items I want," Lydia said. "Maybe you could give out the rest where you see a need."

The bartender nodded. "Need is one thing I see plenty of," he replied.

Without further conversation, Lydia climbed the plank steps to the loft of the storeroom and opened her trunk, which stood in one corner. She was not sorry to leave behind the calico and wool dresses—the memories attached to them were not pleasant ones, since she'd worn them in army hospitals and wrung the blood from their frayed hems like wash water from a rag. She wanted the keepsake photographs of her father and mother, though, as well as the tarnished bronze medal given her by a dying soldier, her journals, her grandmother's

13

mourning ring, and the letters. Lydia tied all her treasures inside a scarf, closed the trunk lid, and descended the stairs with her bundle.

There was no sign of Jim, and she was not really surprised. He had been a good friend, but saying goodbye would be too awkward for them both.

Lydia turned to the slate on the wall, where Jim wrote lists of goods he needed to order for the saloon, took up the nubbin of chalk, and wrote, THANK YOU.

Then she returned to the hotel, taking the long route, so she could get a last look at San Francisco. Only a few short weeks ago, she reflected with a sigh, she'd had high hopes for the city crescented around the bay. She'd planned to take rooms in some decent, respectable house and to start a music school. Now it seemed her destiny lay elsewhere, after all, in a land of timber and savages and men who wore plaid shirts and spiked boots.

The doorman at the Federal Hotel eyed Lydia carefully as she walked past him, this time keeping her chin high, his gaze falling on her pitiful little bundle of worldly possessions. Lydia clutched her belongings closer to her bosom and proceeded into the lobby.

That night, she dined with Mr. Quade in a restaurant renowned for beefsteak, and he took her to see a melodrama in a clapboard theater with a sawdust floor.

Lydia began to wonder when the marriage ceremony would take place, whether she and Mr. Quade would exchange vows there in San Francisco or up north, in Seattle. Since she wasn't particularly anxious for the duties that would come after the wedding, she kept her curiosity to herself and simply let events unfold as they would.

The next day, her future husband didn't put in an appearance at all until dinner, when he seemed harried and distracted. Lydia had spent some of her precious funds to take a carriage tour of the city, and she'd had her palm read by a Gypsy at the waterfront as well. Since she'd deduced from Mr. Quade's manner that he wouldn't care to hear about any of those things, she kept her accounts to herself.

The following morning, when the sun was winking on the waters of the bay, as bright and new as if it had never risen before, Mr. Quade collected his bride and her purchases and they set off for the waterfront by carriage.

Lydia was filled with trepidation and joy. On the one hand, she was very frightened, for she was taking a bold step, as dangerous in some ways as braving Confederate cannon fire to help her father perform surgery. On the other, she sensed that an adventure was beginning. *You will have need of your great strength,* the Gypsy had told her, while staring solemnly into Lydia's palm. *You have already suffered much. Now, you must face an even greater challenge: learning passion and true joy.*

The ship they boarded looked sturdy enough, though it wasn't as large as the one that had carried Lydia around Cape Horn with poor Mrs. Hallingsworth. There were two black smokestacks, and the color had been swabbed out of the wooden decks. Lydia tried not to think about the way the craft would roll and pitch once it left San Francisco Bay for the open sea. She had seen every conceivable horror in wartime surgery tents without folding up, but a few swells in the ocean could send her scrambling for the rail.

Perhaps, she reflected, she would become Devon's wife there, aboard the ship, with the captain officiating.

Mr. Quade made no mention of the event. He simply escorted Lydia to a small stateroom, which contained a narrow bed, a wardrobe very cleverly built into the wall, a washstand and commode. She took her new dresses from the carpet bag she'd purchased the day before and hung them up on a peg, then went out to walk the decks and get her bearings.

The craft was chugging away from the wharf when she came around to the stern and saw Devon standing at the rail. Beside him was a tall, beautiful dark-haired woman, finely dressed, her arm linked with his in a rather familiar fashion.

A cold feeling washed over Lydia's heart, followed immediately by a parching rage. It seemed Mr. Devon Quade would prove to be a scoundrel after all.

She might have jumped overboard and swum back to shore were it not for the fact that Jim the bartender had told her there were hungry sharks in the bay. Summoning up all the dignity she possessed, Lydia joined the twosome and looked up at the man who'd promised to marry her.

Devon beamed, as though nothing were amiss. "Ah, Miss McQuire," he said, patting the kid-gloved hand of the woman beside him, which was resting in the crook of his right arm. "May I introduce Mrs. Polly Quade—my wife?"

2

*D*EVON QUADE ALREADY HAD A WIFE.

Lydia reached out and grasped the railing for support. "You will excuse my presumption, Mr. Quade," she said, with hard-won moderation, "but I did have the impression that I—that we—" She felt herself redden and fell silent, full of humiliation and, yes, relief too.

Devon was the very embodiment of chagrin. He glanced at the lovely Polly, who watched the unfolding drama with neither smugness nor concern. The blood drained away beneath his tanned cheeks, with their high, prominent bones, and he muttered, "Great Zeus, I *did* give that impression, didn't I?"

Lydia enjoyed a brief fantasy, during which she slapped Mr. Devon Quade square across the face. "Yes," she replied simply, tightening her grasp on the ship's railing. Gulls were following after them, squawking and soaring against an untroubled, glacier-blue sky, and Lydia wondered if the captain would turn his vessel back toward shore if he were so bidden.

It didn't seem likely.

Devon sighed, gently disengaged himself from his true

17

bride, and laid his hands lightly on Lydia's shoulders. For some reason, she did not flinch or attempt to pull away.

"I thought I'd explained it all properly," he said, in a hoarse and very earnest tone of voice. "The man I referred to in the handbill is my brother, Brigham. He'll be a fine husband to you, Lydia, once he gets used to the idea of having a wife again. . . ."

Lydia, who had assisted in the amputation of men's limbs without swooning, nearly sank to the deck in a dead faint. *"Once he gets used to the idea?"* she whispered, her horror compounding like interest on a rich man's money. It was bad enough to learn she'd contracted her entire future to someone she'd never met, but the discovery that Brigham Quade wasn't even expecting her made her reconsider the idea of jumping overboard. "How could you do something so . . . so presumptuous and underhanded?"

"That's what I'd like to know," put in Polly. Lydia thought distractedly that the other woman had shown amazing restraint by waiting so long to enter the conversation. "How could you, Devon?"

Mr. Quade let go of Lydia's shoulders to run one hand through his windblown, butterscotch hair. He sighed gravely. "I thought I'd made the situation plain," he reiterated, and to her own great amazement, Lydia believed him. "I'm sorry. You'd be a fine companion to Brigham's children, and you're a handsome woman in the bargain. I'm certain it will only be a matter of time before my brother recognizes your many fine qualities and asks you to marry him."

Lydia nodded woodenly, turned and groped her way a little distance down the railing. Her thoughts were spinning around her like so many chattering birds, and it was a moment before she could settle her mind enough to think.

Soon, for Lydia was no stranger to crisis, she was able to examine the situation calmly. She did not love Devon Quade, though there was no denying that he was a spectacular-looking man with exceedingly fine prospects.

She would not be required to pledge eternal loyalty and obedience to him, nor to share his bed.

Furthermore, since Devon's brother wasn't expecting a potential wife to be delivered to his doorstep, he wouldn't be waiting at the base of the wharf with a preacher and a handful of wildflowers. Lydia had been given a reprieve, uncertain as it was, and perhaps Mr. Brigham Quade would hire her as a governess to his children and expect nothing more of her.

Lydia drew in a deep, restorative breath, watching San Francisco recede from sight, feeling the sea roll beneath her like some great, undulating beast.

Lydia had become expert at adjusting herself to reality, however harsh. For the next few days, she kept to herself, contemplating the adventure that lay before her. She ate, though very lightly, walked along the decks, and was civil to Devon whenever he dared to address her. Which wasn't often.

Seattle turned out to be a ramshackle town, just a few unpainted frame buildings clinging to impossibly steep hills and flanked by dense, primordial forest. Here and there the stump of some ancient evergreen rose in the middle of a muddy street, and piles of clay-streaked dirt, sawdust, and scrap lumber attested to great personal industry on the part of certain citizens. The beer halls, doing a rousing business in those drizzly morning hours, gave raucous comment on the habits of still others. Mill saws screamed and the misty air was thick with the smells of newly sawed wood, fir sap, smoke, and horse manure.

Lydia felt a vague stirring in the depths of her heart, a heart she'd deliberately rendered numb long since, when she'd looked upon her first wounded soldier.

A tendril of hair danced against her cheek, and the wind brought a taste of saltwater to her lips, faintly reminiscent of tears. Lydia could not remember the last time she'd really cried; perhaps it had been at her mother's funeral, when she was a small child.

She stood a bit straighter in her accustomed place at the railing of the steamer *San Francisco*, and even managed a smile for Polly, who beamed upon the crude little country town as though it were Paris.

Apparently, the new bride had found marriage to a complete stranger to be all she'd hoped for. Polly had formed a habit of humming cheery little tunes under her breath, and there was a pinkish glow to her cheeks and a bright shine to her eyes.

The small party transferred to another boat at Seattle's busy harbor, and the last leg of the journey began. In an hour, Devon had told the ladies, they would reach Quade's Harbor, across the Sound.

"You brought me what?" Brigham Quade would have bellowed the words, but shock had knocked the breath from his lungs, and a furious rasp was all he'd been able to manage. He stared at his brother in horrified disbelief, praying he'd misunderstood.

Devon was perched on the edge of Brigham's enormous cherrywood desk, a valuable piece that had come from China aboard a trade ship. "I brought you a wife," he said placidly. "Believe me, Brig, you're going to like Lydia." He held out one hand, palm downward. "She's about this high, with purple eyes and yellow hair, and she's healthy."

"Next you'll be telling me she has good teeth!" Brigham burst out, nearly upsetting his chair when he stood. "Good God, Devon, you make this woman sound like prize breeding stock!"

His younger brother, generous to a fault but often misguided, shrugged. "Lydia is no brood mare, of course," he allowed, "but she *would* produce strong children. I have no doubt of that."

Brigham rounded the desk. "I already *have* children, Devon," he pointed out. "Two. Or has that fact escaped you?"

Devon's eyes were clear of any guilt or guile. "Charlotte and Millie are girls," he reasoned. "They'll marry and set up households of their own. You need sons to take over the timber business when you get old and—"

"Devon," Brigham broke in quietly. It seemed to him

a miraculous thing that he hadn't strangled his brother already. "I've still got a few good years left to me, believe it or not." Beyond the windows of his study a soft summer rain shrouded the view of the snowy mountains, the dark indigo water, the thick, seemingly endless carpet of evergreen trees spilling over the land to the horizon. He stood looking out at the spectacle, which was beautiful to him even in that gloomy weather. "We built the company together, you and I," he said finally. "And we'll run it together."

He heard Devon's sigh behind him, knew what was coming next.

We didn't build this business, Brig—that was your doing. My only contribution was some fetching and carrying, and we both know it. I want something of my own."

Brigham's disappointment came out as impatience. "A general store," he said, with a touch of mockery to his tone, as he turned to glare at his brother.

Devon was the one man he'd never been able to intimidate, and it was plain that nothing had changed in that respect. "A general store," Devon confirmed, raising one eyebrow.

"Damn it, Quade's Harbor has no need of a mercantile," Brigham insisted, shoving a hand through his dark hair in frustration. "There's a company store!"

"Afraid of a little competition?" Devon asked, grinning now.

God in heaven but the man had balls, Brigham reflected—walking away from a half interest in one of the largest timber outfits in the territory, starting up a business no one would patronize, bringing a strange woman home for a wife and another to foist off on his unsuspecting brother.

Brigham swore, stormed over to the teakwood liquor cabinet he'd had sent up from San Francisco a few months earlier, and poured himself a brandy. "Competition," he spat. "The company store has everything a man could want. What will you sell, Devon? Tell me that."

"Maybe some things a *woman* could want," Devon

replied, still unruffled, gesturing toward the mountain where Brigham's crews were even then cutting timber. "The Northwest is a lonely place, Brig. Those workers of yours need wives. Women will be arriving from the East—there's a shortage of marriageable men back there because of the war, you know—and from San Francisco, too. They'll want dress goods and flower seeds and paint for picket fences."

Brigham sighed. He couldn't deny his brother's reasoning, much as he would have liked to do just that. The Puget Sound country was changing, day by day, and the few hearty men who were willing to work in the mountains yearned for the comforts of female companionship. Devon himself had spent the winter pacing and drinking, restless as a tomcat closed up in a hatbox, and now there was a woman upstairs, a bargain bride.

This Polly-person was of no consequence to Brig, though; such things were private matters, and if Devon wanted to give a stranger his name, that was his business. The other woman, however, the one Devon had so thoughtfully brought home for him, like a souvenir from some exotic attraction, was most definitely his concern.

Isabel, his first wife and the mother of his daughters, had permanently cured him of all misconceptions about wedded bliss. Her death from pneumonia, nine years before, had been a tragic one, and even though he and Isabel had never loved each other, he'd grieved for her. Even after all that time, however, he still felt anger whenever he thought of Isabel, because he knew she'd willed her passing. She'd given up, thrown off her life like a garment no longer needed, forsaken her children and husband without even attempting to survive.

He shook off a swarm of troubling memories and took another sip of his brandy. "The other one—Lydia, I think you called her—will have to go back. That is, unless you're planning to start a harem."

Devon rose from the edge of the desk, at last, and went to pour a drink for himself. His motions were pointed, meant to highlight Brigham's rudeness in failing to offer him a brandy when he got his own. "Lydia *is* beautiful enough to spawn such thoughts in a man's mind," he conceded. Holding a snifter in his right hand, he turned to face Brig, his blue gaze slightly narrowed. "Open your eyes and look at your life, Brig. You're in dire need of a wife, and your children want for a mother."

Brigham had returned to his desk. He set aside his snifter with a thump and reached for a stack of papers. "Aunt Persephone provides all the female guidance and companionship Charlotte and Millie require."

Devon swirled his glass, gazing down at the eddy of amber liquid in its bottom as though it could explain some personal mystery that troubled him greatly. "That still leaves the other. And don't say the whores in Seattle are enough, because that's a load of horse shit and we both know it. Lydia is a beautiful and very feminine woman," he said slowly, after a long interval of further consideration.

"If she's such a paragon," Brigham growled, bracing himself against the inner side of the desk with both hands, "why the hell didn't *you* marry her?"

His brother was thoughtful, unmoved, as usual, by Brigham's quiet rage. "She's very strong, both mentally and physically. To tell you the truth, I wanted someone who would lean on me just a little. I think Lydia's been taking care of herself for most of her life."

Giving another sigh, Brigham gathered up some documents and slapped the shiny surface of the desk with them. Why any man would want some wilted violet clinging to the back of his collar with clenched fingers, choking him, was beyond his imagining. It seemed to Brigham that a wife should be a partner of sorts, as well as a bedmate. Which wasn't to say he found the militantly self-reliant types all that attractive, either. If there was one thing he couldn't tolerate, it was a horse-faced bluestocking ranting about her rights.

He decided Lydia McQuire probably fell into the militant category and shuddered. He'd just as soon encounter the ghost of Hamlet's father in an upstairs hallway.

Devon, who had been able to read Brig's thoughts

since they were boys, or so it sometimes seemed, laughed aloud. "You'll be pleasantly surprised when you finally see her," he said. Then he set his empty snifter on the liquor cabinet and left the study.

Brigham might have worked happily over his ledgers for the rest of the afternoon if it hadn't been for the encounter with his brother, and for the troubling knowledge that there was a woman upstairs who no doubt expected to become Mrs. Brigham Quade before the week was out.

His charcoal gaze kept shifting to the ceiling as the spare bedrooms were directly overhead. Finally, he gave up trying to work, wiped his pen and returned it to its stand, carefully closing the bottle of black ink he'd been using.

He crossed the room to the double doors of the study, opened them, and was startled to find a small, feisty-looking blonde woman standing there, one hand poised to knock. Her eyes were a dark, velvety blue, almost purple, and a fetching blush pinkened her high cheekbones. Her chin was set at a stubborn angle, and Brigham found himself hoping against all good sense that this was not Polly, the woman his brother had chosen for a bride.

The violet eyes widened, the small fist descending slowly to her side. She was wearing a prim gray dress with plain sleeves and collar. "Mr. Brigham Quade?" she inquired, with all the dignity of a princess who's lost her way among peasants.

Brigham was holding his breath, feeling as though he'd just stepped onto a rapidly rolling log in a treacherous river. Still, a stern and solemn countenance came naturally to him, even when he was feeling cheerful. He was sure the wench could not guess from his sober nod of acknowledgment how she'd unnerved him.

"I am Miss Lydia McQuire," she announced, putting her chin out as though she expected to be challenged on the matter.

Relief Brigham would never have admitted feeling rushed through him with the force of a prairie wind. "I believe you," he replied.

The lovely eyes widened, then narrowed, but her color was still high. It was some consolation to Brigham to know she also felt the strange and dangerous dynamics at work between them, that he was not the only one to be stricken.

"You wanted something?" he asked, with exaggerated politeness, putting his hands on his hips because he was afraid he would lay his palms against her soft cheeks, or the gossamer cloud of her hair.

The query seemed to befuddle her for a moment. Then, summoning up every inch of her strictly average height, she gave him another regal assessment. "I will not marry you, Mr. Quade, under any circumstances," she informed him. "I would, however, like to discuss your objectives concerning the education of your daughters."

Brigham smiled indulgently. "I don't recall proposing, Miss McQuire," he replied.

Again, rich color flooded her face. "Very well," she said briskly, after a moment of obvious grappling for composure, "that's settled, then. We can discuss what is to be done about your children's schooling."

The master of the house leaned indolently against the doorjamb, arms folded. He was more comfortable now, feeling that he had the upper hand. "Aunt Persephone has taught them to read, write, and cipher quite nicely. To be forthright, Miss McQuire, neither Millie nor Charlotte possess any aspirations that set them apart from other young ladies. To my way of thinking, the practical thing would be to teach them to run a household."

For one delicious moment Brigham actually thought his luscious house guest might kick him in the shins. Wisely, she reconsidered. "Naturally, your daughters would not have aspirations, Mr. Quade. Children tend to regard themselves as their parents do, which means Charlotte and Millie probably feel about as capable as a pair of long-haired lapdogs."

Instantly furious, Brigham leaned down so that his nose was within an inch of Lydia's and practically snarled, "I will not have my daughters taught to be ambitious! I won't see them hectoring politicians for the vote and making speeches in public places!"

She didn't retreat, even though he was leaning over her, deliberately trying to make her take a step backward. No, she stood her ground, like a small soldier, evidently unable to speak for her fury. Her chin quivered and tears glistened in her eyes, and somewhere in the far, far distance, Brigham could have sworn he heard a bugle blow a call to battle.

3

*L*YDIA'S DISLIKE OF BRIGHAM QUADE HAD BEEN BOTH AR-
dent and instantaneous, and her cheeks pulsed with the
anger he'd stirred in her as she turned, sped up the
stairway in high dudgeon, and took refuge in her room.

It was a moment before she noticed the child sitting
cross-legged in the middle of her bed.

The girl was about ten, and beautiful, with familiar
coloring—dark hair and gray eyes, like Brigham's. Her
tresses fell in ribbon-woven ringlets well past her waist,
her fragile cheeks glowed with good health, and her gauzy
white dress with its yellow satin sash made her look as
though she'd just stepped out of some sentimental
French painting. All she needed was a hat with a floppy
brim, and a small dog to rest in the crook of her arm.

"Hello," she said. "My name is Millicent Alexandria
Quade, but you may address me as Millie."

Lydia's mouth curved wryly and she executed a half
curtsy. "I am Lydia McQuire," she replied, "and you
may address me as 'Miss McQuire.'"

Millie frowned, tugging at one of the golden ribbons in
her hair. "I had quite expected to call you 'Aunt Lydia,'"

she confided, bemused. "But I'm ten, after all, and I realize Uncle Devon couldn't have brought home two wives. Are you to be second choice, just in case the other one doesn't suit?"

Lydia might have been insulted, were it not for the guileless puzzlement in the child's eyes. "I'm to be your governess," she answered, regretting the words a mere instant after she'd uttered them. For all she knew, Mr. Brigham Quade intended to put her on the next outbound ship.

The little girl sighed. "Oh, fuss and bother. I've already learned quite enough from Aunt Persephone," she said.

Lydia had heard that name before, from Brigham, and she anchored it in her mind by repeating it silently. *Per-seff-any.*

"I can read grown-up books," Millie went on, "and do sums as well. I know how to play the spinet, too." She extended one foot, which was shod in a small velvet slipper, and wriggled it. "I'll be better when I can reach the pedals, though," she speculated, with a frown. Her face was bright, however, when she looked up at Lydia again. "Do you know how to fish, Miss McQuire?" she asked hopefully.

Lydia laughed and sat down on the edge of the bed. "Yes," she answered. "When I was a child in Massachusetts, I used to fish for brook trout sometimes, with my father. I always caught more than he did."

Millie looked very pleased, but then her smile faded. "Did your father like you?" she asked in a small voice.

The pang of anger Lydia felt then was, of course, directed at Mr. Quade and not his daughter. "Yes," she replied forthrightly, but in a gentle voice. "I believe he did. Does your father like you?"

"Papa is very busy making lumber," Millie said with resolve, sitting up straight and smoothing her small skirts. "And I don't imagine he finds me especially interesting. Not like that woman he visits in Seattle sometimes."

Lydia felt mild heat touch her cheeks from the inside. She reached out and took Millie's hand lightly in her own. "I think you're very interesting indeed," she said. Millie Quade was by all accounts one of the brightest children she had ever encountered. "Perhaps you and I can be friends."

"Perhaps," Millie agreed philosophically. "I have my sister Charlotte, of course, but she can't precisely be called a friend because there are times when she hates me. And Aunt Persephone's bones hurt when it rains, so she spends a lot of time in her room."

A tiny muscle deep in Lydia's heart twisted. It wasn't difficult to imagine how lonely the vast, gracious house could be, set square in the center of this wild and unsettled country the way it was. "Aren't there other children in Quade's Harbor?" she asked, stricken.

Millie shrugged one small shoulder. "Only Indians, and Aunt Persephone won't let us socialize with them because they have lice." She leaned closer to add in a confidential whisper, "And they *don't* use chamber pots."

Lydia held back another smile. "Mercy," she remarked, because the daring information Millie had imparted called for some comment. "What about the lumbermen? Don't any of them have families?" She recalled the row of sturdy saltbox houses she'd seen from the mail boat when she and Polly and Devon had arrived in Quade's Harbor earlier that day. She'd been struck by how much the town resembled long-settled villages in the East.

Millie shook her head. "Most of them don't have kinfolks to speak of, and if they do, they don't want to come here."

Lydia was about to offer a reply when there was a rustle of sateen at the open doorway of her room. She looked up to see a tiny white-haired woman standing there, gazing at her with energetic, speculative eyes. This had to be Aunt Persephone, she thought. Despite Millie's earlier statement that the woman often suffered from painful bones, she didn't look as though she'd ever spent so much as an hour reclining on a sickbed.

Lydia rose, straightened her skirts, and extended a

hand. "Hello," she said. "I am Miss Lydia McQuire—the governess."

The gracious lady in the dark blue dress inclined her head slightly. "Yes," she agreed, in a thoughtful tone. "The governess. My name is Mrs. Persephone Chilcote. Brigham and Devon are my nephews." The sweetly imperious gaze swept to the child sitting on the bed. "Millicent, get down from there at once. One does not invade another person's chambers and muss their coverlet with one's feet."

Millie obeyed readily and fled the room in a sudden and quite staggering burst of energy, shouting, "Charlotte! There's a ship in the harbor and it's going to take you all the way to China because Papa's sold you to a tribe of bandits with long mustaches!"

Mrs. Chilcote rolled her eyes, but her expression was gentle. "I do what I can," she sighed, "but I'm afraid my grandnieces have become too unruly for an old woman to handle."

Lydia privately thought that a whole brigade of whooping Confederate raiders probably wouldn't prove "too unruly" for Mrs. Chilcote, but of course she didn't voice this conclusion. Devon and Polly were newlyweds, concerned wholly with each other, and the master of the house was hardly civil, let alone companionable. Lydia needed an adult friend.

She indicated the two straight-backed chairs near the window, and Mrs. Chilcote took one.

"This town, this house," Lydia marveled softly, sitting across from her welcome visitor. "It's as though some genie lifted them whole from some coastal village in New England and set them down here, in the woods of the frontier."

Mrs. Chilcote smiled, and Lydia had no doubt that the woman had been a significant beauty in her youth. "Quade's Harbor doesn't have the raw look of Seattle, does it?" she agreed. "My nephew—it's Brigham I refer to now—had a vision of how he wanted this place to be before he ever staked claim to his first stand of timber.

Things tend to take shape the way Brigham imagines them."

"Yes," Lydia said.

Mrs. Chilcote leaned forward in her chair, hands folded serenely, eyes dancing. "Am I wrong in guessing that you've already met Brigham and found him difficult?"

It would have been impossible to lie to the woman, Lydia concluded, even if she'd been so inclined. "He's very officious and overbearing," she allowed, looking away.

The Quades' elderly aunt laughed, the sound soft and rich, like the patter of summer rain on the roof. "Brigham is strong-willed," she agreed. Her look became more solemn. "But please don't judge him too harshly. His life has not been easy, despite a fortunate birth, and he's built the beginnings of an empire in these woods, with more hindrance from the fates than help, I'm afraid."

Lydia was puzzled by this last remark, but she didn't pursue it. The excitement and drama of recent events had finally begun to catch up with her, and she wanted nothing so much as a warm fire on the hearth, a pot of strong, sweet tea, and a long, blissful nap.

"You must be very weary," Mrs. Chilcote said pleasantly, and Lydia added astuteness and perception to the qualities she'd already ascribed to the lady. "Would you care for some refreshment?"

"Tea would be wonderful," Lydia answered. "Thank you." Her hostess rose resolutely and left the room, and Lydia went to the marble fireplace, where small bits of dry bark and sticks of kindling rested on the grate. She found matches on the mantelpiece, in a porcelain box with violets painted on the lid, and lit the fire. When the blaze had caught properly and she'd adjusted the damper to her liking, she added several small, seasoned logs from the brass basket at her side.

She was warming herself, hands outspread, when Mrs. Chilcote returned with a tray. This she set on a sturdy table of highly polished, ornately carved pine, and Lydia caught the wondrous scent of tea. There was also a dish of cinnamon pears, a small sandwich with the crust cut away, and a bowl of savory-looking stew.

"I'll leave you to get settled," Mrs. Chilcote said, her voice as warm as the crackling fire on the hearth. "Dinner is at seven, as uncivilized as that seems. Brigham declares he'll starve if he has to wait until eight, as would be proper."

Lydia measured the man in her mind; he seemed as tall and burly as a bear, though in truth he had the same lean grace and broad shoulders as his brother. She'd sensed a controlled energy about him, as though there were a furnace burning in his spirit, growing hotter and hotter, threatening to burst free in an explosion of molten activity.

She nodded her thanks to Mrs. Chilcote, and when she was alone, settled down on the side of the bed to consume the food. When every crumb was gone, she fed the cheerful fire more wood and then stretched out to nap, covering herself with a brightly patterned quilt.

When she opened her eyes again, hours later, the room was in shadows and she could hear rain whispering at the window glass. There was a dank chill in the air, and the fire had reduced itself to a few forlorn embers.

Rubbing her arms in an effort to warm herself, Lydia sprang from the bed and went to the hearth to add kindling, then another log. In the glow of the resultant blaze, she found the kerosene lamp on her bedside table, turned up the wick, and lit it.

She was just replacing the beautifully painted globe when there was a knock at her door. Expecting Mrs. Chilcote, or perhaps Millie, Lydia smoothed her hair and crumpled skirts and went smiling to admit her company.

A slender young woman, just into adolescence, stood in the hallway, where two lamps burned at either end of a long cherrywood table. She was as beautiful as Millie, though in a different way, for her hair was maple-colored and her eyes a soft brown.

Lydia felt an unexpected twinge, surmising that her

caller had to be Charlotte Quade, Brigham's older daughter, and she was somehow certain that the child resembled her mother.

Unmistakable hostility glinted in the wide, fawn-soft eyes. "Papa says you're to come down to dinner or we'll eat without you," she said.

Inwardly, Lydia sighed. If she hadn't been so hungry, she'd have sent Mr. Quade an equally rude message via this irritable little messenger. Instead she simply said, as though having a pleasant encounter at a tea party, "How do you do, Charlotte? I'm Miss McQuire, and I'll be most happy to join you for supper, if you'll just lead the way to the dining room."

Charlotte tossed her lovely head, narrowed her eyes for a moment, and turned on her heel. "I don't understand why Uncle Devon had to bring you here in the first place," she said, without looking back, as she progressed toward a rear stairway in long strides. "We certainly don't need you."

Lydia made no reply, since any comment she might make would certainly be met with more of the thirteen-year-old's brutally direct logic.

They started down the stairs, passed through a kitchen where a man in overalls, suspenders, work boots, and a plaid woolen shirt sat at the table. Dirty pots and pans were everywhere, and he was perusing a thin, crumpled issue of the Seattle *Gazette*.

"That's Jake Feeny, the cook," Charlotte said idly, as though Mr. Feeny were inanimate and unaware of their passing. "Papa hired him after the Indian woman left."

Lydia nodded at Mr. Feeny, and he smiled at her, bright, wry eyes twinkling.

In a dining room as tastefully ostentatious as the rest of the house, the Quade family had gathered at a long table. A blaze chattered on the hearth of a large brick fireplace, and Devon rose at Lydia's appearance, followed reluctantly by Brigham.

She took the only open place, at Brigham's left, and felt unaccountably self-conscious when he drew back her chair before returning to his own.

The conversation resumed, a merry flow of laughter and talk, and the food was delicious. Lydia concentrated on putting away her share of chicken and dumplings and canned green beans cooked with bacon. She wanted to put on a few pounds of insulation in case her fortunes took another unexpected divergence and she found herself out in the rain.

"I think we should send Miss McQuire back wherever she came from," Charlotte proclaimed suddenly, and the tide of happy interchange dried up instantly.

"Let's send Charlotte instead and keep Miss McQuire," Millie countered, pausing to put out her tongue at her sister.

Lydia lowered her fork to her plate and sat with her hands folded in her lap. Although she would have done anything to prevent it, her gaze swerved to Brigham. She wasn't looking for a champion, needed no defense from the silly attacks of a child, and yet she expected something.

Mr. Quade glowered at his elder daughter, taking a white dinner napkin from his lap and setting it aside. "Perhaps you would prefer spending the rest of the evening in your room, contemplating the drawbacks of rudeness."

"I'm sorry, Papa," Charlotte said meekly.

Brigham's response was firm. "It wasn't me you offended," he pointed out.

Charlotte turned her amber eyes to Lydia, and the defiance Lydia saw in their depths belied the child's words. "I apologize, Miss McQuire. I shall not be rude in the future."

Lydia was skeptical of both the apology and the vow to abstain from bad manners, but she nodded, looking solemn for the sake of Charlotte's obviously formidable pride. "Thank you," she said, with dignity.

Soon after, both Charlotte and Millie were excused from the table, and Mrs. Chilcote retired as well. Devon and Polly were lost in each other's eyes, and simply wandered out of the room. Lydia looked after them with an envy that surprised and dismayed her, remembering a time when she'd hoped for a love like that. A time when she'd believed love was possible for her.

"You thought you were going to marry my brother, didn't you?"

Brigham's words so startled Lydia that she spun in her chair, all color gone from her face, the peach-preserve pie that had kept her at the table still untouched before her.

She swallowed. The expression in Brigham's storm-cloud eyes was not unkind, but simply forthright. She cleared her throat. "Yes," she answered, at painful cost to her pride.

The timber baron sat back in his chair, looking at her pensively. "You don't need to worry, you know. You're a handsome woman, and any number of my men would be willing to take you in and give you a name."

Lydia sat up as though lightning had touched the small of her back. A furious blush stung her face. He made her sound like a half-witted waif, or a bedraggled kitten, not the strong and capable woman she was. "I am not looking for a man to take me in, Mr. Quade," she told him, parceling out the words one by one on little puffs of air. "I can look after myself, thank you very much!"

He smiled. "You would have been all wrong for Devon," he said pleasantly. "Polly suits him far better, with her limpid looks and long sighs."

Lydia pushed back her chair to leave, even though it killed her to abandon her pie. She had not had such a treat since before she left the East, and she did not forgo it lightly. "I don't suppose it's occurred to you, Mr. Quade, that Devon might be all wrong for *me*, that *he* might be the one who's unsuited—"

Brigham's palm struck the table with a resounding smack when she would have risen, and she dropped back into her seat, more surprised than intimidated.

"Sit," he said, quite unnecessarily.

Lydia glared at him. It was still raining, and she knew she wouldn't be able to find proper accommodations in a town full of lumberjacks, even if the place had looked staid and settled from the boat.

He waggled an index finger at her. "You and I have

gotten off on the wrong foot, Miss McQuire," he said. "Every time I speak, it seems, you take immediate offense. I was merely offering a comment before; my brother would not know how to deal with a woman like yourself."

A little of Lydia's ire subsided. It was true that Brigham Quade nettled her sorely, but she couldn't imagine why. She was used to the teasing of soldiers with both grave wounds and minor, and besides, he hadn't actually insulted her . . . had he?

She looked at her host out of the corner of one eye. "You have been quite kind, under the circumstances," she conceded, tempted again by the slice of pie awaiting her. The fruit filling was probably both tart and sweet, while the crust looked flaky and light. Lydia tasted humble pie, as well as peach, when she took her first bite. "I'll try to be less sensitive."

There was a smile couched in his voice, or so it seemed to Lydia.

"You do that," Mr. Quade replied.

Lydia savored her pie.

"Devon tells me you were a nurse during the war," said the master of the house, apparently determined to convince her that he could carry on a civil conversation. In truth, Lydia would have been much relieved if he'd simply removed himself from the room.

She chewed, swallowed, dabbed at her mouth with a linen napkin. "Yes." She hated to think about those horrible days, let alone discuss them. There was every possibility that the nightmares would return if she dwelt on the topic too long. "It was not very pleasant, of course."

"I have no doubt of that," Mr. Quade agreed, watching her.

Lydia finished another bite of pie, which didn't taste quite as good as the first. "Perhaps you were involved in the war effort in some way?" she asked, hoping to direct the flow of conversation away from herself.

"Actually," he replied, reaching out for a china pot that looked ridiculously out of place in his brawny, callused hand and pouring himself more coffee, "I sold timber to both sides and kept out of the argument."

She pushed away her pie, unable to believe what she'd just heard. " 'The argument'?" she echoed in disbelief.

Quade leaned forward in his chair, looking baffled. Clearly, he knew he'd offended her again but couldn't think how.

She was about to enlighten him.

"I have seen bodies stacked between trees like cordwood, Mr. Quade," she said coldly, sitting up very straight in her chair. "Sometimes, one of the arms or legs would twitch. We didn't know whether or not some of those men were still alive, and we hadn't a moment to find out, because there were others—so many others—being brought in all the time. At Gettysburg there were corpses so thick on the ground you could barely wedge a foot between them, and they say the water of Antietam Creek ran scarlet with blood. I would not call the War Between the States an 'argument.' Furthermore, I consider your selling lumber to the rebel states an act of treason."

"The war is over, Lydia," he said, his voice quiet and grave.

She barely heard him, she was so flustered. "Have you no conscience? How could you bear to prosper from such carnage?"

Brigham's tones were still level, though a tiny muscle was twitching under his left cheekbone. "I didn't start the conflict, and I couldn't have stopped it by refusing to sell lumber because a man wore gray instead of blue."

Lydia was so horrified that, for the moment, she couldn't speak. She sat clutching the edge of the table, unable to rise from her chair.

Mr. Quade regarded her thoughtfully for a long interval, then said, "I am willing to allow you your opinion, Miss McQuire. Why is it that you are so troubled by mine?"

She closed her eyes, hearing the exploding shells again, the screams, mere boys in farm clothes and mismatched uniforms, covered in gore and shrieking for their mothers. She smelled the powder from the cannons, the blood, the merciless stench made up of sweat, excrement, urine, and infected flesh. She swayed, felt a strong hand grasp her forearm and steady her.

"Lydia!"

She looked, saw Mr. Quade bending close, but she could still hear the screams. Even after she'd walked away from the hospital in Washington City for the last time, she'd heard them, night and day, hour upon hour, until she'd truly thought she'd go mad from the sound.

She was trembling.

Mr. Quade went to a side table. She heard the clinking of glass against glass, and then he returned, shoving a brandy snifter into her hand.

Normally, Lydia did not take ardent spirits, given the havoc whiskey had caused in her father's life, but she was about to topple over and she needed something to revive her. She took an unsteady sip, using both hands to hold the glass.

"What just happened here?" Brigham demanded, crouching beside her chair. As shaken as she was, his nearness had its effect on her. She felt an achy heat deep inside her, in that place a good woman tried hard not to think about. "You look as though you've just taken tea with the devil."

Lydia was beginning to gather her composure. The nightmare was at bay, for the time being at least, and the alcohol had warmed her blood, but in another way she was more frightened than ever. Mr. Quade's distant comfort was quite as intoxicating as opium; she realized she could come to need that comfort to live, the way she needed water and air and food.

She set the brandy down with a shaking hand, pushed back her chair and bolted. In the doorway she turned back, watching as Mr. Quade rose slowly, gracefully to his feet.

"Lydia," he said, and that was all. Just her name. And yet she felt as though he had somehow reached out and caressed her; her blood thundered in the pulse points behind her ears and at the base of her throat.

She shook her head, somewhat wildly, backing away. Mr. Quade did not pursue her when she fled the room.

In the morning, Lydia awakened to a room full of summer sunshine, feeling abjectly foolish. The first thing she remembered was Brigham's handsome face, close to hers, when he'd crouched beside her chair in the dining room the night before. Looking back, she had the strange feeling that he would have listened to every ugly memory she had, and she felt a peculiar ache in her heart. Few people were strong enough to bear the true realities of war, even secondhand, and because of that, she still carried much of the burden.

She jumped out of bed, having long since learned that action was the only remedy for melancholy thoughts, and put on one of the dresses she'd purchased in San Francisco. She looked sensibly pretty in the gray gown lined with faint pink stripes, she decided, as she unbraided her heavy hair, brushed it, and arranged the tresses in a loose knot at the back of her head. The narrow trim of lace around the cuffs and high collar of the dress added just the right touch of femininity.

The house was very quiet when Lydia descended the stairs, and when she passed the long-case clock in the entryway, she was chagrined. It was nearly ten o'clock; Devon and Brigham had probably been about their business for hours, and there was no sign of the children, Polly, or Aunt Persephone.

Worst of all, Lydia thought, with wry grimness, she'd missed breakfast. She'd never get these jutting bones of hers covered with womanly flesh if she didn't catch up on all the eating she'd missed in recent years.

In the kitchen, Lydia found cold toast and eggs. She brought a plate from one of the shelves and ate, aware of the many times, during the war and after, when she would have felt dizzying gratitude for such a feast.

Immediately after, she washed her plate and silverware. There was a cracked mirror on the wall above the pump handle, and she looked quickly to make sure she was presentable. Then Lydia hurried outside.

The land seemed determined to redeem itself, following yesterday's rainstorm. The dense and seemingly endless multitude of trees was rich green, and the sky was a powdery shade of blue. The waters lapping at the shore reflected the heavens, seeming to harbor the light of sleeping stars in their depths, and towering mountains beyond jutted upward, rugged and heavily traced with snow.

Lydia, who had left the house by a rear door, stood stricken on a rock walkway, staring, wondering how even a rain as fervent as yesterday's could have shrouded such beauty. It was as though God had taken a deep breath, pushed up His sleeves, and made a new Eden here, a glittering emerald of a place trimmed in the sapphire of water and sky.

She felt as though her soul had gone soaring like some great bird, out beyond the chain of mountains. A rustling sound high in a nearby cedar tree brought her back with disturbing abruptness.

"Excuse me," Millie said, from somewhere in the dew-moistened leaves above, "but I wonder if you couldn't help me down, Miss McQuire? I seem to have gotten stuck."

Lydia calculated the distance between the treetop and the flagstone path and raised the fingers of one hand to her mouth. "Hold on very tightly," she said, when she could manage to speak, and then she proceeded toward the tree.

"Millicent can climb like a monkey," a masculine voice said from behind Lydia, just as she would have hoisted her skirts and started up through the fragrant branches. She turned and saw Devon standing beside her, the sun glinting in his fair hair. "She probably intended to lure you up there and then leave you until there was no danger of being forced to work out a sum or diagram a sentence." He moved to stand beside Lydia, looking up, his powerful arms folded, a wry twist to his mouth. "Isn't that so, Millie?"

A defeated sigh drifted down to them, followed by an industrious rustle of leaves and motion of limbs. Small black slippers appeared first, and then the skirt of a blue calico dress. "You'd think it was a crime to have fun in this place," Millicent complained, bringing a smile to Lydia's lips. "I declare, Uncle Devon, you're getting to be every bit as dour as Papa."

Devon tried to look stern, and held up his arms to receive his adventurous little niece as she made a heart-stopping leap from a perch on a branch three feet above his head. "Impossible," he said, giving the child a brief hug before he set her on his feet and rested his hands on his hips. "Now, no more tricks, Millie-Willie. You want Miss McQuire for a friend, don't you?"

Millie smoothed her hair, which was filled with leaves and twigs, giving her the impish charm of a wood fairy. "Charlotte says it's impossible to like one's governess."

Devon touched the tip of his niece's nose. "Since when do you listen to Charlotte?"

Millie shrugged one shoulder, evidently willing to concede the point, and reached out for Lydia's hand. Her small, grubby fingers were remarkably strong. "Come along, then," she said, with cheerful resignation. "I'll show you Quade's Harbor, what there is to see of it, at least." With that, Millicent started down the brick driveway, pulling a beleaguered Lydia behind her.

4

"WHO LIVES IN THESE HOUSES?" LYDIA ASKED. SHE AND
Millie were standing side by side in the muddy street,
their backs to the glorious, sun-splashed waters of the
Sound. The pretty row of six saltboxes, with their tidily
painted white trim, and walls of blue, pale yellow, or
gray, stood stolidly in the aftermath of the storm.

"No one, really," Millie replied, sounding disinterested. "Papa had them built for families, but so far no
one has come except for bachelors. They live in the
camps up on the mountain."

Lydia felt sad. Such fine houses should have flowers
growing in their yards and smoke curling from their
chimneys and children climbing the maple and elm trees
planted out front. Devon had been right, the community
needed nothing so much as women. With female residents would come schools and churches and, eventually,
lending libraries and hospitals.

She thought of all the disappointed spinsters and
lonely widows back in the East and guessed that few of
them would be willing to brave the hardships of the
journey west. Despite this dismal conclusion, a sense of

wild elation stirred within Lydia, a hope she had not known since before the war.

She took an involuntary step toward the white picket fence lining the street, her hands closing around two of the pointed staves.

Millie tugged firmly at Lydia's skirt. "Come along, then, and I'll show you where Papa works when he isn't cutting timber. I vow you've never seen anything like it."

Lydia smiled and let the child lead her toward a nearby cove, where an ocean of tree trunks rolled and bobbed on the water. Even as they approached, a roar filled the air and an enormous tree thundered down a flume on the side of the mountain. At the bottom men were waiting with large poles to maneuver the unprocessed lumber into the logjam in the Sound.

Lydia stopped to shade her eyes from the bright sunshine and watched as another log coursed noisily down the flume. Men shouted and mules brayed and the whistling screech of a mill blade pierced the sawdust-and-salt-scented air. Again she felt a surge of excitement and wonder, a sense of being a part of some grand scheme.

"There's Papa's office," Millie said, pointing out the strangest structure Lydia had ever seen. The shack was carved right out of a giant tree trunk, at least twelve feet in diameter, with its roots still reaching into the ground like determined brown fingers. The roof was of weathered shingles, and there was a single narrow, rusted chimney pipe. One set-in window gave the place an impudent appearance, like a rogue winking at a lady.

Lydia was delighted. The tree-stump house looked like something from a storybook, a place where a talking rabbit or wood rat might live.

She was just standing there, enjoying the novelty of her thoughts, when suddenly Brigham strode out through a doorway that had obviously been shaped to accommodate his unusual height. Instantly, his gray eyes swung to Lydia and lingered, unreadable, on her face.

Finally, he came toward her, no hint of a smile

touching his well-shaped, faintly sensuous mouth. "What are you doing here?" he asked, as though Lydia had invaded sacred territory. Then, without giving her a chance to answer, he went on. "This is no place for women and children, Miss McQuire. I will thank you not to bring my daughter here again."

A dangerous place. Lydia thought of Gettysburg, and Second Manassas, and she would have laughed if her recollections hadn't been so grim.

In the next instant, she recalled that Mr. Quade had sold lumber to the southern side as well as the Union, no doubt helping to prolong the conflict and thus the suffering for both Federal and Confederate soldiers. She stiffened, standing her ground only because she sensed that he expected her to turn and flee.

"Go home, Millicent," he said, without glancing at his daughter. Brigham's eyes, gray as General Lee's best coat, held Lydia's Union-blue ones fast.

To Lydia's distress, the child obeyed without question, letting go of her hand and scampering away.

Lydia swallowed, holding her shoulders so straight they ached. She'd once come face-to-face with a Confederate picket, while seeking a few minutes of peace in the woods near one of the battlegrounds, and even that nervous young sentinel hadn't frightened her the way this man did.

"How do you expect to bring women and children to this place, the way you treat them?" she somehow found the nerve to inquire.

Brigham—she wasn't certain when she'd begun to think of him by his given name, but she had—glowered down at her for a long interval, then startled her completely by giving a hoarse shout of laughter. "I thought the Union won because of superior numbers and better supply systems. Now I realize it was because they had you on their side."

Lydia flushed, but beneath her anger was a current of quiet pride. "I don't think it's wise to discuss the war, sir," she said, raising her chin. "It is unlikely that we will ever agree."

He raised curved, callused fingers to within an inch of her cheek, as if meaning to caress her, even though his eyes and the set of his jaw were still full of mockery. At the last instant, probably remembering the presence of his men, Brigham let his hand fall back to his side.

"You're right," he said gruffly. Despite his conciliatory words, there was an unspoken challenge in his tone and his manner. He seemed to find her amusing, to look upon her with a sort of indulgence, and that was infuriating. "We'll never agree."

She suspected that few people, with the exceptions of his aunt and his brother, ever dared to venture an idea contrary to his own. "You should be more open to the opinions of others, Mr. Quade," she said. "You might learn something."

His grin was slow and molten, and the heat of his presence reached deep inside Lydia's being to touch virgin places she'd never been aware of before that moment. "I could say the same thing to you, Miss McQuire," he replied. "Now, take yourself back to the house, please, and read a book or sew something. I've got work to do."

Such a charge of anger went through Lydia that she rose onto the balls of her feet for a moment with the force of it, then she narrowed her eyes and folded her arms. "This is your property and you may certainly order me off it if you wish. However, before I go, I must say that I think you are a pompous and arrogant man, and your attitudes will certainly bring you to grief."

Again that lethal, knee-melting smile flashed white in his tanned face. "You are in sore need of taming, Miss McQuire," he drawled, and even though she knew his words were designed to make her furious, she fell right into the trap.

"Of all the nerve!"

He laughed. "As if you lacked for gall," he scolded mockingly. "Go home and behave yourself."

"I will not be dismissed like a child," Lydia replied evenly, seething. She couldn't remember the last time she'd felt such dangerous anger. "I am not your ten-year-old daughter!"

Brigham's gaze traveled leisurely to the pulse point at the base of her throat, her well-rounded breasts, and then back to her face. "No. You are definitely not my daughter. But I run Quade's Harbor and you will find that it's best to obey me."

Lydia could not remain without doing bodily harm to Brigham Quade. So, turning, she lifted the skirts of her pink and gray dress above the mud and marched away, hurling intermittent looks back at him as she went.

A shout of laughter followed her.

Millie was waiting behind a blackberry bush, just past the last of the six empty saltbox houses, her eyes wide.

"I've never heard anybody besides Uncle Devon talk to Papa like that," the child said, admiration plain in her voice. "If Charlotte or I sassed him that way, we'd probably have to sit in our room for a week."

Lydia smiled, even though Brigham had thoroughly ignited her temper. Until she'd met him, she thought she'd never be truly angry again, and the emotion thrummed painfully beneath the veneer of numbness she'd so carefully cultivated. "You're a child, Millie," she said, in a remarkably normal tone. "It is fitting that you and Charlotte should speak respectfully to your father." *Even if he is an insufferable ass,* she added to herself.

Millie looked up at her in honest question. "Don't you have to speak respectfully, too? Uncle Devon does, and so does Aunt Persephone."

Lydia automatically took Millie's hand. She'd developed a strong affection for the child already, and hoped she would somehow be able to find common ground with Charlotte as well. "I don't think I was impolite," Lydia pointed out, and she supposed she sounded a little defensive. Brigham had ordered her back to the house, and for that very reason she would have gone to China to avoid the place. "What else is there to see in Quade's Harbor?" she asked.

"Uncle Devon's building a mercantile," Millie replied excitedly, her eyes shining. "He promised to have hair ribbons and peppermint sticks and storybooks. All Papa sells at the company store is dried beans and long underwear and those boots with spikes on the bottom."

"Pretty dull fare," Lydia agreed.

Millie pointed to a fenced cemetery, high on a green knoll. "There was an Indian fight right there, when Charlotte was three years old and I was just about to be born. Mama and Papa lived in a cabin, behind where the big house is now, and Papa hid Mama and Charlotte under the floor until the fighting was over. Uncle Devon has a scar on his right shoulder, where an arrow hit him."

Lydia wondered if Millie was making up the story, until she looked down into the child's sad, earnest face. "Aunt Persephone says Mama never got over the terror of that day. She just walked and walked alongside the water. Charlotte says Mama wanted a ship to come and take her away from here forever."

They rounded the base of the knoll and came to the skeleton of a building formed of newly planed lumber. Between the boards, the blue water of the harbor was visible, sparkling in the bright light of morning, and Devon straddled the high center beam, shirtless, his legs dangling.

Lydia looked around for Polly, but there was no sign of her.

Devon grinned down at the pair. "Hello," he called good-naturedly, and again Lydia felt a pang. If she'd sat down at God's elbow and designed a husband for herself —provided she'd wanted a mate in the first place, of course, which she most certainly didn't—the end result might well have been Devon Quade. He was gentle and industrious, and it would probably never occur to him to boss people around the way his brother did. Nor, she reflected, would he have been so coldly avaricious as to sell timber to each of two warring armies.

Millie waved and called back exuberantly, "Hello!"

Lydia seldom indulged in self-pity, at least not for more than a few moments at a time, but as she watched Devon climb nimbly down a support beam and stride toward them, she had grave doubts about her lot in life. It seemed to her then that happiness was something meant only for others.

"Smile," Devon said, shrugging into his shirt and then touching her chin with brotherly affection. "Have I brought you to such a bad place as all that?"

She swallowed. Quade's Harbor could never be described in such a way; it was too beautiful, a living poem from the pen of God Himself. "No," she said, lips trembling with the effort. "Where is Polly?"

Before Devon could answer her question, Millie sniffed and said, "Probably still lying in bed, like Charlotte."

Lydia looked down at the child and spoke with gentle disapproval. "Millicent, that was a very unkind remark."

Millie's chin was set at an obstinate angle, making her look more like Brigham than ever. "It's the truth."

Devon's expression was somewhat sheepish. "Polly is . . . delicate," he said.

"See?" Millie challenged, her lower lip jutting slightly. This gesture, when coupled with the little girl's likeness to Brigham, was comical. Just imagining the imperious Mr. Quade making such a face brought a peal of laughter swelling into Lydia's throat.

"And what of Charlotte?" Lydia asked, trying to hide her amusement. "Is she delicate, too?"

Millie gave a snort. "No. Charlotte is just lazy. And she likes to stay up late, reading about ships and pirates and magical kingdoms. Sometimes she walks around for days, sighing a great deal and pretending she's a princess. When she read about Robin Hood, she was Maid Marian for a solid month!"

Both Lydia and Devon laughed, and Lydia was grateful. Unknowingly, Millie had smoothed over a somewhat awkward moment.

Lydia was just about to say she'd look in on Polly and make sure she was all right when the insistent clanging of a bell echoed through the crisp, clean air.

"Food," cried Millie, letting go of Lydia's hand and bolting back toward the big house overlooking the harbor and the brave beginnings of a town.

Devon smiled, but there was concern in his eyes as he and Lydia walked along the rutted road to the base of the driveway. "I know Brigham can be impossible—remember, I grew up with him—but he's a rare man, Lydia. Like you, he has a strength of spirit that carries him through experiences other people couldn't begin to survive."

Lydia was struck by the implication that Brigham had suffered in some fundamental and poignant way, but she didn't know Devon well enough to pursue the thought. That would have been prying. "Perhaps that 'strength of spirit,' as you describe it, is really just plain, stubborn pride," she said. She'd sounded bitter as she spoke, but the words were already out before she realized that.

Devon's response was gentle, and by that very fact it shamed her. "Is that what makes you so strong, Lydia? 'Plain, stubborn pride'?"

"Maybe," Lydia confessed, flushing. He was right; she held tightly to her pride, fearing that she would be weak without it.

When they were halfway up the brick driveway, they encountered Charlotte, who wore a flowing gauze dress and had draped herself in thin silk scarves of all colors. She stared dreamily ahead, not seeming to notice them, and Lydia was amazed.

She started to follow the girl, only to have Devon grip her elbow lightly and stay her.

"Don't worry," he whispered, his eyes full of warm laughter. "Charlotte is pretending again—my guess would be that she's been reading some story set in Arabia."

Lydia felt an upsurge of joy. After the horrors she'd seen in Union field hospitals and prison camps, it was wonderful to be reminded that young girls still played dress-up and cloaked themselves in dreams. Being in Quade's Harbor was like waking up to sunshine after a frightening and tempestuous night.

"Maybe she'll be an actress when she grows up," Lydia speculated.

Devon touched an index finger to his lips. "Don't let

Brig hear you say that. He has very conventional ideas where his daughters are concerned—he'd rather see them join the circus than tread the boards, I think."

They had reached the house, and instead of using the formal front entrance, they went around to the back and stepped into Jake's kitchen. He'd set the big oak table next to the window for five, but only Millie was there.

Devon washed at the pump in the sink, while Lydia used a basin of warm water Jake had set out for her.

The meal consisted of cold meat, bread, applesauce, and vegetables preserved at the height of last year's gardening season. Charlotte drifted in midway through, like a beautiful ghost, and ate delicate portions without ever acknowledging the others at the table with so much as a look.

"We're invisible," Millie explained in a stage whisper.

"Oh," Lydia replied.

After they'd eaten, she helped Jake clear the table and tidy up the kitchen, but the cook refused to let her wash the dishes. Devon had gone back to his building project, Millie was curled like a kitten in one of the big chairs in her father's study, sound asleep, Aunt Persephone was reading in the main parlor, and Charlotte was still wandering about looking tragic. Lydia climbed the main stairway and tapped discreetly at doors until she found the newlyweds' room.

Polly was standing at the window, gazing out at the endless panorama of sea and sky and mountains. She was still wearing her dressing gown, and her hair trailed down her back in a gleaming tumble of dark curls.

"Polly?" Lydia inquired softly. "Are you ill?"

When the other woman turned to look at her, Lydia saw pain in the beautiful hazel eyes. A single tear slid down her cheek. "No. No, I'm well enough. Considering."

Lydia stepped into the room and closed the door, even though Polly had not actually invited her. "Then why are you crying?"

Polly sighed. "It would seem silly to someone like

you." Lydia had told the other woman something of the suffering she'd seen in the war, while they were sailing up from San Francisco.

Lydia shook her head. "No one's troubles are unimportant," she said.

Devon's bride suddenly covered her face with both hands, sobbed, and collapsed onto the edge of the bed. "Oh, dear God," she wailed. "You don't know what I've done! *He* doesn't know what I've done!"

Lydia went to sit beside Polly on the mattress, cautiously putting an arm around the woman's trembling shoulders. "What is it?" she asked softly, certain the crime could not be anything really terrible. On the other hand, people often brought secrets with them when they came west; sometimes they were pursued by them.

Polly gave a mournful wail and wept on, so Lydia waited patiently. It was in her nature to give comfort, she thought fleetingly.

"Polly?" Lydia prompted, after a long time.

She swallowed. "I'm in love with Devon!" she choked out miserably.

For a moment Lydia was full of relief. Then she saw the look of torment in Polly's eyes. "Is that so bad?" she asked gently. "He's your husband."

Polly shuddered. "No," she said. "It was all a trick."

Lydia just sat there, staring stupidly, horrified. "A trick?" she asked finally.

Polly bolted off the bed and went to the bureau with resolve. She began jerking open drawers and snatching things out, and for one awful second Lydia thought she was packing to leave Quade's Harbor, and Devon, forever.

"Polly, what did you mean when you said it was all a trick?"

The erstwhile Mrs. Quade disappeared behind a changing screen. "I shouldn't have said even that much," she muttered. Then she peeked around the ornately carved maple frame. "You're not going to tell Devon or his brother, are you?"

By then Lydia's frustration had mounted to a dangerous level. "Devon Quade is a very fine man, Polly. If you do anything to hurt him, you'll have me for an enemy."

Again Polly looked around the screen. This time her eyes were narrowed. "Say. You'd better not have your cap set for my Devon," she said. "If you do, I'll pull your ears off!"

Lydia wasn't intimidated. *"Is* he 'your Devon'?" she persisted.

Again Polly's pretty face crumpled into tears. "I do love him, I swear it."

"But you tricked him somehow," Lydia pressed. "What happened back there in San Francisco?"

Polly came out from behind the screen, wearing a dramatic green gown that set off her dark hair and lovely pale skin. She turned her back and Lydia automatically began fastening her buttons.

"Nat Malachi and me, that's the man I've been with since I came out to San Francisco, we had a good business going. He'd pose as a preacher and pretend to marry me to a miner or a timberman, and I'd steal his wallet after—well, when he was sleeping. We intended to do the same thing to Devon, except—except when he touched me, something changed. *I* changed."

Lydia was stunned. She'd read of such doings in the penny dreadfuls, but she'd certainly never encountered a perpetrator. For a long interval she just gaped at Polly in wonderment.

"You've got to tell him the truth," she finally said, when Polly began to snuffle again.

Polly shook her head wildly. "No. And don't you tell him, either. He'd throw me out in the street!"

Lydia had a hard time imagining such a scene, although there could be no doubt that Devon would be furiously hurt when he learned of the deception.

Polly approached, gripped Lydia hard by the shoulders. "You won't breathe a word of what I've said!" she cried in a hoarse whisper, the words forming both an angry plea and a piteous question.

Rising, Lydia shrugged away the other woman's hold,

forcing Polly to step back. Lydia's dignity was one of the few graces left to her. "I can't promise that I won't speak up," she said evenly. She was still human enough, she noted, for an unseemly sense of triumph to race through her spirit, making her drunk with the knowledge that Devon was unmarried after all. This was fleeting, though, for Lydia knew he loved Polly, she'd seen it too clearly.

Polly's hazel eyes filled with tears. "Dear God, he'll never forgive me," she whispered brokenly.

Lydia had no way of knowing whether that was true or not. She touched Polly's arm in an effort to lend some small reassurance, and left the room.

The bright shine of the day had been tarnished, and Lydia wanted only to retreat to her room and remain there until dinner. She had a personal rule, however: when she wanted most to hide from the world, she must instead wade right out into the middle of it and play her part in things.

Lydia found a shawl, as there was a breeze coming up from the shore, and left the house. Since she didn't want to encounter Brigham, she avoided the mill and his tree-stump office. And of course she wasn't ready to face Devon, either, knowing what she did, so she steered away from his building site as well.

Lydia followed a path behind the great house, through a thicket of blackberry vines that snatched at her skirts, past giant ferns and clusters of hemlock and cedar and pine. Gossamer sunshine soaked through the leaves and, here and there, hearty ivy grew up the trunk of a tree like a green coat. Through it all was woven the secret songs of the birds.

At the top of the high knoll there was a small, tree-sheltered clearing, and Lydia drew in her breath in surprise. There, square in the center, was a tiny cabin of unplaned logs. The door was at the far left, with three stone steps leading up to the high threshold, and a single window was set in at the opposite end.

The place seemed oddly enchanted to Lydia, perhaps because she'd come upon it unexpectedly. It wouldn't have surprised her if Hansel and Gretel's witch had come hobbling out to greet her.

Smiling at the fancy, she put her hands behind her back and called out politely, "Hello? Is anyone at home?"

There was no reply, except for the irritable complaints of the birds, who were no doubt remarking to each other that she had a nerve, coming to call without an invitation.

Lydia walked around the outside of the small house, looking at the neatly made brick chimney of the fireplace. There was no back door, she found, and no other window besides the one in front, but that wasn't surprising. Indian attacks were not unheard of in this part of the country, and the fewer points of entry a place had, the less vulnerable were its inhabitants.

She recalled Millie's story, about her mother and Charlotte hiding under the floorboards when Charlotte was a baby, and laid one hand to the sturdy frame surrounding the door. Surely this was the same cabin, the home Brigham had built for his young bride.

The thought gave Lydia an unexpected sting, and she sat down on a flagstone step, resting her chin in one hand. Sweetbriar clambered lushly up a crude trellis beside her, covered in fragrant pink blossoms, and she watched solemnly as a fat bee fumbled from one flower to another.

She tried to imagine Brigham's wife, but no picture came to mind. She hadn't noticed a likeness on display anywhere in the big house, at least not those parts that she frequented, but then she hadn't been looking for one.

Lydia sat awhile, enjoying the scent of the sweetbriar, then stood, her hands on her hips. The whole time, of course, her newest dilemma had been churning beneath the surface of her thoughts. She could not go to Devon with what she knew about Polly, for he had been kind to her and she wouldn't hurt him so cruelly. Perhaps she might tell Brigham, since he was clearly the head of the Quade family, but she feared his reaction. It was only too easy to imagine him in a towering rage, shouting at everyone, perhaps alienating his brother forever.

Walking back down the path toward the main house, Lydia considered speaking with Aunt Persephone about the matter, but she ruled that idea out as well. The whole situation was simply too delicate, and besides, she knew so little about the old woman's temperament. Perhaps such news would vex her to the point of hysteria, or even apoplexy or heart failure.

Jake Feeny was sitting on the back step, a cigar jutting out of his mouth and a huge basin of potatoes at his side. He peeled one deftly with a paring knife and dropped it into a pot of water as Lydia approached.

Lydia smiled. The cook's methods looked none too sanitary, but she'd already surmised that Mr. Feeny kept his kitchen clean and his person tidy as well. On the frontier, one had to make certain concessions.

She joined him, smoothing her skirt beneath her before she sat. "Is there another knife?" she asked, reaching into the basin for a potato.

Mr. Feeny surrendered the blade he'd been using, giving Lydia a pensive but not unfriendly look as she began to scrape away the thick brown peel. "You scrape many spuds back where you come from?"

Lydia laughed and nodded toward Brigham's peak, with its long, noisy flume and rich stands of timber crowded so close together that it seemed there would be no room for a tree to fall. "Enough to make a pile the size of that mountain over there, Mr. Feeny," she said.

The cook didn't return her smile, but he rubbed his beard-stubbled chin and looked her over with solemn respect. "Jake," he replied gruffly. "Call me Jake."

5

BRIGHAM SWEATED AS HE WORKED HIS END OF THE CROSS-cut saw. Despite years of such labor, the muscles girding his stomach and lower back ached with a poignant violence, and the flesh beneath the calluses on his palms stung where he gripped the handle. He set his jaw and continued to thrust and draw, but his mind would not be so easily controlled as his body; every time he let down his guard for so much as a moment, his thoughts went meandering off after Lydia McQuire.

He'd already considered her womanly figure, which needed some plumping up, in his view, and her soft, glimmering hair, but it was her violet eyes that haunted him. They'd seen much suffering, those eyes, and there were still faint smudges beneath them, shadows of the bitter sights they'd looked upon. And yet he glimpsed a capacity for joy in their depths, as well as an almost pagan capacity for passion.

Brigham shook his head. He was imagining things, he told himself. Lydia was tough and strong, but all the whimsy and the poetry and the fire that went into the making of a woman had been crushed by the ugliness she'd encountered.

If he had any sense at all, he decided grimly, he'd write out a bank draft, load her on the next mail boat out of the harbor, and forget she'd ever existed.

He smiled and ran one arm across his brow to soak up some of the perspiration burning his eyes. Then he took a firm grip on the saw handle again, falling gracefully back into the rhythm. Trust Devon to bring home the sauciest little Yankee ever to sprout in New England, and hand her over like one of those souvenir cards with the silly pictures on the front.

His partner let out a yell, and Brigham was so distracted that he barely thrust himself back away from the tree in time. It fell with a rushing sound, made thunder as it struck the ground, and for a moment the earth quaked beneath Brigham's cork boots.

"Damn it, Brig," the other man yelled, gesturing furiously toward the tree, "that was my own personal lucky saw, and you let it go right down with the timber!"

Brigham wiped his face again. He would have liked to strip away his shirt and work bare-chested, but that was dangerous; the branches of a falling tree could rip a man's hide open like the point of a fine sword. "Quit grousing and try to pry it out," he said shortly. It wasn't Zeb he was riled at, though; he was angry with himself for breaking one of his own rules: a man should never think about whiskey, food, or women when he was working in the woods. The indulgence could get him, or someone else, killed.

Zeb, a skinny young South Carolinian with the testy temperament of a bullwhacker, plunged into the fragrant branches to search for his saw.

Brigham turned away, only to find his nervous clerk, Jack Harrington, hovering behind him. The boy's round spectacles had slid to the end of his nose, and he pushed them back with a practiced middle finger. He had a pencil over one ear, and he clutched a pad of paper to his bosom as though it were the Holy Writ.

"God's balls, Harrington, don't sneak up on me like that! If I'd had an ax in my hand, I might have cut you down like a blue spruce!"

Harrington trembled inside his cheap mail-order suit, and Brig wondered why the little squirrel couldn't wear oiled canvas pants, work boots, suspenders and cotton shirts, like everybody else. "It's about Miss Lydia McQuire," he said. "Mrs. Chilcote tells me the woman has been engaged as a governess, but I can find no written record of your authorization."

An oversight like that could keep Harrington awake nights, Brig supposed, feeling a sort of wry sympathy. "That's because I haven't decided whether to put Miss McQuire on the payroll or buy her passage back to San Francisco. I'll let you know when I make up my mind."

Brigham looked back toward the tree he and Zeb had just felled. Already, men were all over it like two-legged bugs, sawing away the branches, shouting to each other, some of them singing a bawdy song in rough chorus. Then he turned to stride back down the mountain to his office, and Harrington scrambled along beside him.

"I don't know, sir," he blithered. "I don't much hold with such loose ends. It seems to me that a decision should be made and acted upon."

Brigham sighed. "I'll have to speak with the lady before I give you an answer," he said reasonably.

"Does she want to stay?"

Brig's heart swelled slightly. "I don't know," he answered, always pragmatic. "For all I can say, she might be swimming out to meet the next boat even as we speak."

Harrington blinked three times rapidly, smoothed his slicked-down hair with one palm, and said, "Oh. You were *joking,* sir. That was very humorous. Very humorous indeed."

Brigham rolled his eyes. "Haven't you got anything better to do than devil me?" he asked. "Go find the McQuire woman yourself, and ask her if she wants to stay on as a companion to my daughters. Tell her I'll pay her a dollar a week and provide her with board and room."

The clerk nodded again, and scurried off. Harrington was never happy unless he had some crisis to fuss about, be it manufactured or otherwise, but he did his job well enough, and that was all Brigham cared about.

Reaching the bench where the water buckets sat, lined up and kept brimming by a full-grown Chinaman no bigger than Millie, Brig dipped out a ladleful, lowered his head, and poured the icy liquid over the back of his neck. He spat out a swear word at the chill and then shook his head, sending droplets flying in every direction, like a dog that's just been sprung from a washtub.

He was hot and bone-tired and, for the first time since the start of Isabel's decline, he was actually looking forward to going back to that grand house he'd built with such confidence. He went into the office, gathered up a stack of ledger books, and started for home.

Millie was swinging on the gate at the base of the walk when he reached the fence, and the delighted surprise in her small face shamed him. So did the worried expression that quickly chased the joy from her eyes.

"Are you sick, Papa? Did somebody get hurt up on the mountain?"

The questions stung, and he would have hoisted the little girl up into his arms if he hadn't been covered in fir sap and drenched with sweat. "No, child," he said, ruffling her hair as the gate creaked backward, carrying her with it, so that he could pass.

Millie hurried after him, and he slowed his pace so she could keep up. "We could go fishing," she said, with such breathless daring that Brigham stopped in midstep and crouched to face her. "The sun will be up for a long time yet, and I'll bet the trout are biting real good."

Brigham smiled. He wanted a bath, a drink, and some time to assemble his thoughts, but he couldn't bring himself to extinguish the eager light in his daughter's eyes. "Do we have any poles around here?" he asked.

She bounced on the balls of her feet in her excitement, and Brigham thought of all the times he'd told himself it was enough to provide well for his daughters. Foolishly, he thought, he'd expected Charlotte and Millie to realize he loved them because he gave them food and shelter.

"Yes!" she cried. "They're out in the shed, and I know where to dig for worms, too!"

Brigham kissed the child lightly on the forehead and rose to his feet. "You go and find what we need, and I'll clean up a little. Then we'll catch a mess of trout for dinner."

With a whoop, Millie shot off toward the rear of the house, a streak of blue calico crossing the lawn, and Brigham followed at a slower meter. He had never guessed that so little notice from him would please the child so greatly.

Reaching the back porch, he entered the empty kitchen, filled a large basin from the hot water reservoir attached to the big cookstove, and went back outside. He'd stripped off his shirt and was splashing his upper body industriously when he became aware of her, stiffened, and turned his head.

Lydia was standing directly behind him, still as a doe scenting danger, her arms full of kindling, her glorious, tousled hair like a honey-colored cloud around her face. Her breasts rose and fell with the rapid course of her breathing, and her cheeks were as pink as if he'd caught her in some scandal.

He felt his heart thud against his chest, as though trying to break free and somehow bond itself with hers. He shook his head, to clear his mind of the fancy, flung the contents of the basin into the blackberry bushes, and reached for the towel he'd hung over the railing beside the step.

She approached the porch resolutely, giving him as wide a berth as she possibly could, but in the end the whole effort proved futile because he didn't move and neither did the kitchen door. Lydia hesitated again, glanced from Brigham to the doorway and back again, then started for the steps.

He waited until she was so close he could have touched her by taking a deep breath, then stepped back to let her pass. He felt her skirts brush against his thigh, even through the thick fabric of his trousers, and the contact sent a subtle heat surging up into his groin. The scents of castile soap and pine pitch lingered behind her, and suddenly Brigham was overwhelmed by a desire so keen that he broke out in a fresh sweat.

After a few moments of effort, Brigham went inside the house. To his disappointment, as well as his relief, Lydia was nowhere in sight. He climbed the rear stairs, strode along the hallway to his bedroom, and found a clean shirt. When he returned to the back porch, Millie was waiting patiently, a wooden fishing pole in each hand, while Charlotte stood a short distance away, watching.

Brigham whistled as he led the way toward the pond high on the hillside, beyond the old cabin and the Indian burial ground. "Come along if you want, Charlotte," he said easily, and she immediately fell into step beside him, although she kept her chin high and offered no comment on the proceedings.

When they reached the pond's edge, Millie rushed off to dig for worms, and Charlotte and Brigham sat side by side on the grassy bank. Brig was making sure the hooks were secure on the fishing lines, and Charlotte started weaving wild honeysuckle into a chain.

"Are you going to marry Miss McQuire?" she asked presently, without looking at him.

Brigham smiled to himself, making certain his amusement wasn't audible in his voice. "No, Charlotte, I don't think so."

The girl sighed and went on with her weaving, frowning intently as she worked. "She wouldn't be suitable," she declared. "Miss McQuire was a nurse in the Great Civil War and she's seen naked men."

This time Brigham couldn't help chuckling. "And that makes her unsuitable?" he asked, setting the poles aside, stretching out on the grass with a sigh and cupping his hands behind his head.

Charlotte looked over at him with soft brown eyes. "Of course it does, Papa," she said, enunciating the words carefully, as though he'd lost either his hearing or his good sense since breakfast. "No proper lady has ever seen a man without his clothes!"

He raised himself onto one elbow. "In a way, Charlotte, I'm glad you hold that particular opinion. But there are exceptions, and tending the sick and injured is one of them. Miss McQuire could hardly be expected to treat only wounds that weren't hidden under clothing."

Charlotte's high, finely sculpted cheekbones flushed with color, and she averted her eyes. Once again Brigham was quietly angry with Isabel for leaving their daughters the way she had. There were certain things he simply didn't know how to discuss with them.

"You like Miss McQuire, don't you?"

Brigham sighed, recalling the way he'd reacted when Lydia had stepped past him on her way into the kitchen earlier. "I think she's a bullheaded little tyrant with a high regard for her own opinions," he answered honestly. Then, sadly, he smiled. "Yes, Charlotte. I like her."

Charlotte had finished twining the honeysuckle into a floral wreath, and she laid it on top of her head like a crown. "Well, I've decided to keep my distance," she said, making a face as Millie came running back with a handful of squirming pink and brown earthworms. "You can just bet Miss McQuire will decide she misses her naked men and go right back to the war."

"The war is over, Charlotte," Brigham said, grinning as his younger daughter thrust the bounty of the soil into his face. He took a fat worm and baited one of the hooks. "And all the naked men have put on their clothes and gone home."

Millie's gray eyes went wide. "What naked men?"

Brigham laughed, rolled to his feet, and cast a line into the calm waters of the spring-fed pond. "Never mind," he said.

Charlotte flung herself backward with a dramatic sigh and cried, "Oh, life, oh, life, thou art agony of the keenest sort!"

Millie looked askance at her sister, after tossing her own fishing line in after Brigham's. "Oh, Charlotte, oh, Charlotte," she countered, in a high, prissy voice, "thou art stupid as a stump!"

"Enough," Brigham said sternly, when Charlotte

jumped up, prepared to defend her honor, and Millie let out a shriek of delighted terror. "You'll scare away the fish."

As it happened, they returned to the house an hour and a half later with enough fresh trout for a fine supper. Millie was wild with excitement, her cheeks sunburned, her hair all a-tangle, and Charlotte was absorbed in one of the parts she was constantly playing. Brigham's bruised heart felt as though it had been dipped in light.

There was a feast of fish that night, even though Jake Feeny had fixed a pork roast, and everyone ate their share—except for Polly, who was pale and distracted. Lydia saw Devon toss a worried glance in his mate's direction every so often, and she hurt for them both. Mrs. Chilcote remained in her room, claiming a case of the vapors, and Millie chattered incessantly. Charlotte was pining over something, but she seemed to have a good appetite, and there was a quietness about Brigham, an ease she hadn't seen in him before.

He was wearing a shirt now, of course, but in her mind's eye Lydia still saw him half naked in the dooryard, splashing his powerfully muscled torso with water. She had seen plenty of bare, hairy male chests in her time, of course, but the sight had never quite affected her in the same way. She'd wanted to lay her hands to those graceful, corded muscles, to feel them move beneath her palms and fingers. . . .

A surge of embarrassment struck Lydia then, and she closed her eyes against the onslaught, feeling color pound in her cheeks. When she looked again, she found Brigham watching her, his mouth solemn, his eyes full of humor.

It was almost as though he knew what she'd been thinking, Lydia reflected harriedly, but that was impossible, of course. No one could truly know the mind of another.

She reached for a bowl of sliced beets and took a second helping. The serving spoon clattered against the dish as she replaced it, and Brigham's gaze lingered, seemingly on the hollow at the base of her throat. Which, of course, was hidden by the fabric of her dress.

Because it was Lydia's habit to charge when retreat seemed to be the only safe course, she spoke up in a clear voice. "I would like to speak with you privately after dinner, Mr. Quade," she said to Brigham.

He smiled, still amused, and Lydia wondered what it was about her that aroused such merriment. "As you wish, Miss McQuire," he answered.

Lydia quite literally felt Polly's gaze careen across the table to catch hers. Polly's lovely face was white with fear; she obviously thought Lydia was about to betray her confidence. An almost imperceptible shake of Lydia's head had to serve as reassurance.

When the meal was over, Lydia rose and cleared her place at the table. The doors of the study stood open to the rest of the house when she reached them, and Brigham was at the hearth, one booted foot braced against the brass fireguard. He watched the flames solemnly, as though they were telling some fascinating story.

Lydia folded her arms and set her feet a little apart, for there was something about this man that made her flood with weakness just when she most needed her strength.

"I will require six dollars salary per month, instead of the four you offered me through Mr. Harrington," she announced, "and you must build a schoolhouse. There is no reason, of course, why the structure couldn't serve as a church and a community meeting hall as well."

Brigham slowly turned his head to look at her, and she was at a disadvantage because of the way the shadows played over his face, cloaking his expression. "You want a whole building for two children?"

Lydia tried to stand a little taller. "Yes, Mr. Quade," she said with patience, only too aware that her voice was shaking slightly. "It's rather the same principle as hanging a birdhouse in one's garden. At first the entire enterprise might seem futile, but in time one bird appears, and then another. Soon, there are swallows or finches or robins everywhere." She paused, spread her hands as she summed up her point. "If you make a place for children, Mr. Quade, you will make a place for *families.*"

He folded his arms and turned toward her, one thick shoulder resting against the mantelpiece. "I built six fine houses, facing the harbor," he pointed out, arching one eyebrow, "and they stand empty. Do you have another theory to explain that?"

Lydia sighed. "You'll need those and more as soon as there's a heart to the town. A meetinghouse would provide that."

Brigham was silent for a long time, thoughtful. Once or twice he rubbed his chin with the fingers of his right hand. "Six dollars a month is too much," he said after a long while. "How do I know you're worthy of such a salary?"

She stood her ground. "You probably pay that much, or more, to the men who tend oxen and mules in your lumber camps. Is the care of your daughters less important?"

He stared at her for a long moment, as if amazed at her audacity, then gave a low burst of laughter. "Five dollars and fifty cents," he countered. "My daughters are certainly more important than the livestock, but they're also easier to handle. Most of the time."

The bargain sounded good to Lydia. After all, she'd been offered four dollars salary in the first place, and now she was getting five and a half. "And the building?" she pressed.

"You'll have your meetinghouse by autumn," Brigham conceded.

Lydia smiled. "Good. That's exactly when we'll need it. In the meantime, Charlotte and Millie and I will explore the woods and shore and make a study of science."

Brigham shifted his foot from the fireguard. "Science," he repeated, somewhat derisively. "Teach my daughters to sew a neat stitch, Miss McQuire. Teach them to cook. Those are the things they'll need to know."

Lydia's patience was sorely tried, and only moments

before she'd been riding the swell of triumph! "It seems to me, Mr. Quade," she said evenly, "that there are a number of things *you* need to know. The world is changing. Women want a new place in that world, and they'll have it."

He bent his head so close to hers that their foreheads were nearly touching, and she felt that strange, primitive need rush through her again, making her head spin and turning her knees to marmalade. "Are you so certain you know what women want?" he challenged in a low drawl; and then, suddenly, with no warning whatsoever, he kissed her.

More than once before, a soldier, grateful and fancying himself in love with her, had pressed an awkward farewell kiss on Lydia, but there had never been one like this. The contact itself was hard and forceful, yet Brigham's mouth felt soft as velvet against hers, and persuasive as the scent of lilacs on a summer evening.

With gentle, skilled motions of his lips, his hand splayed at the back of her head, he made her mouth open. The invasion of his tongue was both sweet and violent, and her own rose to greet his, to do battle, to welcome, to surrender. Her breasts were pressed flush to the hardness of his chest, her breath ached in her throat, and still he kissed her. Still he conquered.

She might have sagged against him when he finally drew back, she was so dazed and boneless, but he gripped her shoulders and held her upright. For a long, humiliating moment, she could only stare up at him in drunken confusion.

He touched her trembling lips with an index finger, then broke the spell with a chuckle. "Good night, Miss Lydia McQuire," he said. "Sleep well."

There was a quiet arrogance in his words, too subtle to challenge, but Lydia was unsettled nonetheless. She hoped she hadn't set an unseemly precedent, letting Mr. Quade kiss her that way.

Letting? she thought as she turned, nearly stumbling, to make her way out of the room, out of Brigham's sphere of influence. She hadn't only *let* Mr. Quade take an improper liberty, God help her, she'd wanted more. The thrumming heat he'd stirred in her still hadn't subsided.

Since Lydia was so preoccupied, she got a fright when she entered her bedroom a few minutes later and found Polly standing at the hearth.

"Did you tell Brigham about me?" the other woman asked, sounding desperate and a little angry.

"No," Lydia sighed. "And I don't intend to. But you can't keep a thing like this a secret, Polly. You must go to Devon and tell him the truth—now."

"He'll be furious."

"I have no doubt of that. But Devon's not an unreasonable man. Once he's had time to think things through, he'll probably understand."

"Probably." The word sounded miserable, hopeless. Polly sagged into a chair next to the fireplace. "Pa always said my sins would catch up to me, and I guess he was right. He preached the Gospel, and he claimed to know God's opinions on everything from the stars and planets to Mr. Lincoln's necktie."

Lydia sat on the trunk at the foot of the bed, still a little confounded by the kiss she and Brigham had just shared, and tried to focus her thoughts on the present moment.

"I loved my Pa," Polly reflected, gazing into the low flames burning in the grate of Lydia's fireplace. "Oh, he was meaner than a Pawnee with a toothache, Pa was, but I would have done most anything to get one fond look from him."

Lydia waited.

"I was raised in Kansas, in Indian country," Polly went on. "We had a sod house and a few cattle, and when Pa rode out to make the preaching circuit, I had to stay there alone. I told Pa I was scared the Pawnee would come, or maybe a band of outlaws, but he just said the Lord would look after me." She paused. "Instead, the Lord sent Nat Malachi."

Lydia was drawn into the story, picturing the lonely sod hut, the wandering cattle, feeling the especially imaginative fears of a young girl. "The man who helped you deceive Devon," she said, without rancor.

"Yes," Polly replied, with a nod. She seemed barely aware of Lydia as she went on with her story. "I told Nat he couldn't stay, since my Pa wasn't around and it wouldn't be proper, but Nat said he'd seen a half-dozen Pawnee just over the next rise and I'd be needing somebody to watch over me.

"Nat has one of those wicked smiles that tempt a woman to sinful thoughts, even if he isn't handsome the way my Devon is. By the time a week had passed, he'd made me believe I loved him, and that I wouldn't be able to make my way in life without him.

"He made love to me in the prairie grass, with just the sky for a blanket, and after the first time, I started to like the things he did to me, the way he touched me. I started to need it.

"Then Pa came riding home from his preaching, on that old mule that was as mean and stubborn as he was, and he caught me with Nat. He called me a Jezebel and said he never wanted to look on the likes of me again.

"The next day, I rode out with Nat." Polly's eyes glistened with tears, and she was silent for a long time. Finally she finished the story. "Nat isn't a good man, but he can love a woman until she's in a fever, and make her do just about anything he wants. He got us passage to San Francisco when it looked like he'd be conscripted to fight for the Union army, and for a while he worked on the docks, but he soon grew weary of that. It seemed like a lark—just an easy, harmless way to make money—when we started duping miners and sailors and others into thinking they'd married me. Now I'd give anything to go back and change it all."

Lydia swallowed. "Are you and Mr. Malachi married?" she asked, fearing the worst. Devon might be able to deal with finding out that he was still a bachelor, and not a bridegroom, but bigamy could be more than he could come to terms with.

Polly gave a soft, bitter laugh. "No, thank God. When I think of how I begged that man for a wedding band . . ."

Lydia closed her eyes for a moment, only to feel her

relief give way to grim logic. "Will Nat come here, looking for you?"

"He was drunk when I went to tell him about Devon," she said. "I'm not sure he heard a word I said."

"Suppose he did hear?" Lydia pressed. "Suppose he comes to Quade's Harbor to find you. Imagine what that would do to Devon."

Polly covered her face with both hands.

"There might even be violence," Lydia went on. "Think how you'd feel, Polly, if something happened to Devon. Think how you would regret not warning him about Nat."

Slowly, Polly lowered her hands to her lap. She nodded. "You're right. I'd rather have Devon turn his back on me in contempt than see him hurt. And Nat can be as mean as Pa ever was, if he has a mind to be." She rose stiffly from her chair. "I'm not a bad person, Lydia," she said plaintively. "We might have been good friends, you and I."

Lydia touched Polly's arm. "We can still be friends," she said. "You'll see."

Polly nodded again and left the room. Lydia undressed to her camisole and drawers and sat by the fire, a kerosene lamp burning at her side, to read. Occasionally she heard voices tumbling down the hallway, male and female and tangled together, but there was no shouting. She was just beginning to hope Devon had heard Polly's story and understood when a nearby door slammed with an explosive crack.

When Lydia peered into the hallway, unable to resist investigating, she saw the broad expanse of Devon's back as he stormed toward the main staircase. Just the set of his shoulders gave eloquent testimony that the soul of this quiet man brimmed with a rage he could barely contain.

6

S OME INNER ALARM MADE BRIGHAM LOOK UP FROM THE
paperwork spread over his desk when Devon came down
the stairs and passed the study doorway. Even in the
shadow-smudged light of the kerosene lamps, Brig could
see that his brother's stiff composure was only a brittle
shell covering some grievous injury of the spirit. He
pushed back his chair and stepped into the entry hall.

Devon. His only brother, his best friend, his partner.
Although the two men never spoke of their affection for
each other, Brigham would have suffered almost any sort
of pain or privation if it meant sparing Devon.

"Wait," Brigham said, reaching the front door just as
Devon descended the steps.

The other man stopped, his backbone stiff, his head
tilted slightly backward, as if to look up at the stars.
Devon's voice was raw when he spoke, and broken. "I
can't talk now, Brig," he said, without turning around.
And then he strode off down the walk, disappearing into
the noisy darkness of a summer night.

It would be no favor to pursue Devon, so Brigham
turned to go back into the house.

Lydia stood in the doorway, a prim corduroy wrapper

clutched around her enticing figure, her hair braided into a single thick plait resting against her right shoulder. The light behind her made an aura of flyaway strands, and her blue eyes were wide and worried.

"Aren't you going after him?"

Brigham muttered an exclamation better suited to the lumber camps than his front porch, and thrust one hand through his hair. He had the distinct impression Lydia knew something about Devon's trouble that he didn't, and the idea irritated him.

"No," he snapped, running his eyes over the length of her sumptuous person with deliberate insolence. "Are you?"

Even in the thin light making its way through the front windows, he could see her color change. "Why, no—of course not. I was simply concerned."

"What's going on here?" Brigham demanded, without trying to couch the words in the slightest courtesy. "Devon is not a temperamental man, and I've never seen him the way he was just now."

She lifted her obstinate little chin. "I would be betraying a confidence if I answered that question. You'll have to ask your brother, or Polly."

Brigham felt wholly distracted in those moments, and wildly frustrated. All of a sudden his very being seemed to be pulled east from west, one part wanting to go after Devon, another to stay near this woman, always. Along with her fresh-faced good looks and saucy pragmatism, she presented a multitude of intangible mysteries Brig wanted desperately to solve.

Feeling her soft, strong body buck beneath his in the fevered abandon of pleasure was only the beginning of the things he wanted from her. Beyond that primordial yearning were other needs, for solace, for challenge, for laughter and fury. He should have been thinking about his brother, and instead he was feeling things, things he'd never imagined, let alone experienced.

The sudden awareness of the track his thoughts were following wrenched Brigham, slammed him hard against a wall of reason. He didn't know this woman. He didn't even particularly *like* this woman. His brother was wandering in the darkness, bleeding from some wound of the soul. And with all of that, here he stood, his brain full of images too lurid for a dime novel.

Crickets and frogs sang in the darkness, and he caught the scents of saltwater and pine sap on the night breeze. As always, those things were a comfort to Brig, because his soul had rooted itself in this land crowded with trees and shining with bright waters. He had long since given his heart to the place, in the same way a husband pledged himself to his wife. "Damn it, Lydia," he said presently, in an effort to redeem himself to his own standards, "if you're keeping back something I need to know to help my brother, I'll never forgive you."

She touched her wild, beautiful hair self-consciously. "Good night, Mr. Quade," she said in stiff tones. Then she turned and marched herself into the house without another word.

"Good night," he said tersely, long after Lydia had disappeared and he was alone with the frogs and the crickets.

The light of the rising sun was dazzling on the water when Polly approached the framework of Devon's building the next morning. He hadn't returned to their room in the big house the night before, after she'd told him of her deception, and she'd known he would be here.

Sure enough, Devon had built a small campfire in the clearing beside the beginnings of his mercantile, and he was sitting next to it with his back to a large, porous rock. He sensed her approach, looked at her. The expression in his ink-blue eyes, so full of laughter and love before her confession, was flat, defiant, cold.

"You're going," he said, in a voice that had no inflection at all, the words comprising both a statement and a query.

Polly's throat tightened. She heard her father's voice, in the forefront of her mind, quoting his beloved Bible. *Ye shall know the truth, and the truth shall set you free.* In this case, the truth had set only Devon free, but she might well remain its prisoner forever.

"Do you want me to go?" she managed, after a long interval of painful, throbbing silence.

Devon was watching the sunlight dance upon the water, and though his voice was low, and directed elsewhere, Polly heard his response clearly. "I'll pay your passage back to San Francisco."

First her father had made all the decisions about her life, then Nat Malachi, and now Devon. Polly was weary of compliance, but she didn't know exactly what to say. She pretended, just for a moment, that she was Lydia McQuire, who struck her as bold, brave, and decisive.

"I won't be going to San Francisco," she said firmly, surprising herself as much as Devon. "Since it's plain that I'm not wanted here, I'll be traveling to Seattle on the next mail boat. Surely I'll be able to find myself a good husband there, since there is such a dire shortage of women."

She saw Devon's fists clench at his sides, and knew a moment of sweeping satisfaction. When he shot to his feet, she was both frightened and exulted.

But Devon did not come to her, take her by the shoulders, shout that he wouldn't allow her to leave him. He restrained himself, visibly, and set his jaw in a callous, almost cruel fashion. "Go, then," he said hoarsely. "And good riddance."

"Devon . . ."

He turned away, his broad shoulders rigid beneath the smudged, wrinkled fabric of his shirt.

Polly's very soul shriveled within her; she started toward him, stopped herself. Devon was her mate, despite the fraud of their marriage; with him she had discovered what it meant to love and be loved. Now, too soon, it was over, and she was waking from the dream.

She'd wanted to have children by this man, to massage his back and rub his feet when he was weary, to laugh when he made a jest and cry when he felt pain. She would be denied those things, those sweetest of pleasures, because of her own foolishness and deceit.

"I'm sorry," she said, so softly that she couldn't be sure he'd heard her.

Polly went back to the big house on the hill, encountering no one on the way, back to the room where she'd lain with Devon, transported by the fierce ecstasies she'd known with him. She pulled her gold wedding band from her finger, laid it on the bureau beside Devon's brush, and then turned to packing the few things she'd owned before meeting the man she would always think of as her husband.

Standing before the bureau mirror, Polly did not see her own reflection, but that of the bed behind her. Never, no matter what she had to do to sustain herself, would she ever lie with another man. She wouldn't take a husband, or a lover, or sell her body for money, because she knew the touch of anyone besides Devon would drive her to screaming madness.

The mail boat arrived at midafternoon, and Polly was waiting on the wharf when it chugged into the harbor. She had hoped, at first, that Devon would appear and ask her to stay, but there was no sign of him. In fact, in the intervals when the steam-powered saws in Brigham's mill weren't shrieking, she heard the rhythmic pounding of Devon's hammer. Unlike her, he still had a dream to pursue.

"It's unwise to run away," Lydia said.

Polly was so startled that she nearly fell into the water. She hadn't heard the other woman approaching because of the ordinary noises.

"I'm not as bold as you are," Polly replied, with dignity. "I'm not as strong."

"Monkey feathers," Lydia answered, her eyes solemn, her mouth unsmiling. "Of course you're strong. You have to be; you have no other choice."

"Devon doesn't want me," Polly said, lowering her eyes. More than once, since she'd come to the wharf to wait for the mail boat, she'd considered simply jumping off into the water and letting herself drown, but some inner core of strength wouldn't allow her the easy escape. Besides, somewhere deep inside her, flickering like the light of a candle, was the fear that she might miss something tremendous by dying now, even though her life looked hopeless.

Lydia sighed. "Stop thinking with Devon's brain, Polly," she said. "You have a mind of your own, and it will tell you what to do if you listen."

Polly stared at this odd, strong, pretty woman standing before her, wondering where she'd gotten all those outlandish ideas that sprang constantly from her mouth. "You could marry him now, if you wanted," Polly said. "Devon is free, in the eyes of God and man, and I know you find him attractive."

The memory of Lydia's shock when she'd discovered that Devon already had a bride, on board the ship from San Francisco, was plain between the two women, needing no further mention.

Lydia folded her arms. "Very well," she said, in a tone of kindly challenge. "If you truly don't want Devon, if you board this boat and sail off to Seattle, I'll make a point of consoling him."

A venomous pain surged through Polly's system. She loved Devon, and she was fairly certain he felt the same way about her, even though his disenchantment had blinded him to the fact. Still, Lydia was a beautiful woman, and Devon wanted a home and family so much that he had been willing to travel far and wide to bring home a bride. He would undoubtedly hurt for a while, then notice Lydia and begin to court her.

Tears burned in Polly's eyes, blurring the raw splendor of this kingdom nestled in the palm of God's hand. "Devon deserves to be happy, and you could give him what he needs," she said. The mail boat put into port just then, and a crewman jumped onto the dock to secure the craft with rope. A ramp slammed against the shifting boards of the wharf, and Polly leaned down and picked up her single carpet bag.

Lydia touched her arm. "Will you write, at least?" she asked quietly.

The other woman's concern curled against Polly's bruised heart like a warm kitten. They could have been such good friends, if only things had worked out differently. "Yes," Polly said. Then, unable to add a farewell, she boarded the boat and walked to the far side of the small cabin to await departure.

Lydia felt bereft as she went back up the driveway toward the house. She knew she could probably have Devon for a husband, if she waited for his inner wounds to heal a little, then offered him gentle, steady condolences. The trouble was, her initial attraction to him had turned to the quiet regard a sister might have for her brother. It was Brigham who made her blood heat until she thought her veins would be seared through, Brigham who had stirred her fighting spirit back to life.

The fact that the imperious Mr. Quade was quite unsuited to her personal tastes didn't seem to matter.

Midway up the drive, she encountered Millie, who leaped out of a lilac bush, her hair full of dingy chicken feathers, her face streaked with berry juice or rouge.

Dutifully, Lydia cried out in mock terror.

"I'm a savage," the child announced proudly.

Lydia laughed and pulled Millie against her side in a brief embrace. "I think many people would agree," she said. "But you're a very appealing savage, all things considered. Where did you get those feathers?"

"From the floor of the henhouse," Millie replied, pleased with herself. "They were lying all over the place, free for the taking."

Lydia grimaced, thinking of lice and other unsavory things. "I believe a bath would be a good idea," she said, taking Millie's small, grubby hand, and at the same time, plucking away the feathers and tossing them aside.

"Savages don't bathe," Millie told her, but she didn't protest being defeathered. "Not in water, anyway." Her small, dirty face glowed with inspiration. "Blood, maybe," she speculated, one finger to her lips. "I heard Papa say once that some of the Indian women wash their hair with urine and fish oil."

Lydia sincerely hoped Brigham hadn't made such a revolting comment in casual conversation. Children were so impressionable, and they had hearing as sharp as a cat's. She didn't comment on Millie's statement because she didn't want to encourage more of the same.

"Where is Charlotte?" she asked instead.

"Who knows?" Millie countered, with a shrug. "Camelot, maybe. Or Sherwood Forest. Or perhaps a castle in Spain."

Lydia smiled. "You are very precocious for a ten-year-old," she said as they rounded the rear of the house and started toward the back steps. "How do you know about all those places?"

Millie preened at the interest. "I can read, after all," she pointed out importantly. "And Charlotte tells me lots of stories. She plans to be abducted by a handsome sheikh someday and carried off into the desert on the back of a camel. Charlotte says that sheikh is going to love her so much that he'll turn out his whole harem and worship at her feet."

A blush filled Lydia's face. In New England a young girl would not be permitted to develop such scandalous ideas. "Merciful heavens," she said. "What does Charlotte know about harems?"

"Quite a lot, I'm afraid," Millie confided, in a businesslike way that was comically reminiscent of her domineering father. "A good bit of it is made up, of course."

"Of course," Lydia said ruefully.

They had gained the kitchen by then, and Lydia was relieved to see no sign of Jake. She sat Millie down at the table and began filling pots and kettles at the pump, placing these carefully atop the wood cookstove to heat. Then she fed the fire and went out to one of the sheds for a washtub she'd spotted there earlier.

Millie chattered on while Lydia heated the water for a bath, small feet swinging, painted face animated and bright. "Does Charlotte have to take a bath, too?" she asked.

Lydia arched an eyebrow, and in the same moment the whistle of the departing mail boat reached her ears. She felt a stinging sadness at the thought of Polly's tragedy, and Devon's. "Only if Charlotte has painted herself like a savage and spent the afternoon crawling through the underbrush, like you," she answered.

The washtub sat in the middle of the floor, and when the water was warm, Lydia filled it, divested Millie of her dirty clothes, and helped her into the bath.

"Normally," Millie said, settling in obediently, "I only bathe on Saturday evenings. And sometimes I have to use Charlotte's water."

The mail-boat whistle shrilled again, and Lydia closed her eyes for a moment. But then she found a bar of castile soap and began washing Millicent the Adventurous.

"Polly's gone away, hasn't she?" the child inquired, when her head was lathered with suds. Lydia had already inspected her scalp very carefully for ticks and lice. "Is she coming back?"

Lydia tilted Millie's head back gently and began pouring water over her hair from a small saucepan. She shouldn't have been surprised at what Millie knew; the child probably missed very little of what went on in Quade's Harbor. Charlotte, no doubt, was equally well-informed.

"I don't know if Polly will come back or not," Lydia answered honestly, handing Millie the soap. "Here, Pocahontas. Wash your face, please."

"I won't miss her," Millie said, with the blithe callousness of the very young. "She stayed in her room most of the time, anyhow. Like Aunt Persephone."

Lydia had almost forgotten the older woman, in the maelstrom of settling into Brigham Quade's complicated household, being kissed by him, chasing Millie and Charlotte all over the grounds, and seeing poor Polly leave the harbor in disgrace. "Perhaps your aunt is ill," she said with concern.

Millie stood, and Lydia handed her a damask towel. It constantly amazed her how many such small graces existed in this remote place. Lydia wondered if this was due to the efforts of Brigham's late wife, or of the reclusive Aunt Persephone.

"No," Millicent said, drying herself. "Aunt Persephone isn't sick. She's just hiding from Charlotte and me. We wear her out and give her sick headaches."

"I don't doubt that," Lydia said practically. Some statements simply didn't brook denial. "I'll look in on Aunt Persephone while you're getting dressed again." She shook a finger at Millie as the child stepped from the tub and started toward the back stairway, wrapped in her towel. "And if you're planning to be an Indian for any significant period of time, Millicent, kindly be a clean one with peaceful intentions."

Not surprisingly, Millie didn't commit herself.

Lydia emptied and rinsed the washtub before taking it back to the shed, then climbed the rear stairs herself.

She hesitated outside the door she knew to be Aunt Persephone's, torn between concern and a certain reluctance to meddle. In the end, concern triumphed, and she knocked lightly.

"Come in," called a frail voice.

Lydia entered the spacious room and found Aunt Persephone stretched out on a Roman couch, a neatly folded cloth resting on her forehead. The draperies were drawn, and the faint scent of lavender toilette wafted on the draft.

"Mrs. Chilcote?"

A veined hand, plump and strong-looking, rose to touch the cloth. "Yes? Who is it?"

Lydia suppressed a smile. She'd been around enough true sickness and injury to know chicanery when she saw it. "It's Lydia," she said, taking the other woman's hand. "I've come to see if there is anything you need."

Mrs. Chilcote removed the cloth and looked up at Lydia, blinking. Her face had a healthy pink tint to it, and her eyes were bright, not with fever, but with suppressed energy. "I don't imagine I'm fooling you," she said, "so it would seem a waste of time to continue."

This time, Lydia allowed her smile to show. She perched on the foot of the couch as Mrs. Chilcote sat up.

"There must be something troubling you," she ventured, smoothing her skirts. "Otherwise, you wouldn't be hiding out in this room with the shades drawn."

Mrs. Chilcote sighed philosophically, reached out for a small crystal bottle on a nearby table, and touched the bottom of the stopper to each wrist. "I was merely trying to give you a chance to become indispensable," she said. "Miss McQuire, you can have no idea how badly this family needs you."

Lydia wanted to be needed, but she was also wary of it. She'd seen what the incessant demands of others could do to a person, whether those demands were whimsical or justified. Giving was fine, taking care of others was truly noble, but the soul of the giver needed nourishment as well.

"I suppose you know that Polly has gone," Lydia said. She had sized up the formidable Persephone Chilcote carefully, and was certain the other woman knew virtually everything that went on in the household.

Sure enough, Mrs. Chilcote sighed and said, "Yes. I saw her board the mail boat, but of course I have no idea why she would leave her bridegroom that way."

Lydia remained silent. If Persephone didn't know the truth—a possibility that seemed most unlikely, given the woman's obvious astuteness—the new governess would not be the one to tell her.

Mrs. Chilcote eyed Lydia thoughtfully, and her sateen skirts rustled as she rearranged them. "I would like you to call me by my first name," she said, without preamble. "Do you know what Persephone means?"

Lydia shook her head and raised her eyebrows slightly, in order to invite the confidence.

"It is a Greek name, my dear," Persephone said. "It means the personification of spring."

Lydia smiled. "How lovely," she said. Spring. How nice, how soothing, to be in this place where the breeze did not smell of gunpowder and fear, where the grass was not soaked with blood and the sounds of screaming and cannon fire did not assault the ear.

"What is that terrible sadness I see in your eyes?" Persephone demanded, leaning toward Lydia in a way that suggested she would not be denied an explanation.

"You're barely into your twenties, and yet I see the grief of a thousand years in your face."

Caught off guard by the old woman's bluntness, Lydia looked away, her eyes suddenly stinging. "When I die," she replied, in a low, hoarse voice, "God will have no call to send me to Hell, no matter how bad my sins. I've already been there, and shaken hands with the devil."

Persephone drew in a sharp breath at the mention of the most feared of all fallen angels. She also reached out and laid a cool hand over Lydia's fingers. "Tell me what you mean by that, child," she ordered quietly. "Were you caught in that dreadful war?"

Lydia ran the tip of her tongue over dry lips. "We all were," she said miserably. It seemed that Persephone had put her under some subtle, lavender-scented spell, for Lydia poured out the whole story of following her father into the thick of battle. She told about the filthy tents, the mud puddles stained crimson with blood, the horrible rasp of metal sawing through bone. And for the first time, ever, she told another living soul about Captain J. D. McCauley, the Confederate prisoner she'd helped to escape.

Persephone did not look shocked, only sympathetic. "Did the Yankees catch this Captain McCauley?" she asked.

Lydia shook her head. Even remembering the experience made her stomach churn and her skin turn clammy with perspiration. She'd seen Union men hanged for attempting to desert, and she'd lived with the gnawing certainty that her treason would be discovered and she too would be executed. "I'm sure he got away."

"Why did you do it?" There was no condemnation in Persephone's voice, only honest curiosity.

"The government paid a bounty for every amputation a surgeon performed," she said, feeling sicker as she remembered. "One night, just after my father died, the pickets brought Captain McCauley in with just a flesh wound in his left arm. He should have been stitched up and sent off to one of the camps, but Dr. James

Steenbock decided to take off the limb and collect the bounty. I brought Captain McCauley my father's uniform and helped him into it, and told him where to find an unattended horse. Then I distracted the guards while he rode out."

Persephone's eyes were shining, and Lydia suddenly knew where Charlotte had gotten her love of drama. "Why, Lydia, that was positively heroic! Didn't they ever suspect you?"

"Steenbock did," Lydia recalled, with soft bitterness. "But he couldn't prove his allegations, and the other surgeons needed my help at the operating tables too badly to accuse me. About a week later, Dr. Steenbock wanted to rid a young man from Kentucky of a leg that needed only stitches and a splint. I went to one of the other doctors and told him what was about to happen, and he investigated. Steenbock was relieved of his commission and sent to one of the camps, to be dealt with after the war."

Persephone's color had drained away and her eyes had grown big. "Did he know you'd been the one to point the finger at him, this Steenbock fellow?"

Lydia drew a deep breath, let it out slowly. She would never forget the way Steenbock had looked when he was taken into custody in the surgery tent that day. He'd glared at her, letting the full, fathomless evil of his soul show in his eyes.

Sometimes in her nightmares he stood at the foot of her bed, a scalpel in his hand, and like the many soldiers he'd robbed of arms and legs, she was unable to escape him, incapable of moving. She would awaken with shrieks of terror echoing in her throat, knowing she'd held the sound inside her, like the memories and the fear.

Eyes shining with the tears Lydia had never been able to shed, Persephone reached out and embraced the younger woman with one arm. "There now, all that's behind you now. This is a good place, and you'll be safe under Brigham Quade's roof, I can promise you that. Why, anyone who knows my nephew would rather tangle with the big saw down at the mill than with him."

Lydia had already deduced that Brigham was strong, and that he was powerful. But she wouldn't let herself depend on him for protection or anything else. He could send her away at any time, leaving her not only alone in a treacherous world, but dangerously weakened by her own failure to remain independent. "I can look after myself," she said, firmly but with kindness.

"You are planning to stay here for a while, though, aren't you?"

Lydia nodded. She was drawing a reasonably good salary, and she had a safe place to sleep and plenty to eat. She would remain until there was reason to leave. "For as long as I'm welcome, yes," she said.

Persephone's face was bright. "Marvelous!" she said, exultant. "If you're staying, there is absolutely no reason why I cannot pay a long visit to my dear sister Cordelia, back in Maine." With that, Mrs. Chilcote rose from her couch and proceeded to open the draperies and the shutters to the late afternoon sunshine. Apparently, she had instantaneously recovered from her ailments.

7

SOMEONE GOES AWAY, SOMEONE ARRIVES, LYDIA thought, one penny-bright afternoon a few days later, as she watched a bearded man stride down the ramp from the mail boat. A seaman's bag bobbed from his shoulder, and a meek-looking woman followed in his broad wake, a small child grasping each of her hands.

Lydia was pleased, for now there would be someone living in one of the tidy saltbox houses. One of the children, a little girl with pigtails as shiny-dark as a crow's breast, was clearly old enough to attend school. The other, a boy in knee pants, was barely out of the toddling stage.

Charlotte and Millie stood on either side of Lydia—they had not been watching for the mail boat, but instead attempting to identify hermit crabs and other small creatures. Lydia had found a nature book in Brigham's study, and she and the girls had been matching the pictures to the minute, industrious beings populating the shore.

"People!" Millie breathed in wonder, as though she'd never seen another human being until that moment.

Charlotte looked petulant, as usual. "Of course they're people, goose," she said. "What else would they be?"

"Hush," Lydia interceded, although it was peace she wanted from the girls, not necessarily silence. Millie fidgeted eagerly at her side.

"I don't see any reason at all why that girl wouldn't like me," she said solemnly. "Do you, Lydia?"

"Certainly not," Lydia said, smiling slightly. "If I were you, I would go forth immediately and introduce myself."

Millie released her hold on Lydia's hand and raced down the wharf, undaunted by the other girl's enormous father and drab, tentative mother. The child's face lit up when Millie spoke to her, and by the time they all reached the foot of the dock, their arms were linked.

"This is Anna," Millie said, presenting her friend joyously. "Anna, here is my teacher, Miss McQuire, and my sister, Charlotte."

While Charlotte was dreamy and often distracted, she was not unfriendly. She smiled in a warm fashion and said, "Hello."

Lydia looked at the uncertain faces of the man and his wife before bending to offer her hand to Anna in formal greeting. "How do you do, Anna?" she said. Then, turning to the little boy, she added, "And who is this?"

"Rolf," Anna said, sounding proud and shy, both at the same time.

"Hans Holmetz," said the bearlike man solemnly, holding out one enormous, callused paw. "I have heard there is work in this place. I am strong, and Magna can cook and clean."

Lydia had no authority to hire workmen, of course, but she also hadn't any doubt that Brigham would find a place for Mr. Holmetz on one of his crews. Heaven knew, he'd made enough noise about wanting families to come and settle in his ready-made town; it wouldn't make any sense at all to turn one away.

"Welcome," she said, with extra warmth, seeing the frightened hope in Magna Holmetz's thin, plain face. "I'll show you where to find Mr. Quade—"

Hans and Magna had a soft, brisk exchange in a language Lydia didn't recognize, and Hans lowered his bag to the ground. Unless Lydia missed her guess, that patched and tattered duffel contained everything the Holmetzes owned.

"There's no need to go looking for Brigham," a masculine voice interrupted, and Lydia turned to see Devon approaching from the direction of his construction project. He didn't smile; his normally mischievous blue eyes were dull and flat, and he was in want of a shave. "We need all the help we can get. They can have their pick of the houses, and I'll see that supplies are sent over from the company store."

Lydia's heart twisted at the desolation she saw in Devon's face, but at the same moment she felt joy for the Holmetzes.

Magna stepped a little closer to Hans, clearly afraid she'd mistranslated Devon's words. Probably, his pronouncement sounded too good to be true.

"We get house?" Hans asked, frowning.

Devon smiled his broken smile and reached out to ruffle the small boy's corn-silk hair. "Please see that these children have something to eat right away, Lydia," he said, with gentle authority, and just then she sorely wished she could love him, step into the awful breach Polly had left in his life.

After more consultations in their guttural language, Hans and Magna agreed to let the children go with Lydia and the girls, while they followed Devon to the street of waiting houses.

Anna and Millie ran ahead, up the hill toward Brigham's place, chattering as if they'd known each other since babyhood. Rolf walked dutifully at Lydia's side, his thin hand in hers. It was plain that he had his doubts about these towering strangers and the places they might lead him, but he would not have considered disobeying Hans's instructions.

In the kitchen of the big house, Lydia settled the children around the table, Charlotte and Millie included, and then went to the springhouse for a jug of milk, a wedge of cheese, and some cold chicken left over from supper the night before.

When she set her burden on the counter to pour the milk, Rolf and Anna looked at her with wide, wondering eyes. Those were difficult times, for the tentacles of the war had reached even into the West, and there was no telling how long it had been since they'd eaten.

Lydia was quick in dispensing the creamy, yellow-white milk, and the Holmetz children reached for their glasses with grubby, awkward hands. A lump thickened in Lydia's throat as she watched them drink.

She served them chicken, cheese, and bread, all of which they consumed while Millie and Charlotte were still taking delicate sips of their milk.

A shape loomed unexpectedly in the open doorway, and Lydia looked up from the ravenous children, expecting to see Devon or perhaps Jake, the cook.

Instead the visitor was Brigham, and for one fanciful moment it seemed to Lydia that he not only blocked out the sunlight, but absorbed it somehow. Its light seemed to glow in his enigmatic gray eyes and turn itself into a pulsing vitality, barely restrained within his powerful body.

Lydia felt the charge of his presence like a lightning bolt, and she braced herself to keep from being swept away by the sheer force of his personality.

He smiled at his daughters, and at the shy Holmetz children, and finally at Lydia.

She was rocked by this sweet, intangible assault, and she prayed Brigham Quade would never guess the power he held over her. Even then, with a history of just one kiss between them, she knew he could seduce her easily, make her surrender what she had never given to any other man.

"You will have your meetinghouse," he said.

Lydia was mildly disappointed at the practicality of his words, since her soul had been primed for poetry, but of course she was also relieved. It wouldn't do for private things to be said with the children present.

"When?" she said.

Brigham sighed, but his eyes were smiling. "The men will begin cutting and planing the lumber today," he said. "You may have the west side of the clearing between Main Street and the cemetery. I'll stake out the four corners of the building."

Lydia lifted her chin. "Thank you."

He laughed, took the basin from the wall, and went to the stove to fill it from the hot-water reservoir. The children might not have been in the room at all, so intense and strange was the intangible interaction taking place between Lydia and Brigham.

"How grudgingly you speak those benign words, Miss McQuire," he teased, carrying the basin of steaming water toward the back door. "But then, I guess I shouldn't expect anything different from a New England spinster."

Lydia followed him to the doorway, fumed there in the chasm while Brigham stood on the ground nearby, the basin balanced on a sawhorse. He began to splash his face and neck industriously.

Even though she knew Brigham was only baiting her, she hated being called a spinster. The term made her sound like tattered goods, passed over in the marketplace for sounder stuff. "I believe you are a New Englander yourself, Mr. Quade," she pointed out tautly. "And you're none too polite, if I do say so."

He chuckled, looking up at her, his black lashes beaded with water, his jet-colored hair wet and unruly and altogether appealing. She gripped the doorjamb because she wanted to go and weave her fingers into it.

"Go ahead," he taunted with gruff ease, "lose your temper, Miss McQuire. Let out all that rage inside you, and deal with it."

Lydia's throat closed, and her grip on the doorjamb tightened. She'd thought her private fury well-hidden, and to have the likes of Brigham Quade read so deftly from the pages of her soul only increased it. She wanted to fling herself at him, screaming and clawing, kicking and biting, not because he'd done her any real wrong, but because there were so many violent feelings trapped within her.

"I'm not angry," she said, the chatter of the children at the kitchen table seeming far away.

Brigham ran his eyes over her, insolently, making her flesh leap in secret response beneath her dress and underthings. "Liar," he replied.

Rage rocked Lydia. She closed her eyes, struggling against it, afraid as always of what would happen if she ever opened a door on the storm in her spirit. Once let loose, it might never be contained again.

Brigham continued to stare at her, hair dripping, eyes mocking her. Challenging her. Then he turned away to toss the contents of the basin into the deep grass, and inexplicably some barrier within Lydia gave way.

She forgot the children, forgot the tenets of civilization. She lunged from the step, landing on Brigham's back like a wildcat, one hand clutching his shirtfront in a choking hold, the other knotted into a fist and pounding at his back. All the while, a low, barely-audible animal sound surged from her throat.

Brig pressed her down into the grass, bruising it, releasing its sweet green fragrance like a perfume, kneeling astraddle her hips, but he made no effort to restrain her flying fists.

In those terrifying minutes, he represented war, and pain, and hunger. He was the night screams of wounded children scattered over battlefields, he was injustice and cruelty. He was Lydia's own helplessness in the face of those things.

Lydia pounded at his chest until she was exhausted, then lay still in the grass, breathless and horrified at what she'd done. Tears slipped over her cheekbones, to fall away into her hair and trickle into her ears.

Brig backed away slightly, drew her up gently into his arms and held her. She knotted her fingers in his shirtfront, unable to let go.

"Poor little Yankee," he said, his lips warm at her damp temple. "The war's over now. There's no need to be afraid."

Lydia came back to herself then, realized what a spectacle she'd made, leaping on Brigham like a she-wolf from a high rock, carrying on like someone who should be wrapped tightly in a wet sheet and calmed with tincture of opium. Charlotte and Millie were standing in the doorway of the kitchen, watching the scene with unreadable expressions.

"Oh, dear God," Lydia whispered, trying to push Brigham away even though she felt faint.

He rose to his feet, drawing her with him, holding her against his chest. The scent of his hair and skin weakened her further. "It's *all right,* Lydia," he said sternly.

She wanted him to lift her into his arms, carry her up the stairs to his bed and take complete control of her mind and body, at least for a little while, and that wanting was the most frightening thing of all. She pulled free, backed away, smoothed her hair, which was falling around her shoulders, with shaking hands.

Brigham gazed at her for a long moment, chest heaving, shoved a hand through his tousled hair, and then passed her to enter the house. Charlotte and Millie moved to let him go by, and Lydia turned away, unable to face them. She had no answers for the questions in their eyes, no answers for the questions in her own heart.

She sat on the bottom step of the porch, hugging herself, and waited until her composure crept back on cautious feet. Then she went inside.

Mercifully, there was no sign of Brigham, and Charlotte too had wandered off, probably to refuel her imagination from a favorite book. Millie, Anna, and Rolf all looked up at Lydia with worried eyes, though, and she fumbled for an explanation.

And, of course, there was none. She could think of no earthly way to rationalize an irrational action.

Devon drove the final nail into the last of the boards forming the roof of his store. The shingles still had to be put on, but at least the inevitable summer rains would be partially deflected from the floors and roughed-in walls beneath. He looked up at the pristine blue sky, knowing well enough not to trust it, and then, in a burst of grief and frustration, flung his hammer off into the trees.

He climbed down the ladder at the side of the structure, half tempted to lean back on the rungs and let himself go tumbling over the steep, rocky embankment to the place where the tide washed the edges of sharp boulders. All that stopped him, in fact, was the possibility that he might not die from the fall, but only be injured to the point of helplessness. He couldn't bear the thought of lying in bed for the rest of his life, pissing in bottles, unable even to shave himself.

Devon had seen men hurt just that badly in the woods, and he knew most of them would have chosen death over such a fate. So he took care climbing the rest of the way down the ladder, and then he stood for a long while looking over the edge of the cliff.

Maybe he'd built too close to the precipice, he reflected. There was at least a thirty-foot drop to the rocks, and the sweet-scented grass was slick under the soles of his boots.

He sighed, lifted his head and looked outward, beyond the water to the mountains. And even in his angry sorrow he was comforted by the sight of the snowy, rugged mountains out on the peninsula.

"Devon?"

His heart thudded at the sound of a soft, feminine voice. For a moment he thought Polly had come back, and he was more than prepared to welcome her magnanimously, but when he turned, he saw Lydia standing there. She looked as beleaguered as he felt, and she was holding a napkin-covered basket and a jug of coffee.

"I thought you might want something to eat," she said, speaking with a touch of quiet defiance, as though she expected to be sent away.

Devon smiled and rubbed his stubbled chin, but he made no move to reach for the food. It held no appeal for him. "Are you still in the market for a husband, Miss McQuire?" he asked.

Color flared in her cheeks, heartening Devon for a moment, almost turning his wan smile to a laugh. "I don't know what you mean," she said, but he could see that she did know, and very well, too.

"You were prepared to marry me in San Francisco," he reminded her. He didn't love Lydia, but he liked her, and maybe that was better. After all, he'd fallen hard and fast for Polly, and he'd been devastated because of it. "Have you changed your mind?"

"Yes," Lydia said firmly, fussing with the napkin covering the food in her basket. "I was desperate then."

This time, Devon did laugh. Oh, it was a raw and raucous sound, lacking the force it might otherwise have had, but he felt better for it all the same.

Lydia reddened prettily. "I didn't mean exactly—well, I'm not saying, mind you, that a woman would have to be desperate to marry you, Devon—"

He raised one eyebrow. "Oh?"

She drew a deep breath and let it out in an anxious burst, making pale tendrils of hair dance around her forehead. "We're all wrong for each other, you and I. You need a silk-stocking sort of woman, not a woolen work sock."

Devon leaned slightly toward her, his arms folded, looking deliberately pensive. "A woolen work sock? Come now, Lydia. Why would you think of yourself in such a homely way?"

"I didn't say I was homely," she pointed out, her pride obviously stung. "I meant that I'm practical and warm and—and durable." Lydia's whole face was flushed now, along with her neck and ears, and she looked poised to drop the lunch basket and run. "Whereas, you would require a soft and delicate woman." She took another deep breath. "Like Polly."

For a few glorious minutes Devon had been distracted from the pain of his fractured heart, but Polly's name brought back all the old melancholy feelings and some new ones besides. He started to turn away, having no destination in mind, just needing to be alone again.

"Devon," Lydia said softly. Gently. "Go to Seattle and bring her back. Polly belongs here with you."

Devon swallowed. He wanted to make a case for

himself, but when he sorted through the words clustered in his mind, he couldn't find any that were presentable. He stiffened his back and walked away without answering at all.

That night, he moved the most essential of his belongings up the hill to the cabin that had been his original home. In those simple and incredibly difficult days, he'd shared the place with Brigham and Isabel, sleeping in the loft.

He was outside, chopping wood by the light of a single lantern, when he heard a rustling sound on the path below and Brig appeared, seeming to take his shape from the darkness itself.

Brig struck a match against the trunk of a fir tree and lit the thin cheroot clamped between his teeth. "Is the big house getting too crowded for you?" he asked after a long time.

Devon went right on chopping wood. He didn't want to sleep in his room because everything in it seemed to exude the clean, subtle scent of Polly's skin, because the place was haunted by her tender words and soft cries of pleasure. But of course he couldn't explain those things, not even to Brigham.

"You might as well know," he said, swinging the ax, splintering a chunk of wood, putting another on the block. "I mean to court Lydia."

He thought he saw his elder brother stiffen slightly, decided it was a trick of the moonlight and the flickering lantern. Brigham was content with the expensive whore he patronized in Seattle, and the last thing he wanted was another wife.

"Why?" Brigham asked presently.

"Why not?" Devon countered, still chopping. He was soaked with sweat, and he already had more wood than he'd need before the first snowfall, but he felt like he had to keep moving or he'd explode like gunpowder on a pancake griddle. "You don't want her, do you?"

With no warning, the ax was wrenched from Devon's hands. The blade made an ominous thumping sound as it plunged deep into the trunk of a nearby tree. Brigham gripped his brother's shirtfront and yanked him up onto the balls of his feet.

"Lydia's no whore," he breathed. "And *by God* I won't let you use her like one, Devon."

Devon put his hands up between his brother's forearms and freed himself from Brigham's grasp. "I said I plan to court Lydia, not use her for a whore," he responded evenly. "I want her for a wife."

"No."

"What the hell gives you the authority to make a decree like that, Brig? Did somebody make you king when I wasn't paying attention?"

His brother's sigh was deep and raspy, and it told Devon a lot more than Brig had probably wanted to reveal. "If you want Lydia," he said, "you'll have to get past me to have her." With that, he ground out the cheroot, turned his back on Devon and strode down the hill.

"I'll be damned," Devon said, a grin spreading slowly across his mouth. "I'll be damned, stamped, and painted blue."

Lydia was eager for a trip that gloomy afternoon of the Monday following, even though she was sad because Aunt Persephone was leaving for the East. The mail boat was loaded down with so many trunks and bags that Brigham swore it would sink under the weight before they'd even left the harbor.

Charlotte and Millie were going along to see their great aunt off on the big ship that would carry her around the Horn, and they were excited because Anna Holmetz had told them there was a trained bear performing at Yesler's Hall in Seattle. For all their delight, the prospect of parting with Persephone, even for a few months, put a visible damper on their pleasure.

Only Devon was staying home, and frankly, Lydia was relieved. Ever since he'd announced his decision to court her, several days before, he'd been filling her chair at the dinner table with lilacs and generally making a fool of himself.

She tried to be tolerant, well aware that Devon was dealing with the loss of Polly in the only way he knew how, but at the same time she wished he'd just leave her alone. Lydia, as it happened, was trying to sort out some very confusing feelings of her own.

All of which were directed at Brigham, not his younger brother.

Ever since that dreadful day when she'd lost all control of her deportment and launched herself at Brigham from the back porch, like a Chinese rocket from a sarsaparilla bottle, and he'd subdued her in the grass, Lydia had been plagued by sinful and unseemly desires.

Lying in bed at night, for instance, she often imagined Brigham there with her. She felt the weight of his hands on her bare breasts, and even the *thought* of that made her nipples bud and her breath turn quick and shallow. Sometimes she even went so far as to imagine him settling between her legs, and all the rest, too.

At least, as much of the rest as she properly understood. She knew what Brigham would do to her, generally speaking, but she hadn't the vaguest idea why she wanted it so much or how giving herself to him that way could possibly satisfy the awesome need yawning inside her. She only knew she'd go insane one of these muggy summer nights if she didn't get some relief.

Lydia stood at the railing as the mail boat chugged out of port, Millie at her left side, Charlotte at her right. Millie was soon bored with standing still and began to run wildly around the deck, whooping and waving her arms.

"Why does she act like that?" Charlotte asked, with moderate disdain, tossing her lovely mane of honey-brown hair for emphasis.

"Because she's ten," Lydia answered, with a smile. She reasoned that, if Millie wore herself out now, she'd sleep all the more soundly that night at the hotel. "Didn't you like to run and make noise when you were a little girl, Charlotte?"

Charlotte was pleased by the implication that she was no longer a child, just as Lydia had intended. "No. Well, yes. Sometimes. But I never smeared blackberry juice on my face to make war paint, and I never got myself stuck twenty feet up in a fir tree, either. Millie did that, you know. Last summer. Papa had to climb up and get her."

Lydia smiled at the image, but at the same time she was glad she hadn't been around for the actual incident. She didn't like to think of the work Brigham did on a day-to-day basis, as it was; to see not only him but Millie in such a dangerous predicament would have terrified her.

As Millie was about to race past him, Brigham gathered Millie up in his arms and swung her up onto one shoulder. Then he came to stand at the rail beside Lydia, who would rather have avoided the encounter. She looked around, hoping Persephone was with him, but the old woman was happily settled in a special deck chair, with Charlotte as lady-in-waiting.

Brigham said nothing to Lydia; he was engaged in a dialogue with his youngest daughter. Only when Quade's Harbor was out of sight, swallowed up by the crowding trees, and Millie had scrambled down to go and bedevil Charlotte, did he speak to her.

"Will you be marrying my brother?" he asked, and although he had clearly intended to present the question in a casual manner, it had a different sort of effect on Lydia. Rather like a lamp being lit in a dark room.

"I'm not sure," Lydia lied, tugging at the pair of gloves Aunt Persephone had given her just that morning, along with some sachets, a book of poetry, and a few pieces of jewelry she didn't expect to need in Maine. "You must admit Devon can be charming, filling my chair with flowers all the time, and writing poetry the way he does." She'd made up that last part, but she was having too good a time to retract the statement.

"Poetry?" Brigham asked in amazement, practically choking on the word.

It was as Lydia had suspected. The idea of courting a woman in the old-fashioned, romantic way would never occur to Brigham. His method was simply to fling them down in the grass and sit on them, apparently.

Not that she really thought he wanted to court her.

Oh, no. She was certain Brigham's intentions weren't at all honorable.

Any more than hers were, regrettably.

She changed the subject, for fear Brigham would demand that she quote some of his brother's alleged poetry. That would mean making up a verse or two, and she hadn't the required talent. "Millie tells me there's a performing bear appearing at Yesler's Hall," she said.

Brigham stared at her for a moment, as though unable to decide whether to kiss her shamelessly or throw her overboard. "If the bear gets tired of putting on a show, they could always bring Devon in as a replacement. Naturally, you would hold the leash."

Lydia's cheeks flared. "That was a mean-spirited thing to say!"

Brigham shrugged. "You pipe the tune and he dances. Don't try to pretend you don't enjoy the attention, because I know you do."

"Maybe I do," Lydia replied, jutting out her chin. "What business is that of yours?"

"I'll show you," he said. And then, right there on the deck of the mail boat, in front of God and all His angels, Brigham pulled Lydia against him and kissed her so thoroughly that her straw hat fell off and her hair came unpinned.

She stood gaping at him, like a fool, when it was over, and he bent to retrieve her hat, handing it to her with a cocky bow of his head.

"Everything about you is my business," he said, and then he walked away and left her standing there, holding her straw cap, her hair blowing unbound in the wind.

8

AFTER STANDING ON THE DECK IN SHOCK FOR A FEW
moments, Brigham's kiss still burning on her mouth,
Lydia bent to gather up her scattered hairpins. When she
had as many as there was rational hope of finding, she
turned away from the small band of spectators over by
the wheelhouse—Aunt Persephone, Charlotte, and
Millie—and hastily bound her pale gold mane back into
a proper knot at the back of her head. Then she put her
hat on again and stood drawing slow, deep breaths at the
railing until the tempest Brigham had spawned in her
senses had ebbed into a cold and quiet fury.

For two hours they traveled through spectacular scen-
ery, rich green trees crowding the mountains and standing like sentinels along the stony shores, overlooked by
whitecapped peaks that gave better testimony to the
majesty of God than any preacher could have done.
Occasionally Lydia glimpsed squat brown Indians digging clams on the beach or fishing from their sleek
canoes.

In all that time, Brigham very wisely kept his distance.

When they arrived in Seattle, however, he immediately
took charge again. Aunt Persephone, Charlotte, Millie,

and Lydia were all loaded into a muddy carriage, long past its prime, with the bags to be sent along later. Brigham sent the women trundling off over the rutted, stump-strewn streets, toward the Imperial Hotel, and Lydia was relieved that he didn't accompany them.

Mostly.

"Where do you suppose he's going?" she mused aloud, the words escaping her before she could weigh and measure them properly.

Aunt Persephone's smile was a knowing one, but then, it didn't take a legendary brain to recognize Lydia's attraction to Brigham. As hard as she tried to fight that attraction, and to hide it, her feelings would be plainly visible to all but the most obtuse observers.

"Brigham has business associates here in Seattle," the older woman said. "Bankers and the like."

Charlotte sighed dreamily. "He probably meets a mystery woman, one with long, flowing hair and a white dress."

Millie's sigh revealed an entirely different opinion. "Stuff and nonsense," she said, folding her arms and thumping her heels against the front of the wooden seat she shared with her sister. "He meets a woman, all right, but there's no mystery about it. She's a soiled dove and she kisses him for money."

Aunt Persephone looked away, perhaps to hide a smile; Lydia couldn't be sure. She was too stunned by the worldly astuteness of Millie's remark, and too afraid it was true, to follow up anyone else's reaction.

Her voice shook a little when she spoke. "Honestly, Millicent, sometimes I think you're a forty-year-old midget just posing as a child. Where on earth did you get such an outrageous idea?"

"I know about these things all right," Millie said, and the obstinance in her voice and bearing reminded Lydia sorely of Brigham. She turned her indomitable gray gaze to her flushed governess. "Papa kissed you on the boat," she observed. "Will he give you money?"

Charlotte giggled, and Lydia's blush deepened, burning like a fever in her face and neck. She could even feel it beneath the prim calico bodice of the dress she'd selected for traveling.

"Certainly not," she said huffily.

Persephone laughed. "I almost hate to go away," she said, to no one in particular. "I'm probably about to miss the greatest spectacle of our century."

Lydia definitely did not intend to be a part of any spectacle, great or otherwise. "I can't think what you mean," she said to the older woman, in a polite but pointed tone.

"Think harder, then," Persephone answered, without even a moment's hesitation.

Lydia said nothing else, and met no one's eyes, until the carriage stopped in front of the Imperial Hotel. Peter and Eustacia Wallace, friends of the Quade family, were waiting to collect Charlotte and Millie and take them home to spend the afternoon and evening with their daughter, Bertha.

Lydia and Persephone checked into their separate rooms, and Lydia poured the fresh water she found there into a pretty basin and refreshed herself by washing her face and hands. Then she got out her brush, took her hair down, groomed it until it crackled, plaited it neatly, and pinned it up again.

All the time, she was thinking of the way Brigham had kissed her on the deck of the mail boat, and how his tongue had done fiery battle with hers. When she imagined him doing that with another woman, for money or for free, an unreasoning jealousy made her blood simmer. She clamped down her jaw and forcibly changed the direction of her musing.

Her objective for what remained of the afternoon was to locate Polly, and she intended to follow through.

Having no idea where to start, Lydia drew herself up and left the hotel nonetheless, standing on the board sidewalk out front and gazing first in one direction, then the other.

Seattle, for all its bustle, was not a large place. Lydia soon discovered that the timberline came right down to Third Street, and the woods beyond had probably changed very little in centuries. There was a church in the center of the community, the interior coolness inviting, offering solace.

Lydia sat for a while on a bench at the back of the plain sanctuary, her hands folded, thinking. There was a slate board next to the altar, and neat chalk figures and letters proclaimed: *22 regular parishioners. 5 visitors. $1.78 collected.* This information was followed by a hymn number and the chapter and verse of several Bible quotations.

Polly would not have come to this place, Lydia decided. Her guilt over her past and the way she'd deceived Devon wouldn't have permitted the redemption and peace she might have found here.

Lydia frowned, shifting on the hard and splintery seat. On the other hand, Polly might have been drawn through the doorway by those very needs, or thrust inside by her own self-condemnation.

"May I help you?"

Lydia started, turned to find a well-fed woman with a kindly smile and a pox-scarred face standing in the aisle. "My name is Lydia McQuire," she said, after a moment of silent faltering, rising from the pew to offer a hand in greeting. "I'm looking for my friend, Polly . . ." She paused, not knowing her friend's real surname, and used the only one she had. "Polly Quade. Do you know her?"

The woman shook her head, her gray hair, drawn back in a severely plain style, catching stray bits of sunlight from the doorway and the narrow, dusty windows. "I'm sorry, I don't." If she recognized the name Quade, which she probably did, she made no mention of it. "Is your friend traveling somewhere? San Francisco, perhaps, or the Orient?"

Lydia sighed. "I wish I knew."

"Is she alone?"

Lydia felt sad, remembering Polly's grief, and the bleak expression in Devon's eyes when she'd last seen him. "Yes, I think so. She would probably try to find an inexpensive place to stay, and work, too, if she could get it."

The other woman looked mildly inspired. "She could be cooking in the woods for one of the timber companies, or cleaning rooms at the Imperial Hotel. Or maybe she's gotten herself married, though it wasn't in this church, I can tell you that. Any time a single woman comes to Seattle, even if she's ugly and mean, or both, the men line up to propose holy matrimony."

Lydia felt uneasy. Ever since she'd left the hotel in search of Polly, she'd felt speculative gazes following her, and she'd heard a few whistles and hopeful catcalls, too. "The Imperial would probably be too expensive. Is there a rooming house?"

"One, but no Christian woman would stay there. It's behind the States Rights Saloon, and I've heard tell the mattress tickings are crawling with vermin."

With a shudder, Lydia ruled out the States Rights Saloon. She had absolutely no doubt that Polly had at least some money to spend, and although she didn't know Devon's bogus bride very well, she was certain her friend's habits were too fastidious for such a place. Lydia herself would have slept in a hayloft before taking a room in a questionable establishment, and she could only believe that Polly would do the same.

She thanked the lady who had tried so hard to be helpful and left the church. The last fierceness of the afternoon sun uplifted her a little, and she walked with a determined bounce in her step, even though she had no real idea where to go.

Lydia called at the desk of the Imperial Hotel, but they knew of no Polly Quade either registered as a guest or working as a housekeeper or cook.

Women are rare in Seattle, Lydia thought impatiently. Someone like Polly would not go unnoticed.

She crossed the street to the States Rights Saloon and stood hesitantly on the sidewalk, remembering her brief stint as a piano player in just that sort of enterprise, back in San Francisco. She thought of Jim, the kindly bartender who had been her only friend in that city, and how he'd known everyone for miles around, either personally or by reputation. Saloon keepers heard every whisper of gossip, every secret.

Lydia peered over the swinging doors. The place was empty, except for the burly redheaded man behind the bar, polishing glasses with his dingy apron, and a harmless-looking reveler who sat with his head on a table.

"Excuse me," Lydia called shakily. She hadn't liked entering saloons in San Francisco, and she wasn't eager to do it now. "Mr. Saloon Keeper?"

The man behind the bar looked up. His Irish-blue eyes widened, then narrowed. "You wanting a place to stay?" he asked hopefully.

Lydia glanced up and down the sidewalk. Men and the few steely-faced women the community boasted were staring at her, scandalized. "No," she said nervously. "Couldn't you come out here, just for a moment?"

"I've got work to do, lady. If you want to talk with Brendan O'Shaunessy without shouting so the whole town can hear, you'll just have to step over the threshold."

Lydia drew a deep breath, let it out in a huff, pushed the doors open and went in. She gave the drunk, who had passed out at his table with his fingers still curled around an empty bottle of rye whiskey, a wide berth as she approached the crude bar. Unlike the beautifully carved teak creations in the establishments where she'd played bawdy tunes she hoped would never flow from her fingers to the keys again, this bar was constructed of old barrels with boards on top.

"I'm looking for a woman named Polly Quade," she said.

Brendan O'Shaunessy put down the glass he'd been polishing—it still looked filthy to Lydia—and asked in a stage whisper, "That would be Devon Quade's runaway bride?"

Lydia was not surprised that word had traveled so fast; news got around in these pioneer communities, where there was little to do besides work and ponder the doings of others. "Yes," she muttered, and saying the word was like pulling a bandage from a new wound.

"She's cooking for one of the mill crews," Mr. O'Shaunessy said. He ran his too-bright eyes over Lydia with dispatch. "You looking for work yourself, miss? Or a husband, maybe?"

Before answering, Lydia took a judicious step backward. The floor was covered with sawdust, slowing the motion of her feet, but she didn't look down. That would have been an indication of weakness. "No," she said. "I have a perfectly good post, and no desire at all for a husband." She stood as tall as she could. "Thank you for your help," she finished, and turned to hurry out.

It was a measure of her luck, she thought, that she nearly collided with Brigham Quade in the doorway. He folded his arms and arched an eyebrow, regarding Lydia with an inscrutable expression. "I didn't know you suffered from the unholy thirst," he said.

All Lydia could think of was how she'd felt, squashed against him that morning, how he'd conquered her with his mouth. Damn the man, he'd stirred things inside her that *still* hadn't settled. "I don't," she said, calling on bravado to raise her chin and push back her shoulders. "I'm looking for Polly."

"You expected her to frequent the States Rights Saloon?" Brigham inquired.

Lydia wasn't about to explain her theory that bartenders knew most everything that went on in a town. "Perhaps," she allowed, sparing only the merest breath for the word. "Now, if you'll just let me pass."

Brigham stepped aside and gestured politely, and Lydia swept by him, barely able to keep from lifting her skirts and breaking into a dead run. She had no more than gained the boardwalk, however, when he caught her elbow in one hand and turned her to face him.

Mr. Quade looked damnably handsome even in his cotton duck trousers, scuffed boots, suspenders, and open-throated work shirt, and for one wonderful, wicked, and utterly terrifying moment, Lydia thought he meant to kiss her again. Instead he released her arm and let go a mighty sigh.

"You shouldn't be meddling in this," he said through his teeth. "Devon and Polly have to work it out themselves."

Lydia leaned close to him, painfully conscious of the stares of masculine passersby, and stood on the balls of her feet to hiss, "I'm not meddling. Polly is my friend and I want to see how she is."

Brigham reached into the pocket of his trousers, pulled out a thick packet of currency, and removed a twenty-dollar bill. "Give her this," he said.

After looking down at the money in surprise for a moment, Lydia lifted her eyes to Brigham's concerned face, not knowing what to think.

Her employer shoved a hand through his unruly ebony hair and looked exasperated. "Get Polly's address when you see her, and tell her I'll have Harrington arrange for regular bank drafts until she remarries."

Lydia swallowed. She wanted to dislike Brigham Quade—in fact, she was *desperate* to dislike him—but she could not overlook the man's gruff generosity, or his sense of honor and decency. She nodded, turned and walked away.

Lydia's persistence was soon rewarded. She found Polly in the mess tent next to one of the mills, harriedly pouring coffee for at least two dozen men. She pushed up her sleeves, grabbed the second coffeepot, and began to help serving.

"There's a dance tonight," someone said. "You want to go reelin' with me, pretty girl?"

"Will you marry me?" another man asked, his brown, gapped teeth showing in a broad and confident grin. He smelled, his gray hair stuck out all over his head in wild thatches, and he apparently believed the very sight of him would drive Lydia wild with passion.

"Some other time," she said briskly, filling his cup and moving on to the next man. Polly was standing stock-still, staring at her, and she didn't move until one of the other workers slammed his metal cup down on the plank-board table.

For the next hour, while the men ate their supper of biscuits and roasted meat and peas from some nearby garden, Lydia concentrated on avoiding pinches and pats, and she poured more coffee. When the dining tent was finally empty, except for her and Polly, the latter approached her.

"What are you doing here, Lydia?"

Lydia took the money Brigham had given her from the pocket of her skirt and held it out. "Here," she said. "Brig—Mr. Quade asked me to give this to you, and to get your address. He'll have his clerk send you regular bank drafts until you get married again."

Polly looked at the money for a long moment, biting her lower lip, then reluctantly accepted it and tucked it down inside her bodice. "How's Devon?"

Lydia sat down at one of the rough tables and propped her chin in one hand. "I think you already know the answer to that question," she replied, without rancor.

Tears swelled in Polly's hazel eyes. "Is he courting you?"

"Yes," Lydia answered. "But I don't think he means it."

Polly raised the hem of her apron and pressed it to her eyelids. "I miss him so much."

Lydia patted her friend's hand, already chafed and reddened from hard work. "Why don't you go back to him, then? Just get on the mail boat and head for Quade's Harbor?"

After a sniffle and another pass of the apron hem over her puffy eyes, Polly shook her head. "I couldn't. He'd turn me away, and I wouldn't be able to bear that."

Just like the woman she'd met earlier, in the church, Lydia was struck with an inspiration. "You could still go back," she insisted. "Brigham would surely hire you to do the same work you're doing here—I heard him say just the other day that he can't keep a cook in the camps."

Polly looked horrified. "Lydia, I couldn't live on the

mountain with all those dreadful men! They'd be plaguing me to—" A light went on in her eyes, and suddenly, tentatively, she was smiling. "They'd be plaguing me to marry them."

Lydia nodded, her own lips curved into a delighted grin. "If that doesn't drive Devon Quade straight out of his mind, nothing will!"

"Do you really think it would work?" Polly sounded doubtful now, afraid to hope.

Raising one shoulder in a shrug, Lydia replied, "Who knows? But you might as well cook there as here."

Polly thought for a moment, then nodded. "I'll use this money for work clothes and passage back to Quade's Harbor on the mail boat," she said, patting her bodice, "and save the rest in case Devon doesn't come around."

Lydia embraced the other woman briefly, then rose from the bench. "I'd best get back to the hotel now," she said. "Aunt Persephone will be waking up from her nap and wanting company." As she left the mess tent, escorted by Polly, the strains of a fiddle and the twangy, unidentifiable sound of another instrument met her ears.

"There's a dance tonight," Polly said, and Lydia recalled the many invitations that had been extended to them both.

Lydia was thoughtful for a moment, listening to the rough, merry music, intrigued by it. She wasn't even sure she'd know how to dance, since she'd never had the chance—except with imaginary partners in her girlhood room, back in Fall River.

"We're staying at the Imperial Hotel," she said, feeling a strange, eager energy gather in her feet. "You'd best come by in the morning and talk with Brigham before you go back."

"I will," Polly promised. "Do you want me to walk to the hotel with you?"

"You would have to come back by yourself," Lydia reasoned, with a shake of her head. "No, Polly, I'll be fine. And I'll see you tomorrow."

With that, the two women parted. There was a moon, and light swelling into the street from the doorway of the

States Rights Saloon, as well as a plank-board eatery and a place of suspicious enterprise, so Lydia didn't need a lantern.

She tried to ignore the music as she passed the large meetinghouse where the dance was being held, but it pulled at her spirit, like an invisible hand. Lydia was filled with an achy nostalgia for earlier, simpler times, when war was only something mentioned in a history primer and she'd still believed in mystery and magic.

Reaching the Imperial Hotel, Lydia hurried upstairs and knocked at Aunt Persephone's door, which was directly across the hall from her own.

Persephone was enjoying a carry-up dinner at a table next to the window. "Merciful heavens, Lydia, I thought you'd been carried off by white slavers or something. Where in heaven's name have you been?"

Lydia drew up a chair and sat, shaking her head when Persephone offered her a portion of her meal. "I helped Polly serve her lumberjacks tonight, and she gave me supper."

Persephone looked detached, in a crafty sort of way. "Her lumberjacks?"

"She's working as a cook," she said.

The older woman pushed back her plate and sighed contentedly, evidently willing to let the subject of Polly go without further discussion. "What are your plans for the evening, Lydia?"

She thought of the music, and the dancing, and the pure frivolity of the occasion, and took her wanton nature firmly in hand. "I'm planning to retire early," she said. "Charlotte and Millie will be back first thing in the morning, and your ship sails in the afternoon—"

Persephone stood, smoothing her sateen skirts and touching her gray chignon with a girlish gesture of her palm. "I do declare, Lydia, sometimes you are a sore disappointment to me. You've got music in your eyes and you've been tapping your feet ever since you sat down. You'll go to the dance if I have to drag you there!"

Lydia was stunned. "But—"

Persephone interrupted by clapping her hands briskly several times. "No more protests. It'll do you good to go dancing, and probably have a redeeming effect on Brigham as well."

Mystified, Lydia allowed herself to be pushed to the door. In the hallway, Persephone looked her over critically.

"A pink party frock would be just the thing, with that lovely coloring of yours, but God knows you're pretty enough even in calico. Those men will be falling all over themselves to get to you."

Lydia was hurt. She'd had the distinct impression that Aunt Persephone was pushing her toward Brigham ever since their brief acquaintance began. Now it seemed the other woman was anxious to marry her off to the first presentable suitor.

Persephone linked her arm with Lydia's and propelled her down the hallway toward the stairway. Words poured out of Devon and Brigham's aunt in an eager rush. "I dare say I may acquire a beau or two myself." She gave a trilling, youthful laugh as they hastened down the steps. "And wouldn't my sister Cordelia and I have a fine time telling *that* story around Bright Harbor, Maine!"

Music and light still poured through the open doors of the meetinghouse as they approached, moments later, and Lydia couldn't stop the smile that spread over her mouth.

At one end of the hall, on an improvised dais of planks balanced on bricks, a fat, smiling man with a patch over one eye and a single suspender holding up his battered trousers played a fiddle. Beside him, on an upturned tobacco crate, sat a blond giant with an ordinary saw blade quivering between his meaty hands, making the plaintive, oddly lovely sound Lydia had heard earlier, while walking back to the hotel.

On the dance floor, which was really just hard-packed dirt with a little sawdust sprinkled over it, other men whirled gracelessly with plain-faced Indian women. Yet other men danced with each other, in a playful way that made Lydia smile. She would have bolted from the place if Aunt Persephone hadn't been holding onto her arm so tightly.

Almost instantly a crowd gathered, and Lydia blushed self-consciously as the horde of men looked her and Aunt Persephone over like a pair of two-headed hens on display at the fair. Then a tall, muscular, and very handsome young man stepped forward, his red hair glinting in the lantern light.

He bowed low, to the cheers of the other men, and offered Lydia his hand without a word.

She took it, too. She'd never danced with a real partner before, because she'd spent her early years looking after her hapless father, and then the war had come along, but her untrained feet seemed to know how to make the steps.

Out of the corner of her eye Lydia saw Aunt Persephone go barreling by in the embrace of a bald man with arms the size of tree trunks, a pink blush highlighting her cheeks.

After the first partner, another presented himself, and then another. Lydia grew breathless, and a little dazed, but she wanted to keep dancing forever.

When she suddenly found herself in Brigham's embrace, being swept through the steps so gracefully that she couldn't even be certain her feet were still touching the floor, she thought she was imagining things. Then she saw the grim set of his jaw and the angry flash in his eyes and knew he was only too real.

"You're just full of surprises, aren't you, Miss McQuire?" he asked. Another man tried to cut in just then, and Brigham seared him with a look that would have dried up Puget Sound. "What the hell do you think you're doing, making a spectacle of yourself in front of all these men?"

Lydia laughed, intoxicated by the exercise, the unaccustomed attention, the music, and the sheer fun of being the belle of the ball. "Is that what I'm doing, Brigham? Making a spectacle?"

"Yes," he hissed, his breath warm on her face, his hard body pressed close to her soft and pliant one. "I'm taking you back to the hotel, right now!"

The other people in the big room were a colorful swirl around Lydia; she was conscious only of Brigham, and the way he was holding her, and the things he made her want.

"I'm not going anywhere," she informed him.

A resigned look came over Brigham's handsome features, and without any warning at all, he hoisted her over his shoulder like a sack of pearl barley and headed for the door.

Lydia began to kick and struggle, but Brigham was far too strong, and she knew it was hopeless. He carried her over the board sidewalk, across the manure-strewn street, and set her down on the hotel steps with a thump that jarred her bones.

She was mad as a hen doused in winter well water, and for the moment all she could do was stand there, staring up at him and quivering with helpless rage.

If anything, Brigham looked even angrier than she was. "You're lucky you didn't end up in the hold of one of those ships out in the harbor," he snapped, glaring at her, "on your way to some brothel in South America!"

Lydia felt the color drain from her face. "You're just saying that to scare me!" she accused in a furious whisper. "Besides, I was perfectly safe the whole time. Aunt Persephone was there, and not one of those men would have hurt me." She paused. "Aunt Persephone!" she cried, and started back across the street to reclaim the adventurous old woman before she met with a foul fate.

Brigham caught her arm and hauled her back to his side again. "My aunt has been reading in her room all evening," he said.

For a moment Lydia was baffled. Then she realized she'd been tricked. Persephone had obviously wanted Brigham to find her at the dance, but had that been the act of a friend or a foe? On the one hand, Brigham seemed jealous, and the thought was a heady one, filling Lydia with excitement as she entertained it. That could well have been Persephone's aim.

On the other, however, the clever old woman might have been trying to get rid of an unwanted house guest, believing Brigham would send her away in disgrace if he found her enjoying the attentions of other men. Just the way Devon had sent Polly away.

Lydia felt true grief, imagining how it would be to leave the girls and Quade's Harbor and, yes, God help her, Brigham. Still, pride caused her to hold her head high.

Before she could offer to resign, however, Brigham guided her up the stairs and into the lobby of the Imperial Hotel. "It would seem there is only one way to keep you out of trouble, Miss McQuire," he said. "Perhaps I'd better just make you my wife and be done with it."

9

*L*YDIA WAS SO SHAKEN THAT SHE COULD NOT OFFER A REPLY
until they'd reached the upstairs hallway and the door to
her room was within reach. Brigham's blithe assumption
that she would eagerly agree to his proposal was singular-
ly infuriating.

"I'd sooner marry the dancing bear at Yesler's Hall!"
she hissed, folding her arms and glaring.

He seemed undaunted. "I don't doubt that," he replied
evenly, the light of humor flickering in his gray eyes.
"You could teach that mangy, toothless critter some new
tricks and make him follow you around by yanking on
his leash." Brigham paused, sighed. "You wouldn't be
happy with a man you could dominate, Lydia, and you
damn well know it."

Just being so near this exasperating man made Lydia's
rebellious flesh tingle with the desire to be touched, but
she hefted her chin another notch and stoked the fire in
her eyes. "I am willing to concede that point, Mr.
Quade," she said. "I would not want a man who let me
run roughshod over him, but neither do I require one
who would do the same to me!"

Brigham leaned closer still, and Lydia felt a flush rise, like a flash flood, from her knees to her forehead.

"Is that what you think?" he drawled. "That I'd be a domineering husband?"

Lydia thought of the stern, efficient way Brigham ran his timber operation, and Quade's Harbor as well. There wasn't a person in the community, with the possible exception of Devon, who didn't have to do as Brigham said or give an accounting for the lapse.

"I have absolutely no doubt that you'd be a domineering husband," she said. She'd backed up to the door of her room now, trying to gather the momentum to clutch the knob and escape inside.

Brigham braced himself against the woodwork, one hand on either side, fencing Lydia in with his arms. There was a dent in his chin, she noticed, and it accented the square strength of his jaw.

"I'm the master of my house," he agreed quietly, "and that isn't going to change. But I could give you a fine home, Lydia, and security." His thundercloud eyes focused disconcertingly on her mouth, causing it to tremble. "I could give you children."

A sweet shiver went through Lydia, because she knew Brigham wasn't talking about Charlotte and Millie. He was referring to babies he had yet to sire.

Lydia pressed her spine to the door, her heart thudding in her throat. He hadn't mentioned love; she must remember that.

Brigham's lips weren't even an inch from hers. He meant to kiss her again, and if he did, her will would be washed away in a tide of passion and she would probably agree to any scandalous thing he might suggest.

"You want children of your own, don't you, Lydia?" he asked, in a sleepy voice that drained away nearly all of her remaining strength. "Sons. Daughters." His lips brushed hers, teasing, making her want so much more. "Lots of babies."

She squeezed her eyes shut, fighting for control of her mind and body. "Yes," she whispered, in an anguish of yearning. They were still in the hallway, and anyone could have come along and seen them in that compromising stance, but Lydia didn't care. Couldn't move.

Lightly, with a gentleness she wouldn't have suspected of such a large and powerful man, Brigham cupped her right breast in his hand. With the thumb, he made the nipple ready for a pleasure Lydia didn't begin to comprehend and yet wanted with her whole soul.

"Think about it," Brigham said, touching, just touching, his mouth to hers for the merest part of a moment. Then, unbelievably, he stepped back.

Lydia stared at him for a moment in utter consternation, fearing she'd slide right down the door panel like a rag doll now that he was no longer holding her up, then fumbled in her pocket for the room key and opened the door. When she turned to look, Brigham was already disappearing down the stairs.

She thought of Seattle's infamous Skid Road, which Millie had obligingly pointed out from the deck of the mail boat on their arrival, with its seedy brothels, beer parlors, and gambling dens. And she hoped Brigham wasn't on his way there to find comfort with some woman of unwholesome inclinations.

His last words echoed in her mind as she turned up the wick in the bedside lamp and lit it. *Think about it,* he'd said. What he'd meant was, think about the way you feel when I kiss you—think of how it would be to lie naked under my hands—to make a baby with me.

Lydia sat down on the edge of her bed with a miserable sigh. Thanks to Brigham Quade and his improper effect on her senses, she would think of little else throughout the night.

It was a fine, sunny day for sailing, and there was a steamboat anchored in the bay, as well as a majestic clipper ship. Charlotte imagined boarding that clipper and racing over the seas, seeing faraway lands and exotic people, and all of a sudden she felt like a bird shut up in a bread box. She loved her father, her Uncle Devon, and even Millie, but she longed to fly away, too. As long as she could remember, she'd ached to leave Quade's Harbor and all its unromantic dullness behind her.

Aunt Persephone was about to board a small tug that would carry her and the other passengers out to the steamer, and Charlotte longed to stow away in a lifeboat on the big, lumbering ship, or in a corner of the hold. Sometimes she thought if something exciting didn't happen to her soon, she was going to go stark-raving mad.

Even with her talent for fancy, however, she couldn't imagine how she could manage such an escapade, with her father standing close by and the steamer way out there in the harbor. She wouldn't be able to board the tug unobserved, and swimming to the steamboat was out of the question, too, even though she had a strong, sure stroke.

She hugged and kissed her tearful great-aunt, but her mind was roving over the seaport, back to the big clipper ship in the harbor. She turned, while Aunt Persephone was walking up the ramp to the deck of the tugboat and everyone was calling farewells and waving, and admired the clipper's tall mast and the netting of rope stretching from there to the deck. On the sleek hull someone had painted the word *Enchantress* in ornate gold letters.

Charlotte was charmed.

She walked, unnoticed, along the wharf to the boardwalk that edged the shore, to stand beside the *Enchantress*'s berth, shading her eyes from the sun as she drank in the pure splendor of the vessel. Her papa had once remarked that clipper ships would soon be mere relics of the past, replaced by the able steamers, and the idea filled Charlotte with bitter sadness.

She imagined that the captain of this glorious ship was a handsome pirate, a man as at home in the crow's nest as Aunt Persephone was in the front parlor. Uncontrollable and largely unrecognizable emotion rode high in her throat, and tears filled her eyes.

It seemed to Charlotte that everyone was traveling

somewhere, doing something, having grand adventures. Everyone except her.

"Charlotte!" The familiar voice rang across the short distance between the two wharfs, blending with the squawks of the gulls and the whistles of boats entering and leaving the harbor.

Shading her eyes from the sun, Charlotte turned and faced her father. "Coming, Papa," she called back obediently. Perhaps it was then that the plan began to take shape in her mind; she would never know for sure.

"We're going to see the bear now!" Millie cried, her small face bright with excitement, when Charlotte joined her family and Miss McQuire on the other dock. "It costs a whole nickel, just to go inside for a look."

Charlotte sighed. Some people were so easily entertained.

Miss McQuire smiled at Charlotte, warming her in the same special way the sun did when it made an unexpected appearance during the long gray months of winter. She wanted Lydia for a friend, but she was afraid to like her too much, for fear she'd leave.

They took the midday meal in the dining room at the Imperial Hotel, and then made the short walk to Yesler's Hall to pay their admission and see the bear.

Charlotte's melancholia deepened when she saw that poor creature awkwardly dancing on top of an old washtub. It had a worn red collar around its neck, and patches of the animal's coat had rubbed away in places, leaving bare spots. On instructions from his handler, the bear opened his muzzle and "talked," and his mouth was void of teeth.

Charlotte, seated on a bench like all the other spectators, turned and rested her forehead against the outer part of her papa's muscled arm for a moment.

Her father gave her a brief squeeze. "It's all right, Charlie," he whispered, using the nickname that was a secret between them. "Nobody's hurting the bear."

Charlotte felt her eyes fill with tears. It wasn't the animal's performing that troubled her, but his lack of freedom and dignity. He should have been roaming the high country, hunting in summer and hibernating in winter. . . .

"May I go out?" she asked.

Her papa considered briefly, then nodded. "Stay close by, though. The mail boat puts in in about an hour, and we'll be leaving for home then."

Charlotte nodded, cast one last pitying look at the bear, and hurried along the board floor to the open doorway at the back of the building.

The towering masts of the *Enchantress* immediately caught her eye, drew her thoughts away from the bear. The berth was not far from where she stood—she could go and have a closer look and be back long before the others came out of Yesler's Hall.

Minutes later Charlotte was standing at the base of a narrow wooden ramp, gazing up at the clipper ship in wonderment. She supposed it had sailed to China, and Hawaii, and maybe Europe and Australia, too. She squeezed her eyes shut and tried to imagine what it would be like to stand at the railing and watch some grand and exotic city take shape on the horizon.

A peculiar kind of excitement jiggled in the pit of Charlotte's stomach. If anyone was aboard the ship, they weren't visible, and one glance back over her shoulder told her no one was paying particular attention to her.

She started up the ramp, holding onto the rope railings on either side as she went, and then she was on the deck. It rocked slightly under her feet, that ship, but Charlotte loved the sensation. She pretended to be on her way to London to have tea with the Queen.

"Hello?" she called, as a salty breeze slapped at the skirts of her best dress, a blue taffeta trimmed in lace at the collar and cuffs.

No one answered, and Charlotte tilted her head back to look up at the mast and the netting of rope. Suddenly, the craving to see far and wide overwhelmed her. Pretending to be Maid Marian, scaling a network of vines to warn Robin Hood that the sheriff of Nottingham had laid a dastardly trap for him, Charlotte began to climb.

The feeling of power, of freedom, was glorious. Charlotte tilted her head back, clinging nimbly to the ropes, and let the wind rush through her light brown hair. Higher and higher she went, until she could see homesteads and Indians' shacks in the forest.

"Hey!" a voice shouted. "You! What are you doing up there?"

Charlotte looked down, and that was her mistake. She might as well have been on a mountaintop, so far away did the deck seem to be. There was a young man standing down there, with longish dark hair, fitted britches, and a flowing seaman's shirt.

She gulped, and her hands froze on the ropes. She had the terrifying feeling that no matter how tightly she held on, it wouldn't be tight enough to keep her from plunging to her death.

"Help me," she said, but the words were only a whisper, and the man on the deck couldn't possibly have heard them.

Still, Charlotte felt motion in the ropes, and when she could bring herself to look again, she saw that he was climbing toward her as nimbly as a spider on a web. She slipped her arms through the spaces in the net and hugged herself.

Soon he was beside her. "Come on, little girl," he said, with exasperated gentleness. "I'll get you down."

Charlotte ran her tongue over dry lips. "Are you the captain of this ship?" she asked, her voice shaking. It was that or give in to panic and start screaming like a saw tearing into gnarled wood.

He did look like a pirate, with his dark hair tied back at his nape. His eyes were so blue that Charlotte thought for a moment that she'd tumble into them, instead of downward to the hard wooden deck, and his straight white teeth made a jolting contrast to his tanned skin when he grinned. He looked to be twenty-two or so.

"No, lass," he said, putting one arm firmly around her waist. "But the *Enchantress* will be mine someday, when my uncle is satisfied that I can handle her. Come on, now. Let's go down."

Charlotte started to tremble. "I'm scared."

"Too bad you didn't have sense enough to get scared sooner," he observed impatiently. "What's your name, anyway?"

"Ch-Charlotte," she stammered. "Charlotte Quade."

Again the grin, blinding and bright. "Hello, Charlotte. I'm Patrick Trevarren. May I have this dance?"

She stared at him, baffled, then realized he was trying to make things easier by jesting. She held onto the ropes as she would the rungs of the ladder and took a faltering step downward, thankful to the core of her spirit for the hard strength of Patrick's arm around her waist. "I d-don't know how to dance," she answered, and instantly hated herself for sounding like a stupid child.

They were about midway from their goal when Charlotte looked down again. The deck and the sea and the timer and the sky began to move, like the colored pieces in a kaleidoscope, and Charlotte was sure she was about to disgrace herself by throwing up.

"I can't do this," she said.

"Yes, you can," Patrick replied firmly. "Here, put your arms around my neck and I'll carry you the rest of the way."

Letting go of that rope took all the strength of character Charlotte possessed, but she did it. She flung both arms around Mr. Trevarren's neck and held on with a grip tight enough to choke him.

He secured her close to his side with one arm and used the other to manage the rigging, and he moved as deftly as a monkey in the jungle. The instant they reached the deck, his polite manner disappeared, and he set Charlotte on her feet with a jarring thunk.

"Somebody ought to take you over their knee!" he growled, his hands resting on his hips. "What kind of damn-fool trick was that, climbing up in the rigging that way?"

Humiliation throbbed in Charlotte's cheeks. There was something wounding in Patrick Trevarren's angry contempt, and she wasn't used to being belittled. "If you touch me, my papa will horsewhip you within *this far* of your life!" she warned, making an infinitesimal space between her thumb and index finger. Her outburst was mostly bravado, since she had no real way to justify what she'd done. "And don't you swear at me, either, you—you sea monkey!"

Patrick stared at her for a long, threatening moment, his brows drawn together in an ominous frown, but then he burst out laughing. "You're a bold one, you are. Go home, Charlotte Quade, and play with your china tea sets and your dolls. A seagoing vessel like the *Enchantress* is no place for little girls!"

If there was one thing Charlotte hated, it was being treated like a child. She was thirteen, old enough to marry and have babies in some cultures. Without another word she turned on her heel and strode away toward the ramp.

"You're welcome!" Patrick shouted after her.

"Go to blazes, Mr. Trevarren!" Charlotte yelled back. As soon as she reached the wharf, she began to run, reasoning that her arrogant rescuer was probably ready to drag her back up into the rigging and drop her on her head.

When she reached the shore and dared to turn and look back, however, Patrick was standing at the railing, high above her, an aura of sunshine outlining his leanly magnificent frame. Relief swept over Charlotte, immediately followed by disappointment.

On some level, she realized, she'd *wanted* him to chase her.

She stood on the bank for a long interval, staring up at him, finally recognizing him as the prince in every fairy tale she'd ever heard or read. Knowing she couldn't have Patrick Trevarren because she was too young.

With tears stinging her eyes, Charlotte lifted her skirts and ran for Yesler's Hall.

As Brigham watched Lydia watching the bear, a peculiar thickness rose in his throat. He wanted her, stubborn and opinionated little Yankee that she was, as he'd never wanted any woman before her.

A pulse leaped visibly under Lydia's left ear; the place looked vulnerable and Brigham was possessed with a most inappropriate desire to kiss it. Not that he gave a damn what was proper, but there were other people around, including his ten-year-old daughter.

He shifted restlessly on the hard bench. He might have spirited another woman to his bed, but Lydia was different.

Brigham sighed. Not that he had tender feelings for her or anything. He didn't believe in romantic love, and he'd seen what sappy infatuation had done to Devon, but he'd been sincere all the same when he'd asked Lydia to marry him the night before.

He folded his arms, cleared his throat, then leaned forward with his elbows braced on his thighs. Damnation, he hated just sitting there, like a schoolboy listening to a lesson, and he wanted to go outside and smoke. That would mean leaving Lydia, however, and he wasn't about to do that. Most of the lumberjacks, miners, and mill workers crowding the hall that day were looking at Lydia instead of the bear. Since there was no gold band on her finger, half of them would commence to courting her the minute he turned his back.

Brigham scowled, directed his gaze to Millie, who was watching the show with wide, shining eyes. His scowl faded and his heart gave an extra thud, then fell a little. Now that Aunt Persephone was gone, it flat wasn't proper for him to have an unmarried woman in the house. It was a bad influence on the girls, and God only knew what kind of ideas those two might get in their heads as a result.

At last the show ended, and Brigham cupped one hand under Lydia's elbow, somewhat possessively if the truth were known, and hoisted her to her feet.

"Mail boat should be in," he said gruffly. For the first time in his life he wished he could spout poetry the way Devon did, but plain words were all Brigham knew. "Time to go home."

* * *

Home.

The word conjured no images of Fall River for Lydia, and certainly none of Washington City or Gettysburg, either. No, it brought pictures of Quade's Harbor instead, with its hopeful row of saltbox houses, its noisy mill, its grand view of mountains and water and more trees than God had angels.

She blushed. Home was the big house on the hill, looking down on the beginnings of a town, even though she had no justifiable claim to it.

Outside the hall, Charlotte was sitting on a barrel, swinging her legs and looking guilty. Millie ran to her, chattering an accounting of every trick the bear had performed and a few she thought it could learn with proper instruction.

Lydia's heart constricted. When had she come to love another woman's children, just as if they were born of her own flesh?

Brigham was still holding her arm, and his touch filled Lydia with sweet misery. She almost wished she'd agreed to his proposal, just so she could find out what it was that her body so desperately wanted from his.

The baggage had been brought down to the wharf by wagon, and Brigham didn't give it a second look as he squired Lydia onto the mail boat, Charlotte and Millie scrambling along behind.

"I guess you'll miss your Aunt Persephone," she said when they were standing at the railing watching the first mate and several other men loading freight. It wasn't at all what Lydia had wanted to say, but she knew no words to explain her true feelings, even to herself.

Brigham smiled sadly, without looking at Lydia, and she felt the poorer for it. "Yes, I'll miss her," he said. "But it's time she had a good long visit with Aunt Cordelia, and that grand tour of Europe she's been talking about for five years."

Lydia started to touch his arm, drew her fingers back just short of contact with the tanned, muscle-corded flesh protruding from his rolled shirtsleeves. Her voice came out sounding like it did when she needed to clear her throat.

"Thank you for taking us to see the bear," she said.

At last he turned toward her, and though his tempting mouth was solemn, his eyes were full of humor. "I think you got more attention than he did," he replied. The boat's whistle sounded and the boarding ramp was raised, but the noises seemed far away, like cries at the far end of a long tunnel. Then, just lightly, Brigham reached out and brushed a tendril of hair from Lydia's cheek.

His touch made her close her eyes for a moment and grip the railing so tightly that her knuckles ached.

She looked at him and tried to lighten the moment with a joke. "I guess if I ever decide I want a husband, I know where to get one," she said, thinking of all the male attention she'd had in Seattle.

The mirth drained from Brigham's eyes, turning them the slate-gray color of an angry sky. He started to speak, apparently thought better of it, and walked away.

"What's the matter with him?" Millie asked, talking around a chunk of the rock candy Brigham had bought for her earlier, in the mercantile, when they'd ordered supplies. "He looks really cranky."

Lydia bent down and whispered, "He is. And I'd stay away from him if I were you."

Millie nodded and scampered off in the opposite direction, as at home on the ship as a galley mouse. Lydia turned to look for Charlotte and saw her gazing toward the harbor with the usual faraway, ethereal expression on her face.

She waited a moment, trying to discern whether the girl wanted company or not, then took a chance and approached.

"Charlotte?" Lydia took a wrapped butter-cream candy from her pocket and offered it. "A sweet for your thoughts."

Charlotte looked at the candy, took it, and then offered

Lydia a faltering smile. "Did you ever think that if you couldn't have a grand adventure straightaway, you'd just go right out of your mind?"

Lydia looked back on her own girlhood. There hadn't been much time for dreams and fancies, not with her father barely making a living in his practice and drinking to drown his loneliness and disappointment. "Not really," she replied honestly, "but I think I know how you're feeling—like you can't wait to grow up. Am I right?"

The girl nodded, and Lydia realized for the first time what a heart-stopping beauty Charlotte would grow up to be, with her large, luminous amber eyes, her high cheekbones, and her golden-brown hair. Again she wondered about the children's mother.

Brigham's wife.

"I feel like that bear back there at Yesler's Hall," Charlotte said, her eyes on the outline of the big clipper ship still in port. Aunt Persephone's steamer had long since rounded a bend and disappeared, but the bay was still full of small fishing boats, canoes, and tugs. "I'm just something to look at, and be ordered about."

Lydia slid an arm around the girl's straight shoulders and squeezed lightly. "You're becoming a woman, Charlotte, and that's a wonderful, exciting thing, but it's troubling sometimes, too."

Charlotte looked at her gratefully for a moment, then frowned. "I'll probably just marry some lumberjack and live in one of the saltbox houses," she said.

The idea of having a home in a peaceful and prosperous place like Quade's Harbor held far more appeal for Lydia, but Charlotte was very young, and restless. Her moods probably fluctuated widely, just because of the changes taking place inside her body. No doubt she remembered her mother, as Millie did not, and missed her.

"You won't have to marry anyone you don't want to," Lydia assured the child, even though she wasn't entirely sure. Brigham was an old-fashioned man in many ways, and he might consider it his right to arrange his daughter's marriage when the time came.

The boat sailed on, and Charlotte wandered off to squat by the grocery boxes from the mercantile, with Millie, and plunder the contents for an orange. Lydia smiled as she watched the girls peel the bright skin from the fruit and squirt each other with the juice.

There was still a lot of daylight left when the mail boat put in at Quade's Harbor, but Devon wasn't working on his building, high on the bluff, as Lydia had expected. She wondered if Polly had reached home ahead of them somehow, if the lovers were even now resting in each other's arms.

The boat whistle sounded, and Harrington, Brigham's skinny clerk, came rushing down the hillside, the sunlight catching on the lenses of his spectacles.

"Mr. Quade!" he shouted, as if there could be any doubt who he'd come to see. "Mr. Quade!" Harrington reached the end of the wharf, cupped his hands around his mouth and yelled again, "Mr. Quade!"

"What is it, Harrington?" Brigham demanded impatiently, vaulting over the ship's rail and onto the dock before the vessel had even been tied up to the piling. He crouched and worked the rope through a rusted iron ring, glaring up at his clerk as he made an able knot. "Well, damn it, what do you want?"

Poor Harrington was breathless, his thin chest heaving. "It's Mr. *Devon* Quade, sir," he got out at last. "He was working in the woods yesterday—search me why he'd want to do such a thing—and he fell." Maddeningly, Harrington chose then to pause and push his spectacles back up to the bridge of his nose. "I'm afraid he's rather grievously injured."

Lydia swayed, there at the ship's railing, and watched helplessly as the color drained from Brigham's face. He grabbed poor Harrington by the lapels of his suit coat and hauled him up onto his toes.

"Where is he?" he rasped as the ramp thumped onto the wharf from the deck.

"The house, of course," the clerk choked out. "They carried him to the house."

Brigham cast one desperate look at Lydia, as if accusing her, or imploring her to alter reality by some secret magic, then turned and scrambled up the bank.

10

Brigham raced up the embankment, across the road, along the driveway leading to the house. His throbbing lungs burned as though filled with molten metal, and his heart hammered a single, silent word into his throat with every beat: *no*.

He flung the front door open with such force that it clattered against the inside wall. *Not Devon*, he thought frantically, taking the steps three at a time. *Oh, God, please. Not Devon.*

Only when he'd reached the second floor did Brigham stop himself, gripping the jamb of Devon's open door in his hands. In those moments, Brigham was engaged in the most ferocious struggle he'd ever faced—he battled himself, his own panic and a wild need to alter an unalterable reality.

He took one deep breath, and then another. He thought of Lydia, and her image formed in his mind, sensible and quiet, calming him slightly. He stepped over the threshold into his brother's bedroom.

At the end of the old hardwood bed—the piece had come down to them from their parents, and both

Brigham and Devon had been born in it—he gripped the footboard to steady himself.

Devon's face was so swollen and bruised that his eye sockets had disappeared entirely. A wide gash stretched from his forehead to the crown of his head, and his thick hair was matted with blood. His bare chest looked as though he'd been horsewhipped within a heartbeat of the grave, and his left arm had been placed in a crude sling.

"I done what I could," Jake Feeny said, from the shadows next to the bed, and Brigham looked up to see the cook's tormented face. "It's bad, Brig. It's real bad."

Brigham shoved one hand through his hair and swayed. He wanted to shout, to rampage, to drink himself crazy and rip the whole town down to its foundations, board by board. He wouldn't, though, he couldn't. He was Brigham, the strong one, the elder brother who always knew what to do.

"You've sent somebody to Seattle for a doctor?" he rasped, going to Devon's side now, lightly touching his brother's blood-crusted forehead.

Jake snuffled and wiped his sleeve across his face. "Sam Baker went right away, riding the best horse in the timber camp. We was afraid to wait for the mail boat."

Devon stirred slightly beneath his brother's touch, and Brigham pushed up his sleeves and turned to the basin and pitcher on the bedside table. "What happened?" he asked, taking a clean handkerchief from Devon's bureau, dampening it in the basin, beginning to wash the blood from his brother's face with gentle strokes.

Jake took a moment longer to compose himself. He'd been with the company almost from the first, and if he had a family elsewhere, he was probably estranged from it. The Quades were all he had, when it came to what he called "folks."

"The damn fool," the old man finally sputtered, looking down at Devon with affectionate fury.

From the corner of his eye Brigham saw Lydia in the doorway, and he was made stronger by her presence.

"The cuss-headed idiot went up to top a tree," Jake

said, "wouldn't let Immerson do it, even though nobody's better at it than that Swede, and the blasted thing split on him." A sob escaped Jake, low and rusty, and he ran his cuff under his nose. "He musta fell near to thirty feet, Brig."

Brigham didn't look at Devon, for the moment he couldn't bear the sight, and he knew Jake needed time and privacy to reassemble his dignity. His eyes swung to Lydia, taking refuge, hungry for the solace of her strength.

Charlotte and Millie were huddled in the doorway behind her, but Brigham couldn't think beyond that. His mind was reeling inside itself, off balance.

Lydia spoke gently to the girls, sending them away, and entered the room. Having her there was, to Brigham, like a gentle splash of cool water on a new burn.

"You'd better go and see if you can rustle up some supper," she said to Jake, moving to stand on the opposite side of Devon's bed and touch his forehead with the backs of the fingers on her right hand. "The girls are hungry and tired, and they'll be wanting water heated for baths."

Jake nodded, looking desperately grateful for something constructive to do, and shuffled out of the room.

Lydia's blue eyes rose from Devon's ruined face to Brigham's despairing one.

"Be careful, Brigham," she said in a firm, quiet voice. "You can't control what you're feeling right now, I know, but you *can* manage what you're thinking. That's going to be communicated from your mind to Devon's, because you're closer than most brothers, and I can't stress enough how imperative it is that you believe in his strength and his will to recover."

Brigham didn't absorb all of what she said, but somehow the words steadied his staggered soul, and he stood a little straighter. "I'll do anything to help him," he said, staring at his brother's face, trying to will his own strength into Devon's broken body. "Anything."

Lydia came around to where Brigham stood, the wet cloth still in his hand, and covered his fingers with her own, lightly. He felt a jolt of courage, and some other emotion, burst through his skin, invade his veins and spread into every part of him like fire.

"Fetch more water," she said softly. She took the cloth from Brigham's hand, dipped it into the basin and began to bathe Devon's wounds with gentle deftness. "I'll need soap, whiskey, too, and lots of clean cloth—a sheet would do. Have Jake boil some sewing needles on the stove—Aunt Persephone must have left a few behind." She paused, and when she spoke again, it was to herself more than Brigham. "I don't suppose you have catgut, so I'll have to use silk thread for suturing and watch very closely for infection."

Brigham turned, moved awkwardly toward the door. An emotion he didn't dare unchain burned behind his eyes and constricted his throat.

Lydia gave Brigham a long and searching look, then came to his side and ushered him into the hallway. "Bring me the things I need," she said, as if speaking to a shattered child. "And then it would be best if you went off somewhere, by yourself, and brought your thinking under control. If you do that, your feelings will fall naturally into line, and Devon will sense that. It will give him something to hold on to, a light to follow in the darkness."

He raised his hand, touched her face lightly, and then went to do her bidding. He rounded up the items she'd asked for, from the whiskey to the sterilized needles, but it was much harder to leave Devon.

What would have seemed like silly, sentimental mysticism coming from anyone else made hard sense when Lydia said it. He could not allow himself to communicate the fear and horror he was feeling to Devon; the weight of those things might drag his brother down. So Brigham did as he'd been instructed, walking blindly through a drizzling rain to the cabin on the hill.

There, he lit a kerosene lamp, built a small fire on the hearth, and sat down in an old rocking chair—like the bed where Devon lay, near death, the rocker had been their mother's—his head braced in one hand.

Grimly, methodically, one by one, Brigham began aligning his thoughts. . . .

Devon was young and strong.

Devon had everything to live for. He had dreams, and people who loved him.

Devon would recover.

Lydia bathed Devon's wounds with infinite care, murmuring soft, reassuring words all the while. She stitched up the cut in his scalp, using white embroidery thread, and treated it with whiskey. With help from Jake, who had recovered himself at least enough to follow orders, she wrapped Devon's cracked rib cage, then felt his broken left arm with practiced fingers. It had to be reset, and Devon groaned at the pain, bringing tears of sympathy to Lydia's eyes.

She sent Jake to the icehouse, soothed Devon's dry lips with ice. "You're going to be fine, Devon," she told her patient in a firm voice that would brook no disagreement. "You're strong and good and we need you here, Polly and Brigham, Jake and the girls and I—we all need you very much."

He gave a low moan and tried to lift one hand, and Lydia knew then that he was conscious—not being able to look into his eyes, she hadn't been certain—and had probably been awake throughout the entire ordeal.

She bent and kissed his forehead lightly, her throat aching. She was remembering Devon as she'd first seen him, standing in the doorway of his room in that San Francisco hotel, hair rumpled, eyes sleepy, lips curved into a polite scowl. After that she pictured him on the roof of his general store, framed by the blue and silver flicker of the Sound, a hammer in his hand, grinning down at her.

"The next few days will be very hard, Devon," she whispered, gently smoothing back his hair, which was still damp from the washing she'd given it. "You'll want to give up and quit many times, but you mustn't do it. If you leave now, the good things you're meant to do will never happen. Children won't be born, whole branches of the Quade family will never exist, and the contributions they would have made will be lost."

Some instinct made her look up then, and Lydia saw Polly standing in the doorway, trembling, her clothes rumpled and her hair tousled by wind and wet with rain. Her hazel eyes were big as the lid on Jake's flour barrel, and she was holding onto the doorjamb with both hands, looking as if she'd fall over the threshold at any moment.

Lydia moved swiftly to her friend's side, gripped her arm. "If you come in here crying and carrying on, Polly Quade, you'll undo all the progress we've made," she whispered. "Unless you can be strong—stronger than you've ever been before—Devon would be better off without you."

Polly's fevered gaze seemed to devour the man she loved. She bit her lower lip and finally nodded. Then, after drawing a breath, she stumbled toward the bed, took Devon's good hand in both of her own. She bent forward and kissed him very lightly on the mouth, but said nothing.

Lydia moved a chair into place, and Polly sat, never letting go of Devon's hand.

"Miss McQuire?"

Turning, Lydia found Millie standing in the hallway, her Brigham-gray eyes wide. She touched the child gently on the shoulder.

"Yes, Millie?"

Millie swallowed. "Is my uncle going to die?"

Lydia slipped her arm around the little girl and guided her toward the rear stairway, which led down to the kitchen. She had seen too much death to regard its treachery lightly, and to misguide Millie would be no kindness. "I hope not," she said. "For tonight, the best thing you and Charlotte could do to help would be to have your suppers and your baths and go off to bed without fighting. When you've settled in for the night, think of your Uncle Devon as he's always been. Go to sleep seeing him well and whole in your mind. Can you do that?"

Millie considered for a moment—Lydia's suggestion

was not, after all, one that could be undertaken without some thought—then nodded. "I'll speak to Charlotte," she said, in a very grown-up voice.

Lydia bent and placed a soft kiss on Millie's crown, just where her lovely dark hair parted. "Thank you very much."

Charlotte was waiting at the base of the stairs, looking every bit as frightened as everyone else. She'd overheard Lydia's conversation with Millie, apparently, for she said, "I'll let Millie have the first bath, and I'll read her a story, too. Might we see Uncle Devon in the morning?"

"Perhaps," Lydia answered, touching Charlotte's pale cheek in a gesture of reassurance. "We'll discuss that at breakfast. Agreed?"

Millie and Charlotte looked at each other solemnly, then at Lydia. "Agreed," they chorused.

Once the water had been poured for the girls' baths, to be taken in the privacy of the spacious pantry off the kitchen, Lydia could no longer withstand the subtle force that drew her toward the back door. A soft, pattering rain was falling as she stepped out onto the porch, setting a kerosene lantern at her feet while she draped the cloak she'd bought in San Francisco with Devon's money, over her shoulders. She raised the hood, lifted the lamp, and looked upward, through the dense timber and underbrush, toward the cabin. A single light flickered through the foliage and the gray rain, guiding her.

Lydia's lamp nearly went out several times, despite her efforts to hold it steady, and more than once she tripped and almost fell over a root or branch lying in the path. The thorns of blackberry vines caught at her skirts and reached beneath to snag her stockings and scratch her calves.

By the time she reached the cabin, she was drenched with rain, despite the cloak, and the flame in her lantern had finally guttered and died. She hurried to the door and pounded at it, a little desperately, with one fist.

Just when she was about to step over the threshold, uninvited, the door swung inward, creaking on untended hinges, and Brigham was standing in the chasm, tall, vital, struggling with God only knew how many conflicting emotions.

He stepped back, and Lydia hurried past him, making her way to the fire that blazed on the hearth. The metal lantern made a hollow sound as she set it on the rock floor in front of the fireplace, then she shrugged out of the cloak.

"How is he?" Brigham's voiced seemed to grate on his throat, like a saw chewing into wood.

Lydia whirled, realizing he thought she'd come bearing the worst possible news. "Devon's holding his own," she said quickly, to reassure him. "It's you I've come to see about."

His handsome face looked haunted in the weak light of the fire and the single lamp burning on a table next to the cabin's one window. "You shouldn't have left the house on a night like this," he said coldly. "You might have run into trouble."

Lydia sighed, draping her cloak carefully over the back of the one chair the room boasted and then plucking at the folds of her skirts and giving them a good shake in front of the fire. "If I were afraid of trouble, Mr. Quade," she said lightly, "I'd never have dared to travel west in the first place."

He looked at her for a long time, his throat working, then muttered, "Are the girls all right?"

She smiled. "Charlotte and Millie are behaving like little women. You should be very proud of them."

He turned his profile to Lydia, standing beside her on the hearth, gazing into the flames as though they held him in some grim spell. "Devon is the best friend I've ever had," he said after a long and pensive silence. "When we were little, I used to take his whippings for him, when he got into trouble. I couldn't stand to see him hurt."

Lydia's heart tightened. She edged a bit closer to him, felt the heat of his body as surely as that of the fire before them. "Whippings?" she whispered, as injured by the thought of Brigham's pain as if the blows had struck her instead.

He grinned slightly, though there was certainly no joy in his face, and no humor. "I think those trips to the woodshed really *did* hurt Pa more than they did me," he said. "His heart just wasn't in it."

Lydia was only mildly pacified. "But he let you accept your brother's punishment?"

Brigham took a poker from its holder and stirred the embers in the grate. "I made sure Pa thought I'd been the one to do the mischief," he explained. "And lots of times, I had been."

Folding her arms, Lydia turned to Brigham. "I hope you don't believe in disciplining children in that primitive fashion," she said. "I could not stand by and see Charlotte or Millie struck."

He sighed. "Don't worry, Lydia," he responded. "Neither could I. And that's probably the reason they run from one end of this town to the other like Indians on a raid."

She never knew what accounted for the action, but Lydia let her head rest against Brigham's shoulder for a moment. The contact was orchestrated by a flash of lightning so close that its golden brightness glared in the room. For the length of a fluttery heartbeat, Lydia was unsure whether the combustion had come from within her or without.

Brigham turned to her, took her shoulders in his hands, gazed down at her in consternation, as if trying to formulate a scathing lecture behind those tarnished-pewter eyes of his. Then, with a low, strangled sound, he wrenched her close and kissed her.

The lightning broke its own rule then, striking for the second time in a single place. Lydia's spirit caught fire as Brigham's lips molded hers, prepared them for the fierce invasion of his tongue.

Lydia felt closed places within her tremble tentatively and then grind open, like stone doors in the ruins of some ancient castle. She didn't protest, couldn't have protested, as Brigham's hands cupped her buttocks through her skirts and petticoats, lifted her slightly and dragged her against him.

His masculinity seemed, for a short, breathless stretch of time, to be the home of the lightning that heated her skin and blinded her by the very intensity of its fire.

"Go back," he gasped, thrusting her away from him, gripping her face now, instead of her firm bottom, which still quivered and tingled from the hold he'd taken earlier. "Go back to the house, Lydia. Right now."

Lydia knew very little in those moments; her emotions were churning and her mind was as muddled as if she'd been drinking hard cider. Despite the ferocious, burning aches opening like lakes of lava inside her, she did not think of giving herself to Brigham. She merely wanted to hold him, to be held by him, and temporarily turn her back on a treacherous and uncertain world.

She shook her head. "I'm staying," she said, and slipped her arms around Brigham's waist. He kissed her again, kissed her until she was too dizzy to stand.

"Lydia," he murmured, his voice ragged and harsh.

Lydia raised her hands to his shoulders, spread the fingers wide to feel the straining muscles beneath his shirt. Then she found his heartbeat, thumping against her palm, and a new excitement possessed her.

She began to unbutton Brigham's shirt, and he groaned a senseless protest but did not lift his hands to stop her.

Pushing the fabric aside, Lydia laid her cheek to the place where his heart pounded against his flesh, as if seeking some union with her, her own pulse. The coarse down covering his chest offered a strange comfort, one she couldn't have defined, and at the same time engendered even greater needs.

He dipped one arm beneath her knees, the other like a steel brace at her back, lifted her, held her close against his chest. "You shouldn't have come here," he said.

Lydia didn't know whether he meant she shouldn't have come to the cabin or she shouldn't have come to

Quade's Harbor, and she didn't care. She was under a greedy enchantment, and she wanted as much of Brigham as he would allow her. Her tiresome New England practicality had been thrust into a dark closet of her spirit, imprisoned there, and she had no desire to free it.

Brigham's gray eyes revealed both pride and pleas. Then, with another moan, he mastered Lydia's mouth with his own.

When the kiss ended, he laid her lightly on the quilt-covered bed. His touch was passionate, yet every bit as gentle as if he'd been handling the most precious, fragile porcelain in existence. Slowly, he undressed her.

When Lydia wore only firelight and the chill of a rainy night, Brigham began taking off his own clothes. Unlike the other masculine bodies she had viewed, his was whole, unscarred, and beautifully muscled. He was so magnificent that Lydia dragged in a deep breath and nearly choked on it.

He lay on his side next to her, his hand cherishing her breasts, each in turn, fondling the nipples until they were hard and eager. He caressed her neck and the underside of her chin, and then teased the flat expanse of her stomach, making the flesh leap and quiver beneath his fingertips.

Lydia closed her eyes and arched her head back as he ventured deliciously, dangerously, near the moist delta where her femininity was awakening. The sensible part of her raved and paced inside its closet, protesting, but Lydia did not, could not, heed the warning.

She felt as though this moment had been bearing down on her since the beginning of time; as though she'd been created to make physical music under this man's hands and mouth, like an instrument.

Brigham knelt between her legs, gently gripped her ankles, set her feet so that her knees were high and apart. Then he fell to her belly, kissing the taut-satin skin, teasing her navel with the tip of his tongue.

It was a scandal, and Lydia loved it. Her skin was

moist with perspiration, her heart was racing, and her head moved from side to side as though in a fever.

When Brigham burrowed through the silken shelter guarding her womanhood and boldly took her into his mouth, she cried out in pleasure and thrust her hips upward off the bed. Brigham nestled his hands beneath her bottom, held her firmly to his lips, and continued to enjoy her.

A storm of ecstasy raged inside Lydia's supple body as she twisted from side to side, forward and back, reveling in the merciless flicks of Brigham's tongue and the drawing of his lips. She strained higher and higher off the bed, desperate to maintain the fevered link between them, an ancient and almost continuous cry coming from the depths of her being.

Still supporting her buttocks with one strong hand, Brigham raised the other to caress her breasts while the tempest thundered wildly within her. Her cries became frantic, the motions of her body more desperate still, and then, with a strangled sob, she fell in trembling relief to the mattress.

She lifted her arms to Brigham, fully expecting to take him inside her, to give him what remained of her innocence as a loving gift, but instead of taking her, he lay beside her again and fitted her close against his frame.

"Brigham," she whispered, in a despair of wanting.

His lips moved, warm and firm and soft, against her temple. "Not tonight, love. Not when your feelings are out of control this way."

Lydia's soul shriveled a little, out of loneliness and disappointment, but her reason rejoiced. Brigham's assessment of her mental state had been correct; she was not in her right mind. She had moaned and pitched under his fingers and his tongue like a wanton, raised herself to him like a sacrifice, sobbed in glorious surrender while he satisfied her.

And she'd done all this because she was overwrought, because she'd come to love Devon as a brother and he was so grievously hurt. She'd wanted to give Brigham comfort, as well as take it from him, but it wasn't a choice she would have made in the cool light of good sense, and she knew it.

She began to cry softly, trying hard not to make a sound, but Brigham knew. He caressed her cheek with one callused hand, wiped away her tears with the rough side of his thumb.

"It's all right, Lydia," he said hoarsely, holding her blessedly close. "I went too far, I know, but things won't go any further." He kissed her again, unromantically, on the bridge of her nose. "I'm sorry."

Lydia thought of the way her body had flown while Brigham loved her, and recalled how her very soul had seemed to soar free of her body during those wicked, violently joyous moments while she had been totally his. *Don't be sorry,* she pleaded, in silent grief. She had no excuse to offer, and couldn't have uttered a word even if she had.

Brigham just held her after that, and the experience was like medicine to her troubled spirit. She had always given comfort, though in less intimate forms, of course, but she'd rarely received it herself. In a way, for all its tender peace, the protection of Brigham's strong embrace was headier and more glorious than his bold lovemaking.

Presently, however, it occurred to her that such intercourse between a man and a woman was, by its very nature, reciprocal. She reached out to touch him, brazen in the sudden intensity of her curiosity, and was startled to feel his manhood straining, hard and imperious against her palm.

He gave a strangled cry when she closed her hand around him, the sound hissing through his teeth as if she'd held a hot coal to his flesh. He swore deliriously and curled his fingers around her wrist to free himself.

"I'm trying to be a gentleman," he breathed, after a long interval of deep, ragged breathing. "But if you do that again, I won't be held accountable for my actions. Is that understood?"

Lydia's eyes widened at the note of dangerous sincerity

in his voice, and at the same time she wanted to find out what she was missing. If it was more of what he'd just taught her, and better, he wouldn't have to worry about being a gentleman because she wouldn't be a lady.

"I never knew it felt like that," she marveled.

Brigham groaned, like a man in the throes of cholera, and moved away from her slightly. "Please, Lydia," he pleaded. "Don't talk about it anymore. I already feel as if I've got a lighted stick of dynamite between my legs."

The sudden return of her inhibitions gave her the impetuousness to sit up, turn her back and reach for her clothes, which were lying in a heap beside the bed. Her face went crimson and her lower lip trembled. How on earth would she face Brigham again after the way she'd acted?

His hand closed gently over her right shoulder. "I need a wife," he said, in a tone that might have been warmer instead of coolly practical. "My daughters need a mother, now more than ever. I'm asking you again, Lydia— marry me."

It took all her strength to rise from that bed, walk to the fireside and begin dressing herself. She knew Brigham was watching her every move, but there was no helping that, because the cabin had only one room and a loft, and there was nowhere to hide. "I know I came here on the agreement that I'd marry for my keep," she said, her voice shaking. The tragic truth was that it was all she could do not to return to that bed, surrender to Brigham again, tease him until he finally took solace in her body. "But for the first time in my life I have to go back on my word. I can't be your wife, Brigham."

She heard the rope springs of the bed creak as he sat up, and turned her back swiftly, her motions frantic as she tried to dress.

When he spoke, he was standing so close that she could feel the warmth of his breath on her nape. "Why not?" he demanded quietly.

Lydia bit her lower lip, and her eyes filled with tears. She could not turn around, could not face him. "Because I won't have a husband who doesn't love me," she whispered when she found the force inside herself to speak. "It would be better to have none at all."

Brigham didn't touch her, nor did he reply. She felt him turn away, unable or unwilling to offer her the one shining thing she wanted most in all the world. In the moments that followed, she grieved bitterly for the dream he'd offered and then taken away.

11

*L*YDIA WANTED TO FLEE BACK TO THE MAIN HOUSE ON HER own, without waiting to light the lantern against the darkness or even taking the trouble to drape herself in her cloak as protection from the rain, but Brigham wouldn't suffer an escape. He made her wait, physically barring the door by leaning against it while he wrenched on his clothes, his gray eyes extending a furious challenge: *try getting past me. Just try it.*

Lydia stared at him in embarrassed fascination for a moment, then turned away, her arms folded. By morning, she surmised, her chagrin would have grown to such proportions that she'd be unable to face Brigham Quade at all.

She put a hand to her mouth and gave a small, stifled sob.

To her surprise, Brigham rested his hands on her shoulders, though he did not turn her to face him. "Don't punish yourself," he commanded, his voice low and gruff and full of authority, for all its softness. "It's a natural thing for a woman to carry on like that when she's being loved, and there's no wrong in it."

Lydia flushed deeply at his directness, but at the same time she was marveling at the way he'd seemingly read her thoughts. She might have been thinking of Devon's great trouble, after all, or of some private tragedy just her own.

She lifted her chin and forced herself to speak. "Let's get back," she said. "I want to look in on Devon and find out if the doctor is here yet."

Brigham sighed. "Yes," was all he said. He put Lydia's cloak over her shoulders, lit the copper lantern she'd brought up the hill with her earlier, before her personal fall from grace, and put out the one that burned next to the window.

The rain had intensified, as if stirred to greater fury by human passions, and Brigham was soaked to the skin by the time they reached the kitchen of the big house. His dark hair hung dripping in his face and, for a long moment, he looked at Lydia with torment in his eyes.

Then, still without speaking, he set the lantern in the middle of the table for her to see by and thrust himself up the back stairway, through the darkness.

Lydia took a few minutes to compose herself, or, at least, to make a noble effort. She shook out her cloak and hung it from one of the pegs by the back door. Despite the cover the garment had given her, she was hardly drier than Brigham had been.

She'd be no help at all if she caught pneumonia, she reasoned, her pragmatism in full sail again. And neither would Brigham.

She pumped water into a copper teakettle, set it on the stove to heat, and added kindling to the dying embers in the grate. She had found a jug of lemon juice in the pantry, along with a crock of honey, when she heard footsteps on the stairs.

Brigham, she thought, her heart seizing up in her breast, trying to make itself small and hard and invulnerable.

But it was not the master of the house who stepped from the shadows at the base of the rear stairway. It was Captain McCauley, and Lydia was so stunned by the sight of him that she let the jug and the honey pot tumble to the table and collapsed into a chair. Lydia had not seen the man since the night she'd helped him escape a Union camp.

It couldn't be him, she said to herself, looking through spread fingers.

"Hello, Lydia," the apparition said, with a smile in his voice. He approached, slowly, a thin man with an engaging smile and unruly brown hair.

Lydia laid her hands on the tabletop to anchor herself, fingers splayed as if to take purchase somehow from the smooth, cool oilcloth. "Wh—" was all she managed to say.

His presence was easy, his manner graciously southern. He looked much the same as he had lying in that faraway hospital tent, about to lose his arm to a bounty-hungry surgeon, except that he was healthier, of course. "It constantly amazes me," he said, "how small this old world really is."

Lydia swallowed hard. Captain McCauley was at once a reminder of the horrors she'd seen during the war and a living reassurance that life goes on, as regularly and unchangeably as the seasons.

"What are you doing here?" she finally got up the strength to ask.

The captain sighed. "I'm afraid the late conflict left the South much changed from what I remembered," he said, his tones revealing both sadness and resignation. "My wife and child perished with the fever, you see, and everywhere I looked I saw something to remind me of earlier, more benevolent days. I signed on as ship's doctor with a craft traveling around the Horn—the *Enchantress,* she was called, originally out of South Carolina. I wandered around Seattle for a few days, then encountered a man looking for a physician to bring back to Quade's Harbor." He paused, shrugged his thin shoulders. "And here I am. You did a fine job of looking after that young fellow up there, Lydia," he added, with a nod toward the ceiling. "He's got some rocky days and nights ahead of him, but I think he'll pull through."

Lydia felt a current of relief swirl through the flood of confusion and surprise that had already engulfed her. *Devon would recover.* The kettle began to hiss and sputter on the stove behind her.

"You never mentioned you were a doctor," Lydia said foolishly, staring at the man who had once been an enemy, remembering how she'd orchestrated his escape and prayed he would get past the lines of her own side.

McCauley chuckled. "I was out of my head with pain and fever most of the time, if I recall," he said. Then, with his left hand, he touched his right upper arm fondly, almost reverently, and he smiled. "I owe you a debt, Lydia McQuire. It would seem to me that the benign fates have placed me in an ideal position to repay it."

Lydia searched his lined but still-handsome face, and she wondered how anyone, Union or Confederate, could ever have seen this gentle man as a foe. "Are you planning to stay here in Quade's Harbor?" she asked, rising on shaking legs to get mugs down from the cupboard, spoon in thick honey and add lemon juice to that.

"I might," the captain answered. "God knows, the place could use a doctor, and I could use a place." He knitted his brows together in a thoughtful but not unfriendly frown. "What's that concoction you're mixing up there?"

Lydia's spoon clattered as she stirred hot water into the honey and lemon juice. "Just a simple cold remedy." She sniffled, suddenly very conscious of her wet hair and sodden skirts. "I was caught in the rain, you see, and thought it wise to take preventative measures. Would you like some tea, while the water's hot?"

Captain McCauley smiled wearily. "That would refresh me some, I think," he agreed, rising. "It's going to be a long night."

"You'll be in Devon's room?"

The doctor nodded. His clothes were threadbare, but finely made, and he still held himself proudly. "Yes," he said.

"I'll bring your tea there, then," Lydia replied, turning

away, pretending to be busy. She'd forgotten that Captain McCauley was a perceptive man, and she feared he'd look inside her and guess that she had a wild side to her nature, a facet she'd just discovered in Brigham Quade's arms only that night.

"Thank you," he replied.

Lydia hastened to light another lantern and offer it to him. "It's good that you're here, Captain," she said, avoiding his gaze. "Quade's Harbor needs you."

Tired humor rumbled in his low voice, like faraway thunder. Or the guns of war. "You'll not be calling me 'Captain' anymore," he said, "for I don't wish to reciprocate by addressing you formally as 'Miss McQuire.' My name is Joseph."

"Joseph," Lydia repeated dutifully.

When he'd gone, she made the tea and left it to steep while she carried the lemon-and-honey potion upstairs.

She found Brigham in the hallway outside Devon's room, his back to the wall, staring off into the distance as though he could see into some far corner of the universe. He hadn't changed his clothes, and his hair was still wet and tousled.

"You'll catch your death," Lydia scolded, nudging his upper arm to get his attention.

The gray eyes revealed surprise when he saw her, as though he'd been wrenched back from a far place. And, of course, he had. "What do you want?" he demanded, just as though he had not made tender love to her only a short time before.

Lydia might have felt wounded, if her inner barriers hadn't been so firmly in place. The only course open to her, she'd already decided, was to pretend nothing had happened in that cabin on the hill. "I want you to drink this," she said tersely, shoving the still-steaming mug at him. "And change into dry clothes, if you please. If there's one thing we have no need of around this house, it's another invalid."

Brigham stared at her in bemusement—no doubt few people spoke to him in such a fashion, given his power and authority—then took the mug and scowled at its contents. "Unless there's whiskey in this stuff, I don't want it."

"There most certainly is not," Lydia whispered, in a hiss. Out of the corner of one eye, she saw a door open and a small face appear in the wedge of light. Millie. "You're setting a very poor example for your daughters, Mr. Quade," she finished, turning to walk away. With a mere look, she sent the curious Miss Millicent scuttling back into her burrow.

Brigham stopped Lydia before she'd gone more than two steps, however, grasping her upper arm and forcing her to face him. "We are not going to playact, you and I, and make believe tonight didn't happen, *Miss* McQuire," he said through his teeth, "because it did. I'm not a man to deny the truth. *That*, my dear, would be setting a poor example for my daughters."

Lydia felt a sweet shiver rush through her at his touch, and she was immediately ashamed. Devon was lying only a few yards away, broken and in pain more brutal than any human being should be asked to endure. Joseph McCauley had turned up, bringing with him all the memories of battles past, and here she stood, wanting to be alone with Brigham again. Wanting to lose herself in the fevered distraction of his lovemaking.

"Besides that," Brigham said, breaking the explosive silence, "you're a fine one to be giving lectures, little Yankee. You need drying off and warming yourself."

The words were innocent enough, but they burst inside Lydia like small cannonballs, and brought pictures to her mind that ignited her passions all over again.

She glared at Brigham until he released his hold on her arm, then went on downstairs without speaking.

She drank her own lemon-honey concoction, then banked the fire in the cookstove and went up to her room. Carefully, she stripped away her damp dress and linens, then put on a warm nightgown. When that was done, all by the light of a single lamp burning on the bedside table, she took down her hair, dried it with a damask towel from the bar on the side of the washstand, and then combed out the tangles.

Under any other circumstances, Lydia would have put on a wrapper and gone to Devon's room to look in on the patient. She knew Devon was being well taken care of by Captain McCauley—Joseph—and Polly, however, so she fell into bed instead, utterly exhausted.

Mercifully, sleep took her straight away, and carried her off to a peaceful place of placid dreams. When she awakened, Millie was bouncing on the mattress beside her.

"Oh," the child said, feigning surprise when Lydia's eyes flew open. "You're awake, Miss McQuire."

Lydia smiled. "Isn't that a strange thing, Miss Quade," she countered. She knew Millie wanted reassurance, and that the other adults in the house were too busy to give it. "And how are you this morning?"

Millie gave a worldly little sigh. "Now that the doctor is here—and Charlotte heard him tell Papa that Uncle Devon will probably recover—I feel a lot better." She got under the covers and snuggled close to Lydia, like a warm, wiry puppy, full of restrained energy. "I'm very glad you're here," she said.

Curving one arm around Millie, Lydia embraced her briefly. "Me, too," she replied. "And where, pray tell, is your sister this morning? Or should I say, *who* is your sister this morning?"

Millie giggled happily. "I'm not sure she's anybody but herself," she answered, "but it's still early."

Lydia sighed. "Perhaps it is. Still, maybe we'd better get up and see about breakfast, don't you think? There will be a lot going on in this house today, I should imagine."

Despite this decision, they laid there for a while longer, listening to the light rain tumbling against the roof and the ordinary sounds of morning—a dinner bell clanging somewhere, the horn of a boat either arriving in the harbor or taking its leave, muffled creaks and clatters in the rooms around them.

Finally, Lydia threw back the covers. "I'll wager that I can be dressed and in the kitchen before you can," she challenged, playfully narrowing her eyes at Millie.

Millie narrowed her own gaze, a gaze so like Brigham's that it made something hard and spiky rise in Lydia's throat and twist painfully before going down.

"What do I get if I win?" Miss Quade demanded.

Lydia laughed, mentally reviewing the contents of the pantry. "Cookies?"

"Cookies!" Millicent agreed jubilantly, bounding off the bed and running for the door. "Do I get to help make them, too?"

"Absolutely," Lydia said. She took her time getting dressed in one of the frocks Devon had had her buy in San Francisco, washing her face and cleaning her teeth, doing up her hair in a plain and sensible style.

When she reached the kitchen, Millie was already there, beaming in triumph. "I win!" she cried.

"Indeed you do," Lydia conceded.

Jake had already made breakfast, leaving plates of eggs and sausage and toasted bread in the warming oven, and he'd filled the hot-water reservoir, too. Lydia dished up a meal for herself and one for Millie, and they sat down at the table to eat.

They had barely started when Brigham stumbled down the stairs, still wearing yesterday's clothes. He gave Lydia a defiantly defensive look as he passed the table to take a cup from the shelf and pour himself some coffee.

"I see you didn't take my advice," Lydia said in a tautly sweet voice, moderating her tone only because Millie was present. If she'd been able to speak her mind outright, she'd have told Mr. Brigham Quade off good for sleeping in rain-sodden clothes after she'd warned him of the danger to his health.

"Would you like to know what advice I'd offer you, Miss McQuire?" he inquired with acid politeness.

Lydia blushed as a number of scandalous possibilities rushed into her mind. "No," she said grudgingly.

"Good morning, Papa," Millie chirped, in what was probably an attempt to protect the fragile peace. "Would it be all right if I went up to see Uncle Devon now, please? I'm very worried about him, and I've eaten all I can of my breakfast."

Brigham was a big man, with an ominous bearing and the sternest possible manner, but he seemed to soften before the bright sincerity of that child. He crouched beside her chair, touched her cheek with one callused finger. "Yes, sweetheart," he answered. He hesitated, took her small arms gently in his hands. "Uncle Devon doesn't look like himself," he added, in a voice that pulled strangely at Lydia's heart, "and he won't know you're there. You understand that, don't you?"

Millie nodded solemnly. "Yes, Papa," she said. And then she got out of her chair, as Brigham rose, and Lydia wanted to lunge after her, crying out, *Don't go!*

Of course she did no such thing, and the child disappeared up the back stairway, leaving Lydia alone with Brigham.

He turned before she could speak, narrowed his eyes and thrust a finger at her. "Don't you dare lecture me, woman," he said, just as she was getting ready to point out how lucky he was he hadn't woken up with pneumonia. "I've got enough on my mind without you nagging me to drink lemon juice and wear woolly clothes!"

Lydia stiffened. Not for anything would she have admitted that he'd read her thoughts as surely as any Gypsy fortune-teller could have done. Again. "The idea didn't even cross my mind," she lied, in a snappish tone. "Have you eaten?"

"No." He threw the word at her, and it quivered in the ground at her feet like a battle lance.

A hurricane of emotions rose up inside Lydia. Not trusting herself to speak, she pushed past Brigham and made for the stairs.

She was not sure whether it was a relief or a disappointment when he didn't attempt to waylay her. A little of both, she guessed ruefully, as she made her way along the upper hallway toward Devon's room.

Like some great cosmic hammerhead, the pain struck Devon blow after bone-jarring blow. He was in some sort of a dream state, unable to reach through to the normal world, but he knew *she* was there. He felt the gentleness of her nature even when her touch brought the biting sting of a needle or the realignment of his broken arm.

Lydia.

It was Lydia who had gathered up the pieces and put him back together again, Lydia who had kept a vigil at his bedside through the horrible night, Lydia who had told him over and over again that she loved him.

He loved her as well; he realized that now. He wanted above all else to get well, to marry her, to start his firstborn child growing within the warm shelter of her body.

He tried to say her name.

"Hush," a soft voice said, and something cool and moist touched the torn, bruised skin of his face. "Hush now, darling. I'm here, and nothing could make me leave you again."

Darling. The word and the voice it was spoken in draped themselves over Devon like a magic blanket, woven of the goddess Athena's cloud wool and full of healing. She loved him. She would stay with him, forever.

Lydia.

"You must have something to eat and get some rest," Lydia whispered to Polly, who sat in a chair beside Devon's bed. There were great smudges of shadow under her hollow eyes, her hair was half up and half down, and her normally flawless skin had turned an alarming shade of gray. "Please."

Polly shook her head, stiffening under Lydia's hands, which now rested on her shoulders, and did not so much as look away from Devon's face. "I won't leave him," she said.

"You won't be any help to Devon if you destroy yourself," Lydia reasoned, speaking softly. Millie was sitting on the hooked rug on the other side of Devon's bed, silently playing with a rag doll, keeping a child's vigil. "Please, Polly. Just go and eat something, and sleep for a while. I promise I'll stay with Devon until you return."

Polly raised unnaturally bright eyes to Lydia's face. "You can't have him. He's mine."

Lydia blinked back tears of sympathy, squeezed the other woman's shoulders. "Of course he is, Polly," she said.

Although she seemed to be slightly reassured, Polly still refused to leave Devon's side. Finally Lydia was forced to go and prepare a tray of food for her.

Polly ate, rather like a person in a trance, her gaze unfocused, her awareness so centered on Devon that it appeared she might pounce on his prone form and cling to him.

When Lydia came back for the tray, she brought a bucket of steaming water with her and poured it into the basin on the bureau top. "Come, Millie," she said to the little girl playing on the rug. "It's time to bake those cookies."

Charlotte was in the kitchen, waiting, and the trio spent the next hour or so shaping sugary dough and baking it into tasty morsels. After the mess was cleaned up, Charlotte wandered off somewhere and Millie went into the parlor with her doll.

Lydia immediately returned to the second floor, half expecting to encounter either Brigham or Joseph McCauley in the hallway, but she met no one. In Devon's room she found that Polly had taken a sponge bath at the basin, put on one of Devon's soft chambray shirts for a nightgown, and curled up next to him on the bed. Even in sleep Polly looked ferociously protective, as though any attack on the man beside her would bring her straight up from her sound slumber, clawing and biting like an enraged tigress.

Taking a lightweight woolen blanket from the upper shelf in Devon's wardrobe, Lydia covered her friend gently. Then she took the basin of soapy water and left the room.

The rain continued.

Lydia checked on Charlotte, found her in a window seat in Brigham's study, a sketch pad in her lap. She was gazing out at the rain-shrouded water, a half smile on her lovely face.

Lydia cleared her throat softly, to let the girl know she was there, then said, "May I see what you're drawing?"

Charlotte held up a startlingly good pencil sketch of a clipper ship, sails billowing in the wind. "She's called the *Enchantress,*" she said. "Isn't that a beautiful name for a ship?"

"Yes," Lydia agreed with a smile. "I believe Dr. McCauley came to Seattle on just that vessel."

Turning her gaze toward the water again, Charlotte gave a tragic sigh. "When am I going to grow up, Lydia?" she pleaded. "When will my life truly begin?"

Lydia laid a light hand to the back of the girl's head, still smiling. "Don't wish your days away, Charlotte," she counseled. "Soon enough you'll be grown and gone, and I promise you, you'll miss your father and Millicent and your Uncle Devon very much."

Charlotte turned, looked up at Lydia with her pale amber eyes. "I'll miss you, too," she said.

Touched by the child's openness, Lydia bent and kissed the top of her head. "Oh, and I shall miss you as well, my beautiful, adventuresome Charlotte. I have a feeling your life will be very exciting indeed."

"Will it?" Charlotte offered the words as a hopeful plea. "Oh, Lydia, do you really think that?"

"Yes," Lydia replied, and though she couldn't have explained why she'd come to such a conclusion, she meant what she said. She glanced down at Charlotte's sketch of the clipper ship and thought of a handsome captain, and then, unaccountably, of a distant paradise where giant flowers grew in a profusion of colors.

Her imagination, she concluded, was running away with her.

Late that afternoon, the rain let up and the sun came out, and Lydia's hopes rose. She went out for a walk, taking Charlotte and Millie with her, and, hearing the whistle, they hurried toward the harbor to watch the mail boat come in.

Joseph McCauley was there ahead of them, standing at

the end of the wharf, hatless, his worn coat blowing in the moist breeze.

Lydia's heart seized up again. He was leaving.

He smiled when he turned and saw the girls chasing each other back and forth at the top of the embankment, the grass slick under their shoes, their laughter ringing through the fresh-washed air like music. Lydia approached with dignity, her heels making a lonely sound as they struck the creaking boards of the dock.

Beyond, the mail boat chugged and chortled toward them, its whistle offering intermittent toots.

Lydia managed a smile, but her voice sounded choked when she said, "You're going?"

Joseph McCauley sighed, his eyes gentle and affectionate as he looked at her. "No," he said. "I just came down here to look at the trees and the mountains and the water. This place is beautiful, isn't it? Looks as if it has just tumbled, brand new, from the Lord's own hand."

"It's lovely," she agreed, sweeping the horizon with her gaze. "How is Devon this morning? Have you seen him?"

Joseph's manner was benignly indulgent. "Of course I've seen him, he's my one and only patient. He's still unconscious, and still in formidable pain, I would imagine, but there's an energy there, a stubborn will to fight. I have no doubt at all that Mr. Quade will rejoin us in the world of the living, though he may have certain—limitations."

Lydia felt herself go pale. "You don't mean he'll be crippled?" she whispered, filled with fear, knowing somehow that Devon would rather be dead.

The doctor touched his temple with an index finger. "He's got to make that decision himself, in here."

The whistle sounded again, and Lydia, who had no idea what Captain McCauley had meant by his words, shifted her thoughts to the arriving boat.

When the craft was tied to its pilings and the ramp had been put down, several passengers alighted.

The first was a man with bristly, blue-white hair and a full beard. He wore plain clothes and a round black hat, but his eyes kept him from being ordinary. They were a bright, pale green, and they burned in his weathered face like fire. Behind him came a big woman with coarse features, worn clothes, and two sturdy children clinging to her skirts.

"Matthew Prophet is my name," the white-haired man announced, as though he expected either Joseph or Lydia to challenge the pronouncement. "I'm here to spread the word of God."

"Welcome," said Joseph, his voice filled with warmth and friendly amusement as he shook the preacher's veined hand.

Lydia slipped around him, to greet the woman.

The new arrival thrust out her chin. "Name's Elly Collier," she told Lydia, ignoring her extended hand. "These are my boys, Jessup and Samuel. My man done took up with an Indian woman and left us on our own. I heard in Seattle there might be work here."

Lydia liked the outspoken Mrs. Collier instantly, perhaps because of her courage and her straightforward manner. "I'll take you to meet Mr. Quade," she said.

"He do the hirin' around here?" Mrs. Collier asked, standing stalwart in the middle of the dock, awaiting her answer.

"He owns it all," Lydia replied.

Joseph had taken Mr. Prophet in hand, and Charlotte and Millie won the Collier boys over by promising them cookies. Lydia led the way to Brigham's office, and it seemed fitting to her that the roots of that stump he'd made into a building reached deep into the ground, holding on, immovable and strong. Like Brigham himself.

He came through the doorway as Lydia and Elly Collier approached, and his gray eyes sliced to Lydia's face and made a silent demand.

"Your brother is fine," she assured him quickly. Then she took Elly's solid arm in both hands and thrust the woman forward. "This is Mrs. Collier," she said. "She wants work, and if you've got a brain in your head, Brigham Quade, you'll hire her here and now."

12

ELLY COLLIER STOOD PROUDLY AS SHE FACED BRIGHAM, A
shabbily dressed woman, squarely built, with plain
brown hair and pale blue eyes that had seen much
trouble. "I ain't exactly a missus," she said, after Lydia
had presented her as "Mrs. Collier." "Zach and I never
got around to sayin' the words in front of a preacher and
the like."

This announcement stirred a buzz of gossip among the
few men who were either going to or coming from their
jobs on the mountain and in the mill. More than one
paused to assess Elly with frank interest.

Lydia was watching Brigham, holding her breath to
hear Elly's fate. He smiled, and the effect was like that of
the sun parting storm clouds. Lydia was unaccountably
jealous, wanting even that small sign of favor for herself.

"We could use a washwoman up in camp," he said.

He hadn't spared a second look for Lydia, but she
could tell he knew she was there and was deliberately
ignoring her. She reasoned that he probably had contempt for her because of the way she'd let him bare her
flesh the night before, because of the way she'd moaned
and pitched under his mouth and his hands.

Color rushed into her face, and the conversation became a blur, passing her ears in a hollow rush, but not entering. Lydia hugged herself tightly, recalling the rich, ferocious sensations Brigham had evoked in her on that bed in the cabin, all but reliving them.

"I've got me two boys," Elly was saying, when the daze faded and Lydia could hear again. "I'd want them with me."

Brigham was clearly restless now, ready to end the exchange and move on. "Fine," he conceded. "Just make sure they stay out of the way." At last his gaze shifted to Lydia, but it was cool, like his tone of voice. "See that the Colliers have what they need from the company store," he said.

Lydia started to protest that she wasn't his clerk, or a household servant to be ordered about on his whims, but for once she held her tongue. She was enmeshed in the tapestry of life in Quade's Harbor, she realized with mingled joy and horror, and did not want to be sent away before she could add a few colorful stitches of her own to the pattern.

"Certainly," she said, with a mocking little curtsy. The gesture wasn't lost on Brigham, despite his hard-headedness, for the merest smile lifted one corner of his mouth. "If you'll just tell me where this storehouse is located." It was all she could do not to add *Your Highness.*

He tossed his head toward the office and the cluster of sheds beyond. "Back there," he said, a satirical edge to his voice.

The "company store" turned out to be nothing more than a clapboard hovel with dusty glass windows and a dirt floor. It was crowded with barrels, bags of flour and beans, tins of coffee, and preserved fruit.

"No wonder Devon wanted to open up a mercantile," Lydia remarked aloud, crinkling her nose in distaste as she and Elly stood in the shadowy confines, listening to invisible mice scatter for safety.

Elly's reaction, not surprisingly, was quite different. "Will you just look at all these vittles?" she marveled, her hands on her broad hips, her face shining in the dust-flecked light. "My boys will be happy to put away some of them beans." She paused and frowned. "The boss didn't say how much I could have."

Lydia felt generous, and she was wise enough to hide the pity that ached in her throat. "Take all you can carry," she said. "I'll help you."

A wagon was brought around, and Elly's two boys— they were close in age, seven or eight, Lydia guessed— reappeared, like dogs summoned with one of those soundless whistles. Lydia helped with the loading, watched as the buckboard finally lumbered up the narrow track to the timber camp, Elly beside the driver, the boys sitting happily in the back with their dusty groceries.

Lydia was aware of Brigham standing behind her, aware in every grain and fiber of her being, but she watched the wagon jostle out of sight before she turned to face him.

"You ought to be ashamed of yourself," she said, gesturing toward the hovel.

His straight white teeth flashed in a knee-melting grin. "I knew it," he said. "You're not only a Yankee bluestocking, you're a reformer in the bargain. Next, you'll be wanting the vote."

There was something about this man, despite his appeal, or maybe because of it, that made Lydia quiver with fury. "If the world were left to hard-headed tyrants like you, Mr. Quade," she said, her anger not at all lessened by the fact that she knew she was exaggerating, "things would be in an even worse state of disarray than they are now."

He arched an eyebrow, clearly amused by her outburst. She hoped he didn't see through the bluff, but wouldn't have wagered her supper on it. He stepped close to her, unmindful of the people around them, who were studiously going about their business and missing absolutely nothing.

"You liked me all right last night," he said.

Such a rush of blood spilled into Lydia's cheeks that she involuntarily raised both palms to her face in an effort to cool it. She heard her own cries of passionate surrender echoing in his words as they faded, with excruciating slowness, into the pine-scented air.

"That was an error in judgment on my part," she allowed, in a fierce hiss. "And I would appreciate it if you could somehow scrape up the good grace never to mention it again!"

Brigham's smile was slow and obnoxious; it seemed to pull Lydia toward him like a warlock's spell. He cupped his hand under her chin and spoke in a low voice that set her already-tremulous pulse thrumming. "Ah, but this is the real world, Lydia," he drawled, "and it's not at all the way you fancy it should be, or would pretend it is. The truth is—as we both know so well, little Yankee—last night was only the beginning of whatever is happening between us. When I bed you in earnest, your cries of pleasure will echo off the mountains."

So great was Lydia's outrage at his effrontery and arrogance—and, heaven help her, the shock of her own arousal—that she was momentarily paralyzed. Even had she been able to speak, she'd never learned an insult scathing enough to suit the occasion.

When Lydia finally regained her equilibrium, after what seemed like an eternity, she swept off toward the main house with her chin thrust high in the air. Some of the workers made a path for her, whistling and applauding as she passed, heightening her embarrassment to an almost hysterical pitch.

Not daring even to speculate on how much the men might know about her ill-advised intimacies with Brigham Quade, cocky King of the Mountain, she hurried on, her disturbing thoughts flocking ahead of her like a gaggle of geese.

As she walked, a light, misty rain began to fall, cooling her anger and the prickly heat that danced on her skin. Reaching the house that was, like everything else in and around that town, Brigham's domain, she sat on the top step.

The porch roof sheltered her, but just barely. On either

side of the walk, lilacs bloomed, their sweet scent more poignant for the added, acrid scent of rain mingling with dust.

Lydia let her forehead rest on her updrawn knees, concentrating on her breathing until it slowed to a regular pace.

Then, when she was herself again, she rose and proceeded inside.

Charlotte and Millie were nowhere in sight, but that didn't trouble Lydia, because it was a big house and the children were used to entertaining themselves. She climbed the main staircase and swept along the hallway to Devon's door.

After rapping lightly, merely as a matter of good manners, she turned the knob and stepped inside.

Polly had risen from her nap beside Devon, and she was fully dressed in the fresh clothes Lydia had laid out for her earlier. She stood beside the bed, gently bathing Devon's upper body with a cloth dipped in cool water.

"How is he?" Lydia asked softly.

Polly spared her one glance, then concentrated on ministering to Devon. "He's stirred a few times," she said. "I think he's trying to wake up."

Lydia came and stood at the foot of the bed. "Let me sit with him for a while, Polly, while you go out and get some fresh air."

It seemed that Polly hadn't heard the suggestion. "Dr. McCauley says Devon has the strongest heartbeat of any man he's ever tended," she said, in a bright and brittle voice that was painful to hear.

Lydia stood still, without speaking.

A sob broke, raw and small, from Polly's throat. "He called out a little while ago. He said, 'Lydia.'"

After swallowing, Lydia made herself reply. She just hoped she sounded matter-of-fact and practical. "Devon is confused," she said. "You mustn't place too much stock in what he says right now. The fact that he's spoken is encouraging in itself."

There were tears on Polly's hollow cheeks as she

looked at Lydia. "Don't take him from me," she pleaded
starkly, with a strange, desperate dignity. "Promise me
you won't make him love you."

Lydia went to Polly then, put an arm around the other
woman's waist. "I'm not an enchantress," she said
gently. Reasonably. "I couldn't 'make' Devon or any
other man love me, even if I wanted that. Now, go and
have some time to yourself. You'll be stronger for it."

Polly hesitated a moment, then nodded once, gave
Devon a long look, full of yearning, and left the room.

"Lydia." Devon said the name clearly, though in a raw
whisper, and there was no mistaking it for any other.

Something like despair rose up inside Lydia, but then
she took herself sternly in hand, told herself not to
borrow trouble. "Hello, Devon," she answered, close to
his ear, as she sat down in Polly's chair. She sniffled and
then smiled purposefully, even though she knew he
couldn't see her. She took his good hand in both of hers.
"You're getting to be quite a layabout," she told him. "I
saw that mouse nest Brigham calls a company store
today. You've got to recover as fast as you can, and get
back to work on your mercantile. Believe me, we need it
desperately. Why, there isn't a place between here and
Seattle where I could buy a skein of embroidery
floss. . . ."

The bedroom door opened and closed again, and
Lydia glanced up to see her friend, Joseph McCauley. He
looked more rested than when she'd seen him last, and he
was wearing fresh clothes and carrying a hopelessly
battered medical kit. He smiled.

Lydia felt foolish. "I was just—"

"I know," Joseph interrupted, in his kind, quiet way.
"He wanders far from us, and you're trying to call him
home. I remember hearing your voice sometimes, when I
was in that Yankee hospital. It was like a shimmering
strand of golden thread; I took it in both hands and
followed it back to this side of the shadowy veil."

"You talk like a poet," Lydia remarked. It was a silly
sentiment, but she'd already uttered the words before she
came to that conclusion.

Joseph stood on the other side of the bed, opening his bag and taking out his stethoscope. His manner was strangely serene, given all he'd endured in his lifetime of perhaps thirty-five or forty years. "Every man is a poet," he replied, after listening thoughtfully to Devon's heartbeat for some moments. "When the situation calls for it."

Lydia was not a person to make wishes; after the carnage she'd seen, she couldn't make herself believe in good fairies or guardian angels. Still, for the merest fraction of a moment, she wished she could love Joseph McCauley. He would have made a wonderful husband, with his refined and gentle ways.

She looked away. Few women would have been better suited as the wife and helpmate of a frontier doctor than she herself, with all her training and experience, but it would be a cruel injustice to encourage Joseph when it was Brigham who made her blood heat.

"Lydia."

She raised her eyes at the gentle command in Joseph's voice, met his gaze. "Yes?" she managed, overwhelmed by the variety of emotions filling that room like the notes of some great, thunderous, silent symphony. She was aware not only of her own feelings, confused and fiery, but also of Devon's angry longing to live and Joseph's search for a lasting peace.

"When I stepped into that kitchen downstairs and saw you there," Joseph said, putting away his stethoscope, "I thought to myself, 'Joe McCauley, heaven does take an interest in puny mortals like yourself after all.' I won't lie to you and say I don't want more, but I could content myself for all the days of my life on an occasional smile or a touch of your hand."

Lydia lowered her eyes. "You speak very directly, sir," she said, and her shyness, uncharacteristic as it was, was quite real.

He sighed and went to the window to stand looking out toward the mountains and the sea. "These are direct times, Lydia," he mused, "and the West is a very forthright place."

She remembered Elly Collier, announcing to the world in general that she and her man had never gotten around to "saying the words in front of a preacher," and Polly, who had deluded Devon into thinking of her as his wife. And herself, lying on a narrow bed with Brigham, letting him play her body like a lyre.

Yes, she thought. The West was indeed a forthright place, with social and moral rules all its own. "I don't love you," she said, not unkindly.

Joseph turned his head, gave her a smile that might have awakened ardent feelings in her—before she'd encountered Brigham Quade. "I'm under no illusion that you do," he said. "If I'd taken that Yankee shrapnel in my eyes, instead of my arm and shoulder, I'd still be able to see that you care for someone else." He paused, turning his gaze to the scene beyond the window glass again. "Brigham is a fine man, Lydia. But he's hard and he's ruthless, too. First and foremost, before any woman and before his own daughters, he loves that mountain out there. He takes his energy from it the way tree roots draw water from the ground; he's a part of it and it is a part of him. He'll crush you, eventually, with the sheer force of his will, like a wildflower beneath the heel of his boot."

Lydia's lips were dry, and she moistened them with the tip of her tongue. She could not deny Joseph's words, for she knew they held a tragic truth. If she let herself love Brigham, he might well consume her in his own fiery strength. Hadn't he warned her, that very afternoon, that when he made love to her in earnest, her cries of pleasure would echo off the mountainsides?

She closed her eyes, started a little when she felt Joseph's hand come to rest on her shoulder.

"There's no hurry, Lydia," he said.

She thought she felt Devon's fingers tighten around hers as the door closed behind the doctor she'd once committed treason to help. "Every day," she said, in a distracted whisper, "women marry men they don't love. After a time, if the husband and wife have some common ground, and an honest liking for each other, true esteem develops."

Devon shifted slightly, and made a raspy sound low in his throat.

Lydia shook off her fanciful thoughts and got up to pour water from a carafe on the bedside table, giving Devon a drink, drop by drop, from a teaspoon.

Presently, Polly returned, and Lydia took her leave.

She found Charlotte and Millie squabbling in the kitchen, while poor Jake Feeny tried to cook supper. "Come with me," she said, crooking a finger.

Both girls looked at her as though they expected a strict lecture. Instead, Lydia took them to the parlor, where the spinet was, and sat down to run lightly through the scales.

"This instrument wants tuning," she said, as Charlotte leaned against one end of the piano and Millie the other. "Still, I think we can make some badly needed harmony, don't you?"

Millie put her tongue out at Charlotte.

Charlotte responded in kind.

Lydia struck a chord and began to sing. "Blest be the ties that bind . . . our hearts in Christian love . . ."

Brigham sat at the head of the table that night at supper, as usual, and of course Joseph was there, too, as well as Lydia herself. Charlotte and Millie had eaten earlier, in the kitchen, and gone to their rooms.

It was Matthew Prophet, the visiting preacher, who took center stage.

"Lots of sin in this place," he blustered, looking at Lydia from beneath his bushy white eyebrows as if to hold her personally responsible for every broken commandment between there and the Canadian border. "Yes, sir, lots of sin."

Joseph grinned, but said nothing in Lydia's defense. Brigham was no more chivalrous, as it happened, though he did not let the comment pass unconfronted.

"Personally, Reverend," he said, reaching for the bowl

of mashed potatoes and scooping out a second helping, "I think Quade's Harbor could do with a little more sin, instead of less. A brothel, say, or maybe a saloon."

Joseph made a choking sound that might have been a laugh, and Lydia seethed. Admittedly, the reverend was a tiresome man, but he was also dedicated and sincere, and Brigham had no right to pick on him.

"Mr. Prophet is a guest here," she pointed out.

Brigham skewered her with his laughing gray eyes. "So are you," he parried.

The preacher leaned forward in his chair, as if expecting Lydia's hair to turn to hissing snakes, like a modern-day Medusa, and she wished, just for a moment, for the power to turn him to stone.

"You live here, do you?" the old man inquired. "In this house? Unchaperoned?"

Brigham smiled down at his mashed potatoes.

Lydia wanted to upend the whole bowlful onto his head, because he was enjoying her discomfort so much. She made herself smile. "I'm—the governess," she said.

"Miss McQuire was actually brought here as a mail-order bride," Brigham put in, with helpful exuberance. "My brother delivered her to me as a gift, from San Francisco."

Prophet's stern and wizened face reddened significantly, and his nose twitched, as if sin had a scent and he'd caught it on the wind. "There are two innocent, impressionable children living in this house, are there not?"

Lydia shot a furious glance at Brigham, then flung one at Joseph, too, for failing to come to her rescue, as would have befitted a true gentleman.

"Yes," she said, awkward in her annoyance. "Charlotte and Millie are children, all right."

Joseph chuckled, sipping from his water goblet, and Lydia could feel Brigham's eyes on her, bright with amusement.

Mr. Prophet was concentrating on Lydia, who suddenly felt wanton, a corrupter of virtue. "If you came here to marry Mr. Quade, why haven't you done so?"

Lydia drew in a sharp breath, trembling now, not with

timidity, but with outrage. "You seem bent on performing the marriage ceremony, Reverend," she began, not planning the words she said next. "Well, that's fine. You can join Dr. McCauley and I in holy matrimony, right now, tonight."

Brigham's fork clattered to his plate, and a sidelong glance showed that all the mirth, along with much of his robust coloring, had drained from his face.

Joseph smiled. Lydia was ashamed that she'd spoken so rashly, and so thoughtlessly.

"A fine idea," he said, with a courtly nod.

Brigham crashed his fist down on the table, making cutlery and china clatter in reaction. "No!" he yelled. "There will be no wedding in this house, not between Lydia and the good doctor, that is!"

All eyes were turned to the master of the house.

He shook a finger at Lydia, as though she were a naughty child who'd repeatedly upset her milk. "I vow this by God's eyeballs," he swore, in a dangerous, rumbling, thunderstorm voice, "if you carry on with this foolishness, I'll tell these men—I'll tell the whole damned world, Lydia—why you can belong to no man besides me!"

Lydia swayed in her chair, sick with fury and humiliation. "I hate you," she whispered finally, pushing back her chair from the table to rise on shaking legs. "I despise you!"

Brigham got to his feet with disconcerting swiftness, towering over Lydia, breathing hard, as though she'd led him a chase through the thick underbrush that carpeted the woods beyond the walls of that sturdy house. His gray eyes were like steel, glittering under a layer of new frost.

"Do not challenge me to prove that the truth is otherwise," he growled, tempering the words with a velvety sweetness that only made them more brutal.

She stood still, amazed and furious and afraid to do further battle because she knew he would win. With a look, with a touch, with the force of his mind, he could make her want him desperately.

Showing unexpected mercy, he freed her from the

spell. "Go," he said, on a harsh breath, waving a hand toward the dining room doorway.

Lydia turned and hurried away, her heart burning behind her collarbone, her emotions in such turmoil that she couldn't even begin to make sense of them. She swept up the stairs, moving as rapidly as she could in her cumbersome skirts, and took refuge in her room, leaning against the door and gasping as though she'd been pursued.

The room was dark, and Lydia didn't bother to light a lantern. She didn't want to see her flaming face in the bureau mirror, or the proud defeat in her eyes.

She paced swiftly back and forth, hugging herself and muttering.

For years she'd been able to keep her emotions under tight control, no matter what horrors presented themselves. Now, after she'd come through a war, after she'd traveled around the Horn and been forced to shift for herself in a strange city, after she'd journeyed on to Seattle, bold as a Viking woman, she'd finally met her nemesis.

Brigham Quade.

Lydia moved faster, back and forth, fighting, fighting. Brigham had uncovered all the feelings she'd worked so hard to suppress, bared them to the light, and now they rose within her like the creatures from Pandora's box. The pain was so fierce that it forced her to her knees on the rug, and she began to sob uncontrollably.

He said her name, kneeling in front of her, cupping her wet face in his work-hardened hands.

Brigham.

"Don't touch me," she wailed, using the last shreds of her will to keep from screaming the words.

Brigham drew her onto his thighs, held her tightly, his face buried in her hair as it tumbled free of its pins. "Let go," he said in an urgent voice. "Dear God, Lydia, you can't hold a whole war inside you. Let it go."

Her fingers knotted on his shirtfront, which was already wet with her tears. The agony of the battlefields broke through her crumbling reserve like a river. "Babies!" she sobbed. "Brigham, those soldiers were just babies—"

His lips were warm and firm at her temple, his arms strong around her. "I know, Yankee, I know."

She heard the screams, the thunder of cannon fire, the gnawing rasp of saws severing bone. Her own shriek was muffled by Brigham's shoulder.

He stood, lifting her easily, and carried her to the shadow-strewn bed. She wept in silence now, and would have curled into a tight ball if Brigham had allowed it. Instead, he stretched out beside her, his hard length like a splint securing a fracture, and clasped her close against him. For all his weight, the mattress shook with the force of her grief.

After a while, when exhaustion had calmed her, Brigham rose and gently removed her shoes, her stockings, her dress. She could not protest, but lay trustingly in her linens, spent by emotion.

He filled a basin with water, just as she had done for Devon when first tending his wounds, and began to bathe her skin, cooling and soothing her. She was raw and broken inside, as though she'd had some intangible surgery, but she also knew that from now on she would grow stronger with every day that passed. She had turned a corner, entered some new phase of her life, and would never be quite the same again.

Once Brigham had washed her—and there was something ceremonial about that, just as there had been in her clinging to him in the storm of grief that had swept over her earlier—he lay down with her again.

They had been bonded together in those moments, for good or ill, and even in her dreamy, disoriented state, Lydia knew that cord could never really be broken.

Deep in the night, Lydia awakened from a healing sleep, her blood hot with fever. Brigham lay beside her, fully clothed, his breathing even and deep, and she wanted him.

"Brigham?" Lydia lifted her head, brushed his lips

with hers, let the silky tickle of her hair awaken him. Her hysteria was past, and she was in full command of her senses. "Brigham!"

He opened his eyes, grumbled. "No."

Lydia laughed softly. "You've compromised me thoroughly, Brigham Quade. If I'm to have the reputation, and I surely will, then I want that pleasure you promised me."

Brigham swatted her bottom lightly. "Go back to sleep, Yankee. You don't know what you're saying."

"Yes, I do. You've ruined me by undressing me and lying beside me all night, and I want to know what you intend to do about it." Lydia was quite serious. She was no prude, but certain conventions simply had to be respected, even in this remote wilderness.

"I intend to marry you," he said, as though his plans should have been obvious. He might have been talking about hiring more lumberjacks or ordering a shipment of dried beans, for all the expression in his voice.

"That's very generous," Lydia said acidly.

He patted her again. "You're welcome," he answered, in all seriousness, and then he drifted off to sleep again.

13

*L*YDIA LAY STILL BESIDE BRIGHAM, SOAKING IN THE warmth and strength of his body, listening to the even meter of his breathing as he slept. She recalled the night before, when her rigid New England composure had slipped so badly, and a blush rose in her cheeks at the memory.

The experience had been a difficult one, an emotional transformation that had left her broken and raw in its immediate aftermath, but now she felt happier and more capable than ever before. Her feelings were back, and all of them were keen and vivid.

They filled her with an uncanny energy, and when that became too great to be subdued, Lydia bolted upright and scooted off the bed. She went to the bureau for fresh underthings, to the wardrobe for the prettiest of her simple dresses, a bright yellow and blue calico print.

Brigham lifted his head, made a grumbling sound, and focused bleary eyes on her. "Wh—?" he said.

Lydia smiled. King of the Mountain.

She slipped behind the changing screen in a corner of the room, taking her clothes with her. "It was very kind of you to propose marriage, Mr. Quade," she called sunnily as she dressed, "and I meant to accept your suit. However, I've changed my mind."

A muttered curse word came from the direction of the bed, and the ropes supporting the mattress creaked. "What?"

"I've decided not to marry you after all." Lydia was fully clad now, and she peeked around the edge of the screen as she buttoned the front of her frock. "Of course, it wouldn't be proper for me to go on living in this house—much as I dislike Reverend Prophet, I have to admit he was right about that. Then again, I don't want to leave Charlotte and Millie, just when we're starting to establish a rapport, so with your permission, I'll move into one of the saltbox houses on Main Street. The blue one, if it isn't promised to anyone else."

Brigham was sitting up now, his clothes and hair rumpled, looking at Lydia in irritable disbelief. "You can't be serious."

Lydia reached for a brush and began to groom her hair briskly. Miraculously, she'd been set free of the past, a gift she'd never expected, and she was light-headed with the joy of it. "Oh, but I am."

He reached for his boots, pulled one on with a fierce thrust of his foot. "You're forgetting something, Yankee. You and I just spent the night alone together, in a bedroom. On the same damn bed. If you walk out of this house without my wedding band on your finger, you'll be ruined. You said so yourself."

She put down the brush and began to divide her hair for braiding. "That was what I thought, too, at first," she conceded cheerfully. "However, after some considera-tion, I've come to the conclusion that I was mistaken. Oh, I'm not saying that we should throw off all moral constraints and behave in any way we wish, but we're not in Maine or Massachusetts, after all. This is the frontier, and the rules are a bit more flexible here."

He came to stand behind her, facing the mirror. She was aware of his looming reflection, of course, but she didn't allow her eyes to rise and link with his. He might cast one of his dangerous spells if she did.

"What about Millie and Charlotte?" Brigham asked in a dangerously quiet voice. "They've come to hold you in very high regard. Losing you will be a blow to them."

Lydia allowed herself the smallest smile. She had finished plaiting her hair, and wound the thick braid into a coronet, which she pinned expertly into place. "I have no intention of deserting your daughters, Mr. Quade," she said. "I will devote my days to them. Should one or the other of them fall ill, may heaven forbid it, I will serve as their nurse."

His hands rose, as if to close on her shoulders, but at the last moment he let them fall to his sides. "The houses on Main Street are unfurnished," he said, his head turned slightly to one side, gaze fixed on the window, where a morning breeze ruffled the lace curtains.

"I won't need much in the way of household goods," she replied. "I'm used to making do." Lydia took her travel case from under the bed and set it on the mattress. Then, methodically, she began removing her clothes from the bureau and the wardrobe. Brigham hesitated for a few moments, watching her with troubled eyes, then walked out of the bedroom and closed the door quietly behind him.

Her resolve faltered a little—if personal honor had allowed her a choice, Lydia would have married Brigham and been his wife in every sense of the word. But to offer herself, loving him as she did, knowing full well that he didn't return her feelings, was a compromise she couldn't make.

When Lydia left her room, she went straight to Devon's and rapped lightly on the door.

"Come in," Polly called.

Devon's breathing indicated that he was resting in a degree of comfort. The swelling on his face had gone down, and his many abrasions and bruises were less angry-looking than before. Lydia's well-honed instincts told her this patient would recover handsomely.

Polly, on the other hand, looked like something from a Greek tragedy. She'd lost weight, and there were purple shadows under her eyes. Her hair, usually so glossy, was dull and flat, and her clothes looked as though she'd been wearing them for a week.

"Devon is improving," Lydia said forthrightly. "You, on the other hand, seem to be in a definite decline."

The other woman sighed, her hollow eyes devouring the man sleeping on the bed. She swallowed, started to speak, and then stopped herself.

Lydia stayed a few moments, then went into the hallway and down the rear stairway. She found Jake Feeny in the kitchen, along with Charlotte and Millie, who were simultaneously eating pancakes and arguing over which of them would be taller when they'd both reached their full height.

Ignoring the girls, who needed to learn to work things out without constant adult intervention, Lydia took a plate from the shelf and began filling it for Polly. "If you have the time," she said to Jake, with a bright smile, "would you please heat water for Mrs. Quade to have a bath?"

Jake blushed as though she'd asked him for a waltz, and nodded. When he'd gone out to the shed to bring in a tub, Lydia sat down at the table, smoothed her skirts, and cleared her throat to let Charlotte and Millie know she wanted to speak with them.

Two luminous pairs of eyes turned to her immediately, one set pewter-gray, the other a brilliant amber.

Lydia cleared her throat again. This would be the most difficult part; making these children, whom she'd come to love very deeply, understand that she would never willingly abandon them.

"I've spoken to your father," she began, in a brave but slightly quavery voice. "We've agreed that it would be better if I went to live in one of the Main Street houses, since both he and I are unmarried."

Charlotte looked away, but Millie leaned forward in her chair, a questioning expression on her face.

"That would be easy to solve," she said, as though pointing out the obvious to a slow-witted but much-loved maiden aunt. "You and Papa have only to get yourselves married to each other. Then you could stay and Charlotte and I would have a mother."

A small muscle in Lydia's heart twitched painfully. "I'm afraid it's not quite that simple," she said softly. "A man and woman should not marry unless they love each other."

Charlotte bit her lower lip. "Some people think Papa is handsome," she said. "He has money, and a large house. He never hits and rarely shouts. Couldn't you learn to love him, with time?"

Learn indeed, Lydia thought ruefully. Her enterprise would be quite the opposite, she feared: learning *not* to love Brigham Quade. "I suppose I could," she replied after an interval, "but he would have to love me as well, you see, and he doesn't."

Millie sagged slightly. "Oh."

Charlotte's golden eyes brimmed with tears. "This is dreadful. I've become attached to you, Miss McQuire—in fact, I meant to ask permission to call you Lydia."

She reached out and took one of each child's hands, squeezing them reassuringly. "You may both address me by my first name, except when we are having lessons. And it isn't as though we won't see each other every day, because you'll be coming to my house mornings to learn reading and arithmetic."

Charlotte made a face, but Millie scooted forward to the edge of her chair. "Couldn't Anna and the others have lessons, too?"

Lydia smiled. "Of course. We'll have our own school, the seven of us, right there in my parlor, until the meetinghouse is built."

"I'm going to tell Anna!" Millie crowed, bolting from her chair and hurtling toward the back door in a streak of energy. "We're going to have a school—a real school!" With that, she clattered out.

Charlotte remained in her chair, clearly feeling none of her sister's enthusiasm. She sighed and propped her chin in one hand in a gesture of forlorn acceptance. "You'll tire of Quade's Harbor soon enough," she said. "And then you'll sail away and leave us even lonelier than we were before."

It was on the tip of Lydia's tongue to promise the child she would stay, but she held the vow back, realizing how rash it would be to make such a pledge. Brigham paid her salary, and there was no one else to work for, since he virtually owned the town. If he ran out of patience with her, he could banish her completely.

"I have no plans to leave, Charlotte," she said. "However, you're a young woman now, and you must know that life can be very unpredictable. If I promised to stay, the Fates would delight in making a liar of me."

This brought a slight smile to Charlotte's mouth. "Yes," she agreed, "I am a young woman now, aren't I? Soon I'll be old enough to travel. I'll go to the far corners of the world." She paused and sighed, staring off into the great beyond. "I'll probably marry a pirate who's so handsome that just looking at him will make my heart pound."

Lydia smiled and pushed back her chair. She would save her lecture on the low moral standards and general social unsuitability of the average pirate for later. For now, it was enough that Charlotte wasn't upset about her intention to move out of the Quade house.

Brigham told himself he was glad Lydia was going to live on Main Street. He had enough people underfoot as it was, he thought.

He sent his largest wagon and two teamsters to his place for furniture and other equipment Lydia would need to set up housekeeping. The men were to take their orders from Miss McQuire, loading and transporting whatever she chose to take.

The shriek of the mill saw gave Brigham a headache, so he went into his office and closed the door firmly behind him. There was an enamel crock with a lid sitting on a table behind his desk, and he ladled out some water to cool his tongue, his mind weighted with worries.

His first and foremost concern, at the moment, was

Devon. His brother did seem to be on the mend, but he still hadn't come out of that deep sleep he'd been in since the accident in the woods. Despite Joe McCauley's predictions that Devon would recover, and Lydia's corroboration of that diagnosis, Brigham had a deep-seated sense of foreboding about the whole situation.

Then there was the mess with Polly. She had told Brigham the truth of the matter herself, when she'd sought him out in Seattle and asked him for work. She'd told him how she had duped Devon, and said she wouldn't blame him if he didn't want her ever to set foot in Quade's Harbor again. All she wanted, she'd gone on to say, was an opportunity to make amends and start over.

Brigham had been shocked, of course, and angry as well, but some instinct had urged him to give the woman a second chance, if for no other reason than that Devon had clearly loved her once. Besides, just about everyone he knew had some kind of shameful secret; the West was a magnet for adventurous misfits.

Like himself.

He smiled, sinking into the creaky wooden chair behind his desk, kicking his feet up and cupping his hands in back of his head. His favorite enigma was Lydia McQuire.

Brigham was fairly certain the woman had set her cap for him—after all, she'd nearly come apart in his arms that night in the cabin, when he'd introduced her to a singular pleasure. The memory made him harden, instantly and painfully, and he set his feet apart a little ways on the desk. He sighed and looked up at the ceiling.

Something must be wrong with him, he decided. Maybe he was getting old, set in his ways. He could have made love to Lydia, she would have welcomed him into the sweet solace of her body, and he needed that consolation sorely, but his damnable honor had interfered. Lydia was not a whore, and his conscience would not allow him to take advantage of her.

He frowned, dark brows knitting together. His certainty that Lydia found him appealing, much as she might wish otherwise, was unshaken. However, he was a pragmatic man and he couldn't overlook the fact that she'd refused his offer of marriage, not once, but twice.

Maybe she was leaning toward McCauley, the gentleman doctor, and she'd never made any bones about the fact that she found Devon attractive as well. Devon was a free man, since the marriage to Polly had been a fraud, and when he finally awakened, he might easily turn to pretty, gentle Lydia for comfort.

Brigham's right temple began to pound. Then there were all the drooling lumberjacks who would be knocking at her door as soon as they knew she was fair game, and not the boss's woman, as many of them now believed. He'd be lucky to get close to her again, let alone persuade her to become his wife.

There was a rap at the door, and Brigham brought his feet to the floor and reached for a pen and his ledger book. "Come in," he barked gruffly.

The hinges creaked and Joe McCauley stepped into the office, medical bag in hand.

Brigham opened his ink bottle and dipped the point of the pen, even though he hadn't the first idea what to write. The tidy pages of numbers and notes, set down by his own hand, were as indecipherable now as Egyptian characters.

"I can come back another time," McCauley said, with a sort of cordial dignity, "if you're too busy to talk."

Brigham gestured toward the only other chair in the room, wiped his pen, and sealed the ink bottle again. He braced his forearms on the desktop and touched the splayed fingers of both hands together. "We can talk now," he said, and the words came out sounding hoarser than he would have liked.

McCauley drew up the other chair and sat. "Of course you know I've come here to discuss Lydia," he said. He was a straightforward man, if a soft-spoken one, and Brigham liked him. "We both know that Lydia spoke impulsively last night at the table, when she mentioned marriage to me, but I would gladly have her for a wife."

The deep breath Brigham drew in left his lungs in a harsh rush. "You're in love with her?"

The doctor raised one shoulder in a shrug. "I'm not certain that the sentiments I feel toward Lydia can be reduced to such a simple term. She's the only reason I'm alive today, and not just because she tended my wounds and saved me from that butcher of a surgeon who wanted to take off my arm for the bounty. There hasn't been a day, an hour, since I rode out of that Yankee camp, that I haven't thought of Lydia. Her name was the litany I said when the pain was unbearable, and when I was too discouraged and hungry to take another step. I don't think it was an accident that I happened upon her again, here in Quade's Harbor."

Brigham reached back, massaged the taut muscles at his nape with one hand. "Why are you telling me this?" he asked, even though he knew the answer only too well. McCauley's eloquent words had left him with a feeling akin to despair.

"I am an honest man, Mr. Quade," McCauley answered, "as I believe you are. I cannot go on living under your roof, knowing that your desire for Lydia's favor is as great as my own, without making my intentions absolutely clear. I will stay here, however, either working for you or in private practice, and if I can persuade Lydia to share my life, I will do that, too. Without hesitation."

Suddenly Brigham was possessed of an insane urge to hurtle over the desktop and take the good doctor by the throat, but he sat back in his chair instead. "There's no need for you to leave my household," he said evenly. "I want you close to my brother. Besides, Lydia is going to live in one of the houses on Main Street."

McCauley looked pleased; the same expression of smugness would have earned another man a sound thrashing, but Devon needed a physician, and so did the growing community. "Very well, then," the doctor said, rising and extending one hand. "I won't take up any more of your time. My aim in coming here was to make certain that we understand each other, and it would seem that I've accomplished that."

Brigham pushed back his chair and rose, shaking McCauley's hand as he did so. "I'll prove a formidable adversary," he warned, and there was no boastfulness or conceit in his words, only grim sincerity.

"I'm sure you will," McCauley replied, his voice as warm and genteel as his handshake. "I'm sure you will."

On orders from Brigham, Lydia chose a bed, bureau, and washstand from an unused guest room in the main house, along with a settee, round table, and two chairs from Aunt Persephone's sitting room. She took linens as well, and Jake generously provided her with those kitchen utensils he felt he could spare. By the time Charlotte and Millie had added contributions from their own rooms and the attic, the large wagon Brigham had sent was piled high, the load held in place by crisscrosses of rope.

Lydia walked ahead of the wagon, toward Main Street, Charlotte and Millie hurrying along on either side. A bittersweet sensation gathered under her heart like a cloud when she saw the blue saltbox that would henceforth be her home.

She would miss being in close proximity to the girls and, yes, to Brigham, and yet she had always yearned to set up housekeeping in just such a place. Here she would be mistress; within those walls she would make the decisions.

The house had a small yard, surrounded by a picket fence, and there was a fruit tree of some kind growing in the side yard. The place boasted a veranda with a roof, and beyond the front door was a good-sized parlor with a stone fireplace and plank floor. Behind it were two other rooms, a kitchen and a single bedroom with a little stove in one corner. Well away from the back doorstep stood a privy.

Charlotte explored the house with Lydia, while Millie remained outside to swing on the front gate.

"It's not very big," Charlotte reflected.

The place seemed like a palace to Lydia, who had lived

in rented rooms all her life, and after that in a military tent with her father. "It would look that way to you," Lydia conceded, not unkindly. "After all, you're used to a mansion."

"Is this where we'll have our lessons?" Charlotte asked, spreading her hands and turning around once in the middle of the parlor. The motion had a certain theatrical grace.

"Yes," Lydia answered. She heard the noise of the wagon pulling up outside, with her borrowed furniture. If she just had a piano, she thought, she could be content to live right there in that cozy cottage until she was a doddering old woman. "Your studies will need to be more advanced, of course."

Charlotte's amber eyes showed a spark of interest. "I can already read and write perfectly well," she said. "And I'm rather good with numbers, too, for a girl. What else is there to learn?"

Lydia laughed. "Only a fool believes there is nothing left to learn," she scolded good-naturedly. "There is *everything* to learn. What makes the flowers grow? What holds the stars in their places? What would it be like to live in Marrakesh or, for that matter, in Chicago?"

The girl looked intrigued, but suspicious. "Do you know all those things yourself, Lydia? Because if you don't, you certainly won't be able to teach them to me."

Lydia carried her satchel over and set it down just inside the bedroom doorway, next to the wall. "I know some of them," she replied matter-of-factly, smoothing her hair. "Others I can look up in those marvelous volumes that line the shelves of your father's study."

Charlotte uttered a long-suffering sigh. "Papa won't let you touch his precious books," she said, as if to dispense with the whole subject. "They're mostly about astronomy and geography and mathematics, and he says females don't have any use for such knowledge."

"He's about to get an education himself," Lydia muttered. It galled her to have tender feelings for the likes of Brigham Quade, but she did. How much better if she could have loved Joe instead, or Devon. Alas, there was no sense in stewing over things that couldn't be helped.

Although she didn't offer an argument, Charlotte looked skeptical. She went out to drag Millie off the gate so the teamsters could bring in the furniture.

They carried in the bed first, their grizzled, weathered faces crimson with embarrassment, their eyes averted, and set it up in the place Lydia pointed out. After that they fetched in the bureau, and a stand-up mirror, and Lydia went out to the wagon for the bundle of linens she'd purloined from the upstairs closet at the main house.

She made up the feather bed while the men brought in the table and chairs and the settee, and various items from the attic. Charlotte and Millie concentrated on getting in the way.

Finally the men finished. Lydia ferreted out the kettle Jake had loaned to her and went out into the backyard to the hand pump. In the meantime, Charlotte found a cracked teapot and put in a scoopful of fragrant orange pekoe.

The three of them were sitting at Aunt Persephone's round cherrywood table, sipping tea, when a timid knock sounded at the front door.

Lydia stood, her heart skipping over a beat, to smooth her hair and shake out her skirts. Perhaps the visitor would turn out to be Brigham, though it was a safe wager he hadn't come to pay a social call.

Opening the door, Lydia was taken aback to find a stranger on the porch. The man wore the oiled pants and flannel shirt of a lumberjack, but he'd obviously made an effort to spruce up. He'd slicked back his thinning gray-brown hair, and fresh cuts on his cheeks and chin indicated an honest attempt at shaving. In his right hand he carried a bouquet of wildflowers, grown limp from the earnestness of his grasp.

"I just wanted to bring you these here flowers," he said, with a gapped, tobacco-stained smile. "Word done got around Quade's Harbor that you ain't the boss's woman after all, so you can expect on havin' other callers, ma'am." He paused, touched the brim of his seedy hat. "You won't meet a harder worker than Erskine Flengmeir," he finished. Then, without another word, Erskine thrust out the flowers.

Lydia took them, offering a shaky smile. She was faced with that age-old quandary of wanting to be polite without giving false encouragement. "Thank you, Mr. Flengmeir," she said, watching with reddened cheeks as her caller turned and made his way jauntily down the walk to the open gate.

Charlotte appeared at Lydia's side and bent forward to sniff a daisy. "I've never seen a courtship before," she said. "I should think the next few weeks will be very interesting indeed."

Lydia closed the door a little too energetically and stepped back. "No one is courting anyone," she snapped.

Charlotte looked at her in surprise.

"Yes, they are," Millie argued happily, having taken up her post at Lydia's other side. "I'll bet practically every man in Quade's Harbor will come calling." She took the flowers and started toward the back of the house. "Do you have any vases?"

Lydia rolled her eyes. "No," she said, somewhat pettishly. She hadn't considered the message moving out of Brigham's house would send to the other men in town.

Charlotte laughed. "I think we should go home, Millie," she called to her sister, who was rummaging audibly in the kitchen. "Lydia needs privacy to settle in and get used to her new house."

Millie came out of the kitchen, carrying the wildflowers in a juice glass brimming with water taken from the drinking bucket. Her small brow was furrowed with thought. "You wouldn't marry anybody, would you, Lydia? Anybody besides Papa, I mean?"

Letting out a long breath, Lydia went to the child, took the flowers from her hands, and embraced her lightly with one arm. "I have no plans to marry at all, Millicent," she said patiently. "And I believe we've already discussed this subject once today."

"Charlotte and I would be very, very good, if you married Papa," Millie said in a cajoling voice that made both Charlotte and Lydia laugh out loud. The little girl feigned injury at their amusement and stomped toward the door, closely followed by her sister.

"You'll come to the big house for supper, of course?" Charlotte called from the threshold.

Lydia looked forward to being alone, but at the same time she felt a certain forlorn ache at the prospect. "Jake gave me some bread and cold meat. I think it would be best if I took my evening meal here."

A shadow of disappointment flickered in Charlotte's eyes, but then she smiled, closed the door, and shouted some good-natured challenge to Millie. Lydia watched from the parlor window as the two girls raced down the road, leaving the front gate swinging behind them.

She went out, closed the gate latch, and returned to her quiet, underfurnished parlor. The tea things were still on the table, near the kitchen door, so she gathered them up and took them to the worktable next to the cookstove. Lydia was not used to idleness, and even bustling busy-work was better than just standing there, waiting for something to happen.

At five-thirty, when Lydia was sitting down to a simple supper of cold roast chicken and bread, there was another knock at the door. When she reached the threshold, however, there was no one on the porch. A little trail of dust still hovered over the path, though, and when a curious sound at her feet made Lydia look down, she saw a tiny yellow kitten, curled up in an old woolen cap.

With a smile, Lydia crouched and gathered up her mewling caller, hat and all. She'd always wanted a home of her own, and a cat to curl up in her lap at night, when she read. Now she would have both.

14

"GET OUT." DEVON HAD NO MORE THAN OPENED HIS EYES and looked up into Polly's face when he uttered the words.

Gently, Polly smoothed a lock of rumpled butterscotch hair from his forehead. Her own eyes brimmed with tears of both joy at his awakening and the poignant sorrow of his rejection. She said his name softly.

Devon tilted his head back, his bruised chin at a stubborn angle, and stared up at the ceiling. The next time he spoke, he wounded Polly almost as brutally as before. "Where is Lydia?"

She swallowed, mindful that she'd brought this sorry state of affairs on herself by trying to deceive Devon in the first place, and summoned up a watery smile. "She's moved to the blue house, on Main Street," she answered, her voice shaky and brittle with the effort not to break down and sob on Devon's chest, begging for his forgiveness. "She and Brigham agreed it wasn't proper, their living under the same roof, with no proper chaperon in evidence." She paused and sniffled, encouraged by the fact that Devon hadn't interrupted her chatter. "Of course, now the whole town will probably court her."

At this, Devon's gaze swerved to Polly's face, and his expression sliced at her spirit like a knife. "I want to see her," he said, with a coldness she would never have believed he could manage, after all the tender warmth he'd shown her before her dreadful confession. "Bring Lydia to me. Now."

Polly rose slowly off the bed, swallowed hard. A sense of frenzied panic gathered in her stomach and rushed to the base of her windpipe, but she held on to her smile. "Lydia has come to visit you every day since the accident," she said. "I'm certain today will be no different."

"I want to see her now."

She closed her eyes briefly, opened them again. "There's something I need to tell you, Devon," she said. "You must listen."

He looked away. "I'm not interested in anything you have to say," he told her. "Get out."

Polly hesitated, nearly overwhelmed by his hatred and by the magnitude of the trouble she was in. She actually considered jumping off the wharf at high tide, so great was her despair, but on some level she knew she could not take such a cowardly course.

She made her way into the hallway, her bearing as regal as she knew how to make it. Beyond the threshold, however, when the door to Devon's room had closed behind her, Polly gave a small, hopeless wail and fell against the opposite wall. Her whole body trembled with the force of her weeping, although she made no sound beyond that first moaning cry, and she raised her arms to brace herself lest she collapse.

Presently, the storm of grief began to abate. Polly had been vaguely aware that someone was standing behind her, but because she knew the person could not be Devon, she did not turn around.

Strong hands came to rest on her shoulders. "Mrs. Quade," a masculine voice said.

Up until that moment, Polly had believed her bitter anguish to be nearly spent, but the title she could not claim clawed at her spirit, tearing it like sharp talons. She whirled, sobbing, and looked up into the sympathetic and genteelly handsome face of Dr. Joseph McCauley.

"There now, what is it?" he asked, and his tone soothed her somehow, like balm on a wound. "When I saw Mr. Quade earlier this morning, he seemed to be doing very well, so it can't be that."

Polly brushed away her tears with the heel of one palm. "He's awake," she said brokenly. The doctor's hands were still supporting her, and she began to feel stronger.

"Good," Dr. McCauley said. Then he sighed, reached into his coat pocket and drew out a clean handkerchief. He offered it to Polly before going on. "Often an active man like Mr. Quade becomes—irritable when he finds himself immobilized. Also, we must remember that he is in significant pain. He'll be more tractable once he's adjusted to the reality of his situation."

"I wish it were that simple," Polly said distractedly, drying her face and then blowing her nose with as much delicacy as possible. She almost blurted out the new and fearsome secret she was keeping, but in the end she couldn't confide something so personal to a stranger.

The physician moved away from Polly, watching her with a kindly gaze, opened the door of Devon's room and went in.

Polly smoothed her hair and skirts, drew a deep breath, and set out resolutely for the stairs. When she reached Lydia's cottage, minutes later, she found her friend kneeling on the front porch, coaxing a distressed marmalade kitten to take milk from a saucer.

Lydia looked up when she heard the gate hinges creak and smiled. A light, lilac-scented breeze played with her spun gold hair, and her eyes were blue as the cornflowers on the Quades' best dishes. Polly wanted to dislike the other woman, on account of Devon's fascination with her, but she couldn't summon the necessary rancor.

After dipping the tip of her index finger in the milk, Lydia offered it to the kitten, who lapped hungrily at the droplet. "I was just about to walk over to the main house," she told Polly pleasantly. "I want to borrow some books for the children's lessons. How is Devon today?"

Polly tried to smile and failed. She sat down on the top step, folding her arms around her updrawn knees. "He's awake," she said. "He asked for you."

Lydia came to sit beside her, holding the kitten on her lap and setting the saucer of milk on the step at her feet. She continued to feed the squirming creature with her finger. "I'll be sure to see him while I'm at the house."

Watching the kitten, with its little ears pressed flat to its head, and its tiny, trembling limbs, Polly bit her lower lip and battled back another spate of tears.

Sensing Polly's suffering, Lydia brought her gaze swiftly to her face. The expression in Polly's violet-blue eyes was a questioning one.

"Babies are such helpless little things, aren't they?" Polly looked down at the kitten.

Lydia was still watching her when she raised her head again. "Oh, Polly," she said softly. "Are you saying that you're—that you're expecting a child?"

Polly reached out, took the kitten and sheltered it gently against her bosom. "I think so," she said. "My female-time was due last week, and it hasn't come. I've never been late before."

"Have you told Devon?"

The laugh Polly uttered held no humor, only a rattle of grief. "Not yet. I'm not sure I ever will."

Lydia's whisper revealed shock. "Why not?"

"The first words Devon said to me when he came around were, 'Get out.' He hates me."

"He's angry," Lydia said, "and probably in severe pain as well. The prospect of a child might be a lifeline to him right now."

The soft, weightless kitten had drifted off into a contented sleep against Polly's breast. "It's bad enough that Devon doesn't want me," she said, staring off toward the snow-covered mountains in the distance. "I couldn't bear it if he turned his back on our child, too."

Lydia took Polly's hand, squeezed it. "Suppose he doesn't?"

Polly lifted the snoring ball of silken fur and gently brushed it against her cheek. At the same moment, a horrible possibility dawned on her. Devon might well think she'd already been pregnant when he met her, that the baby was just another facet of the complicated deception she'd perpetrated.

"He may not believe me," she said, with resignation, "and I have no one to thank for that but myself." She handed the kitten back to Lydia and drew a deep breath in an effort to compose herself. "Where are Charlotte and Millie?"

Lydia sighed. "They're with the Holmetz children, and Elly Collier's boys, gathering plant specimens for this afternoon's botany lesson."

Polly stood, watching as a small freighter came steaming around the bend toward the harbor. Perhaps she would board that boat, sail away from Quade's Harbor, make a new life for herself and the baby somewhere else. She could always go back to San Francisco, pretending to be a widow, and find herself another man.

She said a distracted good-bye to Lydia and moved down the dirt walkway to the gate, her emotions hopelessly tangled. Even then she knew running away wasn't the solution to her problems. Besides, she couldn't take another husband, not when she loved Devon so much. Just the thought of being intimate with anyone else made her shiver with revulsion.

Lydia carried the kitten and its saucerful of milk back into the house, but her thoughts followed Polly along the road to the mansion on the hill. She had half a mind to go straight to Devon Quade and tell him just exactly what she thought of him and his stubborn pride.

Even before she'd put the kitten in the little bed she'd made for it, using a small pillow and an apple crate, and before she'd smoothed her hair and splashed water on her face, Lydia knew she wouldn't broach such a personal subject with Devon. He and Polly would have to work it out themselves.

As Lydia walked toward the big house, she stopped to

watch the freighter tie up to the wharf. Several tall men disembarked, followed by two women in plain dresses, sharing a parasol.

Since Mr. Harrington, Brigham's clerk, was on hand to greet the new arrivals, Lydia suppressed her curiosity and went on. She would seek out the women later, and welcome them to Quade's Harbor.

Reaching Brigham's front gate, she lifted the latch and went through. Her thoughts had shifted from the scene on the wharf to Polly's predicament, and she felt a headache taking hold at her nape. It was amazing, she reflected, how very costly pride could be.

The interior of the big house was cool and quiet. Lydia proceeded through the entryway and turned toward the study, with its leather furniture, Persian rug, and tall windows looking out over the water and the mountains. The mantel was a piece of furniture in its own right, ornately carved with small animals, birds, oak leaves and acorns, stretching from the hearth to the ceiling.

Lydia marveled, touching a remarkable image of a squirrel. The creature's bushy tail alone had probably required hundreds of strokes of the carver's knife. The oak leaves were marked with perfect veins, and the acorns looked real enough to spawn seedlings.

She stood for a long time, discovering more images in the mantel. High over her head she spotted a wizard, skillfully hidden among the other carvings, as well as a magnificent stag and a gnarled tree burdened with fruit. Finally, the pull of the many books lining the floor-to-ceiling shelves behind Brigham's desk became too strong to resist.

Lydia found a stool and climbed up to begin examining the titles. She told herself she would not tarry too long, but simply find a good volume on botany, leave a note for Brigham explaining that she'd borrowed it to teach a lesson, and hurry back to her cottage.

For all Lydia's good intentions, she had a fascination with books akin to a drunk's addiction to liquor. She loved to just *look* at books, touching their bindings, reading their titles, sampling just a paragraph or two from the ones that proved purely irresistible.

She was so absorbed in one author's true account of two years spent living among gorillas in the heart of Africa that when two hands closed tightly on her thighs, she screamed and nearly dropped the precious leather-bound volume.

Brigham looked up at her with a smile in his eyes, his hands lingering on her limbs for a moment, setting fire to her flesh despite the layers of calico and muslin covering her. "Hold your temper, Yankee," he said wryly. "That stool is none too steady, and I didn't want to take a chance on startling you." Having said that, he released his hold on her, though he still looked ready to catch her if the need should arise.

Cheeks hot with color, Lydia replaced the gorilla saga on the shelf. The problem now was to climb down from her shaky perch without breaking her neck.

Brigham grinned, gave his head a wry shake, and placed his hands on her waist. Before she could protest, he'd lifted her off the stool. Her bosom brushed against his chest as he lowered her slowly to the floor, and the sparkle in his eyes said he'd done that on purpose.

A searing arousal swirled through Lydia's being, making her personal parts throb with memory's sweet appeasement. She stumbled back, out of his grasp, only to find herself flush against the edge of his desk.

Brigham stepped in front of her. "I didn't know trespassing numbered among your remarkable talents, Miss McQuire," he drawled. His expression grew solemn as he looked at her hair, the pulse at the base of her throat, and then her lips. "May I ask what you're doing, plundering my study?"

A warm shiver took Lydia, and she folded her arms across her chest. "You know very well that I wasn't 'plundering your study,'" she replied, with flustered impatience. "I merely came to borrow a text on botany."

He nodded indulgently, his eyes dancing at her obvious discomfort. "I see. I think the mating habits of gorillas fall under another category, however."

Lydia wouldn't have thought she could summon up another blush; it seemed to her that every drop of blood in her body had already flowed into her face. Still, her cheeks felt even hotter than before. She glanced fitfully up at the spine of the book she'd been reading, then narrowed her eyes and glared at Brigham.

"I was not reading about the mating habits of anything," she said tartly.

Brigham curled one finger under her chin and lifted it. His lips were so close to hers that she could feel their warmth, sense their texture, anticipate their pressure. "Enough of this foolishness," he muttered.

Lydia told herself she should try to escape his kiss, but she made no actual attempt because she wanted it too much. Her whole body sang like a harp string when Brigham's mouth sampled hers. His hands rose from the sides of her waist to the delicate rounding of her breasts as his tongue played over the seam of her lips and then entered her mouth.

A soft and completely involuntary whimper escaped her. Instead of pushing Brigham away, as she knew she should have done, she clasped his shoulders as if to pull him closer. She felt the size and heat of his manhood against her abdomen, and a sweet dizziness swirled up around her as he pressed her against the edge of the desk.

Lydia was certain she would faint if he didn't release her, but the kiss went on and she stayed conscious. She felt as though she was astraddle a lightning bolt, and the beginnings of another scandalous inner explosion, like the one Brigham had brought her to on the bed at the cabin, seemed to be building inside her.

Just in time, just when she would have tumbled right over the brink, Brigham lifted his mouth. His eyes were full of challenge, and Lydia could see none of her own bedazzlement in their depths.

"Enough nonsense," he said hoarsely, his thumbs playing freely with her nipples, which jutted against her camisole, frantic for contact with his fingers and tongue. "You have need of a husband, and I certainly require a wife. I want you to marry me, Lydia. Now. Today."

She squirmed out of his embrace, and although he didn't make it easy, he didn't try to restrain her, either. She straightened her dress and raised her hands to the coronet of hair at the back of her head. That turned out to be a mistake, for Brigham's gaze slipped immediately to her breasts, and his glance proved almost as effective as a caress.

Lydia turned away, struggling to get her breath. When she'd finally succeeded, she lifted her head high, well aware that he was close behind her, that he could easily draw her back against the hardness of his thighs and chest. "You've fallen in love with me, then?" she said, knowing only too well what his answer would be.

"No," he replied, with wounding bluntness. "Love is a fatuous concept, invented by poets. I'm offering you something solid and tangible, a partnership, Yankee— half interest in everything I own. All I ask in return is that you share my bed, look after my daughters, and give me a son or two."

Lydia whirled, her cheeks crimson again, but this time with fury and conviction, not embarrassment. "You may think that love is a 'fatuous concept,'" she flared, "and no doubt you hold patriotism and personal honor in the same low regard. But I, Mr. Quade, will not settle for anything less than a true and deep sentiment from the man I marry!"

His mouth took on a disdainful slant, and he folded his arms. "That must be why you answered that handbill in San Francisco and willingly agreed to wed a total stranger. And what the *hell* does patriotism have to do with this?"

Lydia faltered. Her body was pulling her in one direction, her mind in another. She was a one-woman riot of conflict and confusion. "Marrying Devon would have been different," she hedged. "He's a gentleman."

Brigham pretended to pull a dart from his chest. Then he arched one eyebrow, and gave no sign that he meant to let her pass. "All right," he said generously, "have it your way. But I still want an explanation for that remark about patriotism."

She swallowed, wishing she'd never thrown out a challenge in the first place. When was she going to learn not to rise to the hook every time this man dangled a line in front of her nose? She fell back on bravado, too proud to admit she'd spoken rashly. "While other men were fighting and dying on the battlefields at Gettysburg and Antietam and Bull Run, you were out here cutting timber. Not only did you neatly avoid the danger, you had the brass to sell lumber to both governments!"

She had cause to regret that statement, as well as the earlier one, in the next instant. Brigham's eyes took on a chilly glint, and a white line edged his jaw.

"Are you calling me a coward?" he asked, his voice low and lethal.

"No," Lydia said, and she wasn't trying to appease him. "You're a rascal and a rounder, but you don't lack for courage."

His nod and brief smile were bitter. "Thank you for that much," he said. With that, he backed her up to the desk and stood with his hands braced on either side of her, once again making escape impossible. "You have a fair share of gall yourself," he said, measuring the words, practically biting them off. "You came into my house, like Sherman taking Atlanta, and then you demanded a place of your own, along with a fat salary and a schoolhouse. Now I find you going through my belongings."

Lydia had never been so rattled. She was practically on her back, her thighs pressed shamefully against Brigham's, and all her nerves were leaping beneath her skin. At one and the same time, she wanted to run away and to take him deep inside her, right there on the study desk, and hold fast to him.

"I was not—going through your belongings—" she explained breathlessly. "I've already explained—"

He pulled her upright in a sudden, wrenching motion. "Explain this," he rasped, his nose practically touching hers. "Why is it that I'm such a 'rascal and a rounder' because I refused to take sides between the North and the South? Joe McCauley fought on the enemy side, Yank. How does it happen that you regard him so warmly?"

Lydia ran her tongue over dry lips. "He is a good man, a doctor. We have a great deal in common."

Brigham sighed, then turned away from her, shoving one hand through his hair. While Lydia was still recovering her scattered composure, he went to the bookshelves and took down a thick volume with a green leather binding.

"Botany," he said hoarsely, slamming the book down on the surface of the desk. Then, without another word, he strode out of the study, leaving Lydia to gaze after him and wonder at the wild sensations he'd stirred not only in her body, but in her soul, too.

She remembered nothing of the walk back to her cottage, except that she moved so fast she got tangled in her skirts twice and nearly fell.

The afternoon was pleasant.

Lydia took her six students to a high knoll overlooking the Sound and the site of the meetinghouse Brigham had promised her, and they sat in a circle. The botany text lay open on Lydia's lap, and one by one they identified the leaves and grasses the children had gathered that morning.

"Mr. Feeny told me Uncle Devon asked for you when he took his meal tray upstairs," Charlotte confided, with concern, as they all walked back toward the town proper. The Collier boys would make their own way up the mountain, to the camp where their mother had taken up residence in a tent, and the Holmetzes lived in the yellow house at the opposite end of the street from Lydia's blue one. Millie had gone ahead to play in Anna's yard.

Lydia sighed. She *had* meant to look in on Devon, but after the incident in the study, with Brigham, she'd fled the house in panic. She wouldn't go back until she knew the master wasn't at home.

"Please tell your uncle that I'll definitely come to call tomorrow," she said. The morning would be a good time, she decided, before she began the lessons she'd planned for the children. She knew Brigham would be either in his office or on the mountain before the rest of the household had even stirred. "How is he?"

"He's in a terrible mood," Charlotte confided. "He raised his voice to poor Polly and made her cry. Not only that, but when she went to bathe him, he knocked the basin from her hands and got the floor all wet." The girl's wonderful eyes were wide. "Is it proper for a woman to bathe a man?"

Lydia suppressed a smile. "It's perfectly proper, under the right circumstances."

Charlotte was still pondering that when they passed the towering Quade house. She gave Lydia a distracted wave and headed up the shady driveway.

Reaching home, Lydia found a basket of fruit on her porch, along with a tin of chocolates and an armload of wildflowers. Undoubtedly, the oranges and candy had come in on board the freighter she'd seen earlier, since such treats certainly weren't available in Brigham's despicable "company store."

Lydia gathered up the booty carefully, then turned to scan the street. She was being courted in earnest, quite possibly by several different men, but so far only Mr. Flengmeir had presented himself at the front door and declared his intentions.

With a sigh and a slight shrug, Lydia went inside. The kitten, whom she had named Ophelia, came scampering and tumbling over to meet her, batting ineffectually at her hem. She put the oranges in the center of the table, the flowers in a jelly jar with water, and the chocolates in the top drawer of her bureau.

She would eat two of the oranges herself, she decided, one after supper and one at breakfast time, and offer the rest to the children the next day, as an incentive to work hard on their studies.

Since the kitten was still attached to her skirts when she'd put the candy away, Lydia bent and gently freed its tiny claws from the fabric, then collapsed wearily onto the feather-filled mattress. Ophelia toddled unsteadily up to the base of Lydia's throat and settled herself there with elaborate ceremony.

Lydia's eyes filled with tears, and she caressed the cat lightly, with just the tips of her fingers, delighting in its warmth. A moment later, weary from a busy day and the encounter with Brigham, Lydia drifted off to sleep.

When she awakened, twilight was casting purple shadows through the window, and Ophelia was snuggled close to her right cheek, giving her soft, purring snore. Lydia lowered the cat carefully to the floor and sat up, yawning.

She hadn't meant to doze off; she needed to make supper, heat enough water to fill the hip bath she'd borrowed from the Quades' attic, and plan the next day's lessons. If there was time, she would seek out the ladies she'd seen getting off the freighter that afternoon and introduce herself.

With a sigh, Lydia swung her legs over the side of her bed and pinned a few loose tendrils of hair beneath her sagging coronet. Perhaps the women were unattached, and some of the loggers would turn to courting them instead of her.

She hoped so.

She made a trip to the small privy out back, washed her hands under the pump in the yard, and filled the largest kettle she had. She put the water on the stove to heat.

Supper was simple; Lydia cooked one of the eggs Mr. Feeny had brought to her, and browned a slice of buttered toast on a small griddle. After pouring a glass of milk, she sat quietly at the round table to eat.

Lydia was just finishing her meal when a knock sounded at the door.

Again her heart lurched. She wasn't up to another encounter with Brigham Quade, and besides, it wouldn't be proper for him to visit her. People would start saying she was his mistress, a kept woman.

"Who's there?" she called in an uncertain voice, fully prepared to refuse Brigham admission. Never mind that it was his house, his town. *She* was the one with everything at stake.

"It's Joseph," her friend replied through the closed

door. "I've come calling, Miss Lydia. It is my hope that we could sit on the front porch together for a while."

Lydia's relief was matched only by her disappointment. She summoned up a smile and opened the door. "Hello, Joseph. Won't you come in?"

He was holding a small nosegay made up of buttercups and wild violets, and once again Lydia willed herself to fall wildly, passionately in love with him.

"It wouldn't be proper for me to do that," he said, and there was an indulgent note of scolding in his tone. "We must think of your reputation, darlin'."

Lydia sighed. If only Brigham Quade would concern himself with wild violets and propriety, things would be so much simpler. She smiled and stepped out onto the porch to accept Joseph's offering, and they sat together on the top step.

"How's Devon?" she asked, after taking a delicious sniff of the delicate wildflowers he'd brought.

"Mean," Joseph answered, with a long sigh. "He's making life pretty miserable for Mrs. Quade."

Lydia felt a flare of sisterly indignation. "He ought to be horsewhipped. Maybe Polly made a mistake, but she loves Devon, and he loves her. I just hope he realizes that before it's too late and there's the baby—" She broke off, horrified that she'd betrayed such an important confidence.

"Does Devon know?" Joseph asked after a long time.

Lydia didn't hesitate. Surely Polly had not kept something so vitally important to herself, fearful as she'd been of Devon's reaction. "He must. Polly had almost no choice except to tell him."

The doctor didn't answer.

15

By THE TIME ANOTHER WEEK HAD PASSED, POLLY KNEW only too well that she was indeed going to have a baby. She was wildly, violently ill in the mornings, and in the afternoons such a fatigue overtook her that she could only lie in silent misery on a couch in the corner of Devon's room. At night she couldn't sleep for the worry.

For the most part, Devon ignored her completely, although after a visit from Lydia, he was always especially surly. Physically, however, he was a little improved with each passing day, and soon he was up and walking with a cane.

Polly, curled in a chair next to his private fireplace, knew she could no longer delay the inevitable. Before long Devon's confinement to the bedroom would end, and avoiding her would be much easier.

"Devon." She said his name firmly, although bravery was the last trait she would have claimed at the time.

He was standing at the windows, wearing only the bottoms of his long underwear and leaning on the cane one of Brigham's men had made for him from a sturdy piece of pine.

Polly's heart swelled with tenderness as she looked at the father of the baby growing inside her, the man she would think of as her husband even if he spurned her forever.

"Devon," she repeated.

He stiffened, the muscles in his shoulders beautiful in their formidable power. "Leave me alone," he said.

Polly swung her feet to the floor and stood, smoothing her skirts. "Honestly, Devon, you're behaving like a spoiled child." The last word stung, pertinent as it was, and she drew a deep, tremulous breath. "I have something important to say, and *by God* I'm going to say it, whether you object or not."

Devon turned his head, looked at her with fierce, Viking-blue eyes. Once, he'd regarded her with gentleness and love. Now he could barely tolerate her presence. He said nothing, he simply stared at her with that expression of challenge in his battered but still handsome face.

The whole world seemed to pulse, like one giant heart, and there was a roaring in Polly's ears. She forced herself to gaze directly into Devon's eyes, and said, "I'm going to have a child. In January, I think."

A series of emotions moved in his face, but he'd brought them under control before Polly could identify them. "Congratulations," he said.

The word stabbed Polly like an arrow, but somehow she found the strength to say with dignity, "You are the father of this child, Devon."

He turned away again, to stare out the window. "How convenient," he said, after a long silence that was pure torture for Polly.

She closed her eyes, gripped the side of a table to keep from sagging to the floor. She had guessed what his reaction would be, and yet it came as a brutal shock, too. Polly had not entirely abandoned the hope that he would remember that he'd loved her once, that he'd remember all the plans they'd made together.

Now, however, there was nothing left to say.

Devon reached out, snatched something from the top

of his washstand. Then, laboriously, depending on the cane to keep himself upright, he turned and flung one hand out.

Currency swirled toward her in a storm. "Here. This is what you wanted, isn't it?" he growled. "Take it—take any goddamned thing you want—and get the hell out of my life!"

Polly had done some pretty questionable things in the past, and she knew the days and years ahead might be bitterly difficult for both her and the baby. All the same, she would have starved before taking that money. She lifted her chin, tried frantically to think what Lydia would do.

At the moment of that decision, a peculiar thing happened. A new strength poured into Polly, and she said something she hadn't planned, hadn't even consciously thought before. "I won't make it so easy for you, Devon. I'm staying right here in Quade's Harbor. I'll marry the first man who asks me, and every day for the rest of your life you'll either see me, or the child you denied. Your child."

With that, Polly turned and left the room.

At noon Brigham came down from the mountain. His clothes were stiff with dried sweat, pitch, and ordinary dirt. His best bullwhacker had quit in a drunken rage, he'd been stung on the back of the neck by a wasp, and he was so obsessed with thoughts of Lydia that he was more a hindrance to the men than a help.

Reaching the cool sanctity of his tree-trunk office, he ladled a big drink of water from the bucket and scowled at Harrington, who was sitting at his worktable on the opposite wall, going over papers.

"There's a problem, sir," Harrington announced bravely, after clearing his throat twice and rustling things.

Brigham touched the sting on his nape and cursed. "There are a number of problems, Harrington," he answered in a curt tone.

"This one is rather urgent, Mr. Quade. Two women

arrived on that freighter that came in last week. They're missionaries."

Missionaries. Brigham took a bottle from the bottom right-hand drawer of his desk and, despite the fact that he rarely took a drink before six in the evening, tossed back one fiery swallow and then another. "Where have they been staying?"

"I gave them my cabin," Harrington answered. "But I'm afraid I can no longer tolerate living up in camp with the other men."

Brigham could well imagine how the skinny, earnest clerk would fare among the timbermen; they would bait him mercilessly. He sighed and rubbed his eyes with a thumb and forefinger. "These women have come to save our souls?" He sighed the question, already convinced of the answer.

But Harrington surprised him. "Not exactly, sir. I believe they think we're hopeless pagans, all things considered, and expect a better harvest among the Indians. They're searching for Reverend Matthew Prophet, too."

The reverend had packed up his bags and left on one of the mail-boat runs some days before, and Brigham hadn't given the wild-eyed fanatic another thought since. He had hoped, in passing, that the old man wouldn't do too much harm to the good Lord's cause before someone lynched him out of annoyance.

"What do they want with Prophet?" he finally asked. He didn't give a damn about the answer, but he knew Harrington would not rest until he'd related it.

"The older one claims to be his wife," Harrington said. "The younger, his daughter."

At last Brigham was interested. "Great Zeus," he muttered. "Prophet abandoned his own family?"

"Yes," Harrington said, and this time there was a grudge in his voice.

Brigham smiled. "Is she pretty? The daughter, I mean?"

The clerk flushed and looked away. "Yes." He pushed

his spectacles up to the bridge of his nose. "It's not right, a girl like that wandering around the frontier with only her mother to watch out for her."

The sting on Brigham's neck was still burning. "Maybe not," he conceded impatiently, and headed for the door, "but it's common enough, since the war. Tell the ladies they can put up in one of the Main Street houses, temporarily."

"Yes, sir," Harrington said, with a note of good cheer.

Brigham started toward home, thinking he'd have a cool bath and put a paste of baking soda and water on the wasp sting. Maybe then he'd be able to concentrate on his work.

The musical sound of laughter reached him long before he came to Lydia's gate and stopped there to watch the game going on in the side yard. Lydia was blindfolded with a bright red bandanna, staggering about in the grass, her arms outstretched, while six delighted children dodged her grasp.

Brigham was enchanted. Along with the hot and elemental needs he felt whenever he saw Lydia, there was a sense of tender magic. He wanted to join in the game, to capture Lydia in his arms and kiss that laughing mouth.

As he watched, Millie purposely allowed herself to be caught and as a result became "it." Lydia removed her blindfold and fastened it carefully over the little girl's eyes. Only when Millie was groping after the other children, who taunted her good-humoredly, did Miss McQuire look toward the fence and catch Brigham staring at her.

He saw her draw herself up, smooth her hair and skirts. The womanly gestures were habitual, he knew, perhaps even unconscious. She was obviously gathering her thoughts as she approached.

"Just in case you're about to say blindman's buff is a waste of lesson time—"

Brigham raised one hand, palm out, to silence her. "I wasn't going to say anything of the kind," he said. "The truth is, I was thinking how good it is to see children playing together." It *was* the truth, he reasoned to himself. It just wasn't the *whole* truth.

Her brows puckered together in a frown, and she tilted her head to one side. "Is your neck swollen?"

Brigham felt foolish, wanting her sympathy and gentle touch the way he did. So he tried to hide his feelings. "It's just a wasp sting, that's all," he said.

She stood on tiptoe, bending over the fence. "Such things can be quite serious. Let me see."

He turned his head to give her a better view of the wound, taking unreasonable pleasure from her concern.

"I don't like the looks of that," she said. "Come sit on the porch. I'll take out the stinger and apply some disinfectant."

Brigham opened the gate and followed her obediently up the walk, while the exuberant game of blindman's buff went on without interruption. He sat on the top step and Lydia went into the house, returning in a few minutes with a basin of water, a cloth, and a bottle containing some tincture. She had washed her hands, and the scent of soap was about her.

Her manner was gently efficient. Brigham couldn't remember the last time a woman had touched him with tenderness—passion, yes. Anger, yes. But not in a gentle, caring way.

He went weak at the softness of her attentions, as dazed as if he'd just swallowed half a bottle of laudanum in one gulp.

She made a tsk-tsk sound, full of sympathy, and Brigham couldn't help thinking of her steadfast refusal to marry him. He'd wanted to bed her almost from the first, but now he mourned something else even more deeply. He ached with the knowledge that he might never be entitled to wifely ministrations like this. So many times, his back was sore when he came out of the woods after a long day's work, and it would have been a glorious thing to feel her strong hands rubbing away the weariness and the pain. She might have cut his hair for him, and listened in soothing silence while he told her about things that had gone wrong, and washed that hard-to-reach place between his shoulder blades when he bathed.

"There," she teased briskly, breaking the spell. Leaving Brigham with no ready excuse to linger. "I'm sure you'll survive your injury."

Brigham turned and looked into her blue, blue eyes, and immediately lost his equilibrium again. He spoke sternly, so she wouldn't know how she'd shaken him, just sitting there, smelling of plain soap and touching him with gentle fingers. "Harrington tells me a woman and a girl came to town last week, looking for Reverend Prophet."

Lydia looked toward the children, soft tendrils of hair dancing against her cheeks, watching with a half smile as Anna became "it" and the others pursued her. The pure gaiety of their laughter did something peculiar to Brigham's heart, as did the close proximity of this woman.

"I know," she said. "I called on them after they'd settled into Mr. Harrington's quarters. Quite a situation."

"Harrington is sweet on the girl, I think," Brigham said. He didn't give a damn about his clerk's romantic interests, but he wasn't ready to stand up and walk away, either.

Lydia's smile was more medicinal than the stuff she'd applied to the insect bite. It made his heart bunch up in his chest, then expand with a painful rush. "Love seems to be in the air," she said. "Mr. Feeny has been calling on Elly Collier of late, and a day doesn't go by that some suitor doesn't leave me a present."

A quiet, poisonous rage surged through Brigham's system, virulent as the wasp's venom, and he stood. "I don't want you accepting gifts," he said flatly. "It isn't proper."

She looked up at him without so much as a hint of timidity, and a little yellow-gold cat wriggled over to make its way onto her lap. "Since when have you troubled yourself over what is or isn't proper?" she countered, unruffled. She stroked the kitten, and Brigham was sore with envy.

He had no answer. Brigham Quade had never given a rat's ass about propriety, except where it concerned his daughters, and Lydia obviously knew that.

"Has Joe McCauley come calling?" he asked, his voice gruff. The place where the wasp had struck didn't hurt half so much as the bite Lydia had taken out of his pride.

Lydia nodded. "Yes. He's made no secret of his intentions, Brigham. Not even to you."

That was true enough. McCauley had gone to Seattle just the day before, in fact, looking for a loan to build himself a combination office and house in Quade's Harbor. Brigham had offered to put up the money, since the town needed a doctor if it was going to grow into the kind of place he envisioned, but McCauley had politely refused. He'd said straight out that he didn't want to be beholden; the building and the practice had to be under his own governing.

Brigham had understood that, being of like mind himself, and his respect for the man had risen accordingly, but he'd had a crazy desire to run McCauley off like a stray dog, too. If Lydia married the doctor, she would be all around Quade's Harbor on wifely business, and he would see her everywhere.

Presently, her belly would swell with McCauley's child, and he would have to live with the knowledge that she shared another man's bed, took pleasure beneath another man's hands and mouth and hips.

Brigham didn't think he could stand that, and yet he'd be damned if he'd leave. He'd worked too hard and suffered too much to give up his holdings on account of some saucy little Yankee.

Her laugh, sudden and bright as a bell on a clear morning, jolted him out of his thoughts.

"For goodness sake, Brigham," she scolded, standing beside him on the dirt path in front of her porch steps. "You look as grim as a thundercloud. Are you sure you're all right?"

"I'm fine," he barked. Then he turned and strode away toward the gate.

When Brigham arrived at the house, he went immediately to his brother's room. Devon was sitting up in bed, smoking a cigar and playing poker with Jake Feeny.

It lightened Brigham's black mood a little, seeing his brother looking almost like his old self.

"I guess I'd like to have some of that raisin cake now," Devon said to the cook, the cigar bobbing between his white teeth as he spoke.

Jake took the hint and left, with a cordial nod at Brigham.

Devon reached out and caught the neck of a whiskey bottle in his fingers and a glass in the curve of his thumb.

Brigham frowned.

"Don't say it," Devon warned, before his brother could offer a comment on the early hour. The bottle clinked against the rim of the glass as he poured himself a double shot—not his first of the day, from the smell of him. "I need this. It controls the pain."

Brigham eyed the liquor warily, only too aware of what it could do to a man's life once it took a stranglehold. "Maybe it's time you got out of this room, Dev," he said quietly, pulling up the chair that usually contained Polly. "I'll have a crew finish the general store, and you can send to San Francisco for stock—"

Devon drained the glass and set it aside with an unsteady motion of his hand, bumping it against the bottle. "I won't be needing the store," he said. "I'm leaving Quade's Harbor, Brig. For good."

The words struck Brigham like the trunk of a three-year-old sapling swung hard at his midsection. The dream of building a decent town, a place for people to live and work, had not been his alone. Devon had shared it once.

"What?" he asked stupidly, still reeling on the inside.

"I can't stay here and watch Polly get fat with that bastard's baby," Devon growled.

Brigham stared at him for a moment, amazed. "What bastard is that?" he asked after a long time.

Devon reached for the bottle again; Brigham got up and pulled it from his hand. For a long moment the two brothers glared at each other in fury, and Brigham knew they would have fought under any other circumstances.

"The child isn't mine," Devon finally said, on a long, ragged breath.

Brigham slowly lowered the whiskey bottle onto the marble top of Devon's bureau. "Did she tell you that?"

"Hell, no," Devon answered in an acid rasp. "She says I'm the father."

Brigham struggled for patience. He hadn't been able to help hearing some of the sounds that had come from this room as he'd passed by in the hall in the days after Devon's return from San Francisco. "You probably are."

Devon sighed, and there was something broken in the sound, for all its bitterness. "No. She lied before, and she's lying now."

"What makes you so sure of that?" Brigham wished to God he had Devon's problem. If he'd made Lydia pregnant, she might have married him. *Might.*

His brother ran his tongue over dry, cracked lips. "I'm sure, all right. Miracles like that only happen in those storybooks of Charlotte's, and I don't believe in fairy tales anymore."

"You're a damn fool. That baby is a Quade, Devon, you can't just turn your back!"

Devon said nothing. Nothing at all.

Brigham suppressed an urge to grip his brother by the shoulders and thump his head against the headboard until he'd pounded in some sense. Instead he made a silent decision of his own and walked out.

If Devon wouldn't take responsibility for that baby, which was as much a Quade as any of them, then he himself would. Even if it meant putting some of his own dreams aside forever.

Lydia dropped the potato she'd been peeling and stared at Polly, who was perched on the porch step beside her. It was twilight, the mail boat had come and gone, and the mill saw was blessedly silent, but the peace had been shattered by a few simple words.

"You're what?"

Polly wouldn't look at her. "I'm marrying Brigham. He called me into his study a little while ago and asked me. We aren't going to live together, of course, but the baby will have the Quade name, and Brigham has promised to help me get started in business as soon as the general store is finished."

Lydia made no attempt to pick up the naked potato, which was now brown with dust from the path, even though the idea of never wasting food was ingrained in her. She was dizzy with bewilderment and shock, and the fact that Brigham and Polly didn't plan to share a bed was of no comfort at all. Brigham was a vital, healthy man, and Polly was a beautiful woman. It would only be a matter of time before Brigham claimed his rights as a husband.

"What about Devon?" Lydia asked when she could manage to speak.

Polly bent down, picked up the potato, and tried to wipe it off with her skirt. A tear rolled down her cheek and dropped off onto her bodice. "Devon is leaving Quade's Harbor. He thinks I'm lying about the baby." She turned her head, looking so despondent that Lydia couldn't be angry with her. "I—I wouldn't have said yes to Brigham's proposal," she added, "except that you've made it so clear you won't have him for a husband."

Lydia was undergoing a major shift in attitude in those moments. She loved Brigham Quade, ornery and hardheaded as he was, and the rest of her life loomed long and lonely without him. She wished she'd accepted his suit, and left the winning of his more noble affections until later.

"I see," she said.

Polly rose to leave, shaking out her skirts. "I'm not strong like you, Lydia," she told her still-stricken friend.

"I couldn't make my own way in the world, not with a baby to look after."

Lydia couldn't speak; she could only nod. As soon as the gate closed behind Polly, and Brigham's future bride was out of sight, she let the tears come.

That night was neither happy nor restful for Lydia. She cried and paced, the worried kitten tumbling after her, trying to catch at her skirts. In the morning, voice hoarse, eyes red and swollen, Lydia taught lessons as usual, sitting with the children in the side yard.

In the afternoon, Joe McCauley arrived on the mail boat and came immediately to Lydia's door, all smiles, his arms full of packages.

She'd been able to fool the children into thinking the bright yellow Scotch broom growing all over the region irritated her nose and throat, but Joe knew the ravages of tears when he saw them. He broke his own rule of propriety and led Lydia into the house, pressing her into a chair and laying the bundles in her lap.

Then he crouched in front of her. "Brigham?"

She sniffled and then nodded. "He's going to marry Polly. So that her baby won't be illegitimate."

Joe smoothed back a stray lock of her hair. "Has he told you that himself?"

She shook her head, fighting back a spate of fresh tears. "No, the coward. He rode off to Seattle to bring back some preacher friend of his, though. He means to go ahead with this."

"Maybe you'd better go to Brig and tell him how you feel," Joe said gently. It was clear that he cared for Lydia himself, and cared deeply. Apparently, her happiness mattered to him more than his own, which only made the situation that much more ironic, to Lydia's mind.

Lydia thought of how she'd turned down Brigham's proposals; in retrospect, the refusals seemed arrogant, given the fact that she'd come to love him even before he'd offered himself as a suitor. "I can't do that, Joe," she said. "If there's one thing I know about Brigham Quade, it's that nothing can sway him from a purpose once he's made up his mind. He's going to do this thing." She looked at her friend in an appeal for understanding. "Besides, what would Polly do? What would happen to that innocent little baby?"

Joseph reached up, caressed Lydia's chin. "There are a lot of hard choices to make in this life," he said gruffly. Then his face lit up with a smile, and he found her hands among the bundles and squeezed them. "I've got my loan, and I'll be building a house and small surgery just down the street, in that lot on the other side of the Holmetzes."

Lydia smiled through her tears and kissed his forehead, nearly sending her lap full of presents toppling to the floor. "That's wonderful," she said, grateful that he wasn't pressing her to turn to him, now that she was losing Brigham forever.

"Open the packages," he said hoarsely.

Lydia dried her eyes on her sleeve, sniffled again, and opened the first of the gifts, which were all wrapped in brown paper and tied with string. Inside was a beautiful bound book of short stories and essays. The next package contained a mirror with an ornate silver back, and the last one held a lovely shawl, delicately crocheted of turquoise silk.

"How on earth did you find such things in Seattle?" Lydia asked, awed. Even there, the merchants dealt almost entirely with lumberjacks, miners, and mill workers, and pretty trinkets were hard to find.

Joe's smile lifted her spirits. "There was a ship in port a while back—the *Enchantress*. She'd sailed to China on a trading expedition, and made a stop in San Francisco, as well. Along with some other cargo, the captain brought finery for the merchants to sell."

Something in his tone caught Lydia's interest. Maybe she was just desperate to turn her thoughts to something besides Brigham's impending marriage for a few seconds. "What other cargo?" she asked.

The doctor's weathered face pinkened slightly around the cheekbones. "You don't want to know."

"Yes, I do, Joseph," Lydia said, smoothing her skirts. "That's why I asked you."

"Women."

Lydia didn't understand. "Women?"

Joseph went to sit opposite her, on an upturned crate. He looked everywhere but at her face. "Yes, Lydia," he said presently. "Women—fancy ones."

"Surely you don't think I'm so delicate that I don't know what a prostitute is, Joseph," Lydia said, a little impatient with his hedging. What did she care if a few more soiled doves flocked to the crude brothels on Seattle's Skid Road.

He cleared his throat.

"Oh, never mind," Lydia fussed. She hadn't been herself since Polly had brought her news of the wedding, and she couldn't think straight. Before she could come up with anything sensible to say, someone knocked hard at the front door.

Joseph shifted uncomfortably on his crate, then rose and went to answer.

Devon loomed in the doorway, leaning on his pine cane, dressed in a good gray suit with a striped vest, and wearing an elegant hat. Ignoring the doctor entirely, he strode into the room, filling it with his size and the sheer, thunderous energy of his personality.

"I'm leaving Quade's Harbor for good," he said bluntly, removing his hat and looking straight into Lydia's wide eyes. "I'm here to ask you to go with me."

Lydia was struck speechless. For one wild moment she considered saying yes to Devon's proposition, but all the while she knew she couldn't do such a thing. She wouldn't be able to set aside her feelings for Brigham so easily.

"I can't," she said gently.

Devon's jawline tightened, but he accepted the pronouncement with no visible emotion. Lydia suspected he might even be a little relieved.

He bent, carefully, this good and gentle man who had brought her to Quade's Harbor in the first place, and kissed the top of her head. "Good-bye, then," he said. And he was gone.

Just as Lydia was asking herself how Devon could travel overland in his condition, she heard the loud hoot of a freighter's horn, and her question was answered.

16

A SIMPLE WEDDING CEREMONY WAS TO BE HELD IN THE SIDE yard at the big house on the hill, with the bride and groom standing in Aunt Persephone's gazebo, and it seemed that everyone in the territory was invited. While the occasion of Brigham's marriage to Polly lacked a sense of celebration for Lydia, there was a definite buzz of excitement in the air because social events were so rare on Puget Sound. Word had spread rapidly through the area, and every day homesteaders and even Indians arrived to set up camp at the edge of town.

In the midst of all this, a flurry of building was going on. Brigham sent a crew to finish the general store, and it was common knowledge that stock had been ordered from as far away as Boston and New York. Joe McCauley's house was under construction at the end of Main Street, too, and the meeting-and-schoolhouse had been begun, as well, along with a large structure meant to be a hotel, according to Charlotte. The echoes of constant hammer blows rang out over the water, the steady rasp of saws adding to the din, and Lydia paced her little house when she wasn't busy teaching.

All the while, Lydia alternately cursed Devon for

failing to return and claim his wife and child, and Brigham, for his unshakable sense of honor. It seemed remarkable now that he'd taunted *her* for her stern New England mores. Polly was the only one she held no rancor toward; on the frontier, women did what they had to do to make a place for themselves. For most, it was a matter of survival.

Lydia avoided Brigham carefully, although he tried to talk to her on several occasions. The first time, when he'd come brazenly to her door, she'd simply pretended not to be home.

Soon after, Brigham had sent Harrington in his stead, with a politely worded invitation to meet with Mr. Quade on neutral ground, at his office near the mill.

Lydia sent Mr. Harrington away with a response that turned the tops of his ears red.

Finally, Brigham even stooped so low as to ask his daughters to do his dirty work. Charlotte and Millie had come to Lydia, after lessons one afternoon, and invited her to supper at the main house.

The children were as confused as Lydia herself, and she loved them devotedly. She phrased her refusal very gently, but volunteered no explanation.

Mail boats and unscheduled freighters came and went in the harbor, and finally the dreaded day arrived.

Lydia donned her best dress, the gray one with pink stripes, and took special pains with her hair that morning. Although her preference would have been to stay home and weep, she meant to sit in the front row of chairs with her head held high and her eyes dry and defiant.

She pinned her new straw bonnet in place—like the many other things crowding the blue saltbox cottage on Main Street, it was a gift from one of her admirers—and studied her reflection in the bureau mirror. She did not look the least bit like an embittered spinster, she assured herself silently, although she certainly felt like one.

Presently, Joe McCauley came to fetch her, offering his arm in that suave way he had, and the two of them walked up the hill to Brigham's house together. Lydia felt like a lady outlaw being led out for hanging, but she had a broad smile for everyone they encountered on the way.

The preparations for the wedding were simple enough; someone had brought out every chair from the house, or close to that number, and lined them up in rows facing the gazebo. There were several big, unfrosted cakes, and red punch was being served from a tin washtub teetering on top of two sawhorses. A few forlorn flowers in fruit jars had been set at the base of the gazebo steps.

Joe seated Lydia in the front row of chairs and took his place beside her. The immediate family and close friends would be seated first, she surmised, and lumberjacks and farmers, mill workers and sailors, Indians and a few traveling peddlers, were already claiming places in the grass.

Mr. Harrington appeared, proudly escorting his missionary, the delicately pretty Esther Prophet. The rumor was that Harrington and Miss Prophet planned a ceremony of their own, one day soon.

Lydia smiled, even though her heart was weighted, almost crushed, by a furious sorrow that would not be reasoned away.

It was a sunny day, with a salty-velvet breeze blowing in from the harbor, and she heard the whistle of yet another freighter but took no real account of the sound. Holding up the facade that hid her bruised and bleeding pride took all her concentration.

Brigham appeared, looking heart-wrenchingly handsome in a dark suit and white linen shirt, and although Lydia took care not to glance in his direction after that first time, she felt the intensity of his gaze. Joe got up and went to talk with the groom, after patting Lydia's hand once in a surreptitious attempt at reassurance.

Someone played a fiddle, somewhere, and there was much talk and boisterous laughter among the guests. Finally, Elly Collier dropped heavily into a chair beside Lydia and said, with typical rough grace, "This here's the damnedest fool sitchy-ation I've ever run across. Brig should be marryin' you. Why, his eyes has been all over you ever since he stepped out of the house. If lookin' was chewin', he'd have eaten you up already."

Lydia blushed. "He's made his decision," she said, shifting primly in her chair. "He'll just have to live with it." *And so will I,* she thought miserably in the next instant.

Vaguely, she heard the sounds of more arriving wagons and horses, and her charges, the Holmetz children, Elly's two boys, and Charlotte and Millie, ran wild through the festivities. At any other time Lydia would have gotten them by the ears, one by one, and given them a lecture on polite deportment. As it happened, though, she could only sit there in that chair purloined from the small parlor and wish it would all be over.

Finally, Polly came out of the house, looking lovely in an antique lace dress. Lydia knew the gown had belonged to Brigham's first wife, Isabel, and that Polly had rescued the beautiful garment from a trunk and altered it to fit. The bride was truly breathtaking, with her dark hair wound into a single thick plait, through which she'd tucked bits of baby's breath and wild tiger lilies and violets that grew in the woods.

Lydia's eyes filled with tears. Polly was a good woman who had made some errors in judgment, that was all, and even then, while her own heart splintered inside her, Lydia could not despise the other woman for what she was doing. She genuinely hoped Polly would be happy as a wife, though if she wished anything for Brigham, it was a toothache that would last until he was eighty.

The strains of the wedding march began, played not only by fiddle, but with the wavering whine of a saw blade, and the eager spectators took their places. Joe patted Lydia's hand again, then got up to move to the back of the grassy aisle between the rows of chairs and take Polly's arm. The preacher, a pleasant-looking middle-aged man with a bald spot and a homemade suit, took his place in the archway of the gazebo.

Brigham stood at the foot of the steps, facing the pastor, his broad back to the guests and ramrod stiff.

Inwardly, Lydia wept, though her demeanor was proud, even haughty.

Joe and Polly went by, Polly's gown swishing softly over the grass, and as she passed, the bride met Lydia's gaze. A bittersweet emotion arched between them, and then Polly was standing beside Brigham.

The pastor began saying the holy words, eliciting the sacred vows that, as far as Lydia was concerned, bound a woman and man to each other until the end of time.

There was a stir at the back of the gathering at one point, but Lydia paid no attention. Her throat was so tightly constricted that it hurt, and it took all her determination to hold back tears.

Finally, fatefully, the pastor looked out over Polly's lace-veiled head and Brigham's dark, bent one, and asked in a clear voice, "Is there anyone here who can give just cause why these two should not be joined in holy matrimony?"

Lydia had certainly never planned to stand up, or, God forbid, to speak—but she did. She was on her feet, and the words were leaving her mouth before she could stop herself.

"I can," she said, in chorus with a masculine voice making the same statement. Out of the corner of her eye Lydia saw Devon standing in the aisle, leaning on the top of his cane.

There was a furor, of course. The guests chattered among themselves, and Brigham and Polly both turned to face the congregation.

Brigham was grinning brazenly at Lydia, while Polly watched Devon with an expression of mingled fear and hope.

"This marriage is a fraud," Devon said clearly, obstinately. "I won't let my brother throw away his life this way."

Polly stumbled toward Devon, clutching her bouquet of wildflowers, and he stiffened when she stood before him. Brigham was still watching Lydia, mouth curved, pewter eyes bright with amusement.

"I'll marry you myself first," Devon said, without a shred of kindness or love in his voice, and Polly sagged a little.

"Wait a minute," Brigham interrupted, stepping away from the gazebo altar to approach. "I want to hear Miss McQuire's objection to the marriage."

Lydia's face went crimson, and she lifted her chin. "It's a simple one. Polly deserves far better than you, Mr. Quade!"

Brigham laughed, but his glance would have seared steel when he turned it on his prodigal brother. "I came here today to take myself a wife," he said, raising another excited outcry of speculation from the guests. "And Polly hasn't stated her preference of a husband."

Polly looked wildly from Brigham to Devon, then to Lydia.

Lydia had already gone so far that there was no point in turning back. She drew a deep breath. She'd almost let Brigham get away because of her pride before, and she wasn't going to make the same mistake again. "You proposed to me recently, Mr. Quade," she said to him, wishing the ground would open so she could disappear. "Were you serious?"

"Yes." Brigham answered in a clear voice, and that insufferable grin still flashed on his face.

"Then I . . ." She paused, swallowed hard. "I accept, if it's not too late."

Brigham held out his hand to her. "Better late than never," he assured her, in a gruff and surprisingly tender voice.

Lydia stepped into the aisle as a cheer rose from the crowd, and went to him. She glanced back once at Joe McCauley, who responded with a sad smile and a shrug, and let Brigham lead her to the altar.

Although later Lydia would hear varying accounts from Charlotte, Millie, Elly, and some of the others, she was aware of very little during the double ceremony that followed. Lydia married Brigham, and Polly took Devon for a husband, legally this time.

Polly and Devon disappeared soon after the vows had been exchanged, and Lydia didn't think either of them looked particularly happy.

For her part, she was in a daze of joy, and stricken with the pure brazen audacity of what she'd done. The gold band Brigham had bought for Polly was on her finger instead, and for the moment that was all that mattered. She would face the awesome ramifications of what she'd done later, when she'd found her balance.

An enterprising photographer had sailed into Quade's Harbor on a recent mail boat, having heard about the upcoming wedding while taking pictures of working men in Seattle. He posed Lydia beside Brigham, in front of the gazebo, and imprinted their sober images on magical photographic plates.

There were so many explosions and flashes of light that Lydia was nearly blinded. Finally, Brigham took her by the hand and led her away to have cake and punch.

Lydia's vision was finally clearing when Charlotte and Millie approached, one on either side of her, and caught her in an embrace. Seeing the joyous acceptance in the faces of her stepdaughters did a lot to settle Lydia's jangling nerves.

"I didn't even dare *hope* to have you for a mama!" Millie confided, after tugging at Lydia's practical skirts and gesturing for her to bend down.

Lydia planted a kiss on the child's forehead. "You're the best part of this bargain," she whispered back, "you and Charlotte."

Only when the girls had dashed away again, to enjoy the yard full of guests, did Brigham reveal that he'd heard his bride's remark. He arched one brow, his eyes shining like polished silver, and said, "I consider it my duty to prove to you, Mrs. Quade, that there are other things to like about this 'bargain' of ours than my daughters."

His words made Lydia very nervous, just as he had intended. She blushed. "I merely meant—"

Brigham cupped his hand under her chin and cut off the flow of words, gently but firmly. "Here's what *I* mean," he said, his voice as low and intimate as a caress, audible only to her, in spite of the crowd. "You've been a sweet torment to me from the moment I laid eyes on you. Pleasuring you on that bed in the cabin, without being able to take you completely afterward, was such an exquisite torture that my nerves hummed with the strain for days. Now, my dear and lovely little Yankee, you are my wife, and I intend to keep my promise."

Lydia swallowed hard. She felt overheated and a bit faint and it was all glorious. "Wh-What promise?" she whispered.

Brigham leaned down, tasted her mouth with his own, and then spoke close to her ear. "I'm going to make love to you so thoroughly, Mrs. Quade, that even the mountains will hear you calling my name in passion."

A hot shiver went through Lydia, and she tried to pull away in sheer embarrassment, but Brigham wouldn't let her go. He nibbled at her earlobe for a moment, sending a sweet fire rushing through her veins from that vulnerable point, and as innocent as she was, she knew this was a portent of what he meant to do to her later.

Her nipples jutted against the gray-striped fabric of her dress, and a low, desperate sound escaped her.

Brigham laughed and then kissed her so deeply that she was like a drunk person when he let her go, and the wedding guests cheered raucously.

There was more fiddle music, accompanied by the strains of the mournfully sweet saw blade, and the celebrants danced in the grass. Brigham whirled Lydia through one waltz, never taking his eyes from her face, and pulled her away toward the back of the house when the song ended.

This was it, Lydia thought, with excited resignation and not a little fear. Her bridegroom was about to take her upstairs to his room, where she would be expected to remove her clothes and surrender to his attentions.

Except that Brigham pulled her up the path toward the old cabin instead. Somewhere in the middle, he swept her up into his arms.

Lydia was practically breathless. She'd come to see a wedding, and ended up a bride herself, and now her groom was carrying her off for deflowering. It was quite a lot to happen in the space of one day, and she was overwhelmed.

"Do you suppose we could wait?" she asked after they reached the cabin. Brigham stooped to work the latch, then kicked the door open. "Just a little while?"

"Wait for what?" he countered, standing just over the threshold, still holding her. He was watching her lips, as though he found them fascinating.

"I didn't plan on getting married today," Lydia pointed out, somewhat lamely.

He bent close to her ear and told her something else she could plan on getting that day, and his audacity incensed her.

Brigham laughed at her huffy response, set her on her feet and pushed the door shut with the heel of his boot. Then he folded his arms. "What's the matter, Yankee? Having second thoughts?"

Lydia recalled how she'd stood up and stopped the wedding, and was unconsoled by the fact that Devon had spoken up at the same time. "What if I am?" she bristled, smoothing her crumpled dress.

He shrugged. "It won't change anything. I bargained for a wife, and I'm not letting you out of my sight until we've consummated this marriage."

She closed her eyes, feeling another blush flood her face. "Must you be so blunt?"

Brigham made no answer. Instead he reached out and loosened the strings of her bonnet with his finger. Then he let the hat fall back to the floor, and began removing the pins from her hair.

Lydia stood, trembling with docile defiance, while he arranged her blond tresses, running his fingers through their silky length, arranging them on her bosom.

"You are so very lovely," he breathed, resting his hands lightly on her shoulders, beneath the cascade of hair, and then pulling her close. He kissed her, his tongue first teasing her lips to open, then invading and conquering her.

Lydia's knees turned to crumbly paste, and her heart was beating so rapidly that she felt sure it would derail itself.

When the kiss ended, she could barely stand. Brigham held her upright by wrapping one arm around her waist. She leaned back lightly into the curve of his elbow as he used his free hand to open the buttons at the front of her dress.

"It's important that you listen to me now, Lydia," he said, with tender hoarseness, continuing to undress her. "This first time might be a little painful for you, but I'm going to give you all the pleasure you can bear beforehand. In a day or two there will be no hurt at all, I promise you that." He paused to nibble her earlobe again and, at the same time, slipped his hand inside her camisole to cup a bare and eager breast.

The nipple thrust against his palm.

"Did you hear what I said?" he asked, with stern affection.

She could only nod. She'd heard, all right, but she didn't care. The craving for completion was too primitive and all-consuming to allow room for fear. "I—I'll probably cry out, like the other time," she managed, as he proceeded to taste her neck.

Brigham's chuckle was a deep, rich sound, welling from the center of his being. "Oh, yes. I can guarantee that you will, Yankee. I'm going to give you a going-over you'll never forget."

Lydia whimpered again. His words were as treacherous as his caresses, making her dance on the tips of invisible flames. "They'll h-hear me—at the wedding party—"

He leaned down, still supporting her in the curve of his arm, and teased a nipple with the tip of his tongue for a long, torturous interval before answering. "No, Yankee," he assured her, as she moaned in response. "The walls of this cabin are thick, and there's music down there, and laughter and a lot of talk. No one is going to hear you but me." With that, he closed his mouth over the morsel at the peak of her breast and enjoyed it in earnest, and Lydia gave a lusty cry at the assault of pleasure and leaned back over his arm.

He took advantage of that by sliding his free hand down inside her muslin drawers and taking a brazen grip on her femininity.

Her eyes flew open in ecstatic shock, but her vision quickly blurred as he reached through to stroke the moist place. He went right on drawing at her breast.

Lydia's breath came hard and harsh through her throat, and a low whining sound began to bubble out of her, rising from somewhere so deep inside her that it seemed like another world, a separate reality.

Brigham licked her nipple thoroughly before lifting his head. "This first time, Mrs. Quade, I want to be looking straight into your eyes when you finally surrender."

"Oh!" Lydia cried. Her hips were moving faster and faster against his arm, her knees were wide of each other, her back arched. "Oh—God—Brigham—"

He continued to stroke her, but his voice was firm. Even brisk. "Look at me, Lydia," he commanded.

She opened her eyes again, focused on his face, and then the ceiling seemed to splinter, along with the sky beyond it. She shouted in joyous response as Brigham thrust his fingers inside her and her body buckled around them in a greedy clasp. "Oh—oh—oh—" she said, peaking with each separate cry.

Brigham caught her when she sagged against him in relief, carried her to the bed where he had mastered her once before, and began removing his own clothes. When he was fully, magnificently naked, he took away all that remained of Lydia's garments—her drawers and stockings.

"Feeling better?" he asked, with deceptive sweetness, stretching out beside her and planting slow, audacious kisses on her belly.

"Yes," Lydia gasped. "No. I don't know." And she

didn't, for deep in its most secret places, her body was still responding to this newest lesson from Brigham.

He parted the veil of silk and kissed her there. "Does that help?"

Lydia moaned like a woman taken by fever. "No—oh, *no*—"

He began to enjoy her, slowly, and with obvious enthusiasm.

"Brigham," she pleaded breathlessly, even as her hands flew up to grip the iron bed rails above her head. "Oh, Brigham—not yet—don't make me—"

But Brigham was merciless. He pried her fingers loose from the bedstead, turned her over and brought her down onto his mouth.

The muscles in her buttocks tensed and untensed as the relentless licking and sucking went on. And on.

"Oh, God!" Lydia cried in desperation, clasping the bed rails again and writhing.

The loving intensified. By the time Brigham was ready to consummate their marriage, he'd turned Lydia's body to pleasure with such precision and skill that she hardly noticed the pain of taking him inside her. There was another violent, glorious upheaval within her, in fact, although this one was spiritual as well as physical. From that moment on, Lydia knew she was truly Brigham's wife, a separate being and yet part of a whole, too.

Beyond the cabin's single window the world grew dark and silver stars sprouted in the black sky. Music, singing, and laughter still rolled up the hill from the wedding place, and a boat's horn sounded from the harbor.

Polly Quade—and now she truly *was* Polly Quade, for she had a signed paper to prove it—sank into the chair where she'd kept her vigil when Devon was hurt, and looked down at the bouquet of wilting wildflowers in her lap. The room was dim, but Polly didn't light a lamp. Nor did she feel drawn to the merriment still going on below the windows, in the yard.

She leaned back and closed her eyes, and it was as though Devon was standing there in front of her as he had that afternoon, after their marriage, leaning on his cane and glaring at her.

"You wanted a husband," he'd growled, his eyes dark with contempt, his jawline hard. "Now you've got one. Your baby will have a name. I hope you're satisfied."

Polly had gazed at him in stupefaction and pain, blinking back shaming tears. From the moment Devon had interrupted the first wedding, earlier, she had known he hadn't returned because he loved her, but because he wanted to save his brother from the clutches of a wicked woman. Still, she'd hoped for something more than the acid bitterness of his anger.

"You did it for Brigham," she'd said. It hadn't been a bid for sympathy, just a simple statement of fact.

"And for Lydia," Devon had replied coldly. "Now, you have the name, you have the store, you can have all of Quade's Harbor for all I care! There's a boat waiting for me at the wharf, and I'm leaving."

Polly had swallowed. "So soon?"

His look had been almost cruel. "Did you want me to stay and consummate this marriage, Polly?" he'd drawled. "Well, you can forget that idea. Brigham and Lydia will do all the honeymooning the situation calls for, I'm sure. Good-bye."

With that, he'd made his way to the door, quite gracefully, considering he still needed the stick to walk. Polly had wished, in those desperate moments, that Devon could have applied such determination to forgiving and loving her.

She had bolted out of the chair when she heard the door close behind him, but in the end she'd dropped back into the seat, shut her eyes and gripped the chair arms with all her strength.

If she'd asked Devon to stay, to give her another chance, if she'd *begged* Devon to stay, he would only have mocked her, and she knew she wouldn't be able to bear any more of that. So she just sat there, grieving, knowing he was leaving her, knowing he might never be back.

Now, when he'd been gone long enough for shadows to stream across the floor and wind themselves at her feet like the black ribbons of mourning, she finally raised her hands to her face and wept.

Joe McCauley stood at the end of the wharf, looking out at the dark water, which was spattered with the wavering reflections of stars. Never, except for those black days of misery following his closest brush with death during the war, and the staggering moment when he'd learned that his wife Susan and their children had perished of the fever, had he ever felt so hopeless.

His disappointment was a grinding, searing thing within him, and yet he was a reasonable man and he knew Lydia was happy. For this night, at least. He would not have taken that from her.

He pulled a cheroot from his coat pocket, lit it with a wooden match struck against the piling, and drew in the soothing smoke. He supposed tobacco would turn out to be bad for him, like most of the other things he enjoyed, but on this particular night he needed comforting.

Joe figured no one would blame him, least of all himself, if he just packed up his few belongings and moved on, started over somewhere else. But he'd taken out a loan in Seattle, and his combined house and office were well under way, and for the first time in a long while he had things to look forward to—even without Lydia.

He sighed, drew on the cheroot again. Maybe what he felt for her wasn't true love anyway. Maybe it was gratitude, for the way she'd saved his arm during the war, or plain friendliness, because she was living proof that there was indeed a Deity somewhere, one kindly disposed toward humankind.

Finally, he tossed the thin cigar into the water, where it would disintegrate into nothing, or be eaten by dogfish and cod and other creatures of the Sound. Joseph McCauley would stay in Quade's Harbor, because he

liked the place, and because there was always the chance
that Lydia might need him one day.

He lifted solemn eyes to the big house on the hill, the
windows shining with light, the sounds of celebration
rising like a fragrance from the yard. He raised one hand
in a solitary, drinkless toast to the bride.

"Be happy," he said in a raw whisper.

17

When Lydia awakened on the morning after her impromptu wedding, the single room of the cabin was gilded in golden sunlight. She sighed happily, stretched, and turned, expecting to find her husband in bed beside her.

Instead Brigham was up and fully dressed, though in plain trousers, a work shirt, cork boots, and suspenders, instead of the fine suit he'd worn the day before. Evidently, someone had brought him fresh clothes from the house.

He came to the bedside with an enamel mug of steaming, fragrant coffee and bent to kiss Lydia's forehead when she sat up.

She was careful to keep herself decently covered with the sheet, and that brought a smile to Brigham's mouth. "Good morning, Mrs. Quade," he said.

Lydia blew delicately on her coffee, stalling, and averted her eyes for a moment. "Good morning," she murmured. She'd spent most of the night tossing and moaning in this man's arms, but in the daylight she suddenly felt shy, and more than a little ashamed of her unbridled responses.

The legs of a simple wooden chair scraped against the floor as Brigham drew it close by hooking his foot under one of the rungs. He turned it backward and sat astride the seat, his arms resting across the back.

"Lydia."

She raised her eyes to his face, embarrassment heating her cheeks. "Yes?"

Brigham smiled, reached out and took her coffee before answering. A moment after he'd set the mug aside on the floor, he tugged the sheet down to reveal her full, warm breasts, with their hard tips of dusky rose.

"Don't hide yourself from me," he said. His gaze moved over her bounty boldly, without apology, and yet there was something reverent in his expression, too. "You're too beautiful for that."

Lydia reddened under his perusal, but she didn't try to yank up the blankets, even though instinct demanded it, because she knew Brigham would only wrench them down again.

He made a sound that was part chuckle, part groan. Then, shaking his head like a man who's just intercepted a right cross from a grizzly bear, he stood and put the chair back in its place. He even bent down to fetch Lydia's coffee and hold it out to her.

She still didn't cover herself. Brigham's perusal made her feel as beautiful as a stage actress, and the sensation was addictive.

"I'd appreciate it," he said, from the area of the door, "if you would move your things back into the main house as soon as possible. Charlotte and Millie can help you—bring whatever furniture you want, and leave the rest for the next tenant."

Lydia might have resented the offhandedness of his command, or the very fact that it *was* a command, however politely phrased, if she hadn't still been under the influence of his lovemaking. She felt as though she'd taken some magical potion, forbidden to all but wizards, goddesses, and angels.

Only when her husband had been gone for some

minutes did she finally rise from the bed, wash at the white enamel basin, and get dressed. She left her long hair free around her shoulders, since there was no brush in evidence.

She couldn't help smiling as she looked at herself in the cracked, undulant mirror. She'd been the same woman the day before, in the same gray-and-pink-striped dress, and yet she was a very different person, too.

She stripped the sheets from the bed, not wanting anyone else to see the evidence of her surrendered virginity, and stuffed them into one of the pillowcases. She couldn't very well carry that particular laundry to the big house, where Charlotte and Millie were, and some guests probably still lingered, let alone bring it to the cottage for washing.

Thus, Lydia went to the stream that ran through the dense trees and blackberry thickets behind the cabin. She scrubbed the sheets carefully, pounding them clean with a rock the way she'd done so many times while traveling with the hospital corps, and draped them over bushes to dry in the sunlight.

That done, she went down the hill to the house, sneaked in through the side door, where the screened sun porch was, and hurried up the stairs. In Aunt Persephone's dressing room she found brushes, combs, and pins. She put her hair up in a soft, flyaway style, and then proceeded downstairs to the kitchen.

"Mornin', Mrs. Quade," Jake Feeny greeted her, with a friendly grin.

The name warmed Lydia's soul like sunshine on frosty ground. "Good morning, Mr. Feeny," she replied. "Are the girls around?"

"They're down watchin' all the buildin's go up," the cook answered, ladling oatmeal into a bowl. "You sit down now, Mrs. Quade, and have yourself some breakfast."

Lydia was not used to being waited on, and she didn't intend to make a habit of it, believing that would have a poor effect on her character. Nevertheless, she was hungry, and she had a lot of work ahead of her, so she thanked him and reached for the cream pitcher and the sugar bowl.

"The general store will be finished and open for business soon," she commented, and immediately thought of Polly and Devon. She was chagrined to realize this was the first time either of them had crossed her mind since the wedding.

"Yes," Jake answered, pouring coffee for Lydia and for himself, and joining her at the table. "There's the doc's place, too. He's going to have a nice little house there at the end of Main Street, with two good rooms and a place in the back to do his doctorin'."

Lydia set down her spoon and lowered her eyes for a moment. She hadn't thought about Joseph McCauley, either, and the prospect of facing him was not an appealing one. She would have to go to Joseph immediately and apologize for any embarrassment or injury she might have caused him the day before, when she'd sat beside him at the wedding and then bolted up and married Brigham.

Jake evidently hadn't noticed her introspection. "The school is takin' shape, too, and then there's the, er, boardinghouse."

Lydia looked at him in question. "Boardinghouse? I hadn't heard about that."

The cook rose to fetch the coffeepot. "I don't reckon you would have," he muttered.

"I beg your pardon?" Lydia asked politely.

"You'd best just go look for yourself, Mrs. Quade. I shouldn't have said anything."

Lydia took up her spoon again. All this fuss over a boardinghouse. As far as she was concerned, it was a good idea; the town badly needed accommodations for travelers and unmarried men and women.

Later, when Lydia arrived in the center of town, she was delighted to see that the meetinghouse was indeed under construction. Men were laying a stone foundation, while others dug a well, and there were stacks of seasoned lumber and kegs of nails on hand.

Lydia permitted herself to imagine the completed structure, with desks and a chalkboard and lots of books, and smiled. At Christmas her students would put on a pageant, she decided, and she'd make sure there were oranges and peppermint sticks for all of them.

"Lydia?"

She started, turned to see Dr. McCauley standing beside her. She hadn't expected to encounter him just yet, and she wasn't prepared. Her tongue rose to the roof of her mouth and cemented itself there, immovable.

"Or should I call you Mrs. Quade now?" Joseph asked, and there was no condemnation in his tone or expression.

Lydia swallowed, pried her tongue loose. It moved awkwardly at first. "Of—of course you'll call me Lydia," she said. She raised her eyes to his gentle face. "Oh, Joseph, I—"

He took both her hands in his own. "Don't, Lydia. You needn't explain. Just tell me that you and I can still be friends."

She felt tears form in her eyes. They had a history together, she and Joseph, forged in the fearsome blood and dust and noise of war, and it was something of a miracle that they'd found each other again. She cherished the bond between them. "I expected you to be angry," she said, turning her head slightly and blinking a few times.

Joseph sighed. "No, darlin'—I couldn't be angry with you, not ever. I won't say I'm not disappointed, but I've suffered worse things and always gotten over them in due time."

His words gave Lydia pause, unsettled her a little. She tried to imagine Brigham saying he couldn't ever be angry with her and failed utterly. With this man there would have been peace and poetry; with Brigham for a husband, she would know passion, perhaps even violent passion, and any fool could safely predict the occasional loud argument.

She stood on tiptoe and kissed Joseph's cheek lightly. "Show me this house of yours," she said. "I've already heard a little about it from Jake Feeny, but I want to see for myself."

The framing was already up for Joseph's simple cottage. There was a well being dug, and, at some distance of course, a pit for the privy. He would have two rooms, one to sleep in, the other for cooking, reading, eating, and the like.

"I'll be needing some help sometimes," Joseph said, looking out at the water and the jagged white peaks of the mountains as he spoke. "I don't suppose you've ever delivered a baby, for all your experience, have you? Once people start moving into Quade's Harbor in earnest, I'm going to need some help."

A tendril of hair blew against Lydia's cheek, tickling, and she brushed it away. "Your soldiers shot ours with rifles and cannon and sometimes plain old ordinary field stones, Dr. McCauley," she said wryly. "They didn't make them pregnant."

Joseph laughed, and the last of the tension between them dissipated, like a fog burned away by sunshine.

Lydia touched his arm, still smiling, glad the rough spot had been smoothed over. "As it happens, I have done some midwifing in my time. My father was a doctor, you will recall, and he had a practice in Fall River before the war. I often helped at birthings."

The physician looked pleased, then a thoughtful frown came over his face. "But you weren't married then," he pointed out after a moment's consideration. "Your husband might have serious objections to your serving as a nurse."

The idea! Lydia straightened her spine and lifted her chin a notch. "I feel certain Mr. Quade will understand my desire to practice the healing arts," she said, though she didn't feel certain at all. When it came right down to it, she didn't have any idea what her husband expected of her—besides more of the glorious mischief they'd engaged in the night before, that is—because she didn't know *him*. Not the way a wife should know the man she's married, anyway.

"Perhaps he will understand," Joseph conceded in a musing tone, turning to gaze at the rising framework of a two-story building on a spit of land out beyond the mill. A moment later he was looking into Lydia's eyes. "But will you?"

Lydia was chilled by his words, though she tried to pass them off lightly. Standing there in the dusty street—the rain so typical of the Puget Sound country had not come in a while—she shaded her eyes and studied the newest structure. "That must be the boardinghouse," she said.

Joseph coughed, as though he'd caught something in his throat. "Boardinghouse?" he echoed. "Is that what Brigham told you?"

She could see tents on the site, and patches of bright color moving about, like chips of painted glass in a low tide. "Brigham didn't tell me anything," she said, squinting. "Who are those women over there, in those fancy dresses? Are they going to be boarders?"

"You might say that," Joseph allowed, taking his watch from the pocket of his vest and consulting it soberly.

"When did they arrive?" Lydia's heart was beating a bit faster than usual, and there was a niggling sensation in the pit of her stomach.

"Yesterday," her friend answered reluctantly. "They probably came in on the same freighter Devon did." He studied his watch again, as though unable to recognize the numerals. "If you have any more questions, Lydia, you'd best present them to your husband."

Lydia had too many other things to do to go trailing after Brigham. Besides, encounters with him took a certain mental energy, and she hadn't had an opportunity to rebuild what she'd expended in the night. She decided to ask about the boardinghouse at supper.

Seeing the children playing happily in the yard of her cottage, Lydia remembered the kitten and hurried toward the gate, full of guilt.

Millie immediately came forward, brought the small creature from the pocket of her pinafore and held her up for Lydia's inspection. "Don't worry," she chimed. "I've already given Ophelia some milk, and she's quite content, riding in my pocket."

Lydia smiled, deeply relieved, and bent to kiss her stepdaughter's forehead. "Thank you."

Charlotte approached. "Must we have lessons today?" she asked, giving the question a plaintive note. "The weather is so splendid!"

After pretending to consider the idea solemnly, having taken Ophelia from Millie's grasp and begun stroking her, Lydia said, "Well, it's Monday, and it is generally bad form to be idle on that day, since one tends to get the week off to a somewhat slipshod start. A good beginning makes for a good ending, you know. However, since I've just been married, I'll let you have this one holiday."

Millie and Charlotte ran cheering back to the yard, while Lydia proceeded into the cottage that had been her home for such a short time. In the small bedroom, she exchanged yesterday's clothes and linens for fresh things, while the kitten frolicked and tumbled on the bed.

She replaced a few of the pins holding her hair in its soft, loose knot, then got out her satchel and began packing her smaller belongings. She had not been at the task long when someone knocked at the front door.

"It's only me!" Polly called, letting herself in. A few moments later she stood in the doorway of Lydia's room.

There were still shadows under Polly's eyes, and her skin had a disconcerting pallor to it, for all her feeble attempts to look and sound normal.

"Congratulations, Mrs. Quade," Polly said gently. "You have the look of a happy woman."

Lydia flushed, taking a camisole from her satchel, refolding the garment, putting it back. She was happy, she realized, both emotionally and physically. "There are no hard feelings, then?"

Polly laughed, but the sound had a hollow note. "No, of course not." She sighed, and Lydia saw that her sister-in-law was leaning against the doorjamb, her arms folded. "I think Brigham was hoping you would speak up when the preacher asked for objections to the marriage."

"I doubt that," Lydia said, dismissing the idea. She wanted to know about Polly. "How are you and Devon getting along?" she asked, even though she dreaded the answer.

"We're not," Polly answered, with a disconsolate breeziness that pulled at Lydia's heart. "My husband left again, not long after the wedding. I thought you knew."

Lydia had known, of course, that Devon and Polly's problems hadn't been solved by his insistence on marriage, but she'd hoped it meant Devon was willing to make an effort. "Oh, Polly," she whispered, moving toward the other woman and taking her forearms in her hands, "that's dreadful!"

She saw Polly's broken heart in her eyes, in her one-shoulder shrug. "At least the baby will have its proper name, and there's the general store to provide a future for us. I'm better off than most women in my position, I should think."

"Still—"

"I don't want you worrying about me, Lydia," Polly broke in. "It's time I rolled up my sleeves and made something of my life anyhow. Who knows? Maybe Devon's leaving was the best thing that could have happened to me."

Lydia embraced her. "If you need anything, you'll let me know, won't you?"

Polly sniffled and then nodded. "I've always wanted a sister," she said, with a shaky smile.

"So have I," Lydia replied. "Now, let's sit down and have a cup of tea. I want to know what you're planning for the store."

Taking the kitten along in her pocket, Lydia went to the wood box for kindling and built up a fire. Then, leaving the back door open so some of the heat would escape, she carried the teakettle out and worked the pump handle until it was filled with water.

"Have you been over to look at the boardinghouse?" she asked, setting the kettle on the stove to begin heating, and reaching for the tin of tea leaves.

It was only happenstance that Lydia glanced in Polly's

direction a moment after she'd spoken, and saw her go even paler than before.

"B-Boardinghouse?" Polly echoed, sounding distinctly uncomfortable.

Lydia stood still, the china teapot in one hand, the canister in the other. "Yes. That big building around on the other side of the mill."

Polly ran her tongue over her lips. "You're not teasing, are you?"

"Teasing?" Lydia was mystified. "Why on earth would I do that?"

Polly rolled her eyes and sighed heavily. "Dear God, you're serious," she decided in dismay. "Lydia, that isn't a boardinghouse. It's a saloon and brothel."

Lydia's mouth dropped open. She'd been around her share of saloons, even played piano in them for her supper, down in San Francisco, and she was well aware of the seedy establishments on the sawdust-covered ground of Seattle's Skid Road. But this was plain, simple, isolated Quade's Harbor. Having a brothel and saloon there was like putting up a privy in heaven.

"Does Brigham know about this?" she asked in an urgent tone after several moments had passed.

Polly stared at her. "Does he know? Lydia, Brigham owns Quade's Harbor. He imported the women from Seattle himself, and he's backing the saloon financially."

After dragging a chair back from the table, Lydia sank into it. She felt a little dizzy. "I don't believe it," she marveled. "It's like giving his own men poison!"

Now it was Polly's turn to be sympathetic. She reached out and covered Lydia's hand with hers. "I'm the last person who would disagree with you," she said. "But men do see things from a different perspective, you know."

Lydia imagined poor Magna Holmetz, as an example, waiting at home, pregnant, friendless, unable to speak the language, while her husband spent his hard-earned wages on whiskey, cards, and women. From there it was easy to picture the drinking disease spreading, until children were going without shoes and coats and even food, all because of personal vice.

"Lydia?" Polly gave her hand a little shake.

But Lydia was still caught up in her thoughts. Her own father had been too fond of whiskey, and perhaps women and gambling, as well. Because of that, she'd grown up with holes in her stockings and a perennial gnawing in her stomach, which didn't abate until she'd gone to war and had access to the United States Army's mess tents.

"He can't do this," she said, pushing back her chair and rising.

"He can't do what?" Polly countered anxiously, standing, too. "Lydia, your husband can do just about anything, short of murder. This is his town, and every one here depends on him, one way or the other."

Trembling, Lydia raised her hands to her cheeks in a vain attempt to cool them. She was distracted, started in one direction, then the other, then stopped in furious confusion.

She'd been such a fool.

"Lydia?" Polly pleaded, worried.

Lydia sorted out the back door from the front and headed toward the latter, setting the kitten down before she went out. She condemned herself as naive and stupid as she walked toward the gate, Polly scrambling after her.

If Brigham was building that saloon, if he'd brought the fancy women in himself, he was surely planning to patronize the place in the bargain. The thought was absolutely unbearable to Lydia, even though she knew, on a practical level, that most prosperous men kept mistresses and went uncondemned for it, even by their wives.

Just as they passed the site of Joseph's future home, Polly caught up to Lydia and stopped her, gripping her arm with surprising strength. "Listen to me!" she hissed. "You can't go to Brigham now, in this state of mind. You've got to wait until you can think rationally."

Lydia could barely stand still; she was filled with quiet hysteria. She drew a deep breath and let it out slowly. "I'm such an idiot!" she blurted, near tears.

Polly gave her an affectionate shake. "Nonsense. Now, come back to the cottage, Lydia. You and I are going to have our tea."

Although she was still chafing to find Brigham and confront him with all the restraint of a chicken tossed into a washtub full of hot water, she knew Polly was right. She would not do her cause any good by approaching her husband in a scalding rage.

She returned to the cottage, or more properly Polly towed her there, and methodically finished brewing the tea. She even got out the box of chocolates hidden in her bureau; there were still four pieces left, even though the children had eaten most of the candy as rewards for diligence at their lessons.

Lydia forced herself to sit at the table, facing her sister-in-law, repeatedly drawing deep breaths and letting them out slowly. After a time, when the tea had steeped and she and Polly had finished off the chocolates, she began to feel calmer.

Slightly calmer.

They drank their tea, like ladies of the manor, and talked of inconsequential things, such as the fabrics Polly planned to carry in the store. She meant to have chocolates, as well, she said, and books. There was more to life than meat and potatoes, after all, and the finer items shouldn't be dismissed as luxuries. Some things were staples to the spirit, she maintained, like flour and beans were to the body.

After an hour Polly reluctantly took her leave. There was a crew working on the store, and she wanted to make sure they were implementing the substantial changes she'd made in the building's interior design.

"You will be calm," Lydia murmured to herself as she cleared away the tea things. "You *will* be calm."

Finally, when the place was as tidy as if she and Polly had never been there at all, she put the last of the cream in a saucer for Ophelia and went out.

Lydia found her husband in the mill, pulling lumber off a steam-powered conveyer as it came from the saw. He was soaked in sweat and covered with plain dirt and sawdust, and his bride felt her sentiments soften just a little. Brigham was an intelligent man, if stubborn, and he would surely see the brothel-saloon issue rationally once she explained it.

Despite the tender way he had initiated her into marriage the night before, and the way he'd looked at her that morning, making her feel as lovely as Aphrodite, he did not seem pleased to see her.

In fact, after shouting to another man to take over for him—and one was forced to yell in order to be heard over the screech of the huge mill saw—he took Lydia's elbow in a firm grasp. He marched her over the floor, which was covered in fragrant sawdust, and through the great open archway that served as a door. The din was only slightly less irritating there.

"What do you want?" he demanded.

Lydia bridled, pulled her arm from his hand. "There's no need to be rude. I'm your wife, after all, or have you forgotten?" *Already,* she added in the privacy of her mind, thinking of those bawdy women and their "boardinghouse."

A grin split his filthy face. "Not a chance," he replied. "Have you moved your things into my room?"

Lydia folded her arms, feeling a need to brace herself against his damnable charm. "No, and I won't until we've settled the question of that saloon," she whispered in a hiss, only too aware of the curious stares from passing mill workers. "What are they looking at?"

Brigham's grin had become a frown of bewildered irritation. "You. Women don't come to the mill, as a general rule. It isn't safe." He placed his hands on his hips and leaned close to her, smelling gloriously of sweat, raw timber, and man. "Now, about the saloon."

She retreated a step. "Yes," she said. "I'm afraid I'm going to have to demand an explanation."

Brigham threw his head back and gave one raucous burst of laughter, and his silvery eyes glittered when he looked at her again. "You *demand* an explanation?" he inquired, folding his arms now and closing the distance she'd managed to put between them a moment before.

"Forgive me, Mrs. Quade, but I'm the head of this family, and if anybody does any demanding, it will be me."

Lydia flushed hotly. The proud, rebellious blood of her ancestors, who had acquitted themselves well in the Revolution, and again in the War of 1812, stirred like sediment in the bottom of her heart and surged into her veins.

"If that's the way you're going to talk to me, *Mister* Quade," she seethed, "then I'll thank you not to speak to me at all! Furthermore, I will have an explanation, and I will have it now!"

Brigham took her arm again, held it fast when she tried to pull away, and thrust her toward his tree-stump office. They surprised Mr. Harrington and Esther in the middle of a chaste kiss, and Brigham barked, "Go do your sparking somewhere else, Harrington!"

Poor Esther looked mortified.

"That was very rude!" Lydia spat at her husband when the hapless lovers had made their hasty retreat.

Brigham glared at her for a long moment, then relaxed his clamped jaw and turned away to ladle a drink from the water bucket. She could see the powerful play of muscles in his back and shoulders as he lifted the dipper to his mouth, even through the shirt he wore.

Lydia struggled to regain a hold on her temper. Polly had said angry words would get her nowhere, with Brigham Quade at least, and she knew her friend was right.

"Do you understand that those women will sleep with men for money?" she whispered, awed. "Don't you know there will be drinking, and gambling, and carousing?"

Brigham turned to face his wife at last, his eyes dancing with an amusement that infuriated her. He feigned a look of astonished chagrin, a mockery of the sincere one Esther had worn when she'd been caught kissing Mr. Harrington a few minutes before. "You can't be serious, Mrs. Quade!"

Lydia's temper was rising again. "I am quite serious, Mr. Quade," she countered. "I want you to close that saloon down and send those awful women away. Now. Today!"

Her husband placed his hands against the edge of his desk and leaned toward her, his eyebrows about to disappear into the shock of dusty dark hair that had fallen across his forehead. "The saloon stays," he said evenly, "and so do the women. And that's final."

18

*L*YDIA DIDN'T LET HER MISGIVINGS SHOW AS SHE GLARED up at Brigham, there in the shadowy confines of his office. She decided to handle him the same way she'd managed a certain irritable bulldog in her neighborhood back in Fall River—by looking fierce herself and not revealing so much as a hint of trepidation.

Unlike the bulldog, however, Brigham was not intimidated.

Even though some instinct told her to button her lip, Lydia just couldn't obey it. She'd had no real experience at loving a man before, of course, and her feelings carried her along on the crest of a tumultuous flood tide—often to places she didn't want to go.

"I imagine," she said shakily, "that you intend to frequent this—this den of depravity?"

Brigham laughed. Damn him, he actually *laughed*. "'Den of depravity'?" he echoed. "Now you're starting to sound like Reverend Prophet."

Lydia reddened. "Kindly do not try to skirt the point, Mr. Quade," she said evenly. "You vowed fidelity to me, just yesterday, and I would like to know whether or not you still hold that pledge in your heart."

He leaned against the side of his desk and folded his arms, his eyes narrowed thoughtfully as he regarded her. "You sound like a character in one of Charlotte's novels," he observed.

Unwilling to be bested, or shunted onto another track like an empty railroad car, Lydia returned his parry. "How would you know that unless you'd read them?" she asked, neither expecting nor awaiting an answer. "It will do you no good, sir, to hedge my questions."

"All right." The expression in his slate gray eyes was unreadable as he regarded her, and Lydia saw no rancor in his attitude or bearing. "Here is your answer, Mrs. Quade. As long as you are a proper wife to me, I will be an honorable husband to you."

Lydia was reminded of a day spent on an icy pond near Fall River, with the family of a schoolmate. The older boys had worn skates, and pulled the other children around behind them, at dizzying speeds. They'd made a great, screaming snake, twisting and gliding over the bumpy surface, and she had been at the tail end, filled with terror and glee.

The feeling she had now, as she looked up into her husband's face, was much the same.

"As long as I am a proper wife to you," Lydia repeated quietly, pacing like a lawyer in front of a jury box, "you will be an honorable husband to me. That is a perfectly fair agreement, provided your definition of the word 'honorable' is the same as mine."

Brigham shoved a dirty hand through dusty, sawdust-filled hair, and Lydia marveled at how attractive she found him, even in that untidy state.

"I will never turn to another woman as long as you will receive me in your bed."

Lydia blushed at the bluntness of his words, even though she'd wanted the unvarnished truth. She waited, hoping he couldn't guess by her appearance that her whole body was thrumming with the memory of his lovemaking, and with anticipation of welcoming him again. "Suppose I am ill, or otherwise indisposed?"

He sighed, and a tiny muscle under his left temple

knotted, then relaxed again. "You're asking if I would remain faithful if you were sick, or in the last stages of bearing my child, I presume?"

She nodded, wildly embarrassed, and at the same time, desperate to know. "Yes."

The fingers of his right hand thumped against his upper arm. "I want more children, Lydia. You will find me the most devoted of husbands during your confinement. As for illness, I would be unshakably loyal—provided I didn't think the malady you suffered was really a convenience designed to keep me from your bed."

Lydia was still then, facing him, trying to read his remarkable face. "As you come to know me better, Brigham, you will realize that I am not the sort to feign illness in order to gain an advantage."

He leaned toward her, arms still folded, voice lowered to a mocking whisper. "Are we through now, wife? I have a great deal of work to do."

She drew a deep breath and let it out again, slowly. "Not exactly. There is still the matter of the . . . brothel." The last word tasted sour on her tongue, like a dill pickle gone bad. "It would not be fair for me to be satisfied with your promise not to frequent the establishment . . ." She paused, narrowed her eyes as she studied him for a long moment, then continued. ". . . if indeed you've actually *made* such a promise—when other women's husbands most certainly would go there to drink spirits and spend their wages. As your wife, I have as much responsibility to the women of this town as you have to the men. I must take a stand."

A flush glowed beneath Brigham's suntan and the layer of dirt, and the look in his eyes did not bode well for social progress. "I will not close the saloon," he said tersely. "In case you haven't noticed, the great majority of men in this town *have* no wives. If there were no whiskey or women here, they wouldn't stay, and I would be out of business."

Instinct made Lydia retreat a step, but she wasn't willing to concede defeat by any stretch of mind or spirit.

"Nonsense. Your workers have stayed all this while. You've built that fancy house and filled it with fine things from all over the world—"

"When I came here," Brigham broke in, with a voice that vibrated like the gathering of thunder in the far distance, "there was very little competition, and I was able to keep my workers because I was good to them and because there was no place else for them to go. Now there are timber operations being set up all over Washington Territory, and if my people aren't happy, they can simply catch the next mail boat back to Seattle. Before a day passed, they would have new jobs."

Lydia swallowed. "But surely you see—"

Brigham took his watch from the pocket of his trousers and, with a practiced and very irritated flick of one thumb, snapped open the case. "We will talk about this later, Mrs. Quade. I would suggest that you go home."

Lydia stared at him, appalled and amazed at the dismissal. She saw that she had made little or no progress with Brigham, and she was thoroughly discouraged. "What?"

"I said, go home," Brigham told her, rounding the desk and stopping to look down into her furious face. "After I've finished my work, had a long swim in the pond, and eaten my supper, I will be happy to listen to your grievances."

She couldn't think why it surprised her to find herself at the end of his list of things to do that day, but surprise her it did. She opened her mouth to protest, then closed it again.

Brigham touched the front of her dress with his fingertips, causing the nipples to strain against the fabric. "Go home," he said for the third time. "If you don't leave now, I can't promise I won't have you right here."

Lydia trembled, partly from wanting, partly from rage at his presumption. He plainly believed he could seduce her in his office, in the broad light of day. Even worse, he was right.

She turned, too angry to speak, and stormed out.

Lydia walked briskly past the big house and up the hill

247

to the cabin behind it, her skirts catching on twigs and blackberry vines as she went.

As her eyes burned with tears, so her body throbbed with a need that would not easily be denied. Reaching the cabin, she snatched up the sheets she'd draped over the bushes to dry after washing away the stains of her passage into full womanhood, folded them, and took them back inside.

Her knees were trembling, so she sank into the rocking chair where Brigham had sat to admire her that morning, and clutched the worn wooden arms in her hands. She began to rock, furiously at first, then with a quiet, purposeful rhythm.

At the end of the workday, Brigham walked home, his bone-deep weariness assuaged by the prospect of Lydia. He imagined her waiting for him in the master bedroom, her skin and hair scented, her lush body draped in something silky. She was an intelligent woman, despite her inexperience in the ways of men and women; by now she had surely seen reason and come to terms with the idea of a saloon in Quade's Harbor.

He would have a bath—perhaps Lydia would wash his back—and tell her about his day. He'd missed such wifely ministrations sorely, he realized. He wanted to be fussed over, coddled a little, to take Lydia to his bed and satisfy her thoroughly, to be satisfied himself. After that, over a private dinner in their room, they could work out this small resistance she seemed to have toward whiskey and fast women.

When Brigham opened the door of his room, however, a frown creased his face. There was no trace of Lydia or any of her few possessions, not even the distinctive, spicy scent of her. The pit of his stomach plunged as darkness engulfed all the delectable fantasies he'd been entertaining.

"Lydia?" Even though he knew she wasn't there, knew it to the core of his soul, he couldn't stop himself from calling her name.

Another door creaked, somewhere along the hallway,

and Millie appeared. Brigham saw a scolding expression in her slate-gray eyes. They were so like his, those eyes, that they might have been taken from his own face.

"Where is your stepmother?" he asked. It was the child's presence that gave him the impetus to step over the threshold and stride purposefully to his bureau for clean clothes.

Millie stood in the doorway, small and fierce. "She's at the house on Main Street," the child announced.

Brigham fetched a bar of soap from the mahogany washstand, a rough cotton towel from beneath. "I'm going up to the pond for a bath. I want you to find Lydia and tell her for me that she'd better be here, under this roof, when I get back."

Millie regarded her father with calm sympathy, apparently undaunted by the sternness of his words. "I don't think she'll listen," she said, with alacrity. At the raising of her father's eyebrows, she added, "But I'll try."

As she scampered toward the front stairway, Brigham strode in the direction of the rear one. He thundered through the kitchen, ignoring Jake Feeny and the delicious smells of supper cooking, and stormed up the hill behind the main house.

He supposed this was what he got for going against his own better judgment and taking a wife. If he didn't put his foot down, Lydia would have him trotting behind her like an obedient puppy and saying "Yes, dear" every time she issued a proclamation.

He'd die first.

He didn't look at the cabin as he passed it, because he didn't want to think about loving Lydia. He didn't want to recall the quick, feverish murmurs she'd given as he'd pleasured her, the small sighs, the primitive, demanding groans of submission and wanting as she'd approached fulfillment. . . .

Brigham reached the edge of the pond, kicked off his boots, flung aside his shirt. His pants caught on the physical evidence of his thoughts as he wrenched them off, and he swore. He was as hard as an oak billy club, and the cool water in the pond would be little help.

He took the soap and waded into the water until it reached his chest, then began to wash. He scoured himself from head to foot with furious energy, and when he left the water, his skin stung with cleanliness. His manhood towered against his belly like the mast of a ship.

He dried himself, then dressed quickly in the fresh clothes he'd brought from his room. His tousled hair got no more than a brisk combing with the fingers of his left hand; he carried his dirty shirt and trousers in a bundle in the other arm.

As he walked down the hill, Brigham was very careful not to so much as glance toward the cabin. If he did, he thought, he would probably turn to a pillar of salt, like Lot's wife.

Reaching the backyard of the big house, where Jake was pumping water and doing his damnedest not to look amused, Brigham flung down the laundry.

"Is she back?" he rasped.

Jake's grin showed in his eyes, even though he'd managed to keep his mouth sober-looking. "No, Brig. Guess you'll have to go after her."

"You're damned right I'll go after her," Brigham muttered.

"Maybe you'd better cool down a little first," Jake suggested. "After all, this ain't no ordinary woman you're dealing with. You say the wrong thing and rile Mrs. Quade, why, she might just up and sail out of here forever. Or she could visit herself a judge and have the weddin' undone. Don't think Doc McCauley wouldn't be waitin' for her with open arms, neither. He's a good man, and where the lady is concerned, he'd be willin' to overlook a lot, just to have her at his side."

Brigham was seething. He had never encountered a woman so willfully disobedient as Lydia, and he wasn't quite sure how to deal with her. Furthermore, the thought of her bucking beneath the thrusts of another man's hips—even one he liked as much as Joseph McCauley—filled him with sickness and fury.

"Are you through?" he raged at Jake, taking his anger out on the old cook because he was close at hand.

Jake looked sorely miffed as he waggled a gravy-covered spoon in Brigham's direction. "You mind how you treat Mrs. Quade, Brig," he warned, "or you'll have me to deal with."

Brigham folded his arms and arched one eyebrow, to let his old friend know he wasn't intimidated, then turned and moved back through the house, toward the front door.

He was the head of the Quade household, he made the rules. It was time he impressed this upon Lydia, once and for all.

Lydia had gone so far as to set her valise on the bed and open it, but so far she hadn't begun to pack. She wasn't about to go back to Brigham's house, much as she wanted his company; her convictions wouldn't allow it. Nor could she bring herself to leave Quade's Harbor, though that was what she'd intended to do in the first flush of fury.

She couldn't desert Charlotte and Millie, or the other children in her school, or Polly.

She sat, forlorn, in the chair facing the bed. The kitten, Ophelia, had been doing acrobatics in her lap; now the bold little creature climbed the bodice of her dress, digging its claws into the fabric as it went.

Lydia made no move to remove the cat; she was comforted by its presence and amused by its audacity. When Ophelia gained her shoulder, trembled there uncertainly for a moment, like a mountain climber on a slick rock, and then curled up against her mistress's neck, Lydia's heart was won forever.

Ophelia made a soft sound, a mixture of purring and mewing, as she lent her small comfort. Lydia reached up to caress the tiny bundle of silk with a gentle hand.

This soothing interlude was interrupted by a sudden, crashing knock at the front door.

Ophelia gave a little squeal of alarm and shinnied

down Lydia's back, using her claws for purchase as she went. The kitten crouched and wriggled under one of the pillows, until only her ridiculously tiny tail was visible.

"Coward," Lydia said, smoothing her hair. Any human being, she thought, would have said she was a fine one to be calling names, when she was so scared herself that she would have hidden underneath the bed. Had her dignity allowed it.

"Lydia!" Brigham bellowed her name as she crossed the front room to the door.

She reddened with embarrassment and anger. His behavior would be the talk of Quade's Harbor within minutes, and it might be years before the memory receded.

"Hush!" she cried, wrenching open the door. She was crimson-faced, terrified, and hungry for the sight of this man who had won her heart, if not her intellect.

Brigham looked like a summer storm, compressed into the shape of a person. His eyes glinted like New England icicles, and a lock of his hair tumbled over his forehead. His jawline was stony as the snowy mountains out on the peninsula, and he pushed past her without ceremony.

Lydia closed the door briskly behind him and swallowed hard. It was very important to keep her composure, she told herself, and her dignity.

He stood in the center of her humble parlor, filling the room to the corners with his presence and power, like some dark prince. It was as though a gigantic boulder had rolled down the side of Brigham's precious mountain, crashed through the wall, and stationed itself in the middle of her house, not to be moved except by some force greater than itself.

"You needn't behave like Zeus hurling thunderbolts," she said, with a moderation and steadiness that surprised her. "I'm perfectly aware that you're annoyed with me."

Brigham glowered at her, his powerful hands resting on his hips. "I thought I told you to move into our room at the main house," he said. His voice was low, and its softness was lethal rather than reassuring.

Lydia straightened her spine and took charge, as she

had another time, during the war, when a young, fever-crazed Rebel soldier, a patient under her care, had somehow gotten hold of a scalpel. The frightened boy had turned in circles, wavering on his crippled legs, eyes as wild as those of a cornered animal, wielding the blade.

By speaking reasonably, and showing no fear, Lydia had disarmed him and helped him back into bed.

"Yes," she said, meeting her husband's eyes with a courage she was only assuming. "You *told* me to move into your room. Subsequently, I decided against it."

"May I ask why?" His words were carefully modulated, and barely above the level of a whisper, yet the force of them seemed to rock the room as an earthquake would.

Lydia straightened her skirts, even though they didn't need straightening. "Of course you may. And I'll answer you, too. Until you close that saloon, Mr. Quade, I will not live under the same roof with you." It was amazing to Lydia how defiantly she spoke while trembling inside.

He stepped closer, and she could feel the heat and power of his body. She was not afraid physically, for she knew Brigham would never touch her in anger, but he was much the stronger of spirit, as well as muscle. If she weren't careful, he would dominate her thoroughly.

"Are you giving me an ultimatum?" he asked.

Lydia considered the definition of the word. "Yes," she finally replied.

He smiled, making her heart beat faster and bringing a blush to her cheeks. "I close the saloon and brothel, and you will share my house and my bed?" he inquired politely, even charitably.

"That's right."

"And if I don't, you'll live here. As long as I allow that, of course."

Lydia lifted her chin, glad of her long skirts, which hid her unsteady knees. "You are a very discerning man, Mr. Quade," she replied.

He gave a low, rough shout of laughter. "And a determined one, as you're about to find out." With that, he slipped one arm under her knees, curved the other behind her back, and lifted her easily, holding her close against his torso.

Lydia had to shut her eyes for a moment and concentrate on controlling her breathing. "Put me down immediately," she said, once she dared look at him again. The scent of soap and pond water and skin filled her nostrils, and she couldn't help being aware of the unyielding strength of him.

"I intend to," he replied, carrying her toward her tiny bedroom, where the kitten still cowered beneath the pillow, tail protruding and swinging tentatively back and forth like a pendulum. Brigham laid Lydia on the bed, and Ophelia waddled away and skittered down the side of the blanket to the floor.

Lydia struggled to rise, but Brigham had placed one hand in the middle of her chest, fingers splayed, and he held her in place with such ease that he was able to undo the buttons of his shirt even while subduing her.

"You would force me?" she asked, breathless with frustration and something else she didn't want to name.

He smiled. "I won't have to," he said cordially, shrugging off his shirt and holding her pinned to the bed at the same time. "You see, I know what you like, Lydia. You showed me last night, remember?"

"Brigham—"

"Tsk-tsk-tsk," he scolded. "You've set your terms, and now I'm setting mine. If you want to stay here and pretend you're independent, fine. But you are my wife and I will not be denied my rights. Nor will I allow you to blackmail me by withholding yourself."

Lydia was no longer struggling, and she told herself it was because she knew a hopeless effort when she saw one. She had no more chance against Brigham Quade and his damnable charms than the Confederacy had had against the Union after the fall of New Orleans.

"Take your hand off my bosom," she said through her teeth.

He did, only to grasp her, through her skirts and petticoat, at the junction of her thighs. Her traitorous legs parted instinctively, and Lydia bit her lip to keep back the low groan that rose into her throat.

"If you can honestly tell me you want me to leave this bed at the end of five minutes," Brigham said, gesturing toward the small clock ticking loudly on the bureau top, "I will comply with your wishes. Do we have a bargain?"

Lydia stared at him, already partly under his spell, knowing how easily he could defeat her. But if she should manage to meet the dragon of desire and turn away, at the end of those five minutes, she would win the soul battle going on between them. Brigham had not been able to dominate her in any other way.

"We have a bargain," she said in a shaky voice.

He lifted his hand from her and finished undressing. The blazing sunlight of that summer day, late in the afternoon, gilded his magnificent frame and gave him the golden aura of a god.

Brigham stood beside the bed, unlacing one of her shoes, and then the other, tossing them aside, beginning to roll down her stockings.

Lydia ached as the flames of the dragon's fire heated her skin and seeped through to her soul, creating a hunger even there, in the deepest part of her. "You realize," she said, with all the quivering primness she could manage, as she lay beneath his skilled, gentle hands, "that you have only five minutes."

He opened the bodice of her dress, unhurriedly, and slid it off her shoulders, down over her waist and hips. She had only her camisole and drawers for armor now, and she made a desperate glance at the clock. Less than a minute had passed.

"I won't need much time," he finally replied, pausing to caress each of her breasts in turn before untying the ribbons of her camisole.

Lydia flushed with outrage at his confidence, but it was all she could do to lie still, to keep breathing at an even pace.

When Brigham stretched out on the bed beside her and kissed her, his tongue toying with the seam of her lips and finally persuading them to open, she raised one eyelid to check the time.

Who would have thought a mere five minutes could seem like such an eternity?

His kiss left her weak, but a flicker of determination still glowed in her heart. He began nibbling his way down over her neck, her collarbone, the plump roundness at the top of one breast. In the meantime, with his left hand, he worked her drawers easily down over her hips.

Lydia couldn't hold back a little cry of angry pleasure as he found the nubbin hidden in moist silk and began to tease it with his finger.

His chuckle echoed through his chest.

"Damn you," Lydia gasped, writhing, unable to focus on the clock's face.

"Oh, I'm surely damned already," he responded in a gravelly whisper, and then he put his mouth to the hard, straining peak of her breast and conquered it without mercy.

"Are—the f-five minutes—up?" she gasped out as he suckled and, at the same time, teased the very wellspring of her pleasure with velvety, demanding strokes.

Brigham raised himself from her nipple and turned to consult the bureau clock with narrowed eyes. "No. There are still three left."

"Oh, God," Lydia moaned as he laved her other nipple with his tongue and simultaneously slipped his finger inside her.

"Do you surrender?" he asked, between nibbles at her breast.

"No!" Lydia cried, with the last of her defiance.

He laughed and moved downward along her trembling, perspiration-moistened body. "Then I'd better make the most of that three minutes," he said, nuzzling the place he had already stroked into a fever of wanting.

He parted her legs and draped them over his shoulders, then kissed her lower belly, and it was as though he had thrown down the gauntlet.

"Brigham," Lydia whispered, her fingers already entangled in his hair. "This isn't—f-fair—"

"You promised me five full minutes," he said, and then he parted the delta and claimed what could only be his.

Lydia's back arched with the violence of her response, and she clasped her breasts with her own hands, as if to protect some part of herself from the onslaught of sensation, and felt the nipples harden against her palms. A low whine escaped her as Brigham tongued her mercilessly; she was consumed in sweet fire.

He suckled her until she was wild with wanting, then withdrew, making her plead to be tasted again. Finally, he raised his head and looked at her over her heaving belly and full breasts. "The time is up," he said in a hoarse voice. "Shall I take you, Mrs. Quade, or shall I leave you to your lonely bed?"

Lydia had long since forgotten their agreement. She was wet with perspiration and the attentions of Brigham's mouth, and she knew that to have him desert her now would be the worst of all tortures.

"Oh—Brigham—my God—"

He spread her velvet folds again and gave her a brazen stroke of his tongue. "Your decision, Mrs. Quade," he rumbled insistently.

"Have me!" she shouted.

He poised himself over her, and she felt the magnificence of his masculinity prodding her. "Do you want this?" he teased, pretending to be confused.

Lydia was writhing wildly, trying to take him inside her. "Yes, damn you—"

"Where?" he inquired innocently, placing a light kiss on each of her eyelids. "Tell me where you want it, Yankee."

"Inside me!" Lydia cried, surrendering at last, defeated by the dragon and her own husband. "Oh, God, Brigham, I want you inside me!"

He gave her one inch, and then another. "How far?"

Lydia was all but delirious as one primordial sensation after another rolled through her. "All the way," she whispered fitfully, and uttered a loud cry of joy when he complied.

19

*L*YDIA LAY CURLED AGAINST THE HARD WARMTH OF HER husband's side, staring up at the ceiling and waiting for her scattered senses to return. Brigham had taken her outside herself during their lovemaking, shown her other spheres and dimensions, and she was still bedazzled by all she had seen and felt.

He swatted her bare bottom, lightly, and then gave the soft, plump flesh there an affectionate and somewhat proprietary squeeze. "It's all settled, then," he said after a long sigh.

Alarm slithered into Lydia's consciousness, a snake entering the Garden. She raised herself on one elbow. "What's all settled?"

Brigham pressed her closer against his side, one arm curved around her waist. His other hand cupped the back of his head, and the expression on his face was blissful. "Our disagreement, of course," he replied, sounding thoroughly untroubled. "You'll mind your business of being a wife and the mistress of my house, and I'll tend to the timber operation and the running of the town."

A part of Lydia wanted desperately to let the inadvertent challenge pass unremarked. After all, it wasn't such a bad life Brigham was offering. She loved him, and if his feelings for her were not so tender, well, he offered a type of security she had never known before. As his wife, she would have a fine place to live, two lovely stepdaughters, good clothes, and all she needed to eat. Not to mention the glorious experience of fusing herself with him, body and soul, on a fairly regular basis.

But she had seen too much, done too much, learned too much. Hardship and the bitter realities of war had broken many people, but they'd left Lydia strong. She couldn't be otherwise, she found, but if it had been possible, she would have *chosen* to be weak, to rest in the security of someone else's strength.

She studied the confident man beside her. He seemed somehow more than human, as though he belonged on Mount Olympus, with Zeus and Apollo and the other Greek gods. "I'm afraid there has been a misunderstanding," she said bravely, sitting upright now and wrapping her arms around her knees. "I—I admit to a certain weakness where—where intimate relations are concerned. When you touch me, I seem to lose all good sense. . . ." Her voice trailed off.

Brigham arched one eyebrow. "What are you getting at?"

"Unless you're planning to close the brothel, Mr. Quade—and I have the distinct impression you aren't considering any such thing—I still cannot and will not live with you as your wife."

Now it was Brigham who sprang up into a sitting position. "But you just—"

"I know," Lydia said, with a soft sigh. "I just responded to you, without any restraint at all. I can't seem to help that, and I'm sure it will happen again no matter what lofty resolves I might set for myself, but I simply can't turn away from this conflict, Brigham. Don't you see that it would be a betrayal, not only of the women who live and *will* live in this town, but of Charlotte and Millie as well?"

Brigham clearly did not understand or sympathize. He tossed back the covers, reached for his trousers, and began wrenching them on with furious motions. "That's exactly the kind of soft-headed logic I would expect from a woman," he muttered. He snatched his shirt from the floor and thrust his arms, one after the other, into the sleeves. "Without a saloon, this place would be a ghost town in five years!" He began to fasten his shirt, mismatching buttons and holes. "What good would *that* do Charlotte and Millie?"

Lydia rose to her knees on the mattress, clutching the sheet around her in a somewhat belated attempt at modesty.

"You are being utterly unreasonable, Mr. Quade," she said moderately. She could feel her lower lip quivering, but that core of strength was still there inside her, refusing to be denied. "This is your town. You have a remarkable opportunity to fashion something really fine and good!"

"I am not trying to start a new society," he interrupted crisply, sitting down hard on the edge of the bed and shaking mattress, frame, and wife as he jerked on one boot, then the other. He stood, and his steely eyes glinted with glacial sincerity as he gazed down at her. "I want to cut, process, and sell timber, and raise sons who will cut, process, and sell timber after I'm gone. To do that, I have to be able to keep the workmen I hire, and frankly, they aren't happy without whiskey and women!"

"You could bring in *good* women!" Lydia argued, grappling for her own clothes and, at the same time, trying to keep the sheet in place around her. "Brigham, *there has just been a war!* The East is full of ladies who want to marry but can't find husbands."

He waggled a finger at her. "Don't you start yammering about that damn war," he warned, completely missing the point of her statement. "As far as I'm concerned, it was a fool's fight on both sides!"

Lydia's face flooded with hot color. "Only fools would go to battle to save the Union? Is that what you're saying?"

Brigham sighed. "Were you saving the Union, Yank?"

he asked hoarsely from the doorway of the bedroom. He pulled his suspenders up onto his shoulders, one at a time, in measured, angry motions. "Or were you just holding on to a lot of very valuable property?"

With that, he turned away. Tears brimmed in Lydia's eyes.

His attitude about the war was just one more reason why she should never have hoped for a harmonious marriage to this man. And then there was his cavalier manner of making a pronouncement and then striding off.

She couldn't let him go, and even though she knew her words were foolish before she uttered them, Lydia called after him, "Were you building a timber dynasty? Or were you just trying to stay out of the line of fire?"

Brigham came back to the bedroom doorway, his hands gripping the door. His expression was dark and ominous, and while every fiber of Lydia's being was aware and alive with the energy of his silent challenge, she knew he would not harm her physically.

For a long time he just glared at her. Then he arched one eyebrow and said in a dangerous drawl, "Are you saying I didn't take part in that idiotic war because I was yellow?"

Lydia swallowed, reaching for her drawers and camisole without ever letting go of the sheet. "This is your country," she said in an even and, she hoped, reasonable voice. "You should have been on one side or the other."

Brigham seemed to be looking off into some distance invisible to Lydia. "It would be like taking up a rifle and going after Devon," he said, just when Lydia was beginning to wonder if he meant to speak at all. " 'Nation against nation, brother against brother.' "

She had scrambled into her underthings and was edging toward the place where Brigham had tossed her dress earlier. She snatched it up, furious with herself because she couldn't think of a remark to counter her husband's.

He lingered, even after she had turned her back to him

to brush and arrange her love-tangled hair, his reflection hovering like a storm cloud in the mirror. "You needn't think, Mrs. Quade," he said gruffly, "that you are going to get your way by being hard-headed and obstinate. As far as I'm concerned, you can live in this cottage for the rest of your natural life if you wish, but when I want you, I will come to you, and you will not refuse me."

Lydia gulped, putting the last hairpin in place. "You won't send the saloon women away?"

Brigham shook his head, then said, "No," in a hoarse and firmly decided voice.

She whirled, waving her hairbrush at him as though it were a saber. "Don't you dare visit that dreadful place, Brigham Quade!" she blurted, amazed at her own courage even as the words were hurled from her throat. "If you do, you can be sure I'll hear of it, and I swear by God's suspenders, I'll come after you with a horsewhip!"

The image made Brigham chuckle, which only infuriated her more. "So you do care a little, Mrs. Quade?" he countered quietly. His hands dropped from the framework of the door to his sides, in a motion of weary acceptance and the profoundest of frustrations. "You can be sure I'll be very careful of what reaches your ears."

Having said that, Brigham turned and walked away, his footsteps echoing as he crossed the small parlor, opened the front door and went out.

Lydia was sure he would come back and that he would see reason and agree, on humanitarian grounds if nothing else, to close the saloon.

Brigham didn't appear the next day, or the day after that. Lydia saw him at a distance sometimes, and he gazed at her from the depths of Millie's troubled gray eyes during daily lessons, but he did not return to her bed.

Another day passed, then a week, then, incredibly, *another* week. Joe's combination office and house was completed on the outside and habitable on the inside, and a boatload of goods arrived to stock Polly's general store. More families came and cabins began to go up at the edge of town, and Brigham's clerk, Mr. Harrington, ran off to Seattle with Esther and got himself married.

The work went on on the mountain, and in the mill at its foot. The saloon-brothel, now called the Satin Hammer, thrived on its spit of sawdust-littered land. Bawdy piano music flowed through its doors and windows day and night, and sometimes, late, Lydia lay in bed and tormented herself with images of Brigham carousing there with one of the strumpets.

Still, she waited.

As a doctor, Joe McCauley knew enough to catch a good night's sleep wherever he could, but his mind was full of Lydia as he lay beneath the rough cover of his army blanket. The house was small and new around him, raw with freshly planed wood.

It had been a month since Lydia had left her husband, and even the hardened, tobacco-chewing lumberjacks gossiped and speculated, wondering if it would be safe to go back to courting the lady. There were those who said Brigham Quade had already gone to a judge and had the thing nullified, while others said he had taken up with Clover O'Keefe, the lady who ran the Satin Hammer, and planned to keep Lydia at the same time.

Joe sat up on the edge of his cot. The straw-filled mattress was supported by a net of creaky new rope, and the wooden bedposts were still splintery.

"Damn," he said, reaching for his trousers. He pulled them on, raised the suspenders to his bare shoulders, and made his way through the dark house to the back door. The outhouse loomed in the moonlight, and the path leading toward it was still just a shadow in the grass.

He supposed he could just have stood on the back porch and pissed on the ground, but between his genteel upbringing and the years he'd spent in the cavalry and in that Yankee prison hospital, Joe McCauley had had his fill of living like a vagabond. He started toward the privy, the quack grass cool under his bare feet.

Reaching his destination, he grabbed the crude wooden handle and yanked open the door. The bright silvery light of the moon flooded the little shack, revealing a figure crouched on the bench, trying to fade into one corner.

"I'll be goddammed," Joe muttered, though he wasn't a man to swear. He'd already unbuttoned his trousers, and it was embarrassing to be caught in such an ungentlemanly state.

The figure made a whimpering sound and shriveled like a wet spiderweb.

Joe made out that the trespasser was a girl. She wore a ragged dress, and her blond hair hung straggly around a thin, defiant, and thoroughly filthy face.

"Come out of there," Joe ordered.

The girl hesitated, then obeyed, standing square in front of Joe on the pathway. She was older than he'd thought, eighteen at least, and nearly as tall as he was. Her jaw trembled as she looked straight into his eyes, but the set of her face was as obdurate as a Yankee picket on his own ground.

"You've gotta help me, mister," she said, but she was throwing down a challenge, not begging. "My pa means to sell me to those folks over at the Satin Hammer. He says all I'd have to do is sing once in a while and bring the men their beer, but I don't believe him."

Joe's southern gallantry was stirred. He took the girl's arm and shuffled her toward the house, forgetting all about the need to empty his bladder.

"What's your name?"

"Frodine Hearn," the young woman answered, willingly enough. "You're not plannin' to use me or nothin' like that, are you? I didn't come here to get myself used, you know."

Joe smiled as he put his hand to the small of Frodine's slender back and guided her over the threshold. She stood just to one side of the door, shivering and barefoot, while Joe lit the kerosene lamp in the middle of the huge wire spool that served as a table.

"I'm not going to hurt you," he said.

Frodine folded her arms. God-have-mercy but she

needed a bath, and those clothes of hers weren't fit to serve as rags. "I'll carve a hole in your belly if you try," she said.

Joe laughed. "Sit down," he said, gesturing toward one of the two upturned crates that were his only chairs.

Warily, the girl took a seat, and Joe busied himself building up the fire in the small cookstove and setting the kettle on to boil. He found preserves in his pitch-scented pantry, along with a loaf of bread he'd bought from Mrs. Holmetz.

"Hungry?" he asked.

Frodine tore off a chunk of the bread and stuffed it into her mouth. "Whaasss—scht—tme—" she said.

Joe opened the jar of raspberry preserves, given him by Brigham's cook, and set them on the table, along with a knife. "You shouldn't talk with your mouth full," he said.

Frodine's black eyes mocked him. "Well, excuse me, Mr. Fancy Pants. I didn't know I was in one of them mansions with the prissy curtains!"

Joe shook his head, amazed at her audacity and the amount of dirt she'd managed to amass. "I'm Dr. Joseph McCauley," he said. "But you can call me Joe."

She ripped away another piece of bread, slathered it with a thick layer of preserves, and gobbled down the whole mess in no more than three bites. "Thanks," she said.

Heat was beginning to surge through the water in the kettle, and Joe got out a tin of tea and the cheap crockery pot he'd bought from Polly. She didn't have much on the shelves of the general store yet, but it seemed like new goods arrived almost every day on the mail boat. "Do I know your pa?" he asked.

Frodine spoke around another mouthful of bread. "I don't reckon so. He likes to move around a lot, but we come here whenever he runs out of drinkin' money. He's a sawyer, but he's done some bull whackin' in his time, too, and Mr. Quade, he's always willin' to give Pa a job. Pa says that's because Brig knows a good worker when he sees one, but I think it's just that he's always short-handed up there on the mountain."

Joe looked at the girl over one shoulder, figuring that any man who'd go along with the idea of naming a defenseless baby "Frodine" would probably be willing to sell that selfsame daughter to a brothel when he thought she was ripe. "You could get married, you know," he said thoughtfully.

Frodine sighed dramatically. "Sure. That way I'd only have to whore for one man instead of a hundred."

"Frodine!"

"Well, it's the truth!" she wailed, looking at him plaintively with those black, black eyes. "Ain't it?"

"Isn't it," he corrected automatically, taking up the kettle and pouring hot water into the teapot. "And no, it isn't. There are a lot of nice young men on the mountain who'd be thrilled to have a pretty wife like you. Provided you were cleaned up a little first, of course."

Frodine sighed and looked very put-upon. "You try bathin' in a creek or somebody's horse trough," she challenged.

"There've been times in my life when I would have been glad to do just that," he said, entertaining memories of prison camp for only a moment before he pushed them aside. Joe was a pragmatic man, but he didn't feel sorry for himself; he'd seen levels of suffering that went far beyond the trials he'd known. Some of those poor wretches would even have envied his luck.

"You gonna turn me over to Pa?"

"I won't have much choice if he comes here looking for you," Joe said. Under the law, a man could no more confiscate another man's daughter than he could take his horse or his tobacco pouch.

Tears glistened in her great dark eyes, and she brushed back a lock of dirty hair with one grungy paw. "Please," she said. "You gotta help me."

Joe sighed. Leaving the tea untouched, he rose from the table and went out back to get the tub down from its nail on the wall. He set it in the middle of the kitchen with a clatter and reached for the two buckets sitting by the stove.

"All right," he said. "But first you've got to take a bath so I can stand being in the same room with you."

He went back and forth to the pump in the yard until he'd nearly filled the tub, then put the last two bucketsful of water on the stove to heat. Frodine wouldn't get a hot bath, but at least he could take the edge off the cold.

She put a grubby finger into the tub and winced. "Hellfire, Joe, that's cold enough I could write my name in it and have it stay."

Joe was getting out his bar of yellow soap, the stuff he used to scrub up before delivering babies and stitching up torn flesh. "Can you write your name, Frodine?" he asked moderately.

The expression in her eyes was one of chagrin. "No. And I can't read it, neither."

"Then I think you should go to school. I know just the lady to teach you."

Frodine gave a derisive hoot. "School? *School?* Are you blind or somethin', Doc? I'm near on twenty years old! Besides, what need have I got for readin' and writin' and figurin' anyhow?"

Joe found a clean towel, also bought from Polly's general store. "Everybody needs to know those things. They help you look after yourself."

She clenched one fist. "I can look after myself just fine, thank you all the same."

He nodded. "That's why you were hiding in my outhouse like an escaped criminal, no doubt."

Frodine's eyes widened, then narrowed. "I was afraid Pa would send the hound out after me. I figured that would throw ol' Homebrew off the trail, if I hid in the outhouse, I mean, but it turned out your privy was practically new and it don't stink much."

"Thanks," Joe said, biting back a grin. He'd seen chicken coops cleaner than this girl, and yet she brought a certain freshness with her, like a cool breeze blowing in off the water.

She glanced around speculatively, and it was clear that his humble quarters looked pretty luxurious to her. "Where's your wife?"

"Don't have one," he said. Then he cleared his throat because the words had come out sounding so hoarse.

"Oh," said Frodine. "Then you don't got nobody to keep house for you and the like."

With an index finger he tested the water heating on the stove. "I'm content to look after myself," he said.

Frodine made a sound of contemptuous disbelief. "No man likes doin' for hisself. It ain't natural."

Joe took out his pocket watch and saw that it was eleven-fifteen. He wondered if Lydia was sleeping already, or maybe entertaining her husband. In either case, he wouldn't want to disturb her, and yet he needed help.

"You get into the tub as soon as I'm gone and scrub yourself good. I'll see about getting you a decent dress and some night things."

Frodine looked at the water, now steaming on the stove top, and swallowed. "You ain't cleanin' me up just so you can take a turn at me, are you?"

"No," Joe said quietly, aching with pity, which he kept well-hidden. "I'm not going to bother you, Frodine. I just want to help."

She was untying the strings that held the front of her dress together when Joe went out the back door. He rounded the house and walked resolutely to the end of the street, toward Lydia's cottage. To his relief, there was a light in the front window, and as he came up the walk, he could see her sitting quietly in a rocking chair, reading.

He made plenty of noise coming up onto the porch, so he wouldn't startle her.

"It's Joe," he said after knocking.

The door opened readily. Joe saw signs of strain in Lydia's violet eyes and in the set of her mouth, and he wished he could take her into his arms and hold her.

"Is everything all right?" she asked, stepping back to admit him.

"No one's sick or having a baby, if that's what you

mean," he answered, shoving one hand through his rumpled hair. It was only then that he realized he was still barefoot, and wearing only his pants and suspenders. He blushed, more embarrassed than he'd been since his father had presented him with his first mistress at the age of fourteen.

Lydia pretended not to notice his state of dishabille. "Then what's wrong?"

"I found a woman in my outhouse," he blurted out, "and I don't know what to do with her."

Lydia stared at him for a moment, then started to laugh. "You found a woman in your outhouse?"

"A girl, really, for all that she says she's twenty. She talks like a sailor and has about as much education as the average bilge rat, but she's in trouble and I can't just turn my back on her."

"Of course not," Lydia said reasonably. "But what *are* you going to do with her?"

He sighed. "I don't know. She says her father means to sell her to the people over at the Satin Hammer, though, and I can't let that happen."

Lydia's cheekbones glowed with crimson. "At least there's one man in this town with some decency."

By all rights he should have refuted her remark, since he'd been to the saloon several times, and taken his fleshly comfort upstairs with various women as well, but he didn't have the heart. Everybody knew the Satin Hammer was a very sensitive subject with Lydia. "She needs something to wear," he said gruffly, after an awkward silence. "And I told her you'd let her go to school. She can't read or write, either."

Lydia sighed. "There's a big market for brides around here. Maybe she should just marry one of Brigham's men. At least she'd have a home that way."

"I suggested that, but she said . . ." Joe paused, flustered again. He couldn't repeat what Frodine had said when he'd brought up the marriage idea. "She didn't want any part of that."

"Great Scot," Lydia said, but she marched into her room and in a few minutes came out with a neatly folded stack of clothes. Joe could see a couple of calico dresses in the pile, along with a nightdress and some under-things. "You'd better send her over here to stay, or the whole town will be talking by morning."

Joe knew he should have been relieved by Lydia's willingness to take Frodine off his hands, but oddly, he wasn't. During those few minutes with the ragamuffin he'd found in his outhouse, he realized, he'd been free of the grinding loneliness that had possessed him from the moment he'd gone away to war. Even Lydia, with all her gentle practicality, hadn't been able to reach that part of him.

"We'll see," he said. Then he thanked Lydia for the clothes and left again. He knew Frodine wouldn't be through with her bath, so he sat on his back step in the moonlight, holding the pile of clothes and listening with a smile as his house guest splashed happily beyond the door.

When she'd been quiet for a time, he called her name, softly.

"You can come in if you keep your head turned aside!" she called generously.

Joe stood, drew a deep breath, opened the door. He was careful not to look toward Frodine, and yet he was painfully conscious of her nakedness. He caught the pleasant scents of her freshly washed hair and skin, and he felt his groin tighten.

He set the clothes on one of the crates and made his way around the tub like a blind man.

"I'm still hungry," she called after him as he took refuge in the room where he saw his patients. "You got anything to eat around here besides bread?"

Joe chuckled, and a fine mist of tears covered his eyes, though he couldn't think why. "There's some cold meat. I'll get it for you as soon as you're dressed."

"I could eat the north end of a southbound skunk," Frodine marveled.

Joe leaned back against the door of his surgery and smiled in the darkness. "That won't be necessary," he replied.

He heard splashing as she rose from the water. "You could probably use a woman around here," she said. "You know, somebody to cook and clean and sew and stuff like that."

"Like a wife?" he inquired, unable to resist teasing her.

"Well, yeah, except for the part where we'd lie down in the same bed and all," she said.

"You can have my bed for tonight," he answered, anxious to put her at ease. "I can bunk on the floor."

She was quiet for a long time, so long that he began to suspect she'd crept out the back door and vanished into the night. The thought filled him with an unaccountable loneliness.

"You're right nice, for a man," she said. "You can come out now."

Joe was surprised at his eagerness. After all, Frodine was the complete opposite of all he'd ever admired and reverenced in a woman. She wasn't gentle-spoken, Lord knew, and her manners would have embarrassed Genghis Khan. She couldn't even read, let alone discuss the great books, and her appreciation for music probably didn't go beyond jug bands, mouth harps, and fiddles.

Still, when he came out of his office and saw her standing there, wet-haired and wide-eyed in Lydia's white lawn nightdress, something inside him, something long dead, was resurrected.

20

LYDIA STARED AT MR. HARRINGTON, FIRST BEFUDDLED, then infuriated. Brigham's clerk seemed healthier since his elopement a few weeks before; his previously skinny frame was filling out, and his coloring was ruddier. He'd stopped wearing his high celluloid collar and parting his hair down the middle, and there was a disconcerting look of obstinance in his eyes.

"I'm sorry, Mrs. Quade," he said, sounding not the least bit remorseful, "but I have specific orders from your husband. He is to pay your salary personally."

Lydia felt the blood drain from her face, then surge in again in a fresh tide of fury. "This is unacceptable, Mr. Harrington!" she said, pounding one fist on the tidy desk he occupied in a corner of Brigham's office. "I have taught those children faithfully. And for the last three days I've been staying after classes were dismissed to help prepare the new schoolhouse. I deserve to be paid the agreed-upon wages!"

Harrington finally rose from his chair, holding up both hands in an effort to calm the roiling waters. "I agree, Mrs. Quade—absolutely. Totally. But I cannot go against Mr. Quade's orders." His thin chest puffed out a little. "May I remind you that I have a family to support?"

Lydia sighed. Arguing with the man would obviously be a fruitless effort, and she was tired from her hard work at the schoolhouse. "Where is he?" she asked on a long breath.

Mr. Harrington gestured toward the looming mountain, with its dense covering of trees. "In the main camp, I suppose. A couple of the bull whackers quit, and Mr. Quade is assisting with the work."

Lydia's heart beat a little faster at the prospect of confronting Brigham; she hadn't seen him, up close at least, since that wonderful-dreadful night when he'd made thorough love to her. He'd said he would come to her only when he needed her as a husband needs a wife, and a full month had gone by since their last encounter.

Lydia was of two very different minds about that. She yearned to be close to Brigham, to be held by him, to hear his voice. At the same time, she feared facing the man she'd married so rashly, feared looking into those tempestuous gray eyes of his and seeing that he no longer desired her. After all, he could go to the Satin Hammer for his comforts now, and Charlotte had mentioned her father's "meetings" with Clover O'Keefe, the madam, on several occasions. Each time, Millie had given her sister a nudge with her elbow and narrowed her eyes in warning.

A spiky lump formed in Lydia's throat, and she turned away so Mr. Harrington wouldn't see her dilemma in her face. It was nearly suppertime, though the sun would be up for several hours. If she did not go to Brigham that very day and demand fair treatment where her employment was concerned, he would bully her at every turn.

She sniffled subtly, squared her shoulders, and turned to look back at the flustered clerk. "Thank you," she said somewhat contemptuously, causing a rush of chagrined color to flood Harrington's neck and glow along his jawline. "You've been very helpful."

Outside, Lydia stood glaring up at the mountain. It represented Brigham in her mind, huge and impervious and unmindful of the wants and foibles of mere humans.

Then, resolutely, she hefted her skirts and started up the curving track, made by the hooves of oxen and mules and the enormous timbers they dragged behind.

The foliage was thick on either side of the road, for this was a virile land, junglelike in its lushness. Ferns and berry thickets covered nearly every inch of ground, and the trees, hemlock and cedar and fir, mostly, gave each other scant elbow room. The clamor of the mill receded as Lydia progressed up the slope, but ahead she heard the shouts of men, the braying of mules and oxen, the rhythmic rasp of cross-cut saws, the steady thwack-thwack of axes.

After fifteen minutes of steady climbing, Lydia reached the main timber camp, a helter-skelter arrange-ment of tents and wagons. A campfire burned at the center of things, and Elly Collier stood beside it, stirring the contents of the enormous pot suspended over the blaze.

The rough-edged woman smiled when she saw Lydia approaching, and wiped her hands on her apron. Lydia felt a twinge of guilt because she hadn't come to pay a social call.

She smiled. "Hello, Elly," she said. "As I'm sure you know, Jessup and Samuel are making fine progress with their lessons."

Elly beamed. She was not a pretty woman; her features were too coarse, her body too broad and bulky, but when she smiled, it was like stepping close to a warm stove on a chill winter morning. "Seems there might be some hope for the two of them after all," she said, her voice booming like a man's.

Lydia's heart ached, just a little. It was a natural thing for a mother to have aspirations for her children, but life was full of perils. Sometimes, boys grew up to be soldiers, and died screaming on battlefields. If war or disease didn't get them, drink might, or a falling tree, or another man's bullet.

Elly gave the schoolteacher a whack on the shoulder that nearly sent her toppling into the campfire. "You're looking mighty down in the mouth, Mrs. Quade," she thundered. "It's no secret that things ain't right between you and the mister, you know. If you want to talk, you go right ahead. Old Elly will listen."

The scent of the stew bubbling in the big pot gave Lydia some badly needed strength. Her stomach growled, and she recalled that she hadn't taken the time to eat since breakfast. She stifled an urge to ask the gruff, kindly cook if the rumors were true, if Brigham was really visiting Clover O'Keefe.

"I need to speak directly to Mr. Quade," she said. She was so eager, her knees were trembling, and yet she wanted to turn and flee down the mountain at breakneck speed.

Elly gave the stew another slow, thoughtful stir, then gestured toward the woods. "He's up there, bull whackin'. Supper'll be ready in a little while, though, and then the boss and all the rest of them will be down here tearin' into my corn bread. You might just as well sit a spell, and I'll give you some coffee. Got to warn you, though—these timber beasts like the stuff strong enough to strip rust off'n a tobacco tin."

After drawing a deep breath and setting her shoulders at a steadfast angle again, Lydia shook her head. "If I don't go to him right now, Elly," she confided miserably, "I'll lose my courage for sure. And if that happens, I won't have any respect for myself."

Regard glimmered in Elly's faded eyes, but she issued a warning all the same. "Your man ain't gonna like it, you traipsin' around in the woods. He's one to hold firm opinions about such things as womenfolk gettin' in the way of dangerous work."

Lydia sighed. There was no denying that the coming confrontation with Brigham would not be a pleasant one, but she doubted that he'd be surprised by her appearance on this sacred, masculine ground. After all, he'd forced her to come to him by refusing to let Harrington pay her wages like everyone else's.

"I have a few firm opinions of my own," she said

distractedly. Then she set out again, through the camp, along the crude trail leading to the place where the men were working.

Lydia walked perhaps a quarter of a mile up the mountain and presently came into a small clearing. An enormous tree had been felled, and men climbed all over it, sawing off branches, paring the bark away in great curved peelings. Brigham's shirt was soaked with sweat, and his flesh was so dirty that he looked like a performer made up for a road show. With the help of several other workers, he was hitching a team of eight lathered oxen to the half-denuded tree, using a system of heavy chains and ropes.

As Lydia watched, her eyes shaded from the late afternoon sun by one hand, Brigham scrambled up the side of the trunk, which was so big that she couldn't see over it, to attach giant hooks in place. Only when he'd finished did he climb down again and stride toward her.

His pewter eyes snapped with annoyance and a hint of amused triumph. "What are you doing here?" he demanded, raising his hands to his hips.

That stance might have intimidated Charlotte and Millie, and maybe Mr. Harrington, but Lydia was determined not to knuckle under, no matter how fierce her husband looked and acted. "I think you know the answer to that question," she said. "A workman is worthy of his—or her—hire, Mr. Quade. I am owed a month's salary. Mr. Harrington refused to pay me, and he said he was following your instructions."

Brigham's gaze slid over her, heating both her flesh and her temper as it passed, and his white teeth flashed in a brief, quicksilver grin. Immediately after that, he scowled. "I expected you to pay me a call, all right," he said. "I just thought you'd have the good sense to come to the house or to my office. In case you haven't noticed, Mrs. Quade, a timber site is a very dangerous place."

Lydia stood toe-to-toe with him, knowing he would run roughshod over her if she didn't stand her ground. "So is a field hospital," she replied.

He narrowed his eyes. "The war is over," he reminded

her tautly. "This is Washington Territory, not Gettysburg or Richmond or Bull Run, and I give the orders here. Go back to town and wait for me there."

She was intimidated, but she hid the fact as best she could, tilting her head back to look defiantly into his sweat-streaked face. "I will be happy to go back to town," she replied evenly, "as soon as you give me my money. And I will not 'wait for you there' or anywhere else. I am not a child being sent to the woodshed!"

Brigham bent until his nose was nearly touching hers. She could smell sweat, fury, pine sap, and pure, undiluted masculinity, and the combination affected her like strong drink. "You will do as I say," he told her in a lethal whisper. "And I warn you, Mrs. Quade: I will not have my authority undermined in front of these men."

Lydia would have retreated a step, but she was afraid she would lose her tenuous balance and fall. "Fine," she said, summoning all her dignity. "Then all you have to do is pay me my salary, and I will gladly leave."

He glared at her, and there was a sizing-up in his look. "Suppose I told you you're fired?" he said. "Suppose I say I don't want my wife to work?"

"If you fire me, I can go to work for Dr. McCauley, as his nurse. And since you are no kind of husband, sir, it makes precious little difference to me what you might want your wife to do or not do!"

Brigham was fairly seething by then; his nostrils flared, his breathing was shallow and rapid, and there was a steely glint in his eyes. A trickle of sweat streaked down over his temple and cheek, leaving a trail in the dirt. "I will warn you once more, Mrs. Quade. *Go home.*"

Lydia held out her hand, palm up. "Certainly. As soon as you give me my money."

For a moment she thought Brigham was going to spit in her hand instead of giving her the few dollars he owed her. His eyes narrowed again while he assessed her expression and manner. "You're going to make a scene if I don't give in, aren't you?" he asked, his voice dangerously calm.

"One you'll never live down," Lydia promised, smiling

up at him. She had been heartbroken and humiliated by the thought of this man turning to a prostitute for pleasure, and having the whole town know made things infinitely worse. As far as she was concerned, a little embarrassment was no more than he deserved.

Brigham reached into the pocket of his trousers and, for one delicious second, Lydia thought she'd won. Then he laid a shiny nickel in her palm. "There you are," he breathed, as though flinging down a challenge. "With all the charges deducted, that's about what I figure I owe you."

Lydia stared at the coin, then at Brigham. "Charges?"

"Yes," he replied, clearly pleased with himself, and began ticking things off on his grubby fingers. "There's the roof over your head, for instance. And all the food I've provided. The clothes Devon bought for you, and your passage to Quade's Harbor, and the furniture in your cottage—"

"You snake!" Lydia interrupted.

He raised one eyebrow and looked affronted, and Lydia longed to slap him. "Did you think all those things came with the job?" he asked in a damnably reasonable tone.

Lydia clenched one fist at her side. It wouldn't do for her to strike him, no matter how badly she wanted to do just that. She was a teacher, and she would be setting a bad example if she indulged in violence.

"I am your wife," she pointed out, but she'd lost most of her momentum, and they both knew it.

Brigham smiled, folding his arms and regarding her indulgently. "Exactly. All you have to do is move back under my roof, where you belong, and we'll call it square. You'll have a more than adequate allowance, and we can bring in a schoolmaster to replace you."

Lydia's fury was so intense that it made her dizzy. She took a firmer hold on her balance. "I will not share your home, not before you close that brothel, apologize for your supreme rudeness, and pay me what you owe. And if you hire another teacher, after I've worked my fingers to the bone with those children, I swear by all that's holy that I'll make you wish you'd never been born!"

He had the temerity to laugh. "Damn if you're not the stubbornest woman I've ever had the misfortune to run across," he said a moment later. "You'll do as I tell you, and that's the last of it."

With that, he turned to walk away, and Lydia suddenly lost all control. She was so enraged that the world seemed to glow red around her, and she flung herself at Brigham's back, hooking one arm around his neck and pounding on him with the other.

He curved an arm around her waist and wrenched her around to face him, slamming her against his impervious chest and thighs. "That," he told her charitably, "was a mistake."

With that, he hoisted her up over one shoulder, so that her bottom was sticking up in the air. Her hair came unpinned and tumbled almost to the ground. She let out a shriek of shock and fury and began to kick as hard as she could.

Brigham gave her a swat on the backside for her trouble, and a cheer went up from the watching lumberjacks.

In those moments, Lydia thoroughly understood the philosophy behind plain old, spur-of-the-moment murder. If she could have gotten loose, she'd have gone at Brigham like a wildcat, but his arms were hard as manacles around her. His strides were long and easy, as though she were no more trouble than a sack of dried peas.

She hooked her fingers in the back of his belt, as if to hold him still. "Brigham!"

He ignored her shouted protest, so she began to struggle again.

"Do I have to take you over my knee," he inquired in a cheerful drawl, "or are you going to behave yourself?"

"You don't believe in striking women," Lydia reminded him, quickly and furiously.

"In your case," he replied, "I could make an exception."

Lydia closed her eyes tightly, then gulped. "Please, Brigham," she wheedled. "Put me down. I think I'm going to be sick."

He made a sound of rude contempt. "Try something else, Mrs. Quade. I wasn't born yesterday, you know."

She paused for a heartbeat, doing some fast calculations in her head. Then she felt herself go pale. "All right," she said as they bounced down the rutted, bumpy ox trail toward camp. "Here's something else. There's a good chance that I'm carrying your child, Mr. Quade. If that's the case, hauling me around over your shoulder can hardly be considered prudent behavior."

He set her down in front of him with a jarring thump. He looked at her in mingled wonder, distrust, and exasperation for a long moment, then splayed the fingers of his right hand and pressed them tenderly against her abdomen. "You're just saying that," he muttered. "Aren't you?"

Lydia's eyes filled with tears. She was still getting used to the realization herself, and as so often happened when this man was involved, she was brimming with paradoxical emotions—the joy of bringing a child into the world, the fear of raising a baby on her own, or being separated from her son or daughter. Under the present laws, she had only a few more rights than one of Brigham's oxen.

"I think it's quite true," she finally said. "I should have had my—my time over two weeks ago."

A slow grin was spawned in Brigham's eyes, and it spread languidly to his mouth. Then, all of a sudden, he gave a whoop that sent the birds squawking out of the trees in terror, wrapped one arm around Lydia's waist and swung her around in a gleeful circle.

"I'm glad you're happy," she said acidly when he'd calmed down a bit.

"You're damn right I'm happy," he replied. Then, to prove it, he lifted her up into his arms and strode on, whistling, through the camp where Elly was cooking supper and on down the track.

"Brigham, really," Lydia protested when he reached

the edge of town. "Enough is enough. You must put me down."

"I will," he responded, then he went right on whistling and right on walking.

Everybody they passed turned to stare at the spectacle they made, Brigham covered in dirt and pitch from head to foot, Lydia with her face smudged and her hair trailing down her back like a trollop's.

They progressed down Main Street, past Joe McCauley's house and the Holmetzes' and Lydia's own tidy little cottage. By then her cheeks were crimson.

She tried again. "Brigham, this behavior is quite unacceptable. You are behaving like a barbarian."

His eyes were saucy as they moved over her face, rested a moment on her breasts, then returned to her mouth. "Don't worry, my love," he promised cockily. "I'll be gentle with you."

Lydia stiffened as a thrill of mingled anticipation and umbrage moved through her. "If you think for one moment that you're going to—to—"

Brigham laughed. "Bed my wife?" he finished for her.

Lydia swallowed as they approached the front gate at the big house. "Brigham, I'm afraid I must insist that you stop this, immediately. We are estranged, you will remember."

He shifted her weight in his arms and opened the gate latch as deftly as if he made a regular practice of carrying women along Main Street and up his front walk. "Oh, I remember all right," he replied. "It's time we started making up."

Charlotte and Millie stood on either side of the path, gaping. Lydia closed her eyes, wondering how she would ever explain being carried into their father's house like a caveman's woman.

"Brigham!" she cried through her teeth.

He kissed her noisily on the forehead and mounted the front steps. Then he turned to face his staring daughters, forcing Lydia to face them, too. "Tell Jake I'll be wanting a hot bath right away," he said, with a jovial grin.

Charlotte gave a sudden, trilling laugh and bounded around the side of the house to obey, with Millie close on her heels.

"This is reprehensible!" Lydia hissed.

Brigham opened the front door and stepped over the threshold. The inside of the house was shadowy and cool, and a quiver of desire stirred deep in Lydia's being as he started up the stairs. "Remember our agreement, dear," he said pleasantly. "When I want you, I'll have you."

"Shhhh!" Lydia whispered, mortified. "Someone will hear you!"

"It's no secret that I'm taking you to my bed, Mrs. Quade," he pointed out as they reached the first landing and proceeded up from there.

Lydia shook her head in bewildered wonder. She'd started out to collect her salary and let her husband know he couldn't bully her, and ended up being carried away like so much pirate's loot. And the awful part was, she couldn't seem to summon up the will to fight.

"What will Charlotte and Millie think?"

He didn't even pause, but proceeded along the upper hallway to the door of his room, then through it. He dumped Lydia bodily onto his bed before replying. "They're innocent children. They'll think we're kissing."

Lydia blinked and sat up as Brigham closed the door of his room and began unbuttoning his shirt. He was right; the girls would giggle and speculate, but it was unlikely that they would know what their father and stepmother were doing.

Brigham dragged off his shirt, tossed it over a bedpost, and went to the marble-topped washstand, where he poured tepid water from a pitcher into a matching ceramic basin and began to wash his face, hands, and chest industriously.

Lydia calculated the distance from the bed to the door and knew immediately that she wouldn't even gain the threshold before he whirled around and caught her. Brigham was a big man, but he was far from awkward.

"I don't suppose it makes any difference to you that I think this is scandalous, and that I want to leave?"

Her husband snatched a towel from the bar across the top of the washstand and dried his face and chest exuberantly. He'd merely rearranged the dirt, rather than washed it away, and Lydia felt a peculiar softening of the heart as she looked at him. "Of course it's scandalous," he replied. "And you don't want to leave."

She scooted backward, against the headboard. "I don't?"

Brigham shook his head. "No. Maybe you don't *want* to want my lovemaking, Lydia, but you do. You've been tossing and turning in your spinster's bed for weeks, thinking about all the sweet things I could be doing to you."

Lydia began to perspire. What he said was true, but she wouldn't have admitted it to save her skin. "Stop it. All I was thinking was that you're a bastard."

He laughed, caught hold of one of her feet. "You were quite right about that," he drawled, clasping one hand around her ankle, just above her high-button shoe, and sliding it slowly up to the back of her knee, where the skin was very sensitive. "I am a bastard, but you want me. Can you deny that?"

Lydia drew in a quick breath as his fingers moved from her knee to her inner thigh, skimming lightly beneath one leg of her drawers. Arousal clamped inside her like a springing trap, and she bit her lower lip while she fought for control. "Yes," she lied.

He found the nest of moist curls at the crux of her legs and petted her in whisper-soft strokes. "Oh?" he inquired, propping her foot on his shoulder and beginning to unfasten the buttons of her shoe with slow, deft movements of his fingers. He tossed the shoe aside, then unrolled her stocking and threw that away, too. He parted the folds of her femininity, gave her a light, teasing flick with the pad of his thumb, and began telling her in excruciating detail what he meant to do to pleasure her. He said one climax would not be enough, no matter how ferocious it might be; he wanted her to respond over and over again. He wanted to watch her while she strained toward one fulfillment after another, and to hear her cries.

He put both her legs on his shoulders and teased her with one finger while his thumb caressed the quivering rosebud he had uncovered earlier. His other hand supported her bottom, which was trembling with Lydia's effort to keep calm.

"My sweet Yankee wife," Brigham murmured, turning his head to kiss the bare skin of her ankle, which he'd made vulnerable by removing her shoe and stocking. "Were you telling the truth when you said you thought you might be carrying my baby?"

Lydia was tossing her head back and forth on the pillow in an involuntary reaction to the nibbling warmth of his lips against her ankle. She hadn't the strength to lie. "Yes," she gasped. "Yes, damn you, I was telling the truth!" Her hips were moving to the meter he set for them with the slow plunge and withdrawal of his finger.

He pushed back her skirt and tasted the fragile flesh behind her knee, making her moan softly. "If my son isn't growing in you now," he vowed, "he will be by the time this night is through."

Lydia whimpered. She should tell Brigham Quade to go to hell. She should free herself and storm out of that room, out of that house, never to go back again. The trouble was, she needed his touch as much as air and water, and since her knees had already turned to jelly, there was no point in trying to escape.

"You have to—take your bath," she pointed out, in a last desperate effort to save herself from her own passion.

He lowered her gently to the bed, removed her other shoe and stocking, then her drawers. Her skirt billowed around her waist, and she felt her petticoat slide down over the smooth skin of her thighs. "And I will. But I mean to get you dirty first."

Lydia trembled as he bent over her to open her bodice and free her breasts from the thin muslin camisole that had confined them. She arched her back, unable to keep from offering herself, and he bent with a throaty chuckle to sample a reaching nipple.

At the same time, he parted her legs with his hand and began to stroke her again. His face and hair left smudges of dirt on Lydia's breasts, but she was past caring.

Brigham left her nipple only to burrow into her neck, where he whispered of the different ways he would arrange her for taking. Then he attended her other breast, at great leisure, before sliding downward to kiss the top of one of her thighs.

She knew what he was going to do, and she wanted it so badly that she couldn't break away. He knelt beside the bed, finally, hooked his hands underneath her knees and parted her legs, then pulled her forward onto the waiting fire of his mouth.

Lydia arched her neck and choked back a cry of scandalized ecstasy.

Brigham nibbled and tongued her until she was half mad with the need of release. "Once won't be enough, Yankee," he rasped between greedy forays. "Once won't be nearly enough. I won't be satisfied until you've given me everything."

"Brigham," she pleaded, the word muffled by the hand she'd clasped over her mouth to keep from shouting like a savage woman rolling on the ground with her mate.

He stopped, began kissing the insides of her thighs, where the flesh was moist and ready. He soothed her until she'd settled down a little, until her breathing was even, and then he brought her back to the brink. At the last possible moment he denied her again, rising reluctantly to his feet.

"After my bath," he promised, admiring her naked breasts as the tips hardened. "I trust you'll be right here, waiting for me?"

Lydia both loved and hated Brigham Quade in that moment. He had made her want him desperately, and they both knew she *would* wait. Until he was ready to attend her. Until hell froze over.

21

As had happened each time before, Brigham's lovemaking left Lydia in a stricken daze. A long interval had passed before she returned to herself, remembered how to make her heart beat and her lungs draw air, and finally spoke.

"I need to know if it's true, what they're saying," she whispered into the moist warmth of Brigham's bare shoulder.

Brigham gave a long, contented sigh and settled himself more comfortably to the mattress. "I guess that depends on what's being said," he replied after a long pause.

Lydia felt the first stirrings of anger as reality settled over her mind like a net of gossamer cobwebs. "You know," she told him, with a small but fierce nudge to his ribcage. "It's that Clover O'Keefe, over at the Satin Hammer. People say she's your mistress now."

There was another sigh, but this one was ragged. "Cl—Miss O'Keefe is a friend of mine," he acknowledged reluctantly.

Lydia's heart was teetering on the edge of some stony precipice, ready to topple over and smash to bits on the rocks of truth below. She knew Brigham would not lie to her; he always said exactly what he was thinking.

"I have a wife," he said at last, his embrace neither tightening nor growing slack, one hand spread possessively over Lydia's bare bottom. "As yet, I've seen no need to take a mistress."

Relief flooded Lydia's soul, but so did fury. It was hard to face Brigham's power over her, let alone accept it as fact. Some primitive feminine instinct declared that she held equal sway over him, but she dismissed that as wishful thinking. She tried to rise, but her husband held her in place with gentle but inexorable strength.

"It's been over a month since—since we were together," she said. Something in her wanted, needed, to fight, to drive Brigham back beyond walls he'd already scaled, away from ground he'd long since conquered.

Brigham laughed. "I've been celibate for longer periods of time than that, my dear wife," he said after his amusement had waned a little. In a sudden but maddeningly graceful move, he pulled her on top of him and flashed his white teeth in the triumphant smile of a dark-haired Viking claiming the spoils of battle. "Don't you believe me?"

Lydia was wonderfully, miserably conscious of the hard, rough, and entirely welcoming maleness of the body beneath hers. Her nipples had tightened, and there was a sensation of something warm tumbling in the depths of her. "Of—Of course I believe you. You haven't the good grace to lie, not even when it would be the kindest thing to do."

He laughed again, and the sound rumbled under her like an earthquake. "As soon as I work out whether that was praise or damnation, I'll respond." He spread his hands over her buttocks, now quivering with renewed sensation, and pressed her to him. His erection seemed as magnificent and elemental as one of those giant trees he'd felled, and Lydia felt herself expanding to take him inside her.

"It was damnation," she answered, but she had already grown breathless. His hands moved from her bottom to her hips, raising her, positioning her. She gave a tremulous cry as the gentle but inevitable invasion began.

While she straddled him, Brigham traced each of her nipples with the tip of an index finger. "Are you really carrying my baby?" he asked in a low voice. He was still entering her, making slow but incredibly pleasurable progress. "Or was that just a ploy to get under my skin?"

Lydia drew in a sharp breath and held it to keep from crying out in the sheer wanton glory of Brigham's leisurely seduction. "There—is really—a baby," she replied grudgingly, her breath fast and shallow now. She tried to move upon him, but he held her hips firmly, stilling her as the pillar of fire rose inside her. "And it seems to me—oh, *dear God*, Brigham—that you're—under *my* skin—"

He let her have a little more of him, a tantalizing fraction of an inch, then raised his head far enough to drink languidly from one of her breasts. "Indeed I am, Mrs. Quade," he replied in a low voice, gruff with both passion and amusement.

"Oh, Brigham, *please*—"

He lowered her farther and farther onto his shaft, until she sheathed him completely. For the first time the fact that his own control was finally slipping was audible in his voice. "This won't—this won't hurt my child?"

Lydia was touched, but the passion had gone too far for her to stop and indulge in tender emotion. The needing was in her blood, coursing through her system like a fever, and Brigham offered the only antidote. "No, Brigham," she managed, with a certainty that came from some deep, unexplored part of herself. "Your son is safe."

At her words, Brigham's powerful body buckled beneath her, like a stallion trying to throw off a rider. Lydia clamped her thighs on either side of his hips and stayed in the saddle. The sweet battle went on and on, until Lydia and Brigham broke through the invisible barrier, their low cries intertwining like ribbon as they streamed toward the ceiling.

When they finally had their fill, Brigham and Lydia drifted off into fitful slumber, their perspiring bodies still tangled in each other and in the sheets. Lydia awakened with a start somewhere in the deepest folds of the night, thinking a lantern had been lit.

Instead, the light of a late-summer moon was shining through the window, bathing her and Brigham and the whole bed in a silvery glow. Lydia's heart tightened at the beauty of it, and the plain hopelessness of loving the man who slept beside her.

She had to rally her strength, she thought miserably, and save some part of her soul for herself. If she didn't, her identity would mingle with Brigham's, then dissolve entirely, and she would have no more substance than the reflection in a looking glass.

She disengaged herself from her husband, cautiously, limb by limb. He stirred, and she waited, her hand resting soothingly on his side, until he settled into deep sleep again. Then she rose from the bed, dressed with quiet awkwardness, and slipped from the room. Part of her spirit stayed behind, nestled close against Brigham's side.

She wept silently as she made her way down the darkened hallway and the rear stairway, through the kitchen, which was spilling with moonlight, and outside into the night. The sounds around her were companionable ones; a night owl hooted in a tree, and she could hear the faint rustle of the water as it broke on the nearby shoreline. Crickets sang their summer chorus in the grass, and a calico cat rushed past, intent on some urgent feline business.

Lydia would have gone straight back to her cottage if she hadn't seen the light burning in a window on the second floor of Quade's Harbor's brand-new general store. Polly lived there now, in a couple of spacious, unfinished rooms above the mercantile.

Polly might be ill, Lydia reasoned, hurrying in the direction of the large, clapboard store. But even as she went over all the dire possibilities, her friend being with child and all, Lydia knew she was fooling herself. She was not going to Polly to lend aid, understanding, and reassurance, but to ask for those things.

She climbed the outside stairway, smiling as she passed the hand-painted letters on the raw wooden wall. QUADE'S MERCANTILE, the ornate words proclaimed. DEVON AND POLLY QUADE, PROPS.

On the splintery landing outside Polly's door, Lydia's resolve faltered a little. It was thoughtless of her to intrude this way, she concluded. Here it was, the middle of the night . . .

The door swung open before Lydia could shuffle back down the stairs and disappear into the few shadows available on such a brightly lit night.

"Lydia," Polly said. In the shimmer of the lantern inside, and the silver splash of moonlight, Lydia could see that her friend had been weeping. The realization caught Lydia by surprise, partly because she'd been so caught up in her own problems, and partly because Polly seemed so strong and optimistic in the daytime. She had a definite knack for running a business, and sometimes it almost seemed that she didn't care if Devon Quade ever came back.

Now, seeing Polly's face, Lydia realized she'd been wrong.

"I saw your light," Lydia said lamely as Polly stepped back to admit her.

Polly closed the door, then embraced her midnight caller for a moment. "Come and sit down. We'll have some tea."

Lydia nodded. She had no better place to be, except in the warmth and safety of Brigham Quade's bed. Just the thought of returning to her cottage filled her with loneliness, even though she knew she would eventually have to go there.

Polly's quarters were tidy and very sparsely furnished. There was a wood cookstove, a changing screen of silk painted with a delicate Oriental design—no doubt purloined from the main house—a table and two chairs, a chest of drawers, and an iron bed. The covers were rumpled, as though Polly had tried to sleep and failed.

"Have you heard anything at all from Devon?" Lydia asked quietly, accepting a seat at Polly's table while her hostess went to the stove, where a kettle of water was already simmering.

Polly's lovely dark hair was wound into a thick braid that trailed down her still-slender back. "No," she said, without turning to meet Lydia's eyes. "He's got to be the stubbornest man God ever breathed life into."

Lydia smiled in spite of herself. "Second stubbornest," she corrected. "I think Brigham taught Devon everything he knows about being hard-headed and unreasonable."

Polly scooped loose tea leaves into a crockery pot, then added water from the kettle. She left the brew to steep while taking mismatched cups from a cupboard fashioned of stacked shipping crates. "Sometimes I think I should just go and find him," she told Lydia distractedly, "and drag him home by the ear. I declare, he acts like a little boy in need of a spanking."

The image of the suave, powerfully built Devon being hauled up the wharf by an earlobe made Lydia smile. All the same, her words were uttered in a sad tone. "Wouldn't it be a luxury just to be weak sometimes?" she reflected. "I mean, Devon and Brigham aren't monsters. Why can't we just let them steer us blissfully through life, the way so many other women let their husbands do?"

Polly sighed heavily, and her answering smile faltered on her lips. "I guess because once you're forced to learn to survive on your own, you don't ever forget it." She brought the teapot to the table, along with sugar and milk and the unmatched cups, and sat down across from Lydia with another sigh. "Besides, I'm not sure Brigham would be attracted to you if you were nothing but a wilting violet, waiting to hear his will so you can act on it."

Lydia would have laughed if she hadn't been so sure she'd become hysterical. "He's never told me he loves me, and he wouldn't compromise to save his soul from hellfire, he's so blasted obdurate! Why couldn't I love somebody like Joe McCauley? Why couldn't I be expecting *his* child?"

Polly's tired, tear-swollen eyes brightened a little, and she reached out quickly to squeeze Lydia's hand. "Oh, Lydia, you're carrying a baby! That's wonderful—now mine will have a cousin to grow up with."

Imagining two small boys playing in the surf, one with Brigham's dark hair and pewter eyes, one with Devon's tawny shock and piercing blue gaze, steadied Lydia's disoriented heart a bit. Then she began to cry again.

Polly went to her bureau, still slender in her lavender silk wrapper, and returned with a clean handkerchief, which Lydia accepted gratefully. It was a measure of the accord between the two women, Lydia thought, that she could blow her nose with no attempt at delicacy. In the meantime, Polly poured the tea.

"Our situations aren't so similar as you seem to think, Lydia," she remarked presently, in a kind tone. "I miss Devon. I'd gladly let him boss me around if he'd just come back and make a home with me."

Lydia gave an unladylike snort and wiped her nose again, just as a precaution. "You're fooling yourself if you think that. You're every bit as strong and willful as Devon is. You could never live as his lapdog, only as an equal partner."

"I suppose you're right," Polly conceded after long and careful thought. "The trouble is, I miss him so much, I truly believe I'll go mad with it sometimes. I pace and weep and pound at these walls with my fists, as though that could change things."

After stirring sugar and a dollop of milk into her tea, Lydia raised the cup to her lips and took a measured sip. "Where do you figure he's taken himself off to? Devon, I mean."

Polly shrugged miserably. "Who knows? He could be in Seattle, or San Francisco, or halfway to China on a sailing ship, for all I can say." Hope lit her eyes, and her voice quickened a little. "I swear, though, it's like there's a golden cord connecting us. It reaches from Devon's heart to mine, and no matter where he goes, he'll never be able to sever it."

Lydia's eyes filled with tears. She felt the depths of

Polly's love for Devon, and knew the perils of caring so much because of her own feelings for Brigham.

"So you're going to stay right here and wait for him?"

Polly nodded, and her expression held a degree of wryness. "You make it sound like I plan to sit on the front porch every night with a lantern burning at my side. I mean to run the store, make it profitable, and raise my baby with the sense of family and belonging that I never had. It isn't a perfect picture, not without Devon, but it's still so much more than a lot of women ever have that I can't help being grateful."

Lydia thought of women like Magna Holmetz and Elly Collier, and that poor creature Dr. McCauley had found cowering in his outhouse. They had endured hardships all their lives, and would continue to do so, and they weren't married to one of the richest, most powerful men in Washington Territory.

"Brigham still refuses to close the brothel," she said after she and Polly had both consumed a good portion of their tea.

"I suspect he'll never give in on that point," Polly answered.

"He says he hasn't taken Clover O'Keefe as a mistress."

"Then I'd say he hasn't," Polly said matter-of-factly. "If he had, I do believe he'd say so, straight out, and expect you to deal with the fact as best you could."

Lydia nodded. Brigham was still faithful to her, despite the crazy convolutions of their relationship, and she treasured that knowledge. She also knew the situation could change in the space of a heartbeat. If Brigham decided he wanted Miss O'Keefe, he'd go directly to the woman and declare himself, and it was most unlikely he'd be refused.

"I can't leave Quade's Harbor and I can't stay," she finally said. "What am I going to do?"

Polly smiled sympathetically and poured more tea for herself and her guest. "Same thing I'm doing, I suppose," she answered. "You'll do whatever work comes to hand and wait. After all, just because we can't solve our problems all at once doesn't mean we shouldn't chip away at a corner here and there."

Polly's remark made sense.

Lydia debated with herself as she went down the stairs after her visit with her sister-in-law. She could return to the big house and crawl back into bed beside her husband, and no one, not even God and His angels, would blame her. She loved Brigham, she was his true and legal wife, and she carried his child tucked away under her heart. On the other hand, if she gave in so completely, she feared the man would soon own her soul.

Assuming he didn't already.

Devon stood at the end of a long wharf, watching smatters of reflected starlight play over the dark water. Even with the noise of Seattle's infamous Skid Road clamoring in his ears, he felt as though he'd been left alone on the planet. He'd been so sure distance would heal him, that he'd forget Polly and her deception easily. All it would take, he'd reasoned blithely, would be a few gallons of whiskey and a whorehouse full of women.

The trouble was, all of the sudden perfectly good liquor tasted like kerosene to him, and worse, he'd thrown it up like some green kid who'd never taken a drink before. As for his visit to the brothel, well, that had been a plain disaster. He'd worked himself up by imagining the woman he'd bought and paid for was Polly, but there was a part of him that wouldn't be fooled. That part, hard as tamarack only moments before, had melted like snow under a tropical sun.

Just remembering it made Devon go crimson with humiliation. He'd paid the whore double her usual fee, and threatened mayhem if she ever told a soul what had happened. She'd patted his cheek and said she knew ways to put the starch back into a man, but Devon had only shaken his head. It was hopeless, and he knew it. For the time being he was spoiled for any woman besides Polly.

He took a thin cigar from the pocket of his shirt, along with a wooden match, then threw both into the water.

The way things had been going for him lately, an innocent smoke would probably turn his stomach inside out.

Devon dragged in a deep breath, then let it out slowly. He turned his thoughts to Lydia——God, he'd been so sure that he wanted her, in his heart and in his bed——but the love he bore for her was that of a brother for his sister. Lydia had been intended for Brigham from the beginning of time; he could see that now.

He shoved splayed fingers through his hair, and the longing that pulled him in the direction of Quade's Harbor was so strong that he nearly believed the water of the harbor would solidify under his feet so that he could take the most direct route home.

Home.

He had been away more than a month, but the sounds of the place still echoed in his soul. He didn't just miss Polly and his general store, he missed his brother, and Lydia, and those two nieces of his. He'd always envied Brigham his children.

He turned from the water, and the star-shimmered path leading homeward, his eyes burning with tears he would have denied before God Himself. The child Polly was carrying——suppose he really was the father, just as she'd said? Suppose he was letting the legendary Quade stubbornness and pride stand between him and everything he'd ever wanted?

Then again, Polly had certainly lied to him, not only in words, but by going through that pretend marriage ceremony in San Francisco. She probably wouldn't be above proffering another man's baby as his own.

The question was, did he care? His loneliness was so great that it threatened to consume him, and a child was a child. Devon wanted a home and family with a desperation that sometimes frightened him.

He strode along the board sidewalk toward the hotel where he'd been staying since his hasty arrival in Seattle weeks before. There was still some soreness in the muscles in his legs and back to remind him of his accident, and his thoughts returned to Polly as though magnetized. Even though he'd been downright cruel to her once he'd regained consciousness, he knew she'd stayed at his side throughout.

It was just possible that she loved him.

Devon wove his way between passing wagons and buggies and crossed the sawdust-covered street to his hotel. "Fool," he muttered to himself, but the pull toward home was even stronger than before, and there was no telling how long he'd be able to resist.

Joe McCauley hoisted himself up off his examining table with a groan, letting his blankets slide to the floor, and finger-combed his hair. Since Frodine was in his bed, he'd had no civilized choice except to sleep in his examining room—if the ordeal he'd just been through could be *called* sleep. His back was killing him, the wind was howling like a thousand wolves, and somebody was literally flinging themselves at his front door.

Yawning, Joe pulled on his shirt and trousers and put his suspenders up over his shoulders. "I'm coming!" he yelled, murmuring as he made his way through the house. Despite the hard and dangerous work they did every day, some of these lumberjacks were nothing but crybabies. They risked getting themselves torn in two while topping a tree, or pinned underneath one with a branch going straight through their belly, but let them get a sliver or a bee sting, and you'd have thought they were dying.

"Hold on!" Joe said before wrenching open the door. He regretted his impatience immediately when he saw the terrified little boy standing on his front step. The Holmetz kid looked up at him with huge dark eyes, his thin face pinched white.

"My mama," the child blurted. "It's her time."

Joe was instantly as awake as if he'd gulped down a mug of strong coffee. "Is she having trouble?"

The boy nodded. "There's blood."

Silently, Joe cursed, but his voice was even and calm when he spoke again. "You run and get Miss Lydia straight away. Tell her I'm going to need her help with your mama."

Again the boy nodded, then he bounded down the pathway to the road, veering off in the direction of Lydia's cottage.

Joe went back to the kitchen, where Frodine was setting water on to heat. She was already dressed for school, which she attended faithfully every day, and so far there had been no visit from her no-good father.

"Somethin' wrong?" she asked, her dark eyes wide with concern. Her blond hair was wound into a flyaway braid, and she looked like the woman she was in her borrowed dress, which was a size or two too small for her.

"The Holmetz baby is on its way." Joe grabbed a basin and began dipping tepid water from the reservoir on the side of the stove. "I'll need Lydia's help today, so I doubt there'll be any school."

The disappointment in Frodine's eyes was keen; she'd just grasped the alphabet and learned to count to a hundred, and she begrudged every second of education she'd been denied. She followed Joe as he went into his office, stripped off his shirt, and began to wash in the basin of water he'd set on the examining table.

"Miss Lydia said there's no reason in the world I couldn't take another name," she babbled. "Frodine don't suit me, you know."

Joe was splashing industriously, a little annoyed that the girl had lingered while he was washing. It wasn't entirely proper, her seeing him without his shirt on, but then neither was letting her live under his roof without a chaperon.

"I know," he said, reaching for a towel.

"What name do you like?"

Joe snatched up his shirt again, thinking not of Frodine's dilemma but of Mrs. Holmetz, who was probably in considerable pain and might even be dying. "Etta," he said shortly, picking the name off the top of his head. "I like Etta."

With that, he grabbed his bag and his coat, shoved on his boots, and hurried out of the house.

When Brigham woke for the second time, just before dawn, he could hear the wind whistling in the tops of the big trees surrounding the house. It was a sound he'd grown used to, a sound he loved, but today something about it made the pit of his stomach turn cold.

He cupped his hands behind his head and stretched. His body was still languid from the sweet satisfaction he'd taken in the night, but a persistent ache had settled in his heart. Lydia was gone, had been for several hours, and he was pretty sure she didn't intend on coming back.

Brigham cursed. He'd been awake when she'd sneaked out of bed and dressed, after that last feverish bout of lovemaking, but he'd feigned sleep. It had been his pride that kept him quiet, and not any nobility or prudence. He'd known she wouldn't stay, even if he begged, and he'd also known that if he'd so much as opened his mouth, he'd have been pleading with her.

He'd never begged anyone for anything, and he sure as hell didn't plan to start now.

Brigham rolled onto his side and squinted at the window, where pink and apricot shadows were invading the otherwise solid blackness, slowly turning it to gray. The sun would be up in another few minutes, but the moan of the wind told him the weather wouldn't be good. From the sounds of things, there was a storm blowing in, the kind that made it too dangerous to work in the woods.

"Shit," he said. He had a deadline to meet, and the least the weather could have done was hold for another day or two so he could get the lumber ready for the ship that would soon be arriving.

Normally, he would have been out of bed by then, splashing himself awake at the washstand and reaching for his clothes, but today he lingered. He could catch Lydia's scent from her pillow, and the warmth of her passion and tenderness still heated the marrow of his bones.

He smiled. She was going to have his baby. A shout of pure joy rose inside him, pushing past all the doubts and misgivings that plagued his spirit, but he stopped the cry at his throat.

After all, it wasn't as though Lydia loved him or anything. She responded wholeheartedly to his attentions in bed, it was true, and she'd even come up with some innovations of her own that had made him certain he was about to die of pleasure. He knew only too well that the spirit wasn't always willing, even though the flesh might be weak. Lydia was a young, healthy woman, just discovering the delights her body was capable giving and receiving, and it was entirely possible that any man with a reasonable degree of skill as a lover could have made her carry on the way she had.

The thought chased the sparkle of pride from Brigham's eyes. Hell and tarnation, he wouldn't be able to stand it if Lydia were to lay herself down in another man's bed. His reason, rock-solid until the day Devon had brought her home from San Francisco and presented her like a present, would desert him entirely. He swore again and thrust himself out of bed, his legs so entangled in the twisted sheets that he nearly fell on his face.

Stumbling over to the washstand, he poured water from the pitcher into a basin, and then stood studying himself in the small mirror affixed to the wall. He imagined Lydia going on her merry way, visiting his bed when she felt the need, then returning to her cottage on Main Street and her work as a schoolteacher as if she didn't even have a husband. He considered the example he'd be setting for his son, not to mention Millie and Charlotte, letting his wife treat him like that, and the eyes looking back at him from the mirror rounded in proud horror.

No one dared show amusement now, of course, but if Lydia kept up her high-handed eastern ways, he'd soon be the laughingstock of every lumber camp between California and the Canadian border. And he'd be damned if he'd let that happen.

22

A STRAY PAPER BLEW PAST LYDIA LIKE A KITE AS SHE hurried along behind the Holmetz boy, and she held her skirts to keep the rising wind from catching them. The sky overhead was an ominous gray, the harbor seemed restless and expectant of some momentous event, and the trees of the forest that curled around the town like a protective arm rocked alarmingly from side to side.

When Lydia and her escort burst into the Holmetz cottage, the place was as neat as if company had been expected. There were pallets on either side of the small front parlor, where the children slept, along with a few pitiful belongings. Mrs. Holmetz lay moaning on a straw-stuffed mattress in the tiny bedroom beyond, and Joe was already with her.

His shirtsleeves were pushed up past his elbows, and his muscular forearms still glowed from the scrubbing he'd given them. Looking at him, Lydia felt her heart constrict, wishing again that she had fallen in love with Joe instead of Brigham. She understood the doctor, even though they'd been on opposite sides in the war, and had much in common with him.

She went to the kitchen without a word, snatched up a

bucket and hurried into the backyard to the pump. When a large kettle was heating on the stove, she washed her hands and arms in the small amount of water Joe hadn't used and hurried back to the bedroom.

The children were standing at the foot of their parents' bed, small hands gripping the iron railing, eyes wide with fear and a woeful knowledge of the dangers their mother faced.

"Go to school," Lydia told them, with gentle briskness. "Tell Charlotte to work on her geography. Millie is to practice the multiplication tables, concentrating heavily on the sevens. Frodine should practice her alphabet, and all the rest of you will read to yourselves from the primers. There had better not be any lollygagging just because I'm not around to keep an eye on things, either."

The children looked profoundly relieved, and after giving their mother sympathetic glances, they dashed off to obey Lydia's orders. That left Hans, who had every right to stay but was obviously going to be of no help whatsoever.

"Go to the main house and tell Jake Feeny you need all the pots and kettles the two of you can carry, and some clean sheets as well," Lydia told Mr. Holmetz. Magna punctuated the conversation with an unsettlingly shrill scream, and Hans looked furiously toward Joe.

"Is not right for a man to touch my wife that way," Hans said.

"He's a doctor," Lydia argued, maneuvering the big man toward the doorway.

Hans's expression was obdurate, and his rough skin had gone crimson. "Magna never needed doctors before. You look after her. All she needs is woman to help."

Lydia glanced back at Joe, who was examining Magna and paying no attention to Hans, although he couldn't have helped hearing the exchange.

"Not this time," Lydia replied quietly. "Magna is in trouble, Hans. She could die, and so could the child. You must cooperate with the doctor and with me. Now, go and do as I say. Please."

The big man hesitated for a long, suspenseful moment,

staring at his writhing, feverish wife, and Lydia repressed an urge to scream at him in frustration. She knew now it wasn't Magna's well-being he was so concerned about, but her *virtue,* and under the circumstances, that was plainly appalling.

Joe raised calm eyes from his suffering patient to Hans's face. He didn't speak, and yet his message was plain enough.

Hans turned around and left the room.

"We'll have to take the baby," Joe told Lydia, smoothing Magna's sweat-dampened hair back from her forehead. "The poor little mite isn't going to make it without help."

Lydia closed her eyes for a moment, then drew a deep breath and let it out in a rush. "All right. Is there ether?"

"In my bag," Joe said. "Sit with Mrs. Holmetz while I go and find more water to scrub up again, will you please?"

Asking was only a formality, Lydia knew. She'd already approached the bedside and taken Magna's work-worn hand in both her own. "The hurting will stop soon," she said to the half-delirious woman, hoping the promise wasn't a lie.

"My little one," Magna gasped out. "Please don't let my little one die."

Lydia forced back the tears that burned behind her eyes. This was no time to fall apart. "We'll do everything we can," she said.

When Joe returned with the kettleful of hot water, he poured it into the basin on the battered chest against the wall and washed again, the strong yellow soap he used filling the stale air with the smell of some antiseptic. Clean again, he took a pad of folded gauze from his bag and laid it on Magna's pillow. Then he handed Lydia a brown bottle.

"Have you ever administered ether before?" he asked.

Again that mental shift occurred, and Lydia was back in the horrifying din of a Civil War field hospital. "When we had it on hand, yes," she answered, carefully pulling the cork from the bottle. Most of the time, nurses and surgeons had simply had to do without the medical supplies they needed; the conflict had turned out to be so much bigger and more brutal than even the most pessimistic doomsayers had predicted.

Lydia turned her attention to Magna, moistening the gauze carefully and laying it over the patient's mouth and nose. Joe, in the meantime, had tossed back the covers and raised the woman's nightdress to her waist. Her distended belly flexed as the life within struggled to be born.

Please, Lydia prayed silently. She never allowed herself a more specific request when interceding for a patient; in her view, only God could know who should live or die.

As Magna began to breathe in the ether and relax, Joe cleansed her stomach with an alcohol solution and brought a scalpel from his bag. Lydia watched approvingly as he washed the instrument in antiseptic.

By the time Hans had returned with the requested pots and sheets, Lydia had finished putting the patient under anesthesia and replaced the blood-soaked bedding with a plain blanket.

A figure appeared in the bedroom doorway, filling it, but to Lydia's relief, it was Brigham who stood on the threshold, not Hans.

Joe began the incision, after a glance at the visitor. "For God's sake, keep the happy husband out of here until we're through," he said calmly.

Brigham nodded, his look lingering on Lydia for a moment, and then turned and left the room.

Lydia gave Magna more ether to breathe. The smell of blood was thick in the room, coppery and pungent, and she swayed slightly on her feet. Still, her attention didn't waver.

With the outer incision finished, Joe began the inner one, his hands steady and deft as they worked. "How's her breathing?" he asked.

"Regular and a little shallow," Lydia reported. She could hear Brigham speaking calmly to Hans in the other room, the sound accompanied by the clatter and clank of pans being put on the stove. Just knowing her husband was so near, even if they were estranged, was a comfort to Lydia.

Joe reached inside Magna's stomach and pulled out a small, bluish infant covered in blood and a powdery substance. "Hello, little one," he said gruffly, clearing the tiny mouth with his finger.

The baby girl gave a weak little mew, like a newborn kitten, and Lydia held her breath. A second later the child began to squall.

Joe tied off and cut the cord, then turned the baby over to Lydia to tend and called to Brigham for hot water and sheets.

Brigham immediately appeared with the requested items, but when he glanced at Magna, he went completely white under his woodsman's tan, and Lydia honestly thought he was going to collapse. He pulled himself together, however, and left the room without a word.

While Lydia happily bathed and wrapped the Holmetzes' baby girl, Joe quickly closed Magna's incisions with neat sutures. She carried the infant out to the kitchen, where Hans waited anxiously. To her disappointment, there was no sign of Brigham.

"I'd like to introduce you to a very pretty young lady," Lydia said, tenderly lifting the blanket so that Hans could see the baby's face. "This is your daughter, Mr. Holmetz."

Hans's grizzled features softened as he studied his child. "Magna?" he inquired, his tone raspy.

"She survived," Lydia said carefully, knowing only too well how many things could go wrong in the next few hours. "She'll need special care, you know, because we had to take the baby surgically."

Hans met Lydia's steady gaze with a glower. "What?"

Joe came out of the small bedroom and stood in the doorway, his clothes blood-spattered. In a few brisk, no-nonsense words, he explained what had been done and the reasons for it.

Somewhat to Lydia's surprise, Hans subsided, although he was a much bigger man than Dr. McCauley.

He sat down on a makeshift chair and held out his enormous arms. "I hold baby," he said. "You please see to Magna."

Lydia surrendered the infant and raised her eyes to Joe, who nodded almost imperceptibly.

Returning to the bedroom, Lydia gently bathed the still-unconscious woman and replaced the bedding with the things Brigham had brought. The image of her husband's wan, shocked face did not leave her mind for a moment.

Hans came in, tenderly placed his baby in Lydia's arms, and bent over Magna to kiss her forehead. Lydia forgave him for his earlier reluctance to let a doctor see his wife undressed.

"This one we keep," he murmured to Magna.

Lydia's throat tightened. She knew the Holmetzes had lost several babies in the last few years. She held the sleeping infant close to her breast and tried to will some of her own strength into the little body.

Joe appeared in the doorway where Brigham had stood earlier, and, although he looked weary, he glowed as though a lantern burned behind his skin. "I'll send Frodine over to look after Mrs. Holmetz and the baby," he said, ignoring Hans and addressing himself to Lydia. "You'd better get some rest."

Lydia sighed. She probably looked a sight, all right. She hadn't slept the night before, and assisting with the birth of a child was physically and emotionally exhausting. She nodded. "Yes, Doctor," she said softly, with a smile.

He watched her for a moment, then turned and walked away.

About fifteen minutes later Frodine arrived, looking flushed and excited. Her dark eyes sparkled as she showed Lydia her slate board, on which she'd carefully written the name ETTA in block letters.

"It's my new name," she said in a trilling whisper, setting aside the slate and reaching for the baby. "From now on, I'm Etta. Frodine is gone forever."

Lydia smiled. "All right," she agreed. "Etta."

Since it soon became clear that Joe had already given Etta detailed instructions, Lydia stumbled back to her cottage, took off her clothes in the privacy of her small bedroom, and gave herself a sponge bath. Then she put on her nightgown, crawled into bed, and immediately lost consciousness.

Polly stood on the porch of the general store, the moist wind whipping tendrils of dark hair against her cheeks, her eyes fixed on the mail boat as it came into port.

A ramp was put in place, and two men in rough clothes stepped onto the wharf, each with a canvas bag slung over one shoulder. They wore hats, so Polly couldn't make out their features, but it didn't matter. Neither one of them could possibly be Devon.

She turned, wiping her hands on her apron, and went back into the store.

The business was taking shape. She had a coffee grinder now, and cheese and books and calico to sell, among other goods, and every time the bell on the fancy cash register chimed, Polly felt hopeful. Even if Devon never came back—and she prayed he would—she was building something for herself and her baby.

In the privacy of the store, she stood behind the counter and turned her back to the door, pretending to examine the tins of crackers, beans, oysters, and other selections on the shelf while surreptitiously raising the hem of her apron to her eyes. The wind howled and shrieked around the sturdy walls of the unpainted building, and rain began to pound at the roof.

Polly composed herself, went to the potbellied stove against the opposite wall and added a chunk of wood to the dying blaze. The air was chilly, and she felt uneasy.

When two giggling bundles of calico and energy burst into the store, she was cheered. Millie and Charlotte stood just over the threshold, dripping wet.

"What on earth are the two of you doing out in this weather?" Polly demanded, but her scolding was good-natured, and the girls knew it. "Get over here and stand by this stove immediately, before you catch your deaths!"

Brigham's daughters obeyed, their hair, skin, pinafores, and stockings soaking wet.

"Papa said we could each have a peppermint stick," Millie announced, prying her way into a pocket and bringing out two copper pennies.

Polly smiled. Like Devon, she loved these children quite dearly and was always glad to see them. She also knew that Brigham never missed an opportunity to increase her business at the store, even though he was in competition with her, in a sense. She took two candy sticks from the jar on the counter and brought them to her sodden customers, careful to accept the proudly offered pennies with proper respect.

Millie went to the window, leaving a trail of rainwater on the sawdust-sprinkled floor, happily munching on her candy. "The mail boat's in," she observed. "Maybe there'll be a letter from Uncle Devon."

The mention of her husband's name snapped against Polly's spirit like the backlash of a tree branch. She glanced through the foggy, rain-speckled glass and sighed. Then she tried for a cheerful expression. "I wouldn't be at all surprised if he wrote to the two of you, or to your father," she said. Every day she was stupid enough to hope Devon would get off that mail boat when it came in, and every day she was brutally disappointed.

"There're two men coming up the hill toward the store," Millie reported, while Charlotte remained by the stove, trying to dry her skirts, the peppermint jutting out of one side of her mouth like a politician's cigar. "I suppose they'll want to hire on with Papa's lumber company."

Charlotte sighed in a fashion so long-suffering that it bordered on martyrdom. "Why else would anyone come here?" she inquired, leaning closer to the fire now and combing her fingers through her wet hair.

Polly smiled sadly at Charlotte's wanderlust. She marveled that the girl couldn't see what she had, right there in Quade's Harbor—a family who loved her, a wonderful home, plenty of fine clothes, all she could want to eat. "Oh, I think this town has things to recommend it," she said, dusting the counter even though she'd polished it earlier with beeswax.

"Like what?" Charlotte asked. She didn't put the question meanly, for though she was spirited, like her sister, she was neither unkind nor ill-mannered.

Millie answered before Polly could think of a response. "Ask Anna Holmetz when was the last time she had a new pair of shoes," she challenged. "Ask her about the two weeks their whole family had to live on buttermilk because there wasn't any money for food. Ask her—"

Charlotte flushed, probably having at least glimpsed the error of her ways. "There is more to life than shoes and food, Millicent Quade," she said haughtily after a moment of recovery. "You don't understand that because you haven't a poet's soul like I do."

"Pooh," said Millie, reminding Polly more of Brigham than ever. Though, of course, he probably wouldn't have used such mild language. " 'There was a young woman named Puck—' " she began.

"Stop!" Polly cried.

The little tin bell over the front door tinkled as a man came in, hat slouched low over his face, and set his kit down next to the flour barrel. He was obviously one of the new workers who'd gotten off the boat that day, come to buy tobacco or ask where to go to sign on with one of Brigham's timber crews, but there was something disturbingly familiar about him.

Then he removed his hat, and Polly saw his thick, maple-brown hair, his irreverent green eyes, that smile that cocked up at one side in such a deceptively charming way.

She felt the color slip from her cheeks.

"Hello, Polly," he said.

Polly gripped the edges of the counter. It was Nat Malachi, the man who had so captivated her when she was an innocent, foolish girl. The man who had brought her to San Francisco and taught her to deceive good men like Devon. The man she'd never expected to see again, outside her nightmares.

Millie and Charlotte, perceptive children both, were staring at the new arrival. They'd obviously noticed that his appearance had startled their aunt, even though she was making a concerted effort to appear calm.

"You'd better run along home, girls," she said in a voice higher and thinner than usual for her. "Looks like there's a lull in the rain, and who can guess how long it will last."

"She's right," Millie said, though she and her sister still looked intensely curious. "Lydia will skin us if we don't have our lessons ready for tomorrow."

As for Nat, he was just smiling at them, with that crooked grin in place and his hat in his hand.

The children disappeared, and after they were gone, the warm, cozy store seemed to yawn around Polly, dangerous and cold like some cave far under the ground.

"What do you want?" she demanded, taking the rifle Brigham had given her from its place under the counter and cocking it resolutely.

Nat laughed. "Now what kind of greeting is that, after you and I have been apart for so long?" he drawled, starting to round the end of the counter.

Polly shoved the tip of the barrel into the hollow at the base of his throat. "Don't come near me, Nat, I'm warning you!" she hissed. "I'm married now, for real, and I mean to honor my vows."

He drew back gracefully, holding up both hands about shoulder level, mouth curved into an indulgent grin. He looked around at the tidy displays of canned goods, work boots, bolts of practical fabric, and other items. "This is quite a nest you've found for yourself. I don't blame you for being a little bristly."

The trembling in her arms and legs abated slightly, and Polly ran the tip of her tongue over dry lips. "The mail boat will stay about an hour," she said. "When it sails for Seattle, I'd like you to be on board."

"We don't always get what we want in this life, Pol," he

said, with mock ruefulness. "You sure ought to know that by now."

Polly stared at the man she'd thought she loved, the man who had used her so shamelessly in San Francisco. "There's nothing for you here," she said, her palms sweating where she gripped the rifle. "This place is too slow and too decent to appeal to the likes of you!"

He laughed again as a fresh spate of rain clattered against the windowpanes. A few drops dripped down the chimney and sizzled on the hot fire in the stove. "Where is he?" he demanded, folding his arms. "Where's this fine, upstanding husband of yours?"

She swallowed. "Never you mind where Devon is. If he catches you around here—and you can be sure I'll tell him just who you are—he'll hang you up for the birds like a chunk of suet."

"You're a liar," he replied charitably. Even sweetly. "I heard the whole story in Seattle—you told him he wasn't the first, and he left in a fit of righteous wrath. Isn't that true, darlin'?"

It took all Polly's restraint to keep from flying at him, claws bared, hissing like a wild animal defending its den. "He'll be back," she said, wondering at the certainty evident in her voice. She'd never been less sure of anything in her life.

"And when he comes through that door, you'll be here waiting for him." He gave the words a maudlin, cloying sweetness. "Forget that, because it's nothing but an empty fancy. You belong with me, and I'm about to take you upstairs to the bed your fine husband deserted and show you the truth of it."

Polly could not have surrendered to the caresses of any man other than Devon, but the idea of lying down with this one upended her stomach. "Just take another step toward me," she breathed, "and I swear by every angel in heaven that I'll kill you."

For the first time, he looked exasperated. Then he tossed his hat down on the floor in a fit of pique. "Now you're being just plain silly, Polly!" he yelled. "Have you forgotten that I'm the man who took you away from that crazy father of yours? That it was me who taught you to feel real good?"

Color surged back into Polly's cheeks, and she braced the rifle on the countertop, so that the barrel was pointed straight at Nat's chest. "Get out," she said.

He arched an eyebrow and bent down to pick up his hat. Just as he was straightening, the bell jingled again and Dr. Joe came in. Polly hoped she'd gotten the rifle out of sight before he noticed it.

"Thanks for telling me where to find the boss man," Nat said, with buoyant good cheer, scooping up his canvas pack and pushing past the doctor to step out into the rain.

Dr. McCauley removed his round black hat and shook the rainwater from its brim, but there was a thoughtful expression in his eyes.

"Something you needed?" Polly asked, her friendly smile a bit brittle.

The physician smiled wearily. "About three weeks of uninterrupted sleep," he answered, approaching the counter. "Mrs. Quade, is everything all right?"

"Everything is fine," Polly lied. "What can I get for you? Did Frodine send you for something?"

He selected a tin of peaches from one of the shelves, then a sack of tobacco and a piece of rock candy. "She's calling herself Etta now," he replied, "and for her sake, I hope it sticks."

"Oh," Polly answered. She liked Dr. McCauley's pretty ward, though she wondered how long a single man could get away with having a young woman live in his house, even in that rough-and-tumble town.

"I believe she favors licorice," he said, laying his few purchases on the counter and reaching into the pocket of his trousers. "I'll have a stick of that, too, I guess."

Polly took the candy from its jar and wrapped it carefully in brown paper salvaged from the packages and parcels of goods she'd been receiving to stock the store. "I suppose Mr. Harrington met the boat and fetched the mail, like every other day?"

Doc smiled at her, gathered up his tobacco and

peaches and the packet of licorice, and put his hat on again. "I suppose," he agreed gently. "There's been no word from Devon yet, then?"

Miserably, Polly shook her head. She supposed she should be glad Devon was away, now that Nat Malachi was around. Malachi could be mean and vindictive, despite his affable manner, and he just might figure he was entitled to some revenge against Devon.

Joe reached across the counter and patted her hand. "He won't stay away forever," he assured her, and then took the things he'd bought and went out.

Polly rushed across the room to the door, which she would have bolted if she hadn't seen Mr. Harrington mounting the steps with a large parcel in his arms. More supplies had arrived to grace the shelves of the mercantile, but Polly was too distraught to feel the usual excitement.

Nat had found her, and for better or worse, she would have to deal with him. She'd promised herself, and the baby growing within her, that there would be no more running away.

"He took himself over to the Satin Hammer for a drink," Jake Feeny told Lydia that evening, when she came to the back door of the Quade household inquiring for Brigham. The rain had stopped, but the wind was still ferocious, and it made her nervous the way the ancient trees behind the house swayed back and forth.

It was a moment before Lydia registered Jake's words. When she did, she felt a hot, helpless rage surge through her like venom. "I see," she said stiffly, turning to go.

Jake caught hold of her cloak. "Won't you stay, Mrs. Quade, and have some supper? I mixed up a nice batch of biscuits, and we've got chicken dipped in cornmeal and fried up crisp in bacon grease."

The last thing Lydia cared about at that moment was food, even though she hadn't eaten all day. All she could think about was Brigham, breaking his word already, when only the night before he'd claimed he would be faithful.

"No," she said, her voice small and almost too soft to hear over the cries of the wind. "Thank you, but I'm not—I'm not hungry." Again she started to walk away.

"What about that little kitten?" Jake persisted. "Don't it need some nice cream?"

Lydia couldn't bring herself to turn down Ophelia's favorite repast; it wouldn't be fair. "Yes, that would be lovely, thank you."

Jake drew her back into the kitchen while he took a jar of cream from the fancy oak icebox. The warmth of the fire was inviting, and the food smelled heavenly—there was even a thick gravy to pour over the biscuits—but Lydia couldn't linger.

She'd come to reassure Brigham, she thought, in furious amazement, as she hurried through the drizzly twilight a few minutes later, holding the jar of cream close so she wouldn't drop it. She'd seen the horror in his eyes when he looked upon the bloody birth of Magna Holmetz's little daughter, and she'd been certain he feared that she might face a similar ordeal when it was time for their own child to be born. Because she loved Brigham, whatever their political and moral differences, she'd wanted to remind him that she was healthy and strong, assure him there was no reason to be afraid.

She'd come out in the rain, without her supper, just to make Brigham feel better, and how had he repaid her? By taking himself off to the Satin Hammer to revel with liquor and bad women in general, and Clover O'Keefe in particular.

Well, Lydia vowed to herself as she stormed along the street, she'd just confront him in that den of iniquity and find out what he had to say for himself.

She stopped at her cottage long enough to give a mewing Ophelia a saucer of cream, then lit a lantern and set out for the Satin Hammer. Her mood, she guessed, was much like General Sherman's must have been when he crossed the border into Georgia.

23

*L*YDIA WAS NO STRANGER TO PLACES LIKE THE SATIN
Hammer, unfortunately. As a child she'd often ventured
into saloons and brothels to find her father and bring him
home, and in San Francisco, of course, she'd earned
survival wages by playing piano for the patrons.

Still, as she stood outside the slapdash wooden building, just beyond the reach of the lantern light, with the
tinkling, brassy music swirling around her like smoke,
she felt her momentum seeping away into the sawdust at
her feet.

There had always been a next time, no matter how
faithfully Papa had sworn to leave the bottle alone, and
yet she had gone back to rescue him again and again,
causing herself tremendous humiliation and pain in the
process.

She lifted her chin, and the moist night wind played
with her hair. If Brigham wanted to drink and go
whoremongering, he would, and her presence, her words,
no matter how sensible and compelling, would serve no
purpose. Except, of course, to make herself totally miserable.

She turned slowly and began walking back toward

home. Joe McCauley must have seen her passing from his front window, because he came sprinting down the path to fall in step beside her.

"Nice night for a walk," he called, with wry good humor, over the howl of the rising wind.

"Go away," Lydia called back, but she was glad when her friend ignored the injunction, because just then she felt her singular aloneness more keenly than she had in a very long time.

Joe escorted her up the steps to her porch, then followed her through the front door. He waited politely while she lighted a lantern and scooped up Ophelia, who came mewing to greet her.

"Brigham," Joe said, summing up all her troubles in that one name.

Lydia took off her cloak and hung it on the peg without shaking the rainwater off first. She reached up to smooth the back of her hair, just beneath the loose chignon. "Yes," she confirmed disconsolately, without looking at him. "Brigham."

Joe went into the small kitchen, and Lydia heard clanking sounds as he built up the fire and set the teakettle on to heat. She stayed in the front room, struggling to assimilate the disturbing discoveries she'd just made—not about her husband, but about herself.

The doctor came back. "Sit," he said, with brotherly impatience, pressing Lydia into her rocking chair. Then he crouched before her. "You went to the Satin Hammer," he finished.

Lydia scowled at him. "Have you taken to following me about?"

Joe only grinned, apparently undaunted by her hostility. "I gave that up when I realized how much you love that big lumberjack of yours. What's happened, Lydia? Was he there, at the saloon, I mean?"

She shrugged. "I suppose so. In the end, I couldn't bring myself to go in and find out."

He arched an eyebrow. "You're even more courageous than I first thought, Mrs. Quade. I'm not sure I've ever made the acquaintance of another woman—above a certain social standing, of course—who would even consider venturing into such an establishment."

Lydia sighed, meeting Joe's eyes directly for the first time. "I've been inside every sort of saloon at one time or another, either singing for my supper or searching for my weak but well-meaning father."

"I'll ask about singing for your supper later," Joe told her, rising as he heard the heat begin to surge through the kettle on the stove. "Right now, I'd like to hear about your errant sire."

Resigned, Lydia talked about her father's drinking while Joe brewed tea for them both and brought it back in enamel mugs. He sat on an upended crate, listening, not once interrupting the flow of misery Lydia had never really shared with another living soul.

"I guess I should have left Papa in those bars," she said, when the long description of degrading experiences was over. "Instead I made it easier for him to go back the next time because he always woke up in his own bed, thanks to me. The messes had been cleaned up, so he didn't have to face the realities of the things he'd done. I enabled him to live the lie that things were normal at our house."

Joe took a thoughtful sip of his tea. "Did he abuse you in any way?"

Lydia wiped a tear from her cheek. "Not like you mean," she said hoarsely. "He didn't beat me, and he certainly didn't ever touch me in an improper manner. On the other hand, there was never enough food or enough coal for the fire, and I wore my clothes long after I'd outgrown them. Mine was no worse than a lot of children's lives, and much better than many others'."

"You always took care of your father," Joe stated.

Again Lydia had to agree. "I didn't just fetch him home from the saloons. I lied to his patients, and to the grocer and the coal man and anyone else who would have made trouble."

He took her hand. "You did the best you could, Lydia, with who you were and what you knew at the time, and you acted out of love. Don't berate yourself for that."

She pushed with her heels, so that the chair began to rock beneath her, but she found no comfort in the rhythm. "Brigham isn't like Papa. I know he isn't."

Joe sighed and rubbed the back of his neck. "Amen to that, Mrs. Quade. Brigham appears to be a healthy man, with no need of anyone to take care of him, and I think that's part of the trouble, where you're concerned at least."

Lydia stared at her friend with wide eyes, feeling a faint rush of anger sweep through her blood. "What are you saying?"

He didn't falter or hedge. "You're a strong woman, Lydia. You've always had to make your own way, and the concept of leaning on another person, even briefly, is alien to you. I think you'd be more comfortable if Brigham were a weaker man, so that you could look after him the way you did your father."

"That's not true," Lydia immediately insisted.

"Isn't it? Brigham is an equal, every bit as strong as you are. That's what scares you, I'll wager. You were in control, dealing with frightened young soldiers, boys in pain or dying, or both, God rest their souls. You know how to deal with small children, and with women in childbirth. But Brigham needs a partner as well as a wife, and you haven't the faintest idea how to respond."

Lydia shot to her feet and just as quickly sat down again. "He doesn't want a partner," she protested, although she was no longer so certain of her opinions. "Brigham wants a wife he can dominate."

Joe's grin was damnably patient. "Does he? We've had a few conversations over brandy, he and I, and Brigham intimated, even if he didn't say it straight out, that he wasn't happy with his first wife. She was the delicate sort, you know, always fainting and afraid of shadows."

"Shadows?" Lydia wanted to defend Isabel Quade staunchly, perhaps because, without her, there would have been no Millie and no Charlotte. "The woman had to face incredible hardships—Indian attacks, sickness, being a world away from practically everything she knew and loved."

Joe nodded in agreement. "She responded by hiding from her fears, by weeping and wringing her hands and begging Brigham to take her home to Maine. I can't imagine you behaving that way. You see life as a challenge, and an adventure, not an unending threat."

"I've done my share of weeping and wringing my hands, Joseph."

"Yes. I'll wager it was in the privacy of an army tent, late at night, when you'd been relieved of hospital duty and there was no other course of action left to you. Think, Lydia. You yourself are really very much like Brigham, adamant in your opinions, immovable in your determination. You understand how to lead, but you don't know a whit about following."

Lydia flushed, but something stopped her from making a heated denial. "I wish you would just go home," she said petulantly, after a brief silence full of struggle.

Joe smiled, picked up her tea mug and his own, and meandered back into the kitchen. He poured another cup for Lydia and brought it to her in passing, on the way to the front door. "The truth can be a fierce adversary, Mrs. Quade," he said, touching an imaginary hat brim in a gentlemanly gesture of farewell. "I would advise you not to waste valuable energy trying to divert it from its natural path."

Lydia remained in the rocking chair when he'd gone, petting the kitten, which had settled in her lap, and sipping her second cup of tea. Even if she hadn't slept the sleep of the dead most of the day, she wouldn't have been able to rest.

As he walked back toward his own house, shoulders hunched against the wind, Joe McCauley wondered exactly why he'd made such a good case for Brigham, back there in Lydia's parlor. He might have argued for his own interests, persuaded her to petition a judge for release from her hasty marriage, then taken her to wife.

A lamp was glowing in the front window when he reached his gate, and he paused, even though the wind was piercing his shirt and pummeling his ears. He thought of the girl he'd found in the outhouse and smiled.

She was a beauty, he allowed to himself as he made his way toward the porch. She was full of sauce and spirit, like Lydia, and it was certainly plain that she'd suffered during her short time on earth. For all of that, Frodine-now-Etta wasn't carrying an entire war around with her.

The door opened and she filled the doorway, wisps of pale hair dancing around her face. "I reckoned you'd spend the night at her place," she said. Pain lurked in her words, along with a reluctant acceptance that such was the way of the world.

Joe crossed the porch and moved Etta gently out of his way to enter the house. With one foot he pushed the door shut against the wind. "Mrs. Quade is a married woman," he said, with a sigh of resignation. Maybe, he reflected, he was just now coming to terms with that fact, though he'd thought he'd already dealt with it.

Etta's dark eyes were wide, and her throat worked as she swallowed. "Brig ain't nobody to mess with anyhow," she said, with nettling reverence. "He catches any man pickin' petals in Mrs. Quade's petunia patch, he'll probably horsewhip the stupid son of a bitch in the street."

Suppressing a smile, Joe moved to the lamp and turned it down until the room was in shadow. "Is that what you've learned at school?" he challenged benignly, turning to look at her. "To talk like a bull whacker on a bad day?"

Even in the dim light, he saw her blush prettily. She smoothed her borrowed skirts and then squared her shoulders. "You—You want me to be a lady?" she asked, her voice barely above a whisper.

He looked at her for a long moment, and all the loneliness of the difficult years just past threatened to crush him. He did not love Etta, but he liked her, and many a successful marriage had been built on lesser foundations. "Yes," he said. "I want you to be a lady."

She shifted her gaze to the floor, just briefly, then met his eyes with an expression of proud desolation. "Why?"

"Because I need one so badly," he admitted, with more frankness than he'd thought himself capable of displaying. He sighed again, rubbed the back of his neck with one hand. "I'm just realizing that I've been marking time since the day I came home from the war and found my family gone. I've been waiting to die, more or less."

Etta's question was barely audible. "And now?"

"Now I want my life back. I want a woman in my bed and a flock of children who might just make the world a better place when they grow up. Will you stay with me, Etta? Will you let me ask your father for your hand in marriage?"

She swayed slightly in the darkness, took a cautious step toward him. "You want—*me?*"

Joe considered the query carefully, not wanting to base the new start he yearned for on a lie. "Oh, yes," he said gruffly.

"But you love Mrs. Quade—I know you do!"

"I can't deny that," he answered in a quiet voice, "and I won't. Yes, God help me, I love Lydia, and maybe, with some part of me, I always will. But it's plain to me that I'll never have her, and I'm not willing to sacrifice the rest of my days to a few memories. I could learn to love you, Etta, and I'd like the chance to try."

Etta took another faltering step toward him, her hands caught together in front of her in a tangle of nervous fingers. "There's one thing you gotta know first," she blurted in a small, strangled voice ringing with hope and fear. "I ain't—pure. There was a man once—"

Finally, Joe advanced, laid his hands on either side of her narrow waist, pulled her close. She felt lean and wiry against him, but curvy, too, and warm. "Hush," he said. "That's over and done with."

Her eyes, as dusky-soft as the center of a spring pansy, filled with tears. "This is just like one of them stories Miss Charlotte's always spoutin', about princes and pirates and ladies in distress. It can't be real."

Joe bent his head, silently enjoining heaven to damn him for all time if he was using this woman, and touched his lips to hers. "Shhh," he said, and kissed her.

She was an innocent, despite her assertion that she wasn't "pure." Maybe some man had taken solace from her body, but it was as plain as sunlight through crystal that no one had ever made love to her.

Her lips faltered under Joe's, then opened, and he felt a shudder of surprise go through her when his tongue moved against hers. To his own utter and complete amazement, he felt something himself when the intimate contact was made, a sensation of some inner door being opened. Gripping her upper arms, so breathless that he could barely speak, he thrust her away from him.

"Go to bed, Etta," he gasped in rusty tones. "We'll make arrangements tomorrow."

She opened her kiss-swollen mouth to protest, then stepped back. "You'll find Pa in the woods," she said, "working for Mr. Quade. He won't make things easy for you."

Joe gestured toward the bedroom, struggling against the heat and hardness of his body, the insatiable hunger she had roused in his spirit. "Good night," he said, turning away, reaching for the lamp.

When he turned again, holding the lantern aloft to light his way, Etta had disappeared.

He went into the examination room, distractedly washed and stripped to his drawers, then stretched out on the thinly padded table to listen to the wind. It was nothing compared to the howling loneliness and need raging in his own soul.

Sleep eluded him, for although he was physically weary, the essence of his being was just coming awake after a long, deep slumber. For the first time in more than a decade, Joe McCauley was truly glad to be alive.

He had no way of knowing how much time had passed when she came to him, clothed only in lantern glow and shadow, her rich, wonderful hair falling around her breasts and shoulders like a cape woven of light.

She touched his face and he moaned, helpless, stunned at the depths and rawness of his wanting.

Etta bent, kissed the hollow at the base of his throat. When he started to speak, she laid a finger to his lips and pleaded, "Don't send me away, Doc. Please. For the first time in all my days, I feel like I'm in the right place."

With a tentative hand she stroked his chest, making slow circles around his nipples, and then his belly. His manhood thrust hard against the thin fabric of his drawers, and when she touched him, he cried out hoarsely, as though wrung with fever.

She knew what he wanted, what he needed, and Joe McCauley vowed then and there never to ask where she'd learned such skills. He craved comfort and real belonging too deeply to care.

Etta opened his drawers, and he let her peel them slowly down over his hips. She moved his legs so that they dangled over each side of the examining table and he was utterly vulnerable to her. Then she leaned over and began kissing his belly, occasionally teasing his painfully alert flesh with the tip of her tongue. Lightly, ever so lightly, she caressed the soft sack beneath his manhood, while his rod took on a life of its own and strained upward.

Etta chuckled affectionately and closed her hand around him, rubbing her thumb across the moist tip and smiling in the faint flicker of lantern light coming from the next room. He moaned and arched his back slightly.

"Are you still wantin' a lady, Doc?" she teased, just before she bent over him again, this time to lash him mercilessly with her tongue. "Or mightn't a whore be what's needed tonight?"

Joe broke out in a sweat. Surrender of any kind was foreign to him, but he left his legs sprawled to the sides of the table and he let Etta have her way. When he felt her mouth close over his manhood, eager and hungry, he gave a shout of glorious despair and rose high off the surface of the table.

Still drawing on him, Etta stroked his hips with comforting hands, eased him back to the table. He lay trembling while she gave him torturous solace, her hands moving lightly over his inner thighs, accentuating the fact that he was spread for her like a banquet.

Finally, he caught her head in both hands and tried to lift her away, but she clung. In fact she suckled harder, and punished his insurrection with the slightest nip of her teeth, and in the next moment his reason splintered in glittering shards of fire. He cried out senselessly to heaven, and still Etta was ruthless.

Only when he was fully spent did she release him, take one of his hands and place it over her breast.

He squeezed gently, feeling the nipple go hard against his palm, wondering at a universe made completely new. Curving his other hand at Etta's nape, beneath the cascade of bright hair, he drew her down for his kiss.

When he could speak again, when his breathing was somewhat regular and his heart was no longer thudding against his ribcage like a sledgehammer against a wash-tub, he drew her against him and whispered her name like a prayer.

Brigham was sleepless that night, pacing before the study fire, filled with the conviction that something terrible was about to happen. The wet, loud fury of the wind had never troubled him before—he was used to living by the sea, having grown up in Maine and made his fortune on the shores of Puget Sound—but now the pit of his stomach was cold with fear. The howling! It was as though the souls of all the dead on earth had risen from their slumber to wage war on the living.

"Papa?"

He turned at the sound of the small, troubled voice and saw Charlotte standing in the enormous doorway, hair trailing. She was wearing a nightgown and wrapper, but her feet were bare. "Go back to bed," he told his daughter, with brusque affection and an attempt at a smile. "The storm will pass."

She crept closer, curled up in the leather wing chair nearest the hearth. "I'm afraid, Papa," she confided, without pretending to her usual worldly wisdom. "Those big trees outside my window are *swaying.*"

"The framework of this house is sound, Charlotte," he

said reasonably, unwilling to show his own uneasiness lest it worry the child further, "and so is the roof. I made sure of that when I built the place."

Charlotte propped one elbow on the arm of the chair and cupped her chin in her palm. Her gaze narrowed slightly and grew pensive. The sudden shift of subject didn't surprise Brigham at all, for he'd seen it coming.

"If Lydia is your wife, why doesn't she live here—with us?"

Brigham felt a headache take root in the muscles at the base of his neck. "That's difficult to explain," he began, after a few moments of awkward silence. "Lydia and I—er, well, we have our differences."

Charlotte gave an exasperated sigh. "And Uncle Devon and Polly 'have their differences,'" she said, in a tone Brigham would not normally have tolerated. "What is it about the men in the Quade family that makes them such dreadful husbands?"

Despite the knotted ligaments in his nape and his sense of impending calamity, Brigham had to smile. "What brings you to the conclusion that the *men* are at fault?" he countered, sinking into the chair behind his desk. "Is it so inconceivable that it might be the women who are making things difficult?"

The girl arched one perfect eyebrow. She was becoming a woman, and Brigham felt a pang of loss at the prospect. Although he longed for sons, he had never wished that either of his daughters had been born male. In his remote and somewhat awkward way, he adored Charlotte and Millie.

"Yes," she answered pertly, raising her chin from her palm. "You're a very stubborn man, Papa, and Uncle Devon is no better. You have all the poetry and grace of an ox."

Brigham laughed and held up his hands in a gesture of mock surrender, but inside he felt another twinge. When had this wise young woman slipped in and taken the place of his little girl? "Poetry and grace, is it? Well, it's a comfort that you think so highly of your father, Charlotte. Tell me, does your sister hold me in the same lofty regard?"

Charlotte's expression was one of impatient indulgence. "Don't be silly, Papa—you know very well we love you devotedly, but that doesn't mean we're blind, Millie and I. If you'd just go to Lydia and admit that you adore her, a number of problems would be solved right then."

He rose, went to the liquor cabinet, and poured himself a brandy, all in an effort to avoid meeting his daughter's gaze. She had already seen too much, this woman-child, and he feared to reveal more. "Life is not so simple as one of your romantic stories," he told Charlotte, somewhat sharply, as he poured. "As you grow, you will learn that, regardless of what the fairy tales say, love does not necessarily conquer all."

The branches of a tree slammed against the window, then made a clawing sound on the glass, like giant fingers, and Charlotte started violently.

"You're certain none of the trees will fall on the house?" she asked in a small voice, her eyes huge in her pale little face.

Brigham was glad to put the discussion of Lydia behind him. "I'm certain you won't be hurt, even if one does," he answered gently. "Now, go back to bed, Charlotte. It's late."

Charlotte rose from the chair, padded over to him with the innocent grace of a kitten, and leaned down to kiss his cheek. "You shouldn't be afraid to tell Lydia how you feel, Papa," she scolded gently. "She cares as deeply for you as you do for her."

Something like hope buoyed Brigham's troubled heart, at least for a moment. "Good night," he said pointedly.

Although he had apparently managed to reassure his elder daughter somewhat, Brigham was himself as anxious as ever. Leaving his drink unfinished on the desktop, he rose and went to stand at one of the windows, trying to make out the shape of Lydia's house in the darkness.

* * *

Dawn was still a long way off when Lydia finally gave up on sleeping, put on a fresh dress and a warm cloak, and set out through the furious storm for the schoolhouse. She would build a fire in the shiny new potbellied stove and carry in drinking water from the well, then write out the morning's lessons on the big chalkboard behind her desk. The time—please God—would pass quickly, morning would come, and the little flock of children would appear, full of mischief and magic. Then she would be able to forget her private concerns by busying herself with the needs and problems of others.

By the time she took refuge inside the newly completed school, her hair was wet with rain and her cloak was clinging to her dress. She lit only one lamp, though she would have liked to have several glowing about the large room. As teacher, it was her responsibility to make sure expensive supplies like kerosene were never wasted.

Humming, Lydia built a rousing fire in the stove in the corner of the room, then shook out her cloak and draped it over a chair to dry. As the moans of the wind grew more plaintive, and the great trees rustled restlessly in response, Lydia concentrated resolutely on planning the day's arithmetic assignments.

Devon was wet to the skin as he climbed down from the box of Clyde Malcott's wagon and stood looking up at the general store he'd built with his own hands. He'd picked a hell of a night to travel overland from Seattle, he admitted to himself, but then the weather had been good the day before, when he and Clyde had set out.

Clyde touched his hat brim. He was carrying special supplies for one of the lumber camps and still had some hard traveling ahead of him. "Fare thee well, Mr. Quade," he called over the tempest.

"Thanks again," Devon replied, pulling his carpet bag from the bed of the wagon just before Clyde and the team of weary horses rattled away. He paused again, at the base of the outside stairs leading to the second floor of the mercantile, and allowed himself to hope.

He'd spent most of the trip—hell, most of the last few

weeks—planning what he'd say to Polly when the two of them were face-to-face, but all his pretty, carefully rehearsed words were carried away on the breast of the wind as he stood there.

Using his cane because he was tired and his healing muscles were cramped from the long, jolting wagon trip through the countryside, Devon started up the steps. When he'd progressed to the upper landing, he drew a deep breath, held it in his lungs for a long moment, and then knocked.

He saw Polly peer out at him from an upstairs window, and then the door flew open and she was standing there, the storm catching her thin flannel nightgown and molding it to her shapely body.

"Devon," she whispered, as if afraid to believe it was really him.

Devon set the bag down at his feet. "Are you going to let me in, woman?" he demanded gruffly. "Or do I have to stand out here in the wind all night?"

With a cry of anguished elation, she launched herself at him like an arrow from a crossbow, flinging her arms around his neck. He felt the slight roundness of her belly against his midsection as he embraced her, and his throat thickened. He carried her over the threshold and closed the door, leaving his satchel and a great many misgivings outside in the rain.

"It isn't going to be easy, our finding our way back to each other," he warned, setting her on her feet again, his hands lingering on her hips, "but I won't know another moment of sanity unless we try."

She reached up and swept off his sodden hat, her face bright with joy, her beautiful eyes glistening with tears. "That's all I ask of you, Devon." She caught one of his hands in both of hers and pressed it to her abdomen, where the baby was growing. "And it's all your son asks, too. Just a chance."

With that, she began peeling away Devon's rain-drenched clothes, and he stood there, needing the warmth of the fire and of her love, ready for the first time in his life to submit to the will of another.

24

THE BLADE OF A KNIFE PRESSED LIGHTLY AGAINST DEVON'S jugular as he lay beside Polly in the stormy, predawn darkness. An instantaneous calm overtook him; without moving or even changing the meter of his breathing, he looked up through his lashes.

The shape of a man loomed over him, and Polly stirred, sated and untroubled, at Devon's side. The instinct to protect her and the unborn child was ferocious; it pumped energy through his being.

"If it isn't the unhappy bridegroom," the intruder drawled, his white teeth gleaming in the gloom as he smiled.

Devon felt no fear; there was no time to indulge in the luxury. In a motion so fast he never recalled making it, he clasped the stranger's wrist to stay the knife and bolted upright.

Polly awakened with a shriek. "Nat!"

Although he had no time to think about it, Devon registered the name on some level of his mind and knew this was the man Polly had known in San Francisco. And the realization gave Devon a new, even greater burst of strength that sent the night visitor hurtling against the nearest wall.

Still, the fight was far from over.

Nat bellowed like a bull and lunged for Devon, trailing the first gray light of dawn, the blade glinting in his hand.

Devon was naked, and still somewhat slow from satisfaction and sleep. He was not yet fully recovered from the near-fatal accident in the woods, and his assailant was strong. For all those disadvantages, it never occurred to Devon that he might lose.

He felt the point of the knife graze the underside of his chin just before he sent it clattering across the floor with a sharp blow to the other man's forearm. Immediately after that, a fist struck Devon hard in the solar plexus, thrusting the air from his lungs.

The pain only made him more determined.

A table crashed to the floor, and something shattered. Devon heard footsteps pounding down the inside stairway and silently rejoiced. No matter what happened to him, Polly would escape; she and the baby would be safe.

The stranger's hands closed around Devon's neck, cutting off his wind, and he felt broken glass cut into his back as he rolled in an effort to free himself. When that failed, he brought his knee up hard between the attacker's legs. The bastard howled in outraged pain, and Devon got him by the ears and slammed his head hard against the floor. Finally, Devon's opponent went limp.

A second later Devon felt the cold end of a shotgun barrel press against his backbone, and a rush of frustration, fury, and love swept over him.

Polly had not fled after all.

"Put your hands up, Nat," she said, her voice quavering in the darkness. "I swear I'll shoot you if you don't."

It was a moment before Devon could get his breath. "Damn it, Polly," he rasped out, "it's me you're jabbing with that thing, and I'd just as soon you wouldn't pull the trigger if you don't mind."

"D-Devon?"

He stood and took the gun from her hands, and he

thought he felt her trembling reverberating in the stock. "Light a lamp," he said gently. "It's dark as a coal miner's tomb in here."

Polly obeyed, and when Devon got a good look at her, his heart softened. Her hair was still tangled from their lovemaking, and she wore one of his shirts, with just one button fastened. She gazed down at the man on the floor with horrified relief.

"Is he dead?"

There was broken glass everywhere; in the scuffle, a small china figurine had shattered to bits. "No," Devon answered, picking his way through the shards of porcelain to lift his wife off her bare feet and carry her to the safety of the bed, where she wouldn't cut her feet. "I'll tie him up and lock him in the storeroom, and tomorrow Brig and I can figure out what to do with him."

Polly touched Devon's back, and her hand came away bloody. She paled. "You're hurt. Maybe I should get the doctor."

Devon reached for his trousers, stockings, and boots. "You're not going anywhere," he replied. "Just stay put, Mrs. Quade, until I've taken care of your admirer here."

He half dragged and half prodded Nat to his feet, escorted him downstairs, and flung him into the storeroom. Using twine, he bound the other man's hands behind him.

"You got one hell of a right cross for a storekeeper," the prisoner muttered.

Devon didn't answer. He just latched the storeroom door and went upstairs to his wife.

Polly was crouched in the middle of the bed, looking small and terrified, and Devon said a silent prayer of thanks that he'd returned to Quade's Harbor when he had.

"That's him, the man you knew before me," Devon said without rancor, setting the shotgun in the corner of the room.

Polly nodded briefly and patted the mattress with one hand. "Come over here and let me pick that glass out of your back."

Devon obeyed. "Do you still have feelings for him?" he asked calmly. No one would ever have guessed from his tone how important her answer was to him.

"Sure I do, Devon Quade," Polly snapped, kneeling behind him on the bed and taking no particular care, as far as he could tell, to minister gently to his wounded flesh. "I hate him!"

"But you loved him once."

"I thought I did," Polly responded, less heatedly. "I was just a scatter-headed girl then, though. I didn't learn what love was until I met you."

Devon was quiet for a moment. He cared deeply for Polly, wouldn't have returned to Quade's Harbor if he hadn't, but he wasn't ready to say he loved her. Not straight out, anyway. "If that baby you're carrying is a boy, I'll want to name him for my brother."

She paused, her hands on his shoulders, and bent to kiss the nape of his neck. Devon wasn't exactly sure, but he thought he felt her tears on his skin.

"Brigham is a fine name," she said hoarsely.

Lydia was busy at the blackboard, writing out the day's arithmetic problems, when she heard, rolling beneath the incessant chanting of the wind, an ominous, grinding creak. Just as the roof shattered, she lunged beneath her heavy oak desk and instinctively covered her head with both arms.

When she looked up, the schoolhouse was filled with branches, and the festive scent of pine sap. And smoke.

She bit her lower lip and struggled to stay calm. A tree had fallen on the schoolhouse, that much was perfectly obvious, but except for a few scratches, she had not been hurt. No, the threat now was fire; the lamp had been broken, and perhaps the stove had been upset as well.

Lydia started to crawl out of her hiding place, but the broken tree limbs were too dense; she was trapped.

She heard a crackle of flames, and the smell of smoke intensified. Her eyes and throat began to sting, and she pressed the palms of both hands to her stomach, thinking of the child nestled there inside her. Trusting her for life and love.

Tears pooled along her lashes. "Brigham," she said softly, amazed at how small and unimportant their differences seemed to her now. She had been wrong to demand so arbitrarily that he close down the Satin Hammer Saloon, no matter how that might have affected his timber business, but she reserved the right to wring his neck if he ever patronized the place. As for their political quarrel, well, if a broken country could mend itself into a union again, surely two people who loved each other could, too.

Lydia lowered her face to her updrawn knees. It was strange, she thought, with despairing ruefulness, how quickly one could put things into perspective when all other options were closed off.

Brigham had been dozing, but some sound jolted him awake, and he sat up straight in his chair. Instinctively, he rushed to the window, and in the first uncertain light of a rainy dawn, he saw the ancient tree that had fallen across the schoolhouse, crushing it to splinters.

He told himself Lydia wouldn't be in there, couldn't be, that she was safe in her bed in the cottage, but all the while he was thinking those thoughts, Brigham was bounding toward the front door.

He flung it open, left it gaping behind him when he ran down the walk and vaulted over the fence. Flames were roaring in the branches of the downed tree, catching at the broken walls of the school. Devon arrived, ax in hand, just as Brigham did, and there were others coming out of the night, too.

Brigham paid no mind to any of them. She was in there. Damn her stubborn Yankee hide, Lydia was *in that schoolhouse,* and if she hadn't been run through by a branch of that huge tree, she would surely be burned to death in the fire.

"Lydia!" he yelled, fighting his way up the huge, knotted trunk of the fallen fir, clawing at the shingles of the roof with his bare hands. "Lydia!"

Devon was beside him, shoving the ax into his grasp. Brigham only distantly acknowledged his brother's presence, so intent was he on Lydia's situation. "Here!" Devon shouted over the rising roar of the flames. While Brigham chopped at the roof with the wild efficiency of desperation, Devon remained at his side, despite the heat and the danger, using all his strength to clear away boards and branches.

Her voice rose to them, small and precious as the sound of a church bell the day after Judgment.

"Brigham? I knew you'd come for me."

Brigham was soaked in sweat and the drizzling mist, and every muscle in his body screamed in protest, but still he swung the ax. A raw sound, part shout and part sob, tore itself from his throat. He thought he screamed her name again then, but he couldn't be sure.

Men were passing buckets of water up onto the burning roof, and Devon and others fought the blaze while Brigham lowered himself down through the rafters and the clawing fingers of the tree's branches.

"In the name of God, Lydia," he shouted in an anguish of fear, barely able to breathe for the smoke, "where are you?"

"Here, Brigham. Under the desk."

Coughing, fighting his way through a curtain of sharp needles and aged, pitchy wood, he found the desk, wrenched her out. Her face was white in the glow of the fire, except for smudges of soot, and she flung her arms around his neck with a little cry.

He took one moment to hold her close, then shouted, "Hold onto me—no matter what happens, don't let go!" She nodded, and Brigham began the dangerous climb back up through the debris. The heat was hellish, and the fire made a voracious whooshing sound in the timber and the remains of the building.

Devon was waiting on the rapidly disintegrating roof, though everyone else had already fled to safety. He took Lydia from Brigham's grasp and carried her down over the massive trunk of the tree. Brigham hurtled after them only moments before the fire exploded and both the school and the tree blazed like the devil's vengeance.

At a safe distance from the inferno, Devon laid Lydia gently in the damp grass. Joe McCauley knelt at her left side, Brigham collapsed at another. His arms and face were scratched and burned, his clothes torn, and he couldn't seem to get enough air no matter how his lungs grasped for it. None of that mattered now, though, because Lydia was lying too still, and her eyes were closed.

Joe McCauley laid his head to her breast. "Her heart is still beating," he said, rising to look directly into Brigham's burning eyes, "but she's not breathing."

Panic swelled in Brigham's chest; he took Lydia's limp shoulders in his hands and raised her up, so that her mouth collided with his. If she had no breath, he would give her his. Had it been possible, he would have given her the strong, steady beat of his heart as well, and the nurturing blood flowing through his veins. He would, indeed, have surrendered his very life to save her.

No one spoke as Brigham drew air into his lungs and forced it into Lydia's. No one dared touch him, even though he knew they all thought his desperate effort was futile.

Tears mingled with the sweat on his face; he shook her once, out of fury and despair, and then he began to feed her air again. All the while, a litany of misery and hope threaded through his mind, twisting, turning, doubling back on itself.

Don't die—please, Lydia, don't leave me—

Finally, Brigham felt strong hands come to rest on his heaving shoulders, heard Devon's voice in the thundering din of that tragic morning. "She's gone, Brig. Let her go."

Brigham threw back his head and bellowed at the sky, like an animal. "Nooooooo!" And then, like God breathing life into Adam, he pressed his mouth to hers again.

A light rain began to fall then, a misty benediction, and suddenly, wondrously, Lydia stiffened in Brigham's arms and then shuddered. He drew back, saw her open her eyes, watched as she tried to form his name.

A swell of joy rose from the onlookers, though Brigham could not have sworn afterward that anyone made the slightest sound. Joe McCauley rubbed his eyes with a thumb and forefinger and said hoarsely, "Let's get that wife of yours in out of the rain, Brig."

Brigham carried her toward his house, the townspeople trailing behind them in the early light as he held her so close against his chest that he could not guess where his being stopped and hers began. She lay trustingly in his embrace, only half conscious, her head resting against his shoulder.

When Brigham reached his front gate, someone ran ahead to open the door. He carried his bride into the entryway and up the stairs without slowing his pace, stopping only when he'd come to his own room. There, he laid her gently on the bed.

Polly sent Devon to the kitchen for a basin of clean water, while McCauley matter-of-factly began to untie Lydia's shoes. Brigham helped, numbly, only vaguely aware of the cuts and burns on his own flesh.

Lydia smiled up at him, her expression dreamy and fey. "You were right, Brigham," she said, as he and the doctor peeled away the last of her clothes and Polly wrapped her in a blanket.

Brigham made a consummate effort to speak normally. "You don't say," he rasped. "What was I right about, Yankee?"

She sighed. "I don't precisely remember, just now," she told him.

He chuckled, felt surprise that the sound hadn't come out as a sob. "Remember this, then, Yankee—I love you. Do you hear me? *I love you,* and I'm not going to let you forget it, ever. There will be no more wandering, no more living apart. Is that understood?"

Lydia ran her tongue over dry, soot-smudged lips. "Yes, Mr. Quade," she replied sweetly. Brigham knew this docile mood of hers couldn't possibly last. "It's perfectly clear."

335

Joe handed him a cup of water, and Brigham raised Lydia's head, gently touching the rim to her lips.

There was a knock at the door, and then Devon came in, carrying a basin and some clean washcloths. When he was gone again, Polly and the doctor unwrapped Lydia, gently cleaned the soot from her skin and treated her burns and scrapes. Brigham sat with her the whole time, holding one of her hands in both of his, thinking how close he'd come to losing her.

Only when Lydia was sleeping comfortably did Brigham agree to have his own injuries taken care of, but though he felt the searing pain of his burns, he barely acknowledged it. Once Joe and Polly had finally left them alone, Brigham stretched out on the bed beside his wife and gathered her into his bandaged arms.

"Don't leave me." She sighed the plea, without awakening, when his lips brushed her forehead.

Brigham's eyes stung, and the emotions that moved through him then were so powerful that he shuddered in their wake. He held her closer still. "I'm here," he assured her quietly. Tenderly. "I'll always be right here."

Epilogue

*L*YDIA WATCHED FONDLY AS THE TWO BOYS, ONE DARK AND one fair, sat on the wooden floor of the mercantile, within the warmth of the stove, chattering as they made a fort of colored blocks. Fat flakes of snow drifted past the windows, and the spicy smell of hot cider filled the air.

"Devon," she said, when her blond son reached out to steal a block from his cousin, whose name was Brigham. "You promised to share, remember?"

Polly, her stomach huge with Devon's second child, perched happily in a nearby rocking chair, embroidering a tiny nightshirt. She looked as serene as a madonna, sitting there. Her cheeks glowed and her eyes were shining with happiness.

"Don't fuss, Lydia," she said good-naturedly. "Brigham and Devon need to learn to work things out between themselves."

A soft cry from the bassinet beside Lydia's chair distracted her, and she reached down for her younger son, Seth, who was now eight months old. She covered her chest with a small, soft blanket, unbuttoned her bodice, lowered her camisole, and gave the baby her breast.

He took the nipple greedily, as though eager to garner all the nourishment he could get, grow up fast, and make a place for himself in the world. Seth's hair was light, like Lydia's, but his eyes were the same pewter-gray color as Brigham's, and he had already revealed a nature much like his father's.

The door opened and a rush of wintry air swept in, along with Brig. He nodded a friendly greeting at Polly and lifted his elder son deftly into his arms, but his gaze was fixed on Lydia from the first. She felt a sweet heat as he stood there, watching her as if he could see through the blanket that hid the baby and her breast.

He smiled at Lydia's blush of response and hoisted little Devon onto one shoulder. Polly made some fluttery excuse about checking a merchandise list and bustled off into the back room as quickly as she could.

"It's time you took yourself home, Mrs. Quade," Brigham said, his gray eyes twinkling. "On a snowy day like this, a man needs a wife to keep him warm."

"Hush!" Lydia hissed, though secretly she was pleased. She found as much joy and fulfillment in the marriage bed as her husband did. "There are children present!"

Brigham reached up to tickle the little boy riding on his shoulder, and the child shrieked with delight. "All Dev knows is that his mama and papa love each other," Brig said. Then he reached out to tug at the blanket and take a peek at his other son and Lydia's full breast. "As for Seth, there, he's not thinking about anything but that nipple. And I can't say I blame him."

Lydia went crimson. "Brigham Quade!"

Still holding Dev, Brigham crouched beside Lydia's chair and put a finger beneath the blanket. He stroked Seth's tiny head, then Lydia's breast, taking care to tease and excite. "Once our son's had his fill," Brigham promised quietly, "I mean to take you to bed, Mrs. Quade, and have a taste of you myself."

It infuriated Lydia, the way Brigham could send a hot shock of need pulsing through her system so easily. He had only to look at her a certain way, or touch her, or speak to her in a low, husky voice, and she was ready to obey his every whim. For the life of her, she couldn't rebel.

She shifted Seth to her other breast and closed her eyes as Brigham reached beneath the blanket again to play with the nipple his infant son had just abandoned.

"I have some business at the mill," Brigham said idly. "Charlotte and Millie won't be home from Seattle until tomorrow afternoon, and the boys will be asleep before dinner."

Lydia swallowed. She was terrified someone would come into the store, and yet she didn't want Brigham to stop teasing her breast. "And?"

"And I would like you to serve supper in our room, Mrs. Quade."

Lydia imagined how it would be; they would dine beside a crackling fire, with candlelight flickering in the darkness and snow rimming the windowsills. Brigham would insist on eating slowly, savoring every bite of his food with a sensual languor, making an erotic ritual of drinking his wine. By the time he actually made love to her, her senses would have reached such an explosive state of wanting that the merest touch would send her tumbling over the edge.

"I'm not one of your bull whackers, and I'll thank you not to give me orders as if I were," Lydia said. She'd never persuaded Brigham to close down the Satin Hammer Saloon, though she knew he didn't patronize the place except to have an occasional glass of whiskey, nor had she ever gotten him to apologize for selling timber to both the Confederate and Union sides during the war. For all of that, she liked to think she'd made some progress in softening his stubborn ways; he was a tender and thoughtful husband, and he'd sought her advice over and over again when the new schoolhouse was built. He was a fine, attentive father to all four of his children, and it seemed to Lydia that she loved him more with every passing day. Moreover, he freely admitted that he loved her in return, and though he wasn't the sort to compose verse—or recite it, either, for that matter—Lydia often found one of his well-read volumes on her vanity table.

She would open the book to the place he'd marked with a scrap of paper or a colorful leaf and find a passage that moved her to tears.

It was for all those reasons that Lydia almost invariably obeyed her husband, in matters of romance at least. When he opened the door of their room later that night, when the boys were asleep, she was waiting for him in a frothy gown of satin and lace and ribbon.

She had lighted candles and set the logs in the fireplace ablaze, and the covers on the bed had been turned down to reveal fresh linen sheets scented with rosewater.

Brigham closed the door and stood looking at her in quiet amazement. His voice, when he spoke, was gruff. "I always think I'm prepared for your beauty, but when I walk in here and find you waiting for me, looking like a lost angel, the sight of you never fails to take my breath away."

Lydia smiled flirtatiously, but her own heart was swelling with love, and she didn't know how she'd ever wait through a meal before losing herself in her husband's embrace. "You behaved like a perfect scoundrel in the mercantile today," she told him. Her breath caught in her throat as he approached and curved a finger under her chin.

"And you've been thinking about me ever since," he replied. Gently, unhurriedly, he drew one strap of her gown down over a milk-white shoulder. "Haven't you?"

Lydia wanted to deny his words, for the sake of her pride, but she couldn't. "Yes," she confessed. "Damn you, *yes.*"

He lowered her other strap, ran the tip of his finger across the cleavage swelling above her bodice, and smiled as a blush rushed up to her neck and then pulsed in her cheeks. Then, with a teasing tug, he bared one of her breasts and caressed it with a look of wonder in his eyes. She lifted her palms to the sides of his face, clean but stubbled with a late-day beard, and pulled him close for a kiss.

The contact was long and lingering, weakening Lydia's

knees and setting her heart to racing. Brigham pulled down the other side of her gown and fondled the second breast, chafing the eager nipple with the pad of his thumb.

"Please," she gasped, beyond all ability to wait, when Brigham finally freed her mouth.

He continued to caress her for a few excruciatingly glorious moments, then gestured with one arm toward the table. "Supper first, Mrs. Quade," he said. "Then dessert."

Brigham ushered a distracted, flushed Lydia to the small table next to the fire and seated her as graciously as if they were in a fine restaurant in Paris or New York instead of their own bedroom. Awkwardly, she pulled her gown up to cover her breasts again, but Brigham only smiled. He was a patient man.

Just as Lydia had known he would, he took the time to enjoy every bite of his food, every sip of his wine. She was barely able to contain her need by the time he finally set aside his glass and stretched out his hand to take hold of hers.

Gracefully, he drew her to her feet and then onto his lap, astraddle his thighs. Lydia's breath quickened as he brought down her bodice again.

"So beautiful," he said, meeting her eyes. While she stared back at him, mesmerized, he reached out, dipped a finger in the sauce topping the remains of their brandy cake. He touched the sugary substance to her nipple, then bent to lick it away at his leisure.

Lydia tried to wait—she always tried to wait—but this new game sent fire rushing through her veins. She cried out, flinging back her head like a mare calling to her stallion, and clutched Brigham's shoulders. Her legs stiffened on either side of his lap. "Brigham," she whimpered.

He put sauce on her other breast, enjoyed it slowly and thoroughly.

By then Lydia was bouncing shamelessly against his thighs. Brigham slid his hands beneath her gown, grasping her bottom with one, stroking the inside of her thigh with the other. When, without warning, he gave her his finger in a sudden, fiery thrust, she came unwrapped like wire wound too tightly around the spool. Brigham sucked noisily at her breast while she convulsed around his finger, knowing all the while that the night's lovemaking had just begun.

He held her close when the first bout was over, his arms tight around her, his shoulder strong and warm under her cheek. He stroked her and spoke to her soothingly until she was calm again, until her breathing had evened out and her heartbeat had slowed to its normal pace.

She sighed when he carried her to the bed and arranged her there, trembled as he spread her legs wide apart and burrowed in between them to tease her with his tongue. As always, she begged for appeasement; as always, he granted her requests, though he took her through every note of a grand symphony before letting her soar on the crescendo.

Brigham quieted Lydia again, when she'd ceased trembling and the heat of the fire had dried the perspiration from her skin. She cherished those tender times, just as she did the peaks of ecstasy, and wished the night would never end.

He gave her a long, searching kiss when he was ready to put her through the last sweet paces of passion—at some point, he'd gotten rid of his own clothes—then turned her onto her hands and knees in front of him. Lydia gasped in weary delight; the pleasure was always keenest when Brigham took her like this, his hands cupping her breasts while he delved deep into the caressing warmth of her femininity.

The first long, slow stroke was Lydia's undoing. She shuddered violently against Brigham, sobbing with the splendor of her release, only to find that each subsequent sheathing of Brigham's sword set her off all over again. Finally, mercifully, when she was certain she would swoon if her body responded even once more, Brigham lunged deep and stiffened, moaning her name as he spilled his seed into her.

They collapsed, entwined, struggling for breath, and lay spent, watching the snow waft past the windows. It would be a cold night, but within that room, there was only warmth for Brigham Quade and his Yankee wife.

Pocket Books
Proudly Announces

TAMING CHARLOTTE

Linda Lael Miller

Coming from Pocket Books
Winter 1993

The following is a preview of
Taming Charlotte . . .

Even at midmorning, the air of the marketplace, or *souk,* shimmered and undulated with heat. Chickens squawked, vendors shouted and argued, monkeys wearing little vests and fezzes shrieked for attention, and strange, incessant music curled through the stalls in place of a breeze. The smells of spices and unwashed flesh competed with pungent smoke from cooking fires, and the bright silken folds of Charlotte's borrowed robe and veils clung to her moist skin.

She was enthralled.

Her companion, Bettina Richardson, who was a few years younger than Charlotte and clad in a similar disguise, did not share this enthusiasm.

"Papa will *murder* us if he finds out we've come to this dreadful place!" she hissed, the veil covering her pretty face swelling with the rush of her breath. "Why, we could end up being carried off to the desert by some sheikh!"

Charlotte sighed. "We won't, more's the pity," she said, just to annoy Bettina.

"Charlotte!" Bettina cried, shocked.

Charlotte smiled behind her veils. The Richardsons had sailed to the island kingdom of Riz, which lay between Spain and the coast of Morocco, to visit old friends, wealthy merchants they had originally known in Boston. Bettina had wanted to stay in Paris until it was time to sail for London and then the United States, but Charlotte had campaigned against the idea. She wasn't about to miss a chance to visit such an exotic place as Riz, since there was at least *some* potential for adventure.

That, of course, was exactly the factor that vexed Bettina so much. She had had to be coerced into borrowing the robes and veils from their hostess's wardrobe, sneaking out by way of a side gate, and venturing through the narrow, dusty streets, following the odors and the cacophony of sounds to the *souk.*

Standing in front of one of the market stalls, Charlotte touched a crudely made basket tentatively. She would remember this day all her life and, out of desperate boredom, she would no doubt embellish it at some point. She might add a grand sheikh mounted on a fine Arabian stallion, riding to the marketplace to buy slaves, or perhaps even a band of marauding pirates, scattering chickens and merchants in every direction with their swords . . .

A stir at the end of the row of tawdry little booths and crevices in the ancient walls interrupted her colorful musings. Bettina grabbed Charlotte's forearm with surprising strength and whispered, "Let's go back to the Vincents' house, Charlotte, *please!"*

Charlotte stood staring at the tall man striding through the crowd, barely able to believe her eyes. For a few breathless moments she was thirteen again and back in Seattle. She'd climbed up into the rigging of a sailing ship, the *Enchantress,* and high off the deck her courage had fled. She'd clung to the ropes, too terrified to climb down on her own.

Patrick Trevarren had come up to fetch her.

Bettina gave her a little shake. "Charlotte!" she pleaded balefully. "I don't like the looks of that man! He's probably a brigand!"

Charlotte couldn't move, and she was especially grateful for her veils because she knew the fluttery smile trembling on her mouth would be an idiotic one. Patrick hadn't changed a great deal in ten years, though he was broader through the chest and shoulders and the angles of his face were sharper; he still wore his dark hair a little too long, caught back at his nape with a thin black ribbon, and his indigo gaze was as incisive as before. He walked with an arrogant assurance that infuriated Charlotte, and yet her heart was hammering in her throat and it was all she could do not to run to him and inquire if he remembered her.

He wouldn't, of course, and even if he did, she had been only a girl when they'd met last. She had dreamed about him all these ten years, weaving fantasy after fantasy around the young seaman, but he'd probably never given her so much as a second thought.

He drew nearer, and even though there was a smile on his darkly tanned, aristocratic face, his eyes were cold. He plucked a ripe orange from a fruit stand, using the point of a dagger drawn from his belt, and flipped a coin to the crouching vendor.

Charlotte neither moved nor made a sound, except to breathe, but something about her must have given him pause. He came and towered over her and the trembling Bettina, staring down into Charlotte's amber eyes with an expression of bemusement.

Say something, Charlotte ordered herself frantically, but she couldn't. Her throat was shut tight.

Patrick pondered her for another moment, ran his gaze over the clinging robes she wore, and then proceeded around her with a shrug. He peeled the orange as he went, tossing the parings to one of the chattering monkeys.

"That's it," Bettina said firmly. "We're leaving, Charlotte Quade, *this very minute.* That was a pirate if I've ever seen one!"

Charlotte watched as Patrick stopped to look up at a veiled and shapely creature dancing on a board stretched between two large barrels, and she felt a jealousy so intense that her throat opened and her lungs started drawing air again. "And we all know you've seen your share of pirates," she retorted with unusual sarcasm. Bettina was not destined to be Charlotte's lifelong friend and confidante, but she was a decent sort and quite fragile, undeserving of such treatment.

Tears welled in Bettina's green eyes; she responded to a

sharp word the way anyone else would to the bite of a lash. She was an only child, gently raised, and it had not been easy for her to disobey her parents by sneaking out of the Vincents' home to explore a foreign marketplace.

"I'm sorry," Charlotte said gently, feeling broken as she watched a smiling Patrick lift the dancer down from her improvised stage and toss a coin to a robed man slumping nearby. "We'll—we'll go now."

Determined not to look back again, Charlotte squared her shoulders and started off in the direction of the Vincent compound. Her senses were in a riot of shock at seeing Patrick Trevarren so unexpectedly, and she couldn't bear even to consider where he might be taking the dancer.

She was distracted, and conscious of Bettina's rising anxiety, and finding the path they'd blazed only an hour earlier proved difficult, without the noise and flurry of the marketplace to guide her. All the impossibly narrow streets looked the same, and any one of a dozen might have led to the quiet residential area she had left so boldly.

Bettina was sniffling, and she dried her eyes with her veil. "I knew it," she fretted, "we're lost!"

"Hush," Charlotte snapped, impatient. "We'll just go back to the marketplace and ask directions."

"We don't speak the language," Bettina reminded her with maddening accuracy.

"Then we'll simply start out again, trying every route until we find the right one," Charlotte answered. She sounded a great deal more confident than she felt.

Bettina mewled in alarm. "I shouldn't have listened to you," she cried angrily. "I *knew* something terrible would happen if we disobeyed Papa, and I was right!"

Charlotte bit her lower lip to keep from telling Bettina to shut up. "We will get back safely," she said in a purposefully gentle voice, when she had her impatience in check. "I promise we will. But you must be calm, Bettina."

The younger girl drew a deep, tremulous breath and looked around at the empty street. It was eerie how quiet the place was after the clamor and excitement of the *souk*.

"I shall have to drink poison if we are taken captive and forced to live in a harem," Bettina warned quite matter-of-factly, after she'd recovered a little of her composure.

Charlotte might have laughed, under less trying circumstances. The fact was, they probably *were* in grave danger, wandering unprotected in a city where the culture was so profoundly different from their own.

There was nothing to do now but return to the marketplace, try to find Mr. Trevarren, and prevail upon him to rescue her a second time. It would be an exquisite humiliation, especially since he was bound to be occupied in a most scandalous fashion with the dancer, if he was around at all, but Charlotte could see no alternative. She and Patrick had not parted on particularly cordial terms that long-ago day in Seattle, but he was probably the only person in the *souk* who spoke English.

She linked her arm with Bettina's. "Come along. We'll be back where we belong, sipping tea and eating chocolates, before your mother and father even miss us."

The marketplace, crowded before, was swelling with people and donkeys now. Charlotte stood on tiptoe, searching for Mr. Trevarren's bare head among the covered ones of the merchants and customers, but there was no sign of him.

Bettina let out a strangled whimper, and Charlotte controlled her irritation.

It was then that the crush of men pressed around them. A dirty cloth, pungent with some chemical, was placed over Charlotte's mouth and nose, and her arms were crushed to her sides. She heard Bettina screaming hysterically, and then the world receded to a pinpoint, disappeared. There was nothing except for an endless, throbbing void.

Patrick Trevarren laid his hands to the sides of the dancer's trim waist and hoisted her back up onto the board. Feeling especially generous, he favored her with a grin and a surreptitious coin, and in that moment a shrill female scream punctured the thick atmosphere of the *souk.*

In Riz, as well as the rest of the Arab world, women were a

commodity, but Patrick had grown up in Boston and studied in England. As a result, he had been cursed with a strain of chivalry, and even though he sensed that responding to the damsel's noisy distress would be a mistake, he could not turn away.

He made his way through the muttering crowd and found one of two foreign women he'd encountered earlier. Her veil had slipped and, by the nasal quality of her continuous, snuffling wails, Patrick identified her as an American.

Exasperated, he took her shoulders in his hands and gave her a shake. "Stop that sniveling and tell me what's the matter!"

The curious Arabs retreated a little.

"My f-friend!" the girl sobbed. "M-my friend has been k-kidnapped by pirates!"

Patrick clamped his jaw down tight as he remembered looking into the other woman's wide amber eyes earlier. There had been something disturbingly familiar about her. "Where did this happen?" he asked, struggling for patience. "How many men were there? Did you see which direction they went?"

The girl made another loud lament. "There were at least a *hundred* of them," she eventually managed to choke out. Her green eyes were red rimmed and puffy, and the end of her nose already looked raw. "And how should I know which way they went? I can't even find my way back to the Vincents' compound!"

Patrick picked a familiar face from the crowd, an earnest little boy who sometimes ran errands for him, and gave him a few pieces of silver. He knew the Vincents and had visited them on several occasions.

In quick Arabic, he instructed the boy to take the lady home—she would obviously be no help at all in finding her friend. Then he began questioning bystanders.

Despite Patrick's easy command of the local language and the fact that he was well known in the kingdom and received in homes on all levels of the social scale, he was still an outsider. The men frequenting the marketplace would sympathize with the kidnappers, not the girl. To them, the selling of innocent young women into virtual slavery was honest commerce.

Still, Patrick searched the alleyways that snaked away from the *souk* in every direction, a feeling of panic rising in him as he struggled to accept the hopelessness of his pursuit. The girl was lost; there would be no saving her from the fate that awaited her.

In the late afternoon, when the sun glared mercilessly down on the ancient, dusty city, Patrick returned to the harbor, where his ship, the *Enchantress,* was at anchor.

She was in a dark, cramped hole, a place that smelled of rats, mildew, and spoilage. Her head ached as though she'd been felled with a club, and nausea roiled in her stomach. Patches of tenderness all over her body told her she was black and blue, and where there wasn't a bruise, her skin stung with abrasions.

Charlotte wanted to throw up, but she was gagged, and when she moved to uncover her mouth, she discovered that her hands were bound as well. Tears of frustration and fear burned her eyes.

You wanted an adventure, she scolded herself. *Here it is.*

Hysteria threatened, but Charlotte would not surrender. She knew it was crucial not to panic; she had to think calmly, come up with a plan of escape.

Instead of strategy, however, she thought of Bettina. Had the kidnappers taken her, too? Charlotte shuddered to think how terrified the girl would be if that were true, and guilt lanced through her spirit. If Bettina came to harm, it would be Charlotte's own fault and no one else's. She had literally browbeaten her companion into visiting the *souk,* and the result might well be tragic.

Another rush of bile seared Charlotte's throat, and she swallowed. If she kept her wits about her, she might be able to find Bettina, and the two of them could flee their captors together. On the other hand, she might never see her friend again.

Colorful and patently horrifying pictures filled Charlotte's mind. She'd often pretended, in the privacy of her mind, to be a harem girl, with Patrick Trevarren as her sultan. It had been an innocent game, heating her loins and bringing a frustrated blush to her cheeks, but the reality of facing a life of white slavery was no schoolgirl fantasy. Of course she wouldn't be sold to the man she'd dreamed about all these years—oh, no. She would surely become the property of some whoremaster, or a concubine to some sweaty, slobbering wretch who valued her no more than he would a dog or a horse.

Despair would almost certainly have overtaken Charlotte in that moment if she hadn't been given something more immediate to think about.

Door hinges creaked, and a slash of light appeared in the darkness. Then a small man entered the chamber. He wore Arab garb, but that was all Charlotte could make out in the gloom.

Her heart pounded with fear and helpless rage as he approached her, roughly wrenching her off the floor and then pulling off her gag. He produced a cup of tepid water and pressed it impatiently to her mouth.

Charlotte bit back all the inflammatory things she wanted to say, all the frantic questions she yearned to ask, and drank greedily. The heat was intense, and she realized she was wet with perspiration.

"Who are you?" she asked hoarsely, when she'd satisfied her thirst.

The man mumbled something in Arabic, and while Charlotte missed the meaning of the words, she caught the attitude. Her captor was not contemptuous, or even hostile; he was indifferent.

"What is this place?" she burst out, more in an effort to discourage the Arab from gagging her again than from any hope of getting a reply she could understand. "Why are you keeping me here?"

Charlotte's visitor shouted something at her; like his earlier conversation, the remark needed no translation. He wanted her to keep quiet.

To demonstrate this, he put the gag back in place and tied it a little tighter than before, so that the filthy cloth chafed at the corners of her mouth. Then he shoved Charlotte, hard, sending her toppling to the floor.

For the first time, a slow, almost imperceptible sensation of rocking penetrated the fog of fear and anger surrounding her, and she realized she was in the hold of a ship. It gave her comfort that she'd identified her prison, but she also had to face the forlorn reality that escape would be even more difficult.

As Charlotte watched the guard leave her makeshift cell, she was actually glad to be wearing the gag. The scrap kept in the flow of scathing and very colorful invective she'd learned in her father's logging camps. Even though he didn't speak English, the Arab would have known he was being roundly insulted, and his already-thin patience probably would have snapped.

Charlotte forced herself to draw in deep breaths through her nose and let them out slowly through the cloth. Whatever happened, she must stay calm, taking every care not to lose her temper or show fear.

The heat in the dark hold was dense, and now that Charlotte knew the place *was* a hold, she picked out the sound of rats scampering overhead in the beams and foraging in the supplies stored around her. She shuddered and offered up a silent prayer for a miracle to happen.

Soon.

Patrick sighed and turned away from the rail of the *Enchantress*. Usually he enjoyed watching the last fierce light of day shatter into glimmering liquid on the water, but that evening he was troubled.

His friend and first mate, Tom Cochran, was standing behind him. "Do we set sail with the evening tide, then, Captain?" he asked. He was a solidly built man, of medium height, and a gray-white stubble of beard covered the lower half of his face. "I imagine that Khalif fellow will be looking for us to put in sometime tonight."

Patrick gave a distracted nod. He had gone to school with the sultan in England, and Khalif was a good friend, but that night the prospect of visiting his luxurious palace lacked its usual appeal. "Yes," he said, somewhat hoarsely. "Give the order to set sail."

With that, Patrick descended to the lower deck and entered his private quarters, a relatively small chamber holding a bed, a wardrobe, a desk and chair, and several bookshelves. He made no move to light a lamp but instead collapsed into the chair with another long sigh.

He heard the shouts of the crew members above, on the deck and in the rigging, but his mind was stuck on the girl kidnapped in the *souk* that day. What was it about her that troubled him so? Unfortunate though it was, unwary young women were often snatched from marketplaces, ships, and street corners in this part of the world, and most were never seen again.

The nape of Patrick's neck clenched tightly, then began to throb. He cursed and sent a small book clattering against the wall.

A knock sounded at his door.

"Come in," Patrick called grudgingly, knowing that if he didn't speak, the cook's boy would just keep knocking.

That night, however, it was Cochran who brought the captain's dinner tray.

"For mercy's sake, man," the old sailor said, "light a lamp. It's as dark as the devil's root cellar in here."

Patrick reached up for the lamp suspended over his desk, removed the chimney and struck a match to the wick. He knew his expression made it obvious he wasn't pleased at the interruption.

"What's chewing on you?" Cochran demanded, setting the tray down on the desk with a thump. "Didn't you find that little dancer in the *souk,* the one you've had your eye on ever since we dropped anchor?"

A surge of unexpected shame swept through Patrick, though he couldn't imagine why. He was an unmarried man, after all, and he'd betrayed no one by following the girl into her tent and enjoying her feminine attributes.

"I found her," he admitted, dropping his eyes to the tray. Lamb stew, brown bread, and weak tea—again.

Cochran chuckled and made himself at home by folding his arms and leaning back against the closed door, though he hadn't been invited to stay. "Don't tell me she wouldn't have you."

Patrick refused to dignify that idea with an answer. He just glared at Cochran for a long moment and then tore a piece of brown bread between his teeth and began to eat.

"I guess I lost my head." Cochran grinned. "Forgot for a moment that no lady has ever refused Patrick Trevarren. If it isn't the dancing girl, what is it that's troubling you so much?"

Patrick shoved away the tray, tossed the bread down beside his bowl. "This is a merciless world," he said gravely.

The first mate pretended profound shock. "Now there's an insight for you," he replied mockingly. "And here I thought it was all rose petals and angels' wings." Cochran, unlike most of the *Enchantress* crew, was an educated man. In fact, Patrick knew he'd once been a tutor in a boys' school in New York, though his friend didn't talk much about the days before he'd gone to sea.

Massaging the knotted muscles at his nape with one hand, Patrick told Cochran about the kidnapping. He didn't mention how the maple-colored eyes haunted him, though.

"You can't save them all, Patrick," Cochran said when the woeful tale was through. "Besides, some of those girls end up living like queens, you know that. The pretty ones get servants of their own, and fine clothes, and all the fancy food they can tuck away."

Patrick bit the inside of his lip to keep the flood tide of furious despair coursing through him from coming out as a bellow.

Cochran laid a hand on the captain's shoulder. "Was she pretty?" he asked quietly.

"Yes." Patrick's admission was gruff.

"Then she'll be all right," the seaman told him. With that, Cochran opened the door and went out.

Patrick propped his feet on the desk, just to one side of the tray, and tilted his head back with a groan. His headache was getting steadily worse, and even with his own lids stubbornly closed, he could still see those golden eyes looking up at him in the marketplace.

In the next instant, Patrick remembered. He and his uncle had docked the *Enchantress* in faraway Seattle, back in '66 or '67, and stayed a few days to enjoy the local hospitality and unload some of the goods they'd brought from both California and the Orient.

He'd returned to the ship one afternoon, after spending the morning with a local merchant, and looked up to find a scrap of a girl swinging in the rigging.

He'd yelled to her to come down, and she'd called back, in a reasonable enough tone, that she couldn't move. He'd climbed up to retrieve her, of course, and they'd exchanged words.

Patrick didn't remember her name, but those amber eyes were engraved in his consciousness. Impossible as it seemed, that adventurous young woman and the one he'd encountered in the marketplace, just prior to her abduction, were one and the same.

He knotted one fist and slammed it down on the desktop with such force that the silverware rattled on his tray.

Charlotte lost track of time after three days. She was given very little to eat or drink and allowed to relieve herself only once every twenty-four hours or so. Her veil had long since disappeared, and her borrowed gown was twisted around her, torn and dirty. Her skin burned with fever, and the bruises and cuts hurt more with the passing of time instead of less.

No one had come to ravish her—that was some consolation. She could endure hunger, thirst, general discomfort, and a bladder that was about to explode, but the prospect of rape terrified her.

When her irascible guard came to collect her one night, jerking her to her feet with his usual lack of ceremony, she thought her luck had finally dried up and blown away like so much fine sawdust. She fought desperately, though she knew all the while there was no chance of winning, and the Arab finally backhanded her across the face. The blow was so hard that she fainted.

She awakened—whether it was minutes or hours later she had no way of guessing—to find herself squashed inside what felt like a burlap bag. She could see light through its loose weave, then make out the shadowy forms of several men.

They were laughing as they engaged in some game of cards, and Charlotte was practically convulsed with fury. She started to scream that they were all beasts and found that she was still gagged. A second later, her eyes widened as the realization came to her that she was naked inside that scratchy burlap sack.

The gambling went on, and Charlotte dozed, opened her eyes, dozed again. Finally, she felt the bag that enclosed her being slung over some man's shoulder like a bag of chicken feed. She struggled, but that only made whoever was carrying her laugh out loud.

"She's a spirited one, all right," a voice said, in unadorned American English. "Raheem won't be happy when he finds out you lost her at poker, but she might improve the captain's mood some. He's been growling for the better part of four days."

An American, Charlotte thought, nearly faint with relief. Now she could explain what had happened, book passage home to the United States, live a blessedly ordinary life . . .

After a lot of jostling, Charlotte heard a loud knock. Again, she felt the rhythm of a ship beneath her.

"Yes?" someone called, in none too friendly a tone.

"I brung you somethin', Captain," answered the man who carried her. "Me and the rest of the crew, well, we've been lookin' for a way to cheer you up a mite."

Door hinges creaked, and Charlotte felt a peculiar combination of excitement and fear. After all, she'd been stripped of every stitch, and she was in desperate need of a bath and shampoo. When the bag was opened, she was going to make for a very unnerving sight.

The sack landed on the floor with a thump, she felt pulling as the rope or twine at the top was untied. The burlap fell around her in a rough pool, and she snatched it back up far enough to cover herself.

When she finally found the courage to look up, she found herself staring into the astonished ink-blue eyes of Patrick Trevarren.

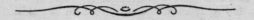

Look for *Taming Charlotte* in Winter 1993
Wherever Paperback Books Are Sold.